Seduction

in Silk

Also by Jo Beverley
Available from New American Library

REGENCY

THE ROGUE'S WORLD
Lady Beware
To Rescue a Rogue
The Rogue's Return
Skylark
St. Raven
Hazard
"The Demon's Mistress" in *In Praise of Younger Men*
The Devil's Heiress
The Dragon's Bride
Three Heroes (Omnibus Edition)

THE MALLOREN WORLD
An Unlikely Countess
The Secret Duke
The Secret Wedding
A Lady's Secret
A Most Unsuitable Man
Winter Fire
Devilish
Secrets of the Night
Something Wicked
My Lady Notorious

MEDIEVAL ROMANCES
Lord of Midnight
Dark Champion
Lord of My Heart

OTHER
Forbidden Magic
Lovers and Ladies (Omnibus Edition)
Lord Wraybourne's Betrothed
The Stanforth Secrets
The Stolen Bride
Emily and the Dark Angel

ANTHOLOGIES
"The Raven and the Rose" in
Chalice of Roses
"The Dragon and the Virgin Princess" in
Dragon Lovers
"The Trouble with Heroes" in
Irresistible Forces

Seduction in Silk

A Novel of the Malloren World

Jo Beverley

A SIGNET SELECT BOOK

ACKNOWLEDGMENTS

This book is special in so many ways, and I thank my husband, Ken, always; my family; my wonderful agent, Meg Ruley, and editor, Claire Zion, and everyone at NAL. And, of course, you, my readers, who fuel the fire. Thank you!

SIGNET SELECT
Published by the Penguin Group
Penguin Group (USA) Inc., 375 Hudson Street,
New York, New York 10014, USA

USA | Canada | UK | Ireland | Australia | New Zealand | India | South Africa | China

Penguin Books Ltd., Registered Offices: 80 Strand, London WC2R 0RL, England

First published by Signet Select, an imprint of New American Library,
a division of Penguin Group (USA) Inc.

ISBN: 978-1-62490-694-7

Printed in the United States of America

Chapter 1

The Honorable Peregrine Perriam approached the deathbed with distaste.

It was early afternoon, but the windows were closed and the curtains lowered, creating gloom and trapping the smells of sickness, decay, and some perfumed stuff designed to hide both.

One branch of candles sat beside the bed, illuminating its massive dark oak posts and crimson velvet hangings. The bed looked to date from the sixteenth century. Perry had gained the same impression of the house. Dark paneling everywhere suggested it was unchanged since the day the feud over Perriam Manor had begun, as if a modern touch might lose a point in the long battle.

He should have ignored the scrawled summons from Giles Perriam, but no one in his family could ignore anything to do with Perriam Manor, especially not a letter that oozed gloating malice.

I've made a new will. Named you as heir. You'd better get here quickly if you want to know what else I've done.

He'd wanted to deny Giles whatever warped pleasure

he sought, but "named you as heir" had brought him here at speed.

That was impossible.

For his branch of the Perriam family this Tudor house and its lands were the "filched estate," its loss the bitter legacy of a division of property seven generations ago. Getting it back was a holy cause, but the only way was if the junior branch, Giles's branch, failed to produce a direct male heir. In that case, by a legal pact, the estate must pass to the senior branch, now headed by Perry's father, Earl of Hernescroft.

The earl had observed Giles's failure to produce a living male heir with satisfaction. When Giles's health had failed, he'd rubbed his hands in anticipation of victory. At last the old injustice would be put right, and in his lifetime too.

"Named you as heir." That wasn't possible. And then there was *"if you want to know what else I've done."*

Giles was no fool. He was a wicked reprobate without a moral scruple of any kind, but not a fool. Whatever scheme he'd devised, it would have teeth and claws.

Perry studied the man propped up on pillows, a skeleton skinned in old parchment. Giles had been fleshy, but now his face was dominated by a blade of a nose and high cheekbones, his sunken eyes emphasized by chiaroscuro. One gaunt hand lay on the crimson coverlet, fingers curled into a claw.

What exactly did Giles seek to grasp, this close to the end?

There were a number of people in the room—a black-and-white clergyman, a coatless doctor, some servants—but Perry focused on the dying man as he walked forward.

When he arrived at the bed, the clergyman leaned down. "Mr. Perriam is here, sir. Your chosen heir."

"Chosen . . . ," Cousin Giles growled without opening his eyes. "Wouldn't have come to this if any of my own get survived."

The chaplain stepped back, stricken. The death of four baby boys left no space for comforting platitudes. Three wives, four sons, but no living heir.

The thin lids raised a little. "Don't tower over me. Sit."

Someone busied himself behind Perry. A hushed voice murmured, "Your chair, sir."

Perry sat. He was famed for his social address, but what to say here?

I'm sorry to find you dying would be a lie. He'd no more than bowed in passing to this man, so any expression of emotion would be hollow.

What malice have you confected? would be honest, but too curt an opening.

Perry chose silence. Let the enemy make the first move.

Giles's eyes had closed again. Perhaps nothing was required.

Then the sagging lips moved. "You married?"

"No." Did Giles seek a marriage alliance? To what purpose? In any case, he had no daughter.

"I'm a cursed man," Giles growled from a dry throat. "Cursed! Breed boys and see 'em snatched away . . . Wives barren or feeble . . . Cursed, I tell you."

"Life's chancy as it is. Queen Anne birthed fourteen and died without a living heir."

"Cursed," Giles insisted. "Supplanted her father, the rightful king. Her sister Mary suffered the same fate. Died in agony from smallpox. Cursed for their wickedness. As am I. As am I!"

His sudden passion triggered a paroxysm of coughing, and the doctor hurried forward to present a drink.

If anyone deserved to be cursed, Giles did, but a belief in curses showed a deranged mind.

Perry glanced at the clergyman and mouthed, *Mad?*

"Not that I know, sir," the man murmured.

Giles pushed away the glass. "Nothing to say, sir? Nothing to say?"

"There are no such things as curses, Cousin. And who would do such a thing to you?"

"Clarrie, that's who. Seemed such a soft, silly . . ." Then his eyes fixed wildly on Perry. "Can still evade the worst. Harpy Mallow showed the way."

Definitely deranged, but the only way was to humor him.

"Who or what is Harpy Mallow?"

"Sister. Arse-faced monster, but Henry married her anyway. Plotted against me . . ." He paused to wheeze in a few breaths. "She claimed to be able to turn the curse. I laughed at her. Then she died. Died! Curse her. Curse her!"

"My lord!" the clergyman protested over a paroxysm of coughing. "Consider the judgment you must soon face."

Giles turned a long-toothed snarl on him. "Cease your bleating. Water. Give me water, damn you all."

The doctor again helped him to drink. "You must rest, sir."

"Soon have eternal rest. Or eternal fires. Henry Mallow has sons and he was as guilty as I. Curse him. Curse him!"

He choked again, then collapsed back on his pillows, eyes closed, each breath wheezing and labored. Perry hoped the tirade had finished him off. The mind had clearly already lost its moorings, so with God's mercy the wasted body wasn't far behind.

He was strongly tempted to leave, but Giles hadn't summoned him here for this babble. There was some plot in hand and he must find out what it was. Perriam Manor must return to his family in truth—that was, to the Earl of Hernescroft, not his youngest son.

He leaned closer. "You wrote that you have willed the manor to me. By the old agreement Perriam Manor must rejoin the principal estate. You must bequeath it to my father or my eldest brother, not me."

The dying man showed no response, but Perry persisted. "Such a mistake will be corrected in the courts, but only think how much money must pour into lawyers' pockets."

Ah.

He leaned back. That must be it. Giles had set up a situation that would suck a small fortune before it was resolved. Lawyers delighted in complicating a case to their own advantage. Sometimes they could even twist the result.

That sent a chill down Perry's spine. He had no idea who else might make a claim to the estate, but a family tree covering seven generations had to hold possibilities. He would not be used in such a malicious device. But what could he do?

Somewhere in the room a large clock ponderously ticked the seconds.

Someone behind Perry whispered.

Clothing rustled, but the man in the bed lay still.

If he shook Giles, could he get a few more words out of him?

Then Giles spoke again, working for each word. "You still there?"

"Yes. Did you hear what I said?"

"Not deaf. That old agreement. Says I must bequeath the manor to Beatrice's line. Nothing about to whom." The strange noise from his throat was probably a laugh. "Create discord in the cozy Herne nest, won't it?"

"If you imagine my family as cozy, you're very much mistaken," Perry said. But Giles was correct. Perriam Manor passing to him would create a new schism, one between his father and him. Thank God the plan wouldn't work.

"Thinking you'll pass it on to Hernescroft?" Giles asked, eyes still shut. "Can't. Written in the will . . . Seen to you lot, I have."

He coughed again and the doctor said, "Sir, I must insist that you rest."

"For what damned purpose? Want to tell my plan while I can still enjoy it. Give me some of that cordial."

"That wouldn't be wise, sir."

"Who pays the bills? Give it me."

Lips tight, the doctor measured a syrupy liquid into a spoon and fed it to his patient. Giles coughed again as he lay back, and he seemed to drift into sleep. But then the potion had some effect and he half opened his eyes. When he spoke, his voice was stronger.

"Fail to keep to the terms of my will and the pact is void. Then the manor can go to anyone I choose. Had my legal people go over that. If you don't dance to my tune, your lot loses Perriam Manor forever."

Perry did his best to conceal his reaction, which was mostly exasperation. He doubted Cousin Giles was lying—he was enjoying the truth too much—which meant that generations ago there'd been some very sloppy legal work. The will itself could be contested, but that too would be a feast for legal vultures.

Giles grinned, enjoying himself now. "Put some other conditions in too."

"If they're outrageous, they can be struck down."

"Not outrageous. But you'll see for yourself when I'm gone. Now, about the curse . . ."

"There are no such things as curses."

"Believe as you wish, but it passes along with the inheritance. Clarrie made it so. Harpy Mallow affirmed it. Perhaps I should let the curse pass to your side of the family. Justice would finally be served."

Mad, bad, and vile.

Perry had had enough.

When he rose, Giles said, "Running away? Don't want to know how to avert the curse?"

"There are no such things as curses."

"Through marriage. Harpy Mallow laid it out. If I married Clarrie's niece, her shade would be appeased."

"Then why didn't you?"

"Dance to Nora Mallow's tune? Anyway, girl too young. Took a new wife, one who could bear sons . . ." Perhaps his silence came from the memory of how futile that had been, but then he spoke again. "Now you'll do it. End the curse. Save us both, or we'll both burn in hell."

"Marry some odd offspring of this insanity?" A laugh escaped. "You must face your fate, Cousin, for I'll have no part of this."

"You don't fear hell?"

"Not as the result of a curse, that's for sure."

"I do."

"Probably with cause."

"I've done some things. . . . But you'll save me."

"I regret, but I must decline the honor."

Giles was weakening, his chest heaving with each breath, but he focused on Perry again. He might even have smirked. "You'll dance to my tune, Cousin, because it's in the will. To inherit this place, you must marry Clarrie's niece. Save us both." He rolled his head. "My will . . . Where's my will?"

A servant began to search drawers.

Giles muttered about their stupidity.

Then the man hurried over with some folded papers.

"Give 'em to him," Giles said, and the man offered them to Perry.

Perry regarded them much as he might regard a bouquet of nettles, but he took them. Marry? He had no intention of marrying anyone.

"It's all there," Giles whispered. "Had time to plan. Might have failed my line, but yours will eat bitter fruit." He began to laugh.

Enough was enough. Perry turned and headed for the door.

A choking sound made him whirl back.

The man in the bed was fixed midcackle, the staring eyes blank of life. The doctor leaned forward to confirm it, but it was a formality. Giles Perriam, forty-seven years old, had gone on to eternal rest or eternal fires, but Perry didn't doubt his last words.

He had done his best to make this victory bitter fruit, and he'd chosen Perry to serve it up.

Chapter 2

Perry wanted to escape—to ride away, back to London—but duty said otherwise. If he'd inherited this place, he must take care of it, for now at least. He spoke to the principal people present, thanking them for their attendance and making the first arrangements. Then he escaped the ghastly room.

When he stepped into the corridor and inhaled fresher air, he was startled by daylight. Why did people draw the curtains on death?

The corridor wasn't bright, for it was lined with the dark paneling that seemed to be everywhere here, and the one window was obscured by ivy. When riding up to the house he'd noted the dark ivy shrouding the walls and windows. It was enough to depress a court jester, but he'd have to stay for at least one night to put some sort of management in place. For decency, he should stay until Giles was buried, so he'd make that soon.

The main order of business, however, was to read the will, identify the poisons, and find antidotes. Perriam Manor must pass into his father's eager hands, and he wasn't marrying the Mallow girl, whoever she might be.

He walked briskly along a paneled corridor to the massive dark oak staircase and descended to the oak-paneled hall. Even the floor was the same—oak planks darkened by the centuries.

Oh for pale tiling and light-colored walls.

And windows that weren't overhung by ivy.

A footman stood on duty.

"Where's Lord Raymore?" Perry asked him.

"In the library, sir." After a moment the man realized this meant nothing and led the way across the hall.

"Thank you. Have bedchambers prepared for both of us, and something to eat. And bring some drink in here immediately." Considering the will in his hand, Perry added, "Brandy."

He entered a modest room with scantily filled shelves and a musty smell. Unsurprisingly, Giles had not been a book lover. There were two good-sized windows of small lozenge-shaped panes, but they too were curtained with ivy. Perry's friend Lord Raymore, seated at the long oaken table, had had to light a branch of candles in order to read a slim tome.

His friend's name in full was Major Lord Raymore, but also Lord Cynric Malloren. To his friends he was Cyn.

Their friendship was recent and had come about when they'd been harnessed into a task by Cyn's brother the Marquess of Rothgar. In many ways they were different, for Cyn had lived a military life and Perry's field of action had been court and politics, but they'd liked each other from the first, and enjoyed each other's company.

Despite his success as a soldier, Cyn was deceptively slight of build and pleasant of feature. As he also had curling russet hair, he could almost be called pretty, but men paid dearly if they said it to his face. Perry was not of much larger build, but his looks were more clearly masculine and his hair dark, so he didn't have to deal with that problem.

Cyn had been with Perry when he'd received Giles's letter and insisted on accompanying him. Now he put aside the book.

"How is he, and has he explained his whimsy?"

Perry tossed the papers on the table. "He's dead and it's not whimsy. It's a thicket of spite."

The footman returned with a tray holding a decanter of brandy and two glasses.

"Requiring strong drink, I see." Cyn took charge of pouring. Once the footman had closed the door, he said, "Tell me all. That's why I'm here."

Perry took the brandy and wandered the room as he gave an account of the deathbed conversation.

"Curses, conditions, and conundrums," Cyn said. "The will must clarify all."

Perry glared at it. "I cling to the illogical feeling that until read, any problems it contains don't yet exist."

Cyn merely raised a brow, so Perry sat and untied the black ribbon that held all together. It loosed two sets of folded papers, and he glanced at the contents of each.

"The will and a document in Giles's scrawl. Which to read first?"

"The will."

"Direct and to the point." Perry smoothed the three sheets flat but looked first at the end of the last one. "Signed only two days ago. I wonder what any previous one contained."

"Irrelevant. Stop delaying."

Perry shot Cyn a look, but he scanned the first page. "The usual preamble . . . Ah. *'Lacking a son to inherit, I am compelled to fulfill an old family pact and pass Perriam Manor along with all its contents and lands to the senior branch of the Perriam family, that of the Earl of Hernescroft. Thus I name as heir Peregrine Charles Perriam, youngest son of the said earl.'* I hope the devil's toasting him."

"Why? An estate like this is hardly a burden."

"No? The restoration of Perriam Manor to the earldom has been a holy quest for two centuries, passed along with a Perriam's first milk."

"So now all is right."

"Don't be dense. My owning it is merely a new schism."

"My apologies for my denseness, but I don't understand any of this."

Perry ran a hand through his hair. "No, I apologize. Of course you don't. Let me try to make it simple. Back in the reign of Henry the Eighth, the Lord Perriam of the time had no sons, so his two daughters were set to inherit."

"Ah, I know something of that. I was reading *A History of Perriam Manor*, which was prominently displayed in the center of the table."

"The Beatrician side of the story."

"Beatrician?"

"The two sisters. Cecily the older, and Beatrice the younger. The Cecilian line and the Beatrician."

"Can the two accounts be different?" Cyn asked.

"Immeasurably so, I suspect. Beatrice wanted the Perriam properties to be equally divided, but Cecily objected, insisting that the future Lord Perriam's estates should not be diminished. Their father had already petitioned the king and gained agreement that the title of Lord Perriam could pass through one or the other of his daughters, going in order of age. Cecily was the older and already had a son."

"Who would be the next baron. Demanding all was somewhat greedy."

"So Beatrice thought. The fighting went on until the king intervened. Beatrice could have only one of the four estates involved, but she could choose which."

"Almost Solomon-like," Cyn said. "I assume she chose this one. Why should it create such bitterness? It was the richest?"

"No. The Worcestershire property was already larger and more productive, but this is the oldest. It was built in the late fifteenth century, but on the site of one dating to the thirteenth. This is the Perriam birthplace."

Cyn whistled. "Clever Beatrice."

"If that's how you choose to see it. Cecily was furious, but all she and her advisers could do was try to limit the damage. A pact was agreed that if Beatrice's line failed to provide a direct male heir, the estate would return to the whole. I presume the document is among these papers. I've never read it. At that point, Beatrice had three daughters and was close to the end of her childbearing years, so Cecily must have hoped for a rapid correction. However, the needed son arrived, and the line has continued to provide a direct male heir for two hundred and forty-one years. Until now."

"So the moment of restoration is at hand, but your inheriting won't be considered complete restoration?"

"It won't be considered any restoration at all. Consider, a Perriam has owned the place for centuries, but not the right Perriam. My father will have an apoplexy when he finds out. It certainly won't increase his fondness for me. Not that I care," Perry said quickly, "but we're an ill-humored family at the best of times."

"Then give him this place," Cyn said.

"Apparently it won't be so easy. Giles said he'd provided for that."

Perry picked up the will to seek the clause, aware that he hadn't yet told Cyn about the marriage threat. He skimmed over the words until he found the part. " '*If Peregrine Perriam sells or passes on the estate before death, any such sale or gift will be negated and the whole will pass to Viscount Nethercote.*' Damn him to Hades!"

"Explain why Nethercote is a particular problem. Bear in mind that I've spent most of my adult life out of the country, and certainly out of the beau monde."

"Nethercote and my father have been at odds for years over some property that's rich in coal, and recently my father won. Nethercote wouldn't sell Perriam Manor to my father for a king's ransom."

"What a family you are for quarrels."

"I can't deny it, and Giles has exploited that." He tapped the will. "This, my friend, is a carefully planned dagger, and he's had time to hone it to perfection."

"Surely you'll be able to will Perriam Manor to whom you wish?"

"I assume so, but may I hope that won't come into force for many decades?"

"Your father won't be willing to wait? Ah, of course. Not in his lifetime."

"Quite. And he's expecting to celebrate soon. In fact, within weeks."

"He can't shoot you."

"I wouldn't be too sure." Perry tossed aside the will and picked up the other set of folded papers. "Let's read the venom in Giles's own words."

My dear Peregrine,

If you are reading this I am dead and discovering the hereafter. I do hope it allows for satisfaction with work done on earth, for I am quite pleased with myself. You are reputed to be clever and adroit in social intricacies, but I believe even your talents will not allow you to evade my traps.

You may question whether I may leave the manor to you rather than to your father, but the pact was carelessly phrased and merely required the return to the senior line. I enclose a copy so you can verify that.

You will have instantly thought of giving the manor to your father, but the will forbids it, and I am advised I may lay such conditions. You must hold the estate till your own death.

I am sweetly anticipating the torture that will cause Hernescroft just as he has tortured me with his gloating over his upcoming triumph.

"Trust Father to make a situation worse," Perry said.

Another requirement is that you must spend a total of thirty days and nights each year in residence. Alas, my legal advisers felt that more would be onerous, and I'll leave no room for escape. As you are fond of Town life and kept busy there in many interesting ways, I hope every one of those thirty days will cast you into despair.

> *What happens if you refuse to comply with my*
> *conditions?*
> *The estate then goes to Viscount Nethercote to be*
> *entailed to his heirs male. Thus, you see, lost to the*
> *Perriam family forever.*
>   *In anticipation of your impotent rage,*
>   *Giles Perriam*

"May he already be roasting in Hades," Perry said, putting the letter down.

"Drooling anticipation on his side too."

"As I said, we're an unpleasant family."

"Not you."

"No? I truly do hope Giles is roasting. Thirty days."

"Not an intolerable burden."

"I don't enjoy bucolic pursuits."

"You like to ride."

"London has parks and open land nearby."

"Have sense, Perry. Everyone leaves London in the summer heat. Spend August here."

"I spend the hot season visiting friends," Perry said, but he heard how petulant that sounded. "I grant you, that condition falls short of torture. However, he mentioned one more matter."

He picked up the will. "Ah, here it is. *'To secure this inheritance, Peregrine Charles Perriam is required, within a month of my death, to marry Claris Mallow, daughter of my old friend Henry Mallow, and niece of a woman I mistreated in my careless younger days. By this I am assured that I will avoid the worst effect of a curse laid on me by my victim, Clarrie Dunsworth: a curse which has slaughtered my wives and children and broken my health. If my heir, that is, Peregrine Perriam, fails in this, he and his line will inherit the curse along with Perriam Manor. Thus Clarrie wrote it. Thus shall it be.'*"

"Now, that is insane," Cyn said, "and could surely be contested."

Perry tossed down the papers. "It all could, but the

case could drag on for years and do nothing but stuff lawyers' pockets, especially with another heir in the wings."

"You're not going to marry this woman, are you? You've said you've no wish to marry."

"I'm too busy to marry, and my way of life doesn't allow for a wife, still less for children."

"Your extremely comfortable gentleman's rooms off St. James's, the clubs, the coffeehouses, court and the beau monde . . ."

"Quite."

"Then don't do it."

"I have no choice!" Perry snapped. "Giles's snare has me tight. If I don't dance to his tune, Perriam Manor is lost forever."

"Then let it be lost."

"I can't do that."

Perry drank some brandy, his mind racing like a rat in a trap. Damn Giles and the whole family saga.

"Marriage is not such a dire fate," Cyn said. "I like it a great deal."

"You're not alone. My sisters seem content, each in her own way, but my oldest brother's union is a battlefield. A clear warning not to marry to oblige the family. Millicent brought a fortune, but he's earning every guinea."

"Perhaps Claris Mallow will suit you. If not, there's many a couple live separate lives."

"My only glimmer of hope." Perry drained his glass and put it down. "Let's seek out any other poisoned points." Perry quickly read through the rest of the will. "Merely minor bequests to trusty servants and such." He refolded the will, picked up Giles's letter, and read to the end. "Ah. He says I should consult the book in the library for further insight."

Cyn picked up the book. "This one?"

"The only one that matters."

"You're supposed to read it?" Cyn flicked through it. A paper fell out. Cyn pushed it across to Perry. It was older than the will and letter and worn along the folds as if opened and refolded many times.

Perry smoothed it out. " 'Struth. It's the curse." The small writing was strangely neat for such words, but both dark and tight, suggesting powerful emotion.

> You have betrayed me, Giles Perriam. You have made me a whore and my unborn child a bastard and your money cannot wash that clean. You'll hear no more from me, but now and with my last breath I wish on you the sufferings that your black heart deserves. May you suffer as I must suffer. May any wife you take die young as I must die, and any children die young as mine must die. May you yourself die young and suffering. May your guilt oppress you every day until Satan comes to carry you to burn in hell, and may this curse pass to your heirs as long as time may be.

Cyn whistled. "An impressive concoction!"

Perry tossed the paper down. "I pity the woman, but that's a cartload of nonsense."

"Giles Perriam does seem to have been plagued by misfortunes."

"Life is chancy for great and small."

"Life can also be odd. In my travels I've come across things that'd make me unwilling to ignore such a well-warranted curse."

"I had no part in the wickedness." Perry was trying to reject the curse entirely, but the direct, powerful words had their effect.

"Perhaps you'll find an escape. Claris Mallow might already be married."

"This will was signed only two weeks ago," Perry pointed out.

"Your malignant relative wouldn't be so careless?"

"He crafted this with precision to do the most harm."

"Is there something written on the back of his letter?"

Perry turned the sheet. "To assist you to marry within the month, I tell you that Claris Mallow is a spinster of twenty-three living in the village of Old Barford, Surrey, daughter of the rector of the parish, Henry Mallow."

"A clergyman's daughter?" Cyn said. "I expected worse. A demure demeanor and a dedication to good works."

"I've known some who break that mold."

"Who still live in the rectory?"

"A point. But in his ravings, Giles mentioned Henry Mallow with rage. I lay odds that rectory is a pit of vipers."

Perry reread part of the will.

"I'm only required to wed the woman. Nothing more." He refolded the papers, stacked them neatly, and retied the black ribbon. "Once that's done, she may stay in the rectory or take up residence here. Though Father will rage, I will have done my best for the family and be free to return to Town and sanity."

Chapter 3

Lavender Cottage, Old Barford, Surrey

"Idling, Claris? You must be sickening."

Claris Mallow turned from enjoying the perfume of the flowers growing up a trellis. "Simply giving thanks for all I have."

Her grandmother Athena Mallow sniffed. "All you have is a rented cottage and a pittance."

"I have enough to live on, and I have harmony. No one—"

"No one will storm out to berate you for every little fault," Athena completed, "nor for many things that aren't faults at all, such as growing sweet peas. You can't build a life on things you don't have."

Athena was ill suited to a cottage garden. Despite wearing plain clothing, she always seemed elegant, and her appearance was impressive. She was a widow of nearly seventy, but her back was straight, her hawk-nosed face only lightly wrinkled, and her dark hair untouched by gray. At market, she used her appearance to tempt women to buy her creams and hair tonic, though Claris had never seen her use the stuff herself.

But then, Claris had known her for only a year, and Athena had shared little about her life. Claris had been embarrassed to ask. On the rare occasions when her father had mentioned his mother, he'd described her as a disgrace to womanhood, and once as a harlot. In truth, when Athena had arrived at the Old Barford rectory on the day after her son's funeral, Claris had been disappointed by a lack of lascivious clothing and face paint.

Athena had shown no trace of grief, but that wasn't surprising, when she'd abandoned husband and son forty-eight years earlier without a qualm. "I have come to nurture the orphans," she'd announced, "but I know nothing of grandmothering and little indeed of mothering. You will call me Athena."

Claris and her two brothers had been stunned but obedient, all relieved that someone had come to their rescue.

Their father's death had been sudden, for Reverend Mallow had suffered an apoplexy in the pulpit when ranting against sin. In an instant his income had ceased and his family had lost any right to live in the rectory. His demented generosity to the poor had left scant savings, and Claris had known of no relations likely to offer refuge to her and her ten-year-old brothers.

Athena had not brought riches, but within days she had persuaded old Lizzie Hubble she'd be better off living with her daughter and had taken over the rent of Lavender Cottage. She'd secured their right to take many items from the vicarage, some of which they'd then sold, and she'd also claimed for them the pension allowed to the orphans of clergymen. She wasn't an easy woman, but she'd been an angel at that time.

"I give thanks for you too," Claris said. "You made this haven possible."

"Perhaps a mistake. Are you to dawdle your life away here? You're twenty-three years old, girl."

"And thus not a girl."

"You're a girl to me as long as you stay here."

"Where could we go?" Claris protested. "We only just manage as things are."

"Because you insist on putting aside money for the boys. Let them make their own way. The world is run for the convenience of their sex."

"They need education and a start in a profession. I'm content here; I truly am."

"Then you're demented. I was younger than you when I escaped my husband and set about enjoying life."

Claris didn't care to think what "enjoying life" might have involved, and yet Athena never showed a trace of shame over her past.

"I have no need to escape," Claris said firmly, picking up her basket of vegetables and flowers and leading the way back toward the cottage. "I enjoy my family and my garden. I enjoy being in the village where I was born, where everyone knows me."

"As the Mad Rector's daughter."

"Father *was* mad," Claris pointed out, for her father's ranting sermons and obsessive guilt could be seen no other way. "I value honesty."

Athena snorted. "And you're tainted by that brutal honesty as long as you remain here."

"What purpose would there be to my leaving? Where would be better?"

"It's time you married."

Claris stopped to stare at her grandmother.

"With such sterling examples before me? You endured only three years of it before fleeing, and my parents were at miserable warfare all their days."

"Extreme examples."

"I've seen others in the area."

"And many good matches too. Your parents were an odd case, and you are certainly not me."

Claris continued toward the cottage. "No, for I'm sure you were a beauty when young. Who will marry me, penniless and without charms?"

"You have charms enough if you cared to use them. You're kind and generous. Often too much so, but that too pleases some."

"With a temper as wild as my father's when stirred."

"There's nothing wrong with a temper when faced with injustice."

"Injustice is part of marriage when a husband has all the power, so I'd likely murder any man unwise enough to wed me. I'm a free woman! I have no man to dictate to me. Why should I change that?"

Claris heard panic in her rising voice and strove to calm herself. "The Mad Rector's daughter" could easily be misunderstood as "the rector's mad daughter."

Athena picked a sprig of rosemary and laid it on the flowers in Claris's basket. "For its soothing powers, child. Clearly I spoke too soon, but you must look to your future. The boys will go away to school, and I . . . Enough of this. I'm off to deliver a tonic to Miss Trueby. I may linger to chat, for she has amusing wisdom for a villager."

"Don't tell her fortune," Claris implored. "We need no more talk of you being a witch!"

Athena ignored her.

She stalked away toward the side path that led to the lane, tall and straight in her plain black gown, a black three-cornered hat on the white cap on her dark hair. Why would a woman who'd fled a cruel husband and lived an adventurous life become cautious now?

Athena's black cat, Yatta, stirred, stretched, and looked as if he would follow, but then he returned to rub against Claris's ankle.

"Why can't you teach her sense?" Claris asked, bending to stroke him.

Somewhere in her adventures Athena had learned herbal lore, and as the previous tenant, Lizzie Hubble, had grown many herbs, she was plying that trade. She took payment in kind from the local people but went to market in Guildford once a month to earn money. The money was useful and her creams and potions seemed effective, but even the grateful villagers talked of her being a witch. They didn't really mean it, but Claris knew country ways. If a disaster happened, if animals died in numbers or a barn burned down, they'd look for someone to blame.

The new rector, Cudlingston, regarded Athena with

suspicion, egged on by the local doctor, whose trade she'd usurped.

Claris was grateful to her grandmother, but she could be a difficult woman, especially if she was going to try to push Claris into marriage. Why on earth would she do that? She remembered the words *And I . . .* And I what?

Must leave here soon? Did Athena think Claris needed a man to take care of her before she could leave?

As she approached the back door to the cottage, Claris wondered how Athena could leave. She seemed to have no money other than her herbal earnings. Surely she wasn't hoping Claris would marry them all into a more comfortable life. That would be a sacrifice too far!

Claris went inside and put the basket on the kitchen table. Perhaps she thumped it down, for Ellie Gable asked, "What's the matter, dearie?"

Ellie had arrived with Athena, having been her companion from her early days. Claris had never sorted out whether Ellie had been her grandmother's lady's maid or a housemaid or even simply a friend, but here, despite her age, she seemed willing to be a maid of all work.

She was a short, wiry woman, with frothy white curls and a face creased by frequent smiles. She seemed to have endless energy. Claris hardly ever saw her sit down, and if she did, she'd have work in her hands.

At the moment she was standing at one end of the table, rubbing something smelly into rabbit skins. The twins had snared three rabbits yesterday, so there'd be rabbit stew today and fur for the winter, but Claris could do without the smell.

If Athena went, Ellie would go too, and that would be a blow. She'd miss Ellie's hard work, but she'd miss her generous nature more, and her sensible advice.

"She told me to marry, would you believe?"

"Athena? Marry who?"

"Anyone."

Ellie picked up another rabbit skin. "She'd never do that, dearie. Too many bad husbands out there."

Claris took down a pottery vase from a shelf and went to the water bucket to fill it. "Exactly, and if there are potential good husbands in the world, I don't see them around here."

"Young Farmer Barnett has an eye on you."

Claris laughed. "If he were so foolish, his mother and grandmother would tie him up, like Odysseus tied to the mast to resist the allure of the siren."

Ellie chuckled with her. "They'd try, wouldn't they, the prating fools, but he's a young man with a mind of his own, and with his father dead he's master there."

Claris put the vase in the middle of the table and filled it with sweet peas. The perfume fought the smell of Ellie's work but was losing.

Gideon Barnett a suitor?

He was a sturdy man and they were of an age. The Barnetts were regular churchgoers, so they'd met on Sundays and feast days all their lives, but no more than that. Her father had never wanted to mix with others, and her mother had refused to mingle with what she'd called the lesser ones—the villagers and farmers.

She realized Farmer Barnett had called at the cottage now and then. Athena provided a cream to help his grandmother's joints and when someone came for it they always brought something from the farm in gratitude. In the past few months, however, it had been Farmer Barnett himself, and last time the gift had been a good-sized piece of choice pork.

A courting gift?

"Barnett has his pick of the young women for miles around," she said, "and thank heavens. I don't want to have to reject him. Shall I wash the vegetables now? If not, I'll hoe around the beans. This warm weather suits the weeds too well."

"You do that, dearie. I've finished these and I want to wash the floors now Athena's not in and out. But wear your hat or you'll never rid yourself of those freckles."

Claris laughed. "I've had them all my life, but very

well." She put on her wide-brimmed straw hat before
going out to vent her emotions on groundsel and chick-
weed.

Then she wondered, *What emotions?*
Panic?
Over the mere mention of marriage?
Or over the idea of leaving here?

She glanced back at the cottage. It was the end one of
a terrace of four, all of which sagged to the right—that
was, to Lavender Cottage. The windows were tiny. The
small panes had glass in them, but it was a thick, rough
glass that distorted the view.

The thatch roof that covered all the cottages needed
repairs, but Squire Callway, their landlord, was ignoring
requests. She didn't know the state of the other cottages,
but hers had damp patches in the upstairs bedrooms.

Everyone pitied them for having to live here after
growing up in the rectory, but Claris had been ecstatic to
escape. Despite the cottage's damp and drafts, which had
made the winter hard, she didn't want to leave.

She was safe here, and if Athena left, so be it. She
could manage on her own.

Chapter 4

Perry approached a terrace of four small cottages, skeptical that one housed Miss Claris Mallow, daughter of the Reverend Henry Mallow, once a friend of Giles Perriam. On arrival in Old Barford, he'd left his horse at the inn and gone to the rectory, which was a handsome house that couldn't be more than forty years old. There he'd learned that Mallow was a year dead and that his family was living at Lavender Cottage.

Sometimes "cottage" was applied to a small house of some style and dignity, and that's what he'd expected. This row lacked both, but the end one on the left was fronted by lavender plants, so that must be his destination. The modern rectory lay only a hundred yards away as the crow flies, but it was a hundred miles away in all other respects. Henry Mallow hadn't provided well for his family, but that could be to his own advantage.

If the family was impoverished, Miss Mallow would be eager to wed. In fact, he'd be an angel to rival Gabriel at the Annunciation. Amused by that image, he walked up to the warped door and rapped on it with the head of his riding crop. He'd soon be back in Town.

In the week since Giles's death, he'd received two reproaches about tasks abandoned when he'd obeyed Cousin Giles's summons. One was indirectly from the king. There'd also been a fuming letter from his father. As usual, his father fumed to no purpose, for there was nothing to be done about Perriam Manor other than this.

He was about to knock again when the door was opened by a maidservant so short he thought her a child until he saw the wrinkled face. Sixty if she was a day, though when she smiled her teeth all seemed sound.

"Good afternoon, sir. Can I help you?"

"Is Miss Mallow at home?"

"*Miss* Mallow, is it?" the maid asked, seeming surprised.

"Yes." Was she married after all? No, for then she'd not be a Mallow.

"She's in the garden, sir. Would you mind going round, for I'm swabbing the floor."

He could see the truth of that behind her. The door opened into a front room with an uneven flagstone floor that was awash with water. A mop was propped against the wall. Oddly, the room contained a large table and shelves of jars and bottles.

A stillroom?

Potions?

The curse returned unsettlingly to mind.

Clarrie had laid a curse on Giles, and her sister, Nora, had claimed to know how to raise it. Nora was Claris Mallow's mother.

Would he be marrying into a family of witches? Witches who knew how to cast curses?

Even so, it must be done.

"A shame to bring Miss Mallow indoors on such a lovely day," Perry agreed. "The path to my left?"

"That's right, sir. She'll likely be down the end."

Whatever that meant. Perry headed for the path.

The cottage was in a poor state, but it had some rural charms. The path was bordered on the right by a bed bursting with colorful flowers, worked over by bees on this sunny afternoon. To his left lay a hedge, twitteringly full of birds.

When he came to the end of the path, he found a contrast. Far less color here, because the garden was devoted to herbs. He had little interest in horticulture, but he was sure everything here had its purpose for cooking or healing, even the brash marigolds crowding along some edges.

Cooking, healing—and magic?

He looked around for other evidence of witchcraft but found none.

A bench sat in one corner with a wooden table in front of it in a position that would catch the afternoon sun. Behind it, a line strung from house to tree carried a full load of white laundry, stirring in the breeze. His life rarely involved lines of laundry, and there was a simple beauty in the movement.

Then he noted the simplicity of the undergarments and that some were patched or darned.

Impoverished.

Excellent.

So where was his bride?

Down the end.

He circled the herb garden and realized that a trellis covered by climbing flowers wasn't the end of the garden but a partition. He went behind to find a gated fence, and beyond that a vegetable garden being pecked over by hens.

Still no sign of Miss Mallow.

Then a movement drew his eye behind a tall frame covered by scarlet-flowered vines. He went through the gate and walked down a side path.

A sturdy woman was hoeing between rows of cabbages as if weeds were imps from hell. She wore a wide hat from which straw escaped around the edge and from which dark hanks of hair escaped down her back. Her shabby black gown was kirtled up to show battered leather shoes and six inches of dirt-splashed white stockings.

Another servant, so Claris Mallow couldn't be in truly dire straits, alas.

Where was she?

As he approached the woman to ask, she straightened. Some hair must have fallen on her face, for she brushed it away, taking a moment's rest and turning to look around. At the sight of him, she stared, and something about her manner alerted him to the astonishing truth.

He bowed. "Good day to you, ma'am. Do I address Miss Mallow?"

He still expected denial, probably a laughing denial in a broad country accent, but she said, "Who are you?" in a well-bred voice.

"Your pardon, ma'am. Your servant advised me to come back here. She's washing the floors."

She laughed then, pushing back her hair again, leaving a dirty streak on her round cheek, and not the first one. She was a mess, but her speech was that of a lady. He'd never imagined his bride with a country burr, but given her appearance it could have been so. He counted his blessings.

"Ellie would do that. I beg your pardon, sir. How may I help you?"

Miss Mallow in the flesh.

His bride-to-be.

How very ordinary she was.

A strange word to come to mind, but appropriate.

She was of average height for a woman, and average build. Her general appearance was below average, but that was because of the dirt, the hat, the extremely unflattering black gown, and the grubby apron. Her face held all the normal features, decently arranged, but her complexion showed that she didn't wear her battered hat often enough. He reminded himself that her physical attributes made no difference. He must marry her.

"My name is Perriam, Miss Mallow, and I believe your father was once acquainted with a relative of mine, Giles Perriam, of Perriam Manor, Berkshire."

The details had merely been intended to ease into his subject, so he was surprised to see her eyes widen, perhaps with fear. She did have quite fine eyes—clear and perhaps hazel.

Had she been in her mother's confidence?

Did she know all about the curse?

She recovered, but her eyes slid from his. "Perriam? Perhaps I do vaguely remember. However, my father is dead."

"I am aware of that, Miss Mallow. It is with you I wish to speak."

She focused on him. "Me? About what?"

"It is both complex and delicate. Perhaps we could speak in the house?"

"Not if Ellie's doing the floors." He thought she might refuse, but then she shrugged. "We can sit outside."

She propped her hoe against the frame and led the way back through the gate. Her straight back was tense, but she moved lightly and her shortened skirts swayed with the movement of her hips in a rather attractive way.

She seemed to be a practical, no-nonsense sort of woman, so this should go well.

She led the way into the herb garden and indicated the bench. "Please be seated, Mr. Perriam. I'll wash my hands and return. Would you like something to drink? We have small beer and cider."

"Cider, if you please."

It was a drink he rarely tasted, but it seemed suited to the setting and might make her more at ease. He sat on the bench and reviewed the situation.

Well-spoken, well-mannered, and not given to drama. All to the good.

Direct and perhaps brave, which could be challenging in an opponent, but a virtue in a wife.

She wasn't a beauty, but he'd have no cause to be ashamed of her once she was decently dressed. There were creams and lotions to soften and lighten a lady's complexion. Given the herbs and the stillroom, it was odd she didn't employ them already.

A brush on his thigh startled him. A sleek black cat had leapt onto the bench and was staring at him with amber eyes, as if seeking the secrets of his soul. The cat licked his fingers, the tongue abrasive; then, as if it had learned something, it butted his hand. Perry took the hint and stroked it. It purred, and he chuckled.

"Do people always do as you command?"

He continued to stroke, for he liked cats. They were elegant and self-sufficient. They didn't fawn or learn demeaning tricks, and they would correct sharply if displeased.

Would the cat's owner have similar qualities?

If so, the marriage might even prove amusing.

Claris hurried into the kitchen, where she poured water into a bowl and washed her hands. She welcomed the blended herbs that made the smell of Athena's soap so soothing.

"Trouble, is he?" Ellie asked, coming into the kitchen with her mop and bucket.

"He's a Perriam."

"Ah."

Ellie had never lived at the rectory, but she'd heard of Reverend Mallow's ravening guilt over some long-ago sin, a sin connected to a Perriam.

"I've offered him cider."

"Right, then." Ellie went into the larder to bring out the big earthenware jug.

Claris reached down two glasses from a shelf. They rarely used glasses, but she didn't feel able to serve that man in a pottery mug. She couldn't find words to express how he alarmed her.

"His dress is simple—leather breeches, brown jacket—but . . ."

"London made and costly." Comments like that always pointed to Ellie being more than she seemed. "Don't you go fussing, dearie. There's nothing he can do to you, be he ever so grand."

Claris wished she could feel sure of that.

"It's not just his clothing. He's . . . he's like a butterfly."

"A butterfly?" Ellie asked, staring.

"Oh, I don't know. But he moves, he speaks, he gestures . . . nothing like any man around here."

"London ways, is all. Likely a court gallant."

"But what's a court gallant doing *here*? And what does he want with me?"

"Best take him his cider and find out."

Claris poured cider into the glasses. "I wish Athena were here."

"You can deal with him. Whatever brings him, it's nothing to do with you."

"I wish I could be sure."

She'd never told Athena or Ellie about her mother's obsession with avenging her sister's death. They knew Claris was named after her dead aunt, Clarrie Dunsworth, but not the rest. It was too demented to be spoken of. Oh, dear heavens, was this man here about her mother's attempts at blackmail? Mother had been dead for eleven years!

Ellie was frowning at her. "Are you truly frightened, dearie?"

Claris found a smile. "No, and you're right. Whatever crushed my father with guilt happened long ago and he did his best to suffer for it on earth."

She hadn't told Athena or Ellie all about his suffering, either.

She picked up the cider and walked toward the door but paused by the window to steal another look through the half-open window. He was sitting on the bench stroking Yatta. Sitting shouldn't be remarkable, but she was taken aback by how elegantly he'd disposed himself, probably without thought.

London ways.

A court gallant.

A court gallant could mean power.

Even the nobility.

Claris had little to do with the local gentry, never mind the nobility, but she'd seen the Marquess and Marchioness of Ashart now and then. They were the local grandees, and their great house, Cheynings, lay not far away, so they sometimes passed by.

Claris realized that was what she'd recognized. This Perriam was from the same mold.

Yatta fancied himself a guard cat, so his verdict was made — Perriam was safe.

Claris feared that this time, the cat was wrong.

His hair should reassure her, for it wasn't darkly dramatic like the marquess's. It was brown, wavy, and simply tied back with a black ribbon, but the sun caught copper and gold, making it seem more alive than was natural, and even fiery. . . .

A hank of hair tumbled over her eye, alerting her to what a mess she must be.

She put down the cider, whipped off her hat, then ran to the tiny mirror to pin up her hair, which always stayed stubbornly brown in even the brightest sun.

"If you're fussing," Ellie said, "your apron's grubby."

Claris whipped it off, but what difference did it make? She was in one of the old mourning gowns she wore for work. She must still look a draggle-tail.

"Oh, don't be foolish," she muttered. Her elegant visitor had no more interest in her appearance than he had in the garden gate.

She hurried toward the cider.

"Your skirt, dearie. You're showing your ankles."

"He's already seen them," Claris retorted, but she unpinned her skirt so it fell to a decent level. Then she picked up the cider and glasses and marched out.

Mr. Perriam dislodged Yatta and rose.

Oh, so gracefully.

Claris set the glasses on the table and sat on the bench, right at one end. He took the hint and sat at the other end, leaving feet of space between them.

Claris took a sip. "Now, Mr. Perriam, how may I help you?"

He too sipped and then put his glass down. "As I said,

Miss Mallow, my distant cousin, Giles Perriam, knew your father in their younger days. He required me to come here."

"For what purpose?"

"May I ask what you know of the connection?"

"You may ask, but I see no reason to answer." Claris realized that was an error, implying that she did know. "Indeed," she added, taking another drink, "how could I know? The acquaintance occurred before I was born."

"Stories are passed down in families. In mine, we gnaw on an event many generations ago, when the Perriam lands were divided between two sisters, which led to one part being lost from the whole."

He'd come to talk of his family's history? At least that seemed safe.

"Lost?" she said. "Weren't both sisters of the same family?"

"I salute your common sense, Miss Mallow, but property goes to the eldest son so that it may be kept whole. Keeping estates whole is a sacred trust."

"Among the grand perhaps. The Perriam family is noble?"

She'd sensed it, but she still hoped it wasn't true.

"My father is the Earl of Hernescroft."

Heaven help her. "Then I'm even more surprised that you think you have business with me, sir."

"Roots and branches can spread a long way. Your parents never spoke of the sad history of your aunt, Clarrie Dunsworth?"

Claris wished she were a better liar. "I know she died young and that my mother believed the blame lay with the man you claim as cousin."

"Very, very distant cousin. The scion, in fact, of the younger of those sister heiresses, as I am a scion of the older. The two branches of the family are not fond."

"Yet you come here at his bidding? Enough, Mr. Perriam. I have work to do. What do you want?"

Oh, he wasn't used to being commanded, this fine gentleman, especially by a woman, and a woman such as she. Claris met his angry eyes.

"I too have work to do. My cousin Giles is recently deceased, and his will requires that I marry you, Miss Mallow. I hope to do it as expeditiously as possible."

Claris stared, truly speechless.

"Marry me?" she managed at last.

"Marry you. I am Giles Perriam's heir, but in order to claim the inheritance, I must marry you. It might be some deathbed attempt to put right an old wrong, or even to deflect a curse—"

"A curse!"

"—but it is assuredly an act of malice. Still, it must be done."

Claris rose to her feet, needing a hand on the table to steady herself.

"I fear you are unbalanced, sir. Please leave."

He too rose but made no move to obey. "I'm as sane as any man in this demented world. Come, come, Miss Mallow, don't cling to the conventional response. The marriage will give you all possible advantages, and I pledge to be an amenable husband."

"Amenable?" Claris echoed. "Be amenable, sir, by leaving this instant!"

For the first time she noted that he wore a sword.

A sword!

She moved to one side, putting the length of the table between them.

"Miss Mallow . . ."

She glanced around for any weapon but didn't even see a trowel.

"Ellie!" she shouted.

Stupid, stupid. What could Ellie do?

Then Ellie came out of the cottage, astonishingly with a pistol in her hands. Though it was a small gun, it seemed too large for her to manage, so Claris snatched it and pointed it, hands trembling.

"Leave, Mr. Perriam, and do not return!"

She'd never held a pistol in her life, and it was shockingly heavy. Could she bring herself to fire it?

"You heard Miss Claris, sir," Ellie said. "You'd best be off before she does something she'll regret."

He suddenly laughed, eyes bright with it. "I'm tempted to test that. But how delightful this is, Miss Mallow. I very much look forward to our further acquaintance."

His eyes in some way held hers, sending a shocking frisson through her.

Fear.

But it didn't feel exactly like fear, even if it did make her knees loosen and her hands tremble. She raised the pistol a little higher, trying to steady it on him.

Without urgency, he picked up his gloves, hat, and riding crop. Then he bowed, in an elaborate style that must surely be from court and power but was all insolence, and walked away. What was worse, he turned his back in complete disregard of the gun. Claris was tempted to shoot him for that alone.

Yatta leapt down and followed, perhaps pretending to himself that he was chasing the enemy away, but Claris knew the truth. They couldn't have forced that man away if he'd not been willing to go. Even so, she kept the pistol trained on him until he rounded the cottage and was out of sight.

Ellie took the pistol from her weakening hands. "There, there, dearie, he's gone now."

Claris collapsed back onto the bench. "He'll return."

"Likely he will."

"Then I *will* shoot him." It was the frisson speaking. "Show me how."

"It's not a skill learned in a day, dearie. This one isn't loaded or primed or I'd not have let you take it."

Claris sank her head in her hands. She'd threatened him with nothing, and perhaps he'd known that. She looked up to glare at the gun. "Where did that thing come from? Why do you have a pistol?"

"We've been in some unruly places, Athena and I." Ellie put the pistol on the table and sat beside Claris to take one of her hands. "Now, dearie, what did he do to set you screeching?"

Claris clutched that hand. "I'd think I'd dreamed it if not for those two glasses. And the pistol. Ellie, he proposed marriage! No, he didn't propose. He stated that he was going to marry me. As if I had no say in the matter at all!"

"Perhaps he thought you'd snatch at the chance."

"That's it! He did. Said how comfortable I would be, how amenable he would be. How dare he?"

"Like I said, he likely thought you'd be honored, a fine gentleman like him. Though that could be a sham. Many a fine man eats oats."

"Eats oats?"

"Or any other poor food. If you're thinking of it—"

"Of marrying him? Of course not!"

"I'm merely saying that if you were, you'd best confirm that he's as prosperous as he seems. But then, why should he deceive you? That's the line a scoundrel takes with an heiress."

Claris shook her head. "I think you're as mad as he is. I have no intention of marrying anyone, be he rich as Croesus, but certainly not a stranger claiming to be forced into it."

"Forced? Now, that's interesting. It'd take a bit to force a man like that." Ellie pushed to her feet and picked up the pistol. "You tell us all about it when Athena's home. But for now, I've the floors to finish and the stew to tend."

"I'll help."

Ellie looked at her. "Perhaps that's best. Keep busy, dearie. And keep an open mind."

"On marriage to that wretch? Closed as a tomb. I'm mistress of my life, and so I shall remain."

Chapter 5

Perry returned to the inn to collect his horse, his amusement fading. Damn Giles Perriam for plunging him into this mess.

He'd not expected this mission to be entirely smooth, but he'd not thought to terrify a lady and be cast as a villain. He shouldn't have let her manner trigger him into making his proposal so abruptly, but Zeus alone knew why it had frightened her so badly. He wasn't the sort of man who frightened women, and he'd never given one cause to scream for help.

May Giles be writhing in hell's hottest flames, he thought. A furnace even fiercer than the one in the village smithy, which blasted out at him as he passed. The smith, stocky and broad, was standing by his door and nodded good day. He was probably keeping an eye on the stranger.

Perry returned the salute, wondering what the man thought of the coven at the cottage. He put aside such nonsense. He'd been driven off by a gun, not a spell, and all in all he admired a woman willing to come to pistols to make her point.

His shabby bride-to-be certainly had fire in her. Given her mother and her aunt, he'd been a dolt not to have expected that, but what a family to marry into! A cursing witch, a vicious harpy, and a pistol-waving virago. He had no choice, however, so he'd return tomorrow better prepared, and win.

It must be an idle day in Old Barford, for the innkeeper was standing outside his hostelry, puffing on a pipe. He was as big a man as the smith, but softer.

"You'll be wanting your horse, sir? Can I offer you some ale before your journey?"

Perry almost rejected the offer, but inn chatter might be useful. If Miss Mallow was as impoverished as she seemed, why had she rejected his offer without a thought?

He went into the taproom and accepted a foaming tankard. The only other person present was a hunchbacked ancient on a settle, whose gnarled hands clutched a tankard of his own. He gave Perry a deeply suspicious look from under bushy white brows but said nothing.

The innkeeper picked up his pipe again and puffed it back into life. "Gather you visited Lavender Cottage, sir." As he'd thought, nothing went unnoted in a village, especially a stranger. "Sad case, them being left orphaned so shockingly."

"Shockingly?" Perry responded, as he was supposed to.

"Well, see, their mother went first. Ten years ago, would you say, Matt?"

The ancient nodded. "Near enough, Rob, near enough. But went quietly in her bed did Mistress Mallow."

"Aye, despite being a restless woman in life."

Old Matt cackled. "More than restless, I'd say. Whenever I pass her grave I expect to see the ground churning."

Perry looked to the innkeeper for a second opinion, but he nodded. "Never happy, sir. Always angry over something, and freely voicing it."

The harpy.

"A difficult wife," Perry said.

"You have the right of that, sir, but Reverend Mallow was difficult in his own way." The innkeeper leaned forward as if to impart a secret, though ancient Matt must know all. "Reverend Mallow had a weight of sin on him, sir. He spoke of it often, though he never said exactly what. He had a mighty fear of death, sir, because he dreaded hell."

"I had a relation who was exactly the same," Perry said.

"The sinner's burden, sir, the sinner's burden. The godly man has no fear of death."

Yet many do, Perry thought.

The innkeeper went on. "Often preached a powerful sermon on damnation, did Reverend Mallow, sir, confessing himself a sinner and begging God for forgiveness. He'd urge us all to follow his example—to forego worldly luxuries and give all we could to the poor."

"He's to be admired for setting such an example," Perry said, but he now had the explanation for the poverty of the rector's dependents.

"Indeed, sir," the innkeeper said, but without sincerity. A noise from the old man indicated a similar doubt.

"But that brought his end," the innkeeper went on. "He was in powerful form one Sunday, describing the horrors of hell, when he turned purple and died. Right there in the pulpit. Or perhaps from the fall," he added thoughtfully, "for he tumbled out to land at his children's feet."

Now, there was an image to stick in the mind.

Especially a sensitive lady's.

Was Miss Mallow mad as well as angry?

Would insanity be an excuse to overturn the will?

"They must have been deeply shocked," Perry said.

"Indeed they were, sir, but there was worse to come. With Reverend Mallow dead, the rectory was no longer their home, even though they'd lived there all their lives. Lost his stipend too."

"A sad case."

"And like to be tragic except that their grandmother turned up. The rector's mother, that is. Never seen here afore, but she took charge. She could do no better than to secure some sort of pension and find them a home in a laborer's cottage, but at least they're not tramping the roads."

Perry drank more of his ale. The story explained much but made Miss Mallow's behavior more peculiar. She'd been raised to a better life and must know her only hope of improvement was through marriage. The grandmother sounded more practical. Perhaps she'd take his side.

"Mistress Mallow wasn't at home when I called. I hope to meet her soon."

Old Matt muttered something and cackled. Perry was about to demand an explanation when the ancient spoke.

"A daft man was Rector Mallow, sir. Told me m'aching joints were a gift from God to wash away m'sins. He'd probably have called Grannie Mallow's cream a work of the devil, but I'll take me chances on the hereafter for a bit of ease today."

Perry's image of a kindly grandmother with round cheeks and smiles shattered.

In rural parlance, "grannie" often designated an old woman skilled in herbal lore—one who in less enlightened times would have been called a witch. And Grannie Mallow wasn't related to Carrie and Nora Dunsworth.

Sorcery on both sides of the family?

The innkeeper turned to Perry. "Mistress Mallow's skilled in plant lore, sir, which she shares with her neighbors at very little cost, as a good Christian would."

"Rector Mallow couldn't abide her," said Old Matt. "Heard him once refer to his mother as the Whore of Babylon."

He pronounced it "wore" with relish.

"You shut your mouth, Matt Byman. There's no call to repeat such filth. A very respectable lady, sir, and from a good family. Her maidservant once said as her father was a titled gentleman."

Perry's vision of Grannie Mallow shifted again.

Grandmother, grannie, lady, and whore?

He couldn't wait to meet the woman, but he'd no idea now of how she'd affect his goal.

He drained his tankard. "My horse, if you please."

The innkeeper went to a back door to shout the order and then returned. "Can I hope you brought the Mallow family good news, sir?"

"I believe so. I'll be returning tomorrow when Miss Mallow has had time to consider matters and speak with her grandmother."

"I hope your matters are to their advantage, then," said Old Matt, "or Grannie Mallow'll put the evil eye on you."

"Hold your wicked tongue, Matt. She does naught but good."

The overhung eyes fixed on Perry. "I'm just warning this fine gentleman not to try any mischief with the Mallows, that's all."

"And that's a fair point, sir," said the innkeeper, amiably enough but meaning it. "No one would take kindly to that." It carried more weight than a wavering and probably unloaded pistol. The villagers cared enough about the family to make life difficult for anyone harming them.

"As I have no ill intentions, I'm at ease." Perry put some coins on the bar. "Another drink for you, sir," he said to Old Matt, "and my thanks for your warning. I know it was well intended."

He left the inn, mounted, and rode off with enough puzzles in his head to occupy a month.

A month he didn't have.

He had only twenty-two days to get his bride to the altar.

His rebellious bride.

His unreasonably rebellious bride, who'd turned a pistol on him. When he returned tomorrow, it would probably be loaded, so he'd best put together the pieces and find the right way to proceed.

Her father had been driven mad by guilt.

Perry had assumed that the connection between Cousin Giles and Claris Mallow was only the betrayed

Clarrie Dunsworth and her vengeful sister, Nora. What if Henry Mallow's dread sin had been his active part in Clarrie's destruction? But if Mallow had helped ruin Clarrie, why marry the sister?

An attempt at penitent restitution?

Possible, but why would she marry him?

The vicious harpy. The angry, tumultuous woman. Old Matt's musings about the heaving earth over her grave could make the hair stand on end. Harpy Mallow had approached Giles, offering to lift the curse if he'd pledge to marry her daughter, who was a mere child. Her mother hadn't considered her happiness. She'd been obsessed to the point of insanity.

Witchcraft on both sides of the family, and insanity as well. All that was needed was a giant helmet falling from the sky for his life to be a piece of nonsense to rival Horace Walpole's *Castle of Otranto*.

He gave thanks that he was a guest at Cheynings. The Marquess of Ashart was a rational man, a scientist with a particular interest in the study of the skies. Perhaps he could refocus this mess into normality.

Claris wore herself out with work, waiting desperately for her grandmother's return so she could discuss the situation. But a short time after Athena returned, the twins came home from their lessons in the next village. Unusually, they were arguing.

"You did," Peter yelled.

"I didn't!" Tom yelled back.

"You are such a dunce!"

"Stop." At their grandmother's voice, they paused. "Or you will get none of the honey Mistress Trueby gave me."

They turned into eleven-year-old angels. Truly they could look angelic, with their clear eyes and skin and tumbling brown curls, but no angel would ever be so noisy. Despite that, Claris would miss her brothers when they left for school, which they must do soon if their education was to progress as it should.

They all sat to rabbit stew followed by bread and honey, talking of their day. Claris didn't mention the visitor in front of the boys and was grateful when Ellie didn't either.

When they'd all finished, she rose to clear the table. "Off to your tasks," she told the twins. "There's a weak spot in the chicken coop and water to bring from the well."

They went willingly enough, still full of energy after a long day. They were probably hoping for encounters with some village lads that might lead to a game. They rubbed along well with the local boys, whereas Claris had never made friends in the village. Her mother had kept her too close for that, and after her mother died she'd had the twins to care for.

Her mother would have allowed her to have friends from the local gentry, but those families had avoided the Mallows as much as possible. Claris couldn't blame them.

"Let's sit outside," she said. "It's a lovely evening."

Only Athena took up the invitation. She sat on the bench and said, "Who was this visitor to have you all on end? Gideon Barnett finally plucking up courage to propose? Or some other suitor?"

Claris laughed but then realized that in a way her grandmother was right. "A threatener, more like." She described the encounter, then asked, "What am I to do?"

"Marry him? It would be a better life than this."

So she *did* want Claris to marry them into comfort!

"I'm sure your life with your husband was 'better' in those terms," Claris pointed out, "but you couldn't bear it."

"A point. A salient point. Let me amend my advice. If this Mr. Perriam is a decent, kindly man, which my husband wasn't, you could marry him."

"If he were a saint from heaven I'd not marry him, so take heed of that."

"Very wise," Athena said, undisturbed. "Saints make poor husbands, quite apart from their having to be dead to be canonized. What of this curse? Do you know anything about that?"

"Of course not. I know nothing of Perriams other than the occasional mention by my father. Do you not know anything?"

Athena stared at her. "I paid no attention to my husband or Henry after I left, but I assume it's possible Henry's mad guilt has some connection to the Perriam curse."

"Even if so, it's not for me to expiate their sins. Yet that man is going to return and try to insist."

"You could shoot him. I gather you waved Ellie's pistol around."

"No jokes. Why on earth does Ellie have a pistol?"

"We've traveled in places where it was wise. Do you think it drove him off?"

Claris would have liked to say yes, but she shook her head. "I think it suited him to leave then."

"To give you time to consider."

"As if I'm some weak-minded fool whose convictions re-form by the moment."

"Claris, resolution is a virtue, but stubbornness is not. Consider well. The life of an impoverished spinster is not to be cherished."

"I'm *content*," Claris insisted, remembering saying that earlier, before her world had been cast into turmoil. "Or I would be if not threatened."

"He can't force you to the altar."

"I thank God for that, but I don't want to be pestered."

"We can't forbid him to visit the village, but we don't have to let him into the house or garden."

"Who's going to stop him? He's a gentleman. Ellie said his clothes were London made. How did she know that?"

"We've spent time in London."

Claris rose to pace the herb garden. "Perhaps I could complain to someone, seek protection. The squire ..."

She dismissed that. Squire Callway was no match for Perriam. "Lord Wishart? The Marquess of Ashart!" she exclaimed. "He'd see him off."

"And how would you approach such a man?"

Claris blew out a breath. She'd not be allowed through the door of Cheynings. "I've heard of people delivering petitions for help to such men."

"To what purpose? What is your complaint? A gentleman has offered you marriage."

"And plans to return, even though I forbade it!"

"When he's returned a half dozen times you might have a case."

"Then what am I to do tomorrow?"

Athena shrugged. "I could stay at home and stand willing to shoot him. We could bury him in the garden with no one the wiser."

"No jokes!" Claris protested.

But later, sleepless in her bed, she wondered if it had been a joke. Her mysterious grandmother might be well capable of shooting a man.

She herself had pointed a pistol at him.

She didn't regret it, but it was the sort of thing to stir a man's anger. He might return similarly armed—or even with a magistrate. That made her sit up in panic. It was probably a crime to threaten the son of an earl with a gun.

She collapsed back down again. Why was this happening to her?

By what justice were her father's sins being invoked to torment her?

Chapter 6

Perry enjoyed riding, so the three miles to Cheynings restored his mood.

When he'd set out on this enterprise, he'd intended to take a room at an inn in Woking, but he'd run into Ashart there and been invited to his home. They weren't close friends, but they'd both lived their adult lives at court and shared many cynical opinions of court and the beau monde.

Perry had been curious to witness Ashart the husband and father, who seemed improbably fond of rural living. Many said that with a beauty for a wife he had reason to spend time at Cheynings, but a wife was a moveable object.

Last evening had answered some questions. Ashart had frankly admitted that Cheynings had needed extensive repairs, which had drained his purse. The beau monde was expensive, but rural living was economical and had allowed him to supervise the work.

It had also been clear that he was enjoying doing so, which was astonishing, even given Genova Ashart's stunning blond beauty and the charms of an infant daughter who might one day rival her mother. That was no puzzle for his investigation, however.

He hadn't told the Asharts the details of his business, only that he needed to visit an old connection of Giles Perriam's. Now, however, he needed help, so once they'd dined and were enjoying coffee in the drawing room, he told the tale.

Ashart laughed. "That almost rivals my family's demented obsessions and feuds. You're truly going to marry this woman?"

"One must suffer for family duty," Perry said, "and perhaps she deserves some good fortune."

"Then why the pistol?" Genova Ashart asked. Perry had discovered that her beauty was matched with intelligence and an independent spirit.

"She hasn't yet recognized her good fortune?"

"Or accurately sees that you are not it."

"She's living in poverty," he pointed out.

"Wealth is not the only consideration in life, or I'd never have married Ashart."

Ashart chuckled. "A true folly, love. One for which I'm grateful."

The Asharts open fondness was distinctly unfashionable. Perhaps that was why they lurked in the countryside.

"In my experience," Perry said, "all women wish to marry, but most especially those without the means for a comfortable life. Why is Miss Mallow so different? A sensible answer, if you please."

"Perhaps she loves another," Genova said.

"Inconvenient if true, but I don't think so. She would have thrown that at me like a spear."

Ashart said, "Perhaps her parents' marriage has given her a distaste for matrimony."

"More plausible, but illogical. She and I are not they."

"Not everyone is ruled by logic," Genova pointed out.

"Alas."

Genova frowned. "Your social skills are famous, Perriam, but I fear you must have mishandled this."

"I did. She seemed so practical that I raced to the point. What now? I have only twenty-two days to get her to the altar, and less time than that before I should be back in Town."

"You have pressing appointments with your tailor and boot maker?" Ashart asked lazily. He knew better.

"I have, but yet more pressing duties for my father." To Genova, he added, "He provides both a salary and sinecures so that I be ready to support the family's interests."

"What does Rothgar pay you?" Ashart asked.

So that was the thrust of his comment, and might be the reason Perry had been invited here. Perry sometimes assisted the Marquess of Rothgar in delicate matters to do with court politics, but Rothgar was Ashart's cousin and until recently they'd continued a family feud of their own.

"Are you still sparring with him?" Perry asked.

"Only for amusement, but I could bear to know what engages him at the moment." When Perry didn't oblige, he shrugged. "Very well, I'll return to your entanglement. I see no hope. It's no longer possible to drag an unwilling bride to the altar."

Genova offered more coffee and refilled cups. "The normal course is to woo. That didn't occur to you?"

Perry spread his hands. "How, if she has more brain than a pigeon, and I assure you she has. Did I glimpse her amid her cabbages in her dismal black gown and tattered straw hat and be instantly slain by passion?"

"As bad as that?"

"I understate the case, but at least her appearance is amendable and by God's grace she speaks well and has respectable manners."

"When not offended," Ashart pointed out. "Pointing a pistol at a guest is not comme il faut."

"If you can't woo," Genova said, "then persuade. You have much to offer."

"And a gift for it," Ashart said. "If challenged, you could persuade the king to dance a jig down Pall Mall, but you can't coax a clergyman's impoverished daughter to the altar?"

"I prefer honest dealings."

"And you a courtier."

"I prefer honest dealings in my personal life, and marriage is personal no matter how practical the cause."

"Then you've a lost cause."

"I reject defeat. I didn't explain the situation or show her the documents. When I do she'll see the sense of it."

Genova rolled her eyes. "Lord save me from illogical men! The documents explain your needs. They don't touch hers."

"I'll lay out the advantages to her, but I hope her grandmother will already have done so."

"Grannie Mallow?" Ashart said with twitching lips. "She's probably toiling over her cauldron, perfecting a spell to turn you into a toad."

Claris spent a restless night, her problems building to horrors, as such things do. Morning light brought some sanity, and she persuaded herself that he wouldn't try to take her to court over the pistol. He wanted to marry her, not throw her in jail, but how could she convince him she'd never marry him, no matter how he pestered her?

When she found herself taking down one of her better skirts and bodices, she put both back on their hooks and dressed in the black again. It suited her mood and she didn't want Pestilential Perriam to think she sought to please.

She went into the garden to let out the chickens, aware that the weather was in tune with her mind. The sky was overcast and threatened rain. Perhaps the fine gentleman wouldn't want to get his London clothes wet. She collected the eggs and returned to help with breakfast. The boys staggered in with fresh water from the village well. Soon they'd eaten and were setting off for the two-mile walk to Hutton Vill and their lessons.

"Study well!" Claris called after them.

Father had insisted on educating them to save money, but he'd not had the patience for it. Despite her efforts to help, they were sadly behind for their age, especially in Latin and Greek. Reverend Johnson was striving to get them ready to go to Dr. Porter's School in Winchester.

She wished she could afford to send them to Winchester College, which had an excellent reputation, but the fees were too high. Peter was clever and might obtain free admission as a poor scholar, but Tom was slower, and she knew they'd not separate.

When educated, what profession could they aim for? Reverend Johnson had suggested the navy, which they could enter soon, with no money needed. She couldn't bear the thought. She returned to the kitchen to make bread. Kneading dough was exceptionally soothing.

Pestilential Perriam did not come.

She knew it was too early, but even so she pounded at him through the dough for drawing out the torture, her temper rising.

Ellie was preparing damsons for jam, and Athena was going between her herb garden and her stillroom. He was keeping them all waiting.

She set the bread to rise and looked for another job. Athena came in from the garden with a basketful of seed heads.

"I want a pistol," Claris said. "Loaded and ready."

Athena considered her and then nodded. "Very well." She went upstairs.

"You sure, dearie?" Ellie asked. "You don't want to do something you'll regret."

"I'll regret it if I let that man force me to the altar. Regret it all my days."

"I'm sure you know best."

Claris wasn't, but she wouldn't be forced. She would not!

Athena returned. "It's not cocked. To do that, you pull back this hammer on top all the way." She did so. It made two clicks. "Half cock then full cock. Now, if I were to squeeze back the trigger with my finger, the gun would fire. Be careful. This trigger is eased to suit my old fingers. To uncock it I pull back again and carefully ease the flint down. Take it outside and practice the action. Don't point it at anything you don't want to kill."

As if alarmed, Yatta ran upstairs.

Claris took the pistol outside. It seemed heavier than yesterday, but then, this was Athena's, not Ellie's. She just managed to pull back the hammer with her thumb.

Click. Click.

She couldn't squeeze the trigger without firing it. She pointed it at the cherry tree and imagined doing it.

Yes, she could.

If threatened, she could.

She very carefully eased the hammer back down.

Click. Click.

Her hands were shaking, but she was ready. If he attempted abduction, she could hold him off. She returned to the kitchen and put the pistol on a shelf; then she looked around for something to do. . . .

There was a rap at the door.

Ellie moved to clean her hands, but Claris said, "I'll go."

She had to rub her hands on her skirt as she crossed the front room, for her palms were damp. She opened the door, and there he was, sword at his side. It was common enough for gentlemen to be armed when traveling, but she felt it as a threat. A pistol, however, must beat a sword any day.

He bowed. "Good day to you, Miss Mallow."

"I told you not to return."

"Alas, my business is imperative."

His manner was amiable, but that threatened as much as a snarl. *See how confident I am? A well-off and highly born male. What resistance can you offer, you little female mouse?*

Claris suppressed a growl. He'd soon see. Today she had Athena, and the pistol, loaded and ready.

"Come through to the kitchen. My grandmother is keen to meet you."

"The keenness is on both sides. Your paternal grandmother, I understand?"

"Yes."

"Do you have grandparents on your mother's side?"

Claris wanted to snap that it was none of his business, but pettiness would be weak, not strong. "No, alas. They both died before I was born." She entered the kitchen relieved to find Athena there. For once she would use the term Athena hated.

"Grandmother, Mr. Perriam has returned."

Athena eyed him without a trace of fear. "A son of the Earl of Hernescroft, I understand."

Perriam bowed. "Correct, ma'am."

"Full of his own importance, as I remember, and he was a young man then."

Claris wanted to applaud. Athena was skillfully establishing her credentials as an equal.

"We must speak here, sir," Athena said, taking command, "for we have only the two rooms and I've commandeered the front one for my potions."

All was going well, but with new eyes she saw how simple the kitchen was. Though it contained some elegant bits and pieces from the rectory, it was their only living space and was both cramped and disorderly. That wasn't helped by Ellie at one end of the plain table, squeezing cooked damson pulp to remove the stones.

"Shall I go?" Ellie asked.

"Of course not," Athena said, sitting at the other end, the head. "Ellie's been with me since before my marriage, Perriam, and knows all I know of my family's affairs. Claris."

Claris obeyed her grandmother's gesture and sat on her right. That put her close to the pistol. Perriam took the seat on Athena's left. Had Athena's directions been deliberate? In the Bible, the sheep were to be on God's right hand and the sinful goats on his left. Claris had always felt that was unfair to goats, but the placement was appropriate for a relentless invader.

Athena turned to him. "Explain yourself, young man. Your intent to marry Claris is extraordinary and unreasonable, but at first glance you appear to be a rational man."

Perriam's eyes narrowed at this attack, but his smile remained. "I was too abrupt yesterday and apologize for it, though in my defense, Miss Mallow did ask me to be brief."

"Because I was busy," Claris protested. "I'd no notion of such insanity."

"I grant you insanity in many aspects of this affair, but permit me to explain. The telling of this story could waste a day, but I'll do my best to make it brief. As I told you, generations ago the Perriam properties were divided between two sisters, there being no sons to inherit. The older daughter was to pass on the title, so her share of the property would be attached to the title, with its own rules. The property taken by the younger daughter would pass on by will. In order to avoid it being lost to the Perriams forever, it was legally settled that if her line failed to produce a male heir, it would pass back to the senior line. Dry stuff, but essential background."

Athena said, "I believe our poor female minds can absorb the facts, wet or dry."

Ellie chuckled.

Perriam's brows twitched, but if anything he was amused, which wasn't a good sign. A powerful opponent wasn't amusing.

"Giles Perriam died recently, leaving no surviving son, despite taking three wives and siring four sons. All died young. I hesitate to mention the next detail because it's foolish, but it's the pin that holds these tattered shreds together. He believed the deaths came about through a curse, a curse laid on him by your aunt, Miss Mallow."

"By Aunt Clarrie?" Claris asked, staring at him.

"Whom he ruined and abandoned. Do you know that tale?"

"I do, and it's a wicked one. Giles Perriam married Aunt Clarrie but later denied it, despite her being with child. She committed suicide and Mother hated him for it, with reason. I know nothing of a curse, however, and don't believe in such things."

"Giles Perriam did suffer misfortune," Perriam pointed out.

"I hope that was this Clarrie's doing," Athena said. "Such wretches should suffer, and I applaud her!"

"As do I," Claris said.

Perriam looked at her. "Even though she might have caused the deaths of four innocent babes and three equally innocent wives?"

Ah, that changed everything.

A portrait of Aunt Clarrie had hung in the rectory. She'd looked so sweet, so gentle.

"The blame rests on the originator," Athena stated. "On Giles Perriam. If there is divine justice, he now burns in hell."

"It does seem likely. However, he's left some poison to trouble the living. The matter of our marriage—"

"There is no such matter!" Claris stated.

"Which can be laid at your mother's door."

"*Mother?* What has she to do with this?"

"When Giles's second wife died, your mother made occasion to visit him to remind him of the curse and to make a demand—that he pledge to marry you when you were of age and thus appease your aunt Clarrie's shade. That, she claimed, would lift the curse from him and his heirs."

Claris laughed in disbelief. "Even she wouldn't do that. Marry me to a wicked debaucher? An old wicked debaucher?"

"A young wicked debaucher would be tolerable?"

"Such as you?" Claris leaned forward to glare at him. "No husband will ever be tolerable, sir, so you might as well leave now."

"I am not a wicked debaucher," he said, lips tight. Good, that had struck home. "Do you truly disbelieve the story?"

Claris wanted to deny every word, but she couldn't. "Mother was obsessed by Perriam wickedness," she admitted, "and perhaps out of her wits over it. She might have gone to such an extreme. But nothing came of her plan."

"When did your mother die?"

She didn't want to answer questions, but it was hardly a secret.

"Eleven years ago, not long after the birth of my brothers."

"So when she made that visit you were too young to marry and Giles was a widower desperate for another chance to get a son. There was never any hope that he would agree. It would have been about then that he married his third wife."

"With the same lack of success?" Athena said.

"Two stillbirths, which drove the poor lady mad. She lingered until a year ago, preventing any further efforts, thank God."

"I'm surprised he didn't rush to the altar as soon as she was buried."

"By then his own health was failing, and willing brides were thin on the ground."

"And you offer me this treat?" Claris demanded.

His eyes turned cold. "I am not him, and with the curse overwhelmed by our marriage, you'll have nothing to fear."

"Women die in childbirth without curses."

"You'll have nothing *exceptional* to fear."

Claris smiled. "But in spinsterhood I have nothing to fear at all. Are you finished?"

He held her gaze, but she would not be quelled, despite the fear beating within her.

He looked away—to take a paper from his pocket.

"Perhaps the words will move you." He unfolded the sheet and placed it before her. It was many years old and worn along the folds as if often handled. The ink had faded.

"Your aunt Clarrie's curse."

"Read it aloud," Athena commanded. She could no longer read without spectacles, but didn't like it known.

Claris picked up the paper, disturbed by the very feel of it. The handwriting reminded her of her mother's, but it was smaller and with loops. The look of it didn't match the harsh words.

"'You have betrayed me, Giles Perriam,'" she read. "'You have made me a whore and my unborn child a bastard and your money cannot wash that clean. You'll hear no more from me, but now and with my last breath I wish on you the sufferings that your black heart deserves. May you suffer as I must suffer. May any wife you take die young as I must die, and any children die young as mine must die. May you yourself die young and suffering. May your guilt oppress you every day until Satan comes to carry you to burn in hell, and may this curse pass to your heirs as long as time may be.'"

Shaken by the force of the words, Claris put the paper down and pushed it away.

"Nonsense," Athena said.

"The logical mind scoffs," Perriam agreed, "but travelers bring tales that challenge logic, and Giles suffered all she condemned him to except oppressive guilt." He looked at Claris. "Did your aunt know anything of curses?"

"I can't imagine how, but she died before I was born. All I know of her is my mother's loving praise and a portrait. She looked sweet and gentle in that."

"May I see it?"

"I no longer have it," Claris said, and didn't explain. "She would never have attempted a curse, however, so your purpose is hollow."

"Not according to your mother."

"She wasn't rational on the subject. This curse is nonsense and you have no reason to attempt to marry me and can leave now."

He picked up the paper, folded it, and put it away. He didn't rise. "I'm driven by nothing so macabre, Miss Mallow. I need to secure Perriam Manor to my family, and Giles Perriam made our marriage a condition of the inheritance. If you and I don't wed within a month of his death, the property goes elsewhere."

"Then it must go elsewhere, sir, for I will not marry you."

He spread his hands, unimpressed. "An impasse."

Claris rose. "For you, perhaps, but not for me. Please leave."

He remained seated. "No pistol this time?"

"It is prepared, in case."

A twinkle lit his eyes. "How delightful! Please be seated, Miss Mallow, so I may tempt you with the many benefits of our marriage."

Claris almost did so. Instead she caught herself, folded her arms, and glared. Why would he not see that she was resolute?

He turned to Athena. "You're a woman of the world, ma'am. You must see how the marriage would improve your granddaughter's life."

"Must I?" Athena said. "I found marriage so intolerable that I fled it."

"Did you? Such a fascinating family." He turned his smile on Claris. "I can't claim great wealth, Miss Mallow, but I can provide a very comfortable life for my wife. What's more, and you seem to have failed to grasp this, I'm at your mercy. You may demand what you will."

"Except, it seems, that you leave and never bother me again."

"Except that," he agreed. "But you may continue to live here if you wish, or I can offer Perriam Manor as an alternative residence. It's of modest size, but in good repair and well furnished, though in an old style. I'm sure it's cozy in winter and pleasant in summer. It's surrounded by parkland and gardens that I would judge adequate but ripe for improvement, if gardening is your true delight."

Claris kept a stony face. "Alas, with you present, sir, all would be spoiled."

"Then you'll be delighted to know that I would rarely

be there. I'm much engaged in Town matters and can only enjoy rural delights now and then."

"Even one day a year would be too much." His amiable confidence was stirring her temper and for once she welcomed it. "Why am I debating this with you?" She loosened her arms to point at the door. "Begone!"

"Consider," he said, completely unmoved. "You would be the mistress of a comfortable domain, and enjoy its income. Did I not mention that?"

"Will you not leave!"

"The income of the manor would be yours to do with as you wish," he continued as if she hadn't spoken. "You would need for nothing."

"Except my independence! I would have a husband, a lord and master."

"Alas, true, but I assure you that I am far too busy to abuse my powers."

"*Busy?* What if you have an idle moment, sir? *Leave!*"

"I must remain until you change your mind."

Breathing hard, Claris saw that he meant it. He was disregarding every word she spoke. "You . . . you . . ." She grabbed the pistol and pointed it.

"Claris . . . ," Athena said.

"Leave," she growled, "or I *will* shoot you."

The smile widened and his eyes lit.

He was *laughing* at her?

She cocked the pistol, the *click, click* loud in the room.

"You won't fire it," he said.

"Oh, won't I?" Claris closed her eyes and squeezed the trigger.

A tremendous *boom* deafened her.

Ellie came downstairs, having finally settled Claris in bed with a soothing draft.

"Perhaps you shouldn't have put powder in the barrel."

"I decided that if she had reason to fire it, it might as well make a bang."

Ellie rubbed her ears. "Nearly deafened me, but grand to see."

"A girl of spirit. Don't know why she's fallen apart over it."

"From knowing she tried to kill a man? And that if she had she'd hang for it?"

"I suppose that would shake her. All very interesting, isn't it? I mean his story."

Ellie returned to her damsons. "You sure he's right for her?"

"Why do you think I am?"

"You reminded him of the twins."

Athena shrugged. "He'll have his way. Best if she goes willingly and on her own terms."

"She'll do it for the boys?"

"Of course she will, and they won't appreciate the sacrifice. Born and bred to be selfish; that's the male of the species."

"Then why help him?"

"Claris is worthy of more than Old Barford and Lavender Cottage."

Ellie gave her a look. "You intend more for yourself too."

"Of course. It's amused me to play at herbal lore among yokels, but I weary of it. Winter looms and I'll not endure that again."

"It wasn't so very bad."

"You nearly died of pneumonia and my bones tortured me. I intend that Claris be mistress of a pleasant country house by then, with all its income in her hands."

"I'll not see her forced into marriage against her will, and I'm surprised you would."

"She isn't me, Ellie. There's no other life for her in this unjust world, and Perriam seems a decent enough man."

"All the same, I might well load a pistol with ball next time."

Chapter 7

Perry didn't dawdle at the inn but rode straight back to Cheynings. He entered the house from the back, coming from the stables, and encountered Genova in the hall.

"Success?" she said with obvious surprise.

"Am I so transparent?"

"I can almost see banners waving. Or bloody heads on pikes."

"The world seems distressingly void of ladies with sensitive minds."

"And of men who understand the complexity of women," she retorted. "What happened?"

"She shot me."

She looked him over. "To little effect, it seems."

"Don't sound so disappointed. I was doing nothing more than trying to persuade her to see sense."

"With a superior tone, I'm sure. A pity she missed."

"She didn't. It was very close range. The pistol lacked a ball."

"Careless of her."

"Or careful of whoever prepared it."

"You seem in remarkably high spirits over it."

"She's a remarkable woman."

"But you also sense victory. You're not going to threaten to take her to court, are you?" She glanced at the footman. "We can't talk here. Come to my boudoir. Ashart's away, but I can't wait for the tale."

Perry went upstairs. He liked Genova's cozy paneled room and it seemed a good place to savor victory.

As they both sat, he said, "Miss Mallow has brothers."

"Who are large and strong and will defend her from vile imposition?"

"Who are eleven years old and likely to have a hard road without money and patronage."

"Oh, by the stars. She'll sacrifice herself for them?"

He was surprised by her outrage. "Her duty, surely."

"Why? Is the family so impoverished that they lack education?"

"Not that I know, but the bare bones of an education are not the same as what I could offer."

"The bare bones will do, however, if they have brains and resolution. Then there's always the navy. They could go now as cabin boys. Many have risen from there to admiral."

"Even there they'll rise more easily with patronage; don't deny it."

Her lips tightened, which was an admission, but Perry had been surprised by her reaction. Of course she wasn't cast from a common mold. He'd heard that she'd shot and killed a Barbary pirate who'd tried to capture her to sell to a harem.

"If you'd had a younger brother, would you have felt the same?" he asked.

"The situation would never have arisen."

"Imagine it. By some disaster you were left orphaned and with little money, with a young brother hardly out of childhood for whom you care. A gentleman offers marriage which will provide comfort and security for you and a bright future for your brother. Would you reject it so absolutely?"

She frowned. "Annoying man. Probably not. Unless the marriage was abhorrent to me."

"There is no reason for this marriage to be abhorrent to Miss Mallow."

"That is for her to judge."

"Unreasonable woman! There's no reason for this marriage to be abhorrent to her, because I've promised that after the vows are said I will leave her completely to her own devices."

Genova cocked her head. "That does remove many objections. However, before the law you would still be her master."

"As Ashart is yours."

"A factor that weighed with me, I assure you. Love is the very devil."

Perry laughed. "Not something that will trouble Miss Mallow and me. And thus, we will both be perfectly comfortable."

She still looked dissatisfied, but she didn't press her point.

"I was reminded of the boys by the grandmother, so I have an ally there. Grannie Mallow is no rural witch but a lady of some stature. I'll discover more when I have time. She said she fled her marriage, and someone in the inn said she was of noble birth. She's certainly ill suited to Lavender Cottage."

"Then she probably seeks improvement for herself, even at her granddaughter's expense. And thus you are triumphant."

"You sound as if you'd prefer that I fail."

"I would."

"Why?"

"Because your path always seems so smooth."

"Dear lady, only because I take care to smooth it before I step forward. Giles Perriam pushed me onto a rough track lined with brambles, but now all is straight again."

Perhaps she growled. "Oh, I do hope she says no."

"And I hope you're wrong. Tomorrow, I put it to the test."

Ashart came in then, and Perry told the tale again.

Ashart found it amusing but said, "If you're going to be a landowner, you might want to accompany me on some business after dinner."

"I intend that my wife manage the estate."

"But you'll want to supervise."

Perry wouldn't, but he didn't argue the point. Riding around the Cheynings estate would be no penance. However, Genova's reaction jangled in his mind. She still hoped for resistance, and he wanted the matter settled.

That evening, as they took coffee in the drawing room, Perry turned to Genova and said, "You mentioned wooing Miss Mallow."

"And you rejected the very idea," Genova pointed out.

"I'm reassessing."

"Not so certain that Miss Mallow will sacrifice herself for the good of men?"

"I wish to ensure it, to persuade her that she, as well as her brothers, will benefit. Thus I will woo her, but not with trinkets and love poems. With samples of the pleasures to come."

"Seduction in a cottage?" Ashart said, brows raised.

"There are other pleasures. I'll seduce her with comforts she must be missing and luxuries she's not yet known."

"You are a devious man," Genova said.

"You would condemn her to her dismal life?"

"Perriam . . . ," Ashart warned.

Genova frowned, but in thought. "Am I doing that? It's only that I resent her being manipulated by an expert."

"To her own good. You'll know better than I what a lady would value as samples of future comfort."

"So now you seek to recruit me?"

"If she's tempted, she's tempted. If she truly doesn't

value comfort and earthly pleasures, she'll disdain the bait."

Genova looked at her husband. "What do you see as the right thing to do?"

"Miss Mallow's current situation offers little hope. Perriam can provide better, though at some cost to himself."

"Cost to himself?" she queried, surprised.

"By all we've heard, Miss Mallow comes from a dubious background. Her father may have been mad, and her mother was deranged by grief. Her aunt could have believed in witchcraft and certainly attempted a curse. Miss Mallow can be driven to a murderous rage and her grandmother dabbles in herbal lore. If she is, as Perriam said, highborn, what story brought her to the ramshackle cottage? She could be any kind of rogue and bring a new scandal into his family."

"Why didn't you point this out before?"

"It seemed obvious apart from the pistol. Add that a husband is legally liable for his wife's debts and crimes and he's paying a high price to keep an old estate in his family."

Genova glared at Perry. "Am I now to see you as the victim? I hope she makes you thoroughly miserable."

"Genova is nothing if not irrational in her passions," Ashart murmured.

"Wretch. Very well, I will advise you, Perriam, but at a price."

"Price?"

"If she agrees to marry you, I will be on her side. She'll need assistance when moving so many steps up in society, and I'll advise her on that. I'll also make sure she knows her rights, such as they are. There will be settlements, sir, carefully written by Ashart's lawyers."

Perry smiled. No wonder Ashart had been smitten into marrying a woman without status or wealth.

"Of course. I truly do not wish Miss Mallow ill. I simply wish this done. May we act now? Will you help me assemble gifts that would tempt any woman down to Hades?"

"That," said Genova, "is not a promising phrase. Let us at least aim at purgatory. For both of you."

Chapter 8

The next day Claris did put on more stylish clothes, for if Perriam returned, she felt the need of some dignity. Even so, she chose her simplest, consisting of a russet skirt, a blue bodice, and a plain, practical apron. Perhaps such clothing would knock home how unsuited she was to be his wife.

Unlikely. Pestilential Perriam didn't want to marry her any more than she wanted to marry him. She could be an uncouth slattern with crossed eyes and he'd still insist. She'd try to resist any pressure, but she knew she'd put a powerful weapon in his hands. Why, oh, why had she given in to her temper and fired that pistol?

Feeling like a condemned prisoner awaiting the gallows, she went downstairs and out to get the eggs. When she returned, Ellie asked what the matter was.

"He'll threaten to drag me to court for trying to kill him. How can I resist that?"

"Lord save us, dearie. You did nothing but deafen us all."

"But I *tried* to kill him."

"But didn't even scratch him."

Athena came down. "Ellie's right. What's more, we're his only witnesses."

"You'd lie for me?"

Athena seemed astonished. "Without hesitation."

A little of the weight lifted. "He'll still pester me to marry him."

"Yes, but remember his words. You hold the power. You can dictate terms."

"I don't want to marry him on any terms!"

Athena rolled her eyes. "Then come and learn the herbal trade. You'll need some means of earning pennies."

Claris went into the front room with her grandmother. "I could set up a school."

"And be paid with eggs and butter."

"I'd need little when I'm alone here."

She tossed that out to see Athena's reaction. The lack of one showed that she did intend to leave. It wasn't surprising, for she and Ellie were used to a wandering life, but also to one better than this damp, drafty cottage. For all their vigor, they were old. Presumably Athena must have enough money set by to afford a more comfortable place to live, but of course it would suit her better if Claris provided a manor house.

Athena gave Claris a bowl of borage and told her to pick the leaves neatly from the stalks, then left her alone with her thoughts.

They were rather dismal. Athena and Ellie would leave, and so would her brothers. When they went to school in Winchester she'd rarely see them. It was fifty miles away and even the simplest travel was expensive.

She could move to Winchester.

Yes, why not? They could even live at home, which would be more economical. Finding one solution heartened her. Surely she could solve the Perriam problem as well.

Athena returned to inspect her work. "You're leaving too much stalk on those. Have you made up your mind?"

"I've told you, I won't marry him. I won't marry anyone."

"Then I leave you to your own devices. I'm off to deliver a cough linctus to Mistress Norris and I'll take Ellie with me. She deserves an outing."

Claris dropped the borage and pursued her grandmother into the kitchen. "You're abandoning me?"

"I've left the pistol on the sideboard. This time it's loaded."

"Ellie?"

Ellie was putting on her hat. "I'm sure you'll do what's best, dearie. You're a sensible girl at heart."

When they'd left, Claris was fixed in place.

Alone already.

Abandoned.

Why was life so unfair?

Yatta meowed, as if to say that he was still there, and leapt up to sniff the pistol. It looked no different than it had yesterday, but now it was loaded. It could kill.

She shuddered at the thought and put it carefully in a drawer.

"I won't hang for him," she said to the cat. "That truly would be a fate worse than marriage."

Yatta leapt down and sauntered over to lie in the sunlit doorway.

"On guard?" Claris asked, but drily. The cat was already asleep.

She went back to the herbs, but that task left too much space in her mind for worry, so she set about an inventory of the pantry, scrubbing shelves as she cleared them.

Someone knocked at the front door.

She froze, heart leaping in panic, and her first impulse was to ignore the knock. Perriam wouldn't hesitate to come in search of her, though, and she'd not be found cowering.

She marched off to open the door.

The visitor wasn't Perriam. It was Farmer Barnett, tall, sturdy, and smiling.

She had to put a hand to the doorjamb to steady herself.

He offered a shallow basket. "We've been slaughtering some lambs, Miss Mallow, and I thought you might like a joint and some sweetbreads. For Grandma Pollock's liniment."

"How kind," Claris said, taking the gift and also seeing a new defense against invaders. "Do you have time to come in and tell me how your family goes along?"

He turned pink, eagerly ducked through the doorway, and followed her through to the kitchen. Too late, Claris remembered that he might be courting her. This gift was too much for liniment. She'd resolved not to encourage him, but marrying someone else would be the perfect defense against Perriam.

At least she knew Barnett and knew him to be honest and true. He was a well-set-up young man in excellent health who owned a sizeable farm.

Head whirling, Claris sat at the table and waved him to a seat opposite. He was the catch of Old Barford. If she rejected his offer, the village would think her the rector's mad daughter in truth.

"Does your grandmother need more ointment, Mr. Barnett? I know where it's kept."

"Nay, she's well enough now, thanks be to God, with the weather still warm. But it did her well in the winter."

"And how is your family?"

"All in fine trim, Miss Mallow, thank the Lord."

"Amen."

"And yours?"

"The same." A silence fell. "How go the crops?" she tried.

"The weather's been fair, so all should go well, the Lord allowing."

"And your animals?"

"Fat and fine, God be praised."

Could she endure such banal conversation? The whole family was the same. They used words sparingly but frequently called on the Lord. Though they attended the parish church, they were more of a Methodist persuasion. They dressed and lived soberly and never took part in village festivities such as May Day and the maypole, calling them pagan.

No, she'd run mad within a month.

Alas, he was a fate worse than Perriam. How was she to get rid of him before he made the offer?

"It's particularly kind of you to stop by," she said. "You must be busy at this time of year."

He blushed again. "I have time to enjoy your company, Miss Mallow."

"And I yours, sir, but I was in the middle of a task, which is why you find me so plainly dressed."

"I'd like to see you more finely dressed. . . ." His blush spread up to his hair. "I mean, all the time. Well, not when in kitchen work . . ."

Struggling with laughter, Claris said, "It's wise to dress appropriately for each occasion, isn't it?"

"What I meant to say, Miss Mallow . . ."

Another knock at the door.

Thank the Lord!

"I wonder who that can be?" Claris asked, leaping up to answer it.

When she opened the door, giggles threatened.

Apparently it was to be the battle of the baskets, but Perriam's would win. His was a wicker box with a lid and latch. Heaven alone knew what it contained.

"Good morning, Miss Mallow. I've brought some gifts for you and your family."

She managed to conquer laughter. "Please come through to the kitchen."

When they arrived there, Barnett rose, glowering. She glanced back to see Perriam had halted and was eying the other man keenly, but with that irritating amusement.

Barnett turned red and she finally understood. He was here today because he'd heard rumors that a fine gentleman was calling on her. He'd wanted to get in first.

Two men fighting over her!

Claris made strangled introductions, thinking she might need the pistol to shoot herself.

"Mr. Barnett, this is Mr. Perriam, an old connection of my father's. Mr. Perriam, Mr. Barnett is one of the local farmers. He very kindly brought me some lamb from a recent butchering."

"How very practical," Perriam said, making the lamb seem ridiculous.

"It is, for I enjoy roast lamb. Do you wish to stay? If so, please be seated."

He took a seat at the end of the table. Barnett sat down again. Claris took the seat she'd used before, a suitor on either side.

Alas, Farmer Barnett was in the goat's seat.

"Have you traveled far, sir?" Barnett asked.

"I'm staying locally," Perriam replied. "Is your farm far from here?"

"But two miles, sir. A connection of Reverend Mallow's, are you? He was a mite older than you."

"The connection is through an older cousin. They were friends in their younger days, enjoying the pleasures of London."

"Pleasures? A den of iniquity, or so I hear. Do you spend much time in London, sir?"

Claris bit her lip, but she was impressed with Barnett's fighting spirit. Perhaps Yatta was too, for he came in, leapt into her lap, and put paws onto the table to observe.

"I do," Perriam agreed, with that easy smile, "for I delight in it. There is everything in Town, good and bad."

"Served Reverend Mallow badly, or so he used to say. May I hope your cousin is served better, sir?"

"Unlikely, but now he's dead."

"Then we must pray that he be enjoying his heavenly reward."

Claris feared he'd start up a prayer, then and there.

"Why?" Perriam asked. "He was a bad man, and I prefer to trust in God's justice rather than assume he can be swayed by pleas."

Barnett's jaw dropped. "That's . . . That's not right, sir. God hears our prayers."

"And may put them in the balance when he judges us.

But if I pray night and day for the salvation of an evil man, should God alter his judgment? You'd as well believe in popish indulgences."

Farmer Barnett's mouth worked, but no words came out.

"Let's not fall into religious debate," Claris said quickly. "Do you have news of events in London, Mr. Perriam? Has the unrest and violence ended?"

"That seems to be the case, Miss Mallow, perhaps because many of the rich and powerful are still away from Town, enjoying their country estates."

"So it's the rich and powerful who cause the trouble?" Barnett challenged.

Heavens, was he a radical?

Perriam's brows rose. "I meant that they are the prime targets for violent destruction. So much more amusing to break the windows of a peer than a peasant."

"Are you a peer, sir, or do you have an honest profession?"

"Mr. Barnett!" Claris protested, but Perriam laughed.

"What a limited view of the world you have, sir. You think all the nobility dishonest?"

"I doubt they do an honest day's work."

"Now, there you'd be wrong. You have a farm. Of how many acres?"

"One hundred and fifty," Barnett said proudly.

"An excellent property, and it brings you hard work and profit, all being well. Imagine an estate of six thousand acres."

"Such a landowner would have many to manage it for him."

"All requiring supervision."

"From fancy London houses and parks?"

"Gentlemen, gentlemen!" Claris intervened. "Enough of this. Mr. Barnett, I must ask you to leave. Mr. Perriam and I have some business to discuss, to do with his cousin and my father, and I must not keep him too long."

Her farming suitor rose reluctantly, but he left as he

must, firing a parting shot. "I'll see you at church come Sunday, Miss Mallow." She could hear the unspoken end of his thought: *when your London gentleman has gone.*

Claris might never attend church again.

Yatta pursued Barnett to the door and beyond, but he'd not manage to keep him away any more than he'd deterred Perriam.

Claris was relieved to close the door, but as she turned back toward the kitchen she realized she was now alone with her prime problem.

Truly alone with him for the first time.

Chapter 9

She entered the kitchen, chin up. "Why must you per-
sist, sir?"

"You know why."

"You think I'll be swayed by gifts?"

"It will be interesting to see."

"How little you think of me." But her nose detected
something from the basket, something . . .

Oranges? Her mouth watered with the remembered
sweet, tangy taste.

He unlatched the basket. "Will you not at least look
at what I've brought?"

When she didn't respond, he flipped back the lid.

The aroma of oranges grew stronger, but she stared at
a lacquered box with a lock. It must be a tea box. Her
mother had owned one. If full, this one must hold a
pound at least of the expensive leaves. She hadn't tasted
tea since her mother died.

What on earth was in that beautiful blue-and-white
jar?

He lifted out the jar and took off the lid. "Ginger from
the orient, in a sweet syrup." He found a long silver fork
in the basket and used it to spear an amber cube and
raise it to her lips. Claris turned her head away, but he'd
touched it to her lips and she licked them. Oh, dear lord!
So sweet, so spicy. Before she knew what she was doing,
she licked her lips again, seeking more.

He smiled, his eyes bright.

With victory?

She stepped back, raising a hand between them. That didn't block whatever made her feel breathless and hot.

"Too foreign for you?" He opened a glass jar full of crimson liquid containing dark objects. "Perhaps you'd prefer an English cherry?"

He speared one and offered it. When she tightened her lips, he said, "It isn't poisoned. That would hardly serve my purpose. Nor is it bespelled to force you to do my will. Do you think a taste of cherry would overcome you?"

Challenged, Claris took the cherry from the fork. Merely a cherry, after all—but this had been steeped in something strong, brandy perhaps, and the complex flavors burst in her mouth. She couldn't hold back an "Oh, my . . ."

"My wife will enjoy such delights at will."

Claris was tempted to spit out the fruit, as if it were the apple in the Garden of Eden or Persephone's pomegranate. That would admit the powerful effect it was having on her, however, so she swallowed it and then said, "There's more to life than cherries."

"Oranges, for example." He took one out of the basket—a large one, and then another, and another. In the end there were five of them. One for each of her family.

How could he have known the power of an orange?

When her mother was alive, there had always been oranges at Christmas. As the twins had grown, Claris had wanted to revive that tradition and had bought some. They'd been only four pence each, but her father had caught the twins eating one and ranted about wicked indulgence. He'd carried those left off to the almshouses. She'd wanted to ask why the indigent were allowed wicked indulgences but his children weren't, but she'd known there was no point. She'd never dared try again.

"Wine," he said, taking out two bottles.

She'd never tasted wine.

"Coffee, and these." He poured pale ovals from a bag into one of his hands.

"Monstrous teeth?" she asked.

"Sugared almonds. And yes, these gifts are designed to sweeten your mind toward your future. All these luxuries and more will be yours to command once we are wed."

He couldn't know how well he'd baited his trap.

She loved sweet things, a weakness inherited from her mother. In her childhood there had been cakes and sweetmeats, no matter how her father railed. Since his death she'd managed to provide some, but now she could have them in abundance. . . .

At cost of her liberty!

She began to put everything back in the basket. "I have no desire for such excess, and I cannot be bought."

"A singularly foolish declaration. Not bought so cheaply, I'm sure, but are you truly beyond price? Beyond thousands, tens of thousands, hundreds of thousands of pounds?"

Claris laughed. "What would I do with a hundred thousand pounds?"

"Not hoe your own garden."

"I enjoy hoeing my garden," she lied, closing the basket. "I am not so foolish as to refuse this"—nor strong enough, alas—"but our business is done. I have much to do today."

Unnoticed, he'd kept an orange, and now he sat down and began to peel it. "Your tasks must wait until you've named our wedding day."

"Which will be never."

But oh, that aroma!

He split the peeled orange in half and separated one segment. "We are going to marry, Miss Mallow, so why draw this out?"

"We are *not* going to marry, and a piece of orange won't change my mind!" Not even when he put it in his mouth and she could almost taste it in her own. "If you won't leave, I will."

She walked toward the stairs, but that took her close to him. He grabbed her wrist. A shock of something went right through her, freezing her in place.

Fear, yes, but something else.

"Mr. Perriam!"

"If you aren't swayed by ginger and oranges, what of a bright path for your brothers?"

She froze and he released her.

She covered her wrist with her other hand. "We have money enough to send them to school."

"To the best school?"

"It will be good enough."

"And university?"

"They will win scholarships."

"Are they bright enough?"

Peter was, but Tom?

"They study hard," she said, knowing it was inadequate.

"Why deny them the benefits I can give them? Not just a fine education, but introductions to the highest circles, where they will make connections that will prove invaluable throughout their lives."

"Two boys raised in a country village?" she scoffed, but he was conjuring a vision that battered at her defenses.

"They probably do lack training in the style and etiquette of the highest circles, but that is easily corrected. It is their birthright, after all."

"They're the sons of an impoverished country rector."

"Impoverished by choice. What is their Mallow line?"

Claris's knees weakened and she sat down. "This isn't fair."

"Life often isn't. All I require in return is your vows at the altar."

"There's more to marriage than that."

"You're thinking of the marriage bed?" Claris hadn't been, and her cheeks heated. "It's not required."

"Not? But . . ."

"Implied, but not required. Unless, that is, you intend to complain to the church courts when I fail to do my duty. Even in that case, I believe I could argue in civil court that I had fulfilled the terms of the will."

Her fists had clenched and now she beat them on the table.

"The will, the will, the *damnable* will!"

He covered her angry hands with his. "We are in accord on that. May we not be in accord on other matters?"

She jerked free, but she couldn't escape his words.

"Remember, I offer you Perriam Manor. Not just a house and estate, but a home farm to supply food. You won't have to depend on charity for roast lamb. Perhaps I didn't make clear that you will have the estate's income. You will be able to purchase all necessities without care, and any luxuries you please. I offer a grand future for your brothers, but many improvements immediately."

"Immediately?" Claris braced herself. She could sense a killing blow.

"They'll enjoy living at Perriam Manor. There's a river that promises fishing and woodlands to explore. There are also stables. The horses there now would be too large, but I can purchase ponies for them if they'd like."

If they'd like.

They didn't complain, but ponies to ride would be a dream come true.

She tried one last shot. "They'll be going away to school soon."

"There will be holidays."

"It will be too expensive for them to travel home."

"You'll be able to afford to bring them home from Scotland if necessary, but Eton College is less than ten miles away from Perriam Manor. They could come home often if they wished."

He spoke in that light, pleasant voice that should carry no threat at all, but his words were flailing her into submission with an idyllic picture of comfort, wealth, and abundance, along with glittering advantages for the boys. And ponies.

She was going to have to agree, but she would set her terms, as Athena had recommended. "You won't live at the manor?"

"My home is in London."

"Yet Perriam Manor is so very important to you and your family."

"Only symbolically. I'd not visited the place until Giles Perriam summoned me to his deathbed."

"What of other members of your family? Won't they want to visit the shrine?"

"I doubt it, but if they do I give you the freedom to deny them. It will only be from idle curiosity. Perhaps my mother will want to inspect you, but I can deter her. She'll not feel strongly about it. We're not a close family, Miss Mallow, and my parents are too involved in court and affairs of state to dabble in their adult children's lives short of dire necessity. I have one sister of whom I'm fond, but she is newly married and absorbed by her husband and his run-down estate in Devon. She may write to you, but if you wish, leave her letters unread."

His words flowed lightly over her and she recognized that the stream was as much to give her time as to convey information. He gave nearly everything and asked hardly anything in return. Simply her vows at the altar.

How could she believe that? But nor could she believe him a shameless liar. Athena too had judged him honest, and she had more experience of the world.

There was still a husband's legal authority to fear, but if Perriam kept his word on the rest, that had weaker teeth.

She realized she was looking at the basket and accepted another truth. She felt all the pressure to make this pact for the twins, but she'd been undermined by his gifts.

Ginger, brandied cherries, and a peeled orange.

What a weak, self-indulgent woman she was. After such a slight brush with luxury, the thought of living in penury all her days made her shudder.

She peeled off a segment of the orange and bit into it, taking the time to savor the sweet juiciness, to admit its power. Taking one last moment to find an acceptable alternative. There was none.

"Very well, Mr. Perriam, I will marry you. But if you renege on any of your promises, I will shoot you, and the pistol will be loaded."

She saw neither triumph nor fear.

Very wise. Even now she might find the resolution to back out if he gloated.

Instead he offered her another segment of orange. "We could wed on Sunday and gain extra blessings."

"Sunday! That's only four days away. We need banns."

He put the segment on the table in front of her. "I don't have time for banns. It must be by license."

"*I* need more time . . ."

"To do what? You can purchase all you want later."

"Not a new gown for the wedding."

"You must have something that would do."

Would do? That showed how little he thought of the matter.

"You're harrying me, Mr. Perriam, and I will not allow it."

"You've agreed, Miss Mallow. What point in delay? I admit my need for haste. I have obligations in London which I've already neglected."

His tone infuriated her, but she liked the words. He wasn't in haste to capture her, but to fulfill the requirements of a will and return to his life and responsibilities—his life far from Perriam Manor.

"If you don't care for a Sunday wedding," he said,

"shall it be Monday? A word to the new rector and it's all arranged."

Claris realized something. "I don't want to marry here."

Before she could explain, he said, "Ah, your father's death. It must be a terrible memory."

For a moment, that puzzled her. The only terrible memory she had of that day was her shocking relief that her father was dead. She supposed her father falling dead at her feet should have shocked a normal woman, but her dislike of marrying there came from something else.

She didn't want to marry in Old Barford because the villagers would stare and speculate on what the Mad Rector's daughter was doing now.

"Marrying elsewhere must delay things," she said.

"Not at all. With a special license we can marry anywhere. A little more difficult to obtain than an ordinary license, but not unduly. We can be wed within the week."

Within the week?

She'd agreed, but not thought it would be so soon.

"May I make a suggestion, Miss Mallow? No, first, may I call you Claris now we're betrothed?"

Claris couldn't see reason to object. "And you, sir? What shall I call you?"

"I was christened Peregrine, but my friends call me Perry."

Too informal by far. "I prefer Perriam."

"As you wish," he said, undaunted. "Now, I suggest that you remove from here to the home of my friend Lord Ashart."

Claris stared. "The marquess? He is your friend?"

"I'm staying at Cheynings. Is it so odd?"

She laughed and then clapped her hand over her mouth before it turned wild. When she'd recovered she said, "Only that I once thought of appealing to him for protection against you."

"He might have obliged, especially as his wife would

have urged him to it. Are you acquainted with Genova Ashart?"

"Hardly."

"You'll like her. She's ready to stand by your side against the oppressive male world. In fact, she has already offered to help you prepare for the wedding and your future life." He rose. "Shall I take you there now?"

Claris swayed away from his outstretched hand. "No! You're like quicksilver, sir. Allow me a more leaden pace."

"Tomorrow, then. I can delay no longer before traveling to London to purchase the license. Thus, I point out, I won't linger at Cheynings to disturb you."

"A great blessing," she said tartly. "But I prefer to stay here. There will be much to do. All our possessions . . ."

He glanced around. "Abandon them. I can provide all you need."

She surged to her feet. "Does it not occur to you, you oaf, that we poor people might have possessions we value? No matter how worthless they seem to you?"

"Oaf?"

Their eyes clashed, but then he smiled.

"My most sincere apologies, Claris. Of course you do. I will arrange for a wagon. Will one be enough?"

It was the first time he'd used her name, and she knew then that she shouldn't have given him permission.

"A very small one will be enough."

"As for possessions, surely your grandmother and brothers can cope?"

She supposed they could. Athena and Ellie would keep an eye on the boys, and together they could pack their belongings.

"I am not harrying you to Cheynings for my benefit," he said, "but for yours. You will be more comfortable with a gradual transition."

"I don't know. . . ."

He seized on her weakness. "I'll come tomorrow morning to take you there."

Claris looked at the orange on the table. It had been like Persephone's pomegranate after all, and clearly she'd already eaten too much to escape.

"Very well," she said. "Tomorrow."

When he'd gone, she shivered, but she also picked up and ate another piece.

Chapter 10

Perry left before the unpredictable woman changed her mind. He waited until he was out of sight of the cottage before blowing out a relieved breath. He knew how such things could show even from the back. He was tempted to dance a jig.

It was done!

She wouldn't change her mind and deprive her brothers of advantages. He wasn't sure how potent the luxuries had been, but she'd not been unmoved by them.

Had she ever tasted an orange before? Or ginger? Or brandied cherries?

How intriguing she was. A shame there'd be scant opportunity to unravel the puzzle. Honor required that even during his thirty days at the manor he avoid her whenever possible.

As he crossed the village green, he paused to consider the rectory that had been her home. It was a modern house with clean, square lines and long windows. It would be light filled and draft free. Ample chimneys implied winter warmth.

On impulse he entered the churchyard through the lych-gate and walked the main graveled path between graves toward the mellow, square-towered church. Clergymen were generally buried close to the church walls, and that's where he found Henry Mallow's grave.

Here lies Henry Richard Mallow,
1718–1764 Anno Domini.
Rector of this parish from 1740 to 1764,
always mindful of Christian charity and
God's mercy.
"Let he who is without sin cast the first stone."

"May I help you, sir?"

A stocky man in shirt, waistcoat, and breeches was coming over. He was probably the sexton, in charge of maintaining this place. Perry didn't attempt concealment. The whole village would have been observing his comings and goings.

"I've been visiting the Mallow family and thought to see their parents' grave. The rector's wife is not buried with him?"

"Ah." The lack of expression was eloquent. "Mistress Mallow died afore, you see, sir. Ten years afore. Buried over here, she is."

Perry followed the man down a side path and then across grass to a different headstone, considering the fact that a wife dying before her husband wasn't adequate explanation for separate graves.

Here lies Eleanora Anne Mallow,
1715–1754
wife of Henry Mallow, rector of this parish.
May God have mercy on her soul.

A conventional enough inscription, but Perry sensed a bitter edge to it, as if she might need a great deal of mercy.

Henry Mallow had died suddenly, so he must have made arrangements ahead of time to ensure that he not lie for eternity with his wife. Such deep enmity, and Claris had lived in the midst of it.

He gave the sexton a coin and retraced his steps, wondering how it had warped her. It had nurtured a murderous temper. The thirty days might well be the torture Giles had intended.

He collected his horse and rode away, planning the next week. Acquiring a special license would provide time in London to deal with a number of issues, including a proposed canal that his father opposed. The Earl of Hernescroft was inflamed enough about the way Perriam Manor was left. No need to stoke the fires by neglecting his causes.

Claris was tempted to hide the basket, that evidence of her weakness. She'd conceal the marriage if she could, renege if she could, but she'd been thoroughly defeated.

When Athena and Ellie returned she said, "It's done. I've agreed to marry him."

Athena looked at the peel. "Bribed by an orange?"

"And tea, coffee, ginger, and cherries. But mostly by the benefits for the twins."

"I hope they'll appreciate it."

"They'll appreciate the ponies." Claris had to sit. "How could I deny them ponies? Oh, God, what have I done?"

"Don't paint yourself the martyr, girl. Tea, coffee, ginger, and cherries are not to be discounted. Is it good tea, I wonder?"

On the edge of bitter laughter, Claris watched her grandmother unlock the tea box and take the lid off an inner container. She took a pinch and rolled it beneath her nose.

"A very promising blend. Set the kettle to boil, Ellie. We have tea! Claris, reach down the teapot and wash it."

Claris obeyed while Ellie built up the fire beneath the kettle with equal excitement. They'd missed tea so much? Clearly they had been used to a much better life. No wonder they were cock-a-hoop now.

As she washed her mother's teapot it brought back memories. It was made of delicate china and ornamented with pretty pink flowers. When her mother died, her father had sold all her possessions—those he hadn't buried with her. The teapot spout was chipped, however, so he'd thrown it out.

Claris had rescued it, perhaps because her mother's lessons in the etiquette of tea were among the few good memories of her. They would sit in the rectory parlor with china, silver, and her mother's box, which contained four canisters of tea. Her mother would blend a certain amount from each and then pour boiling water into the pot to warm it.

A lady must know the art of it, and you are a lady, Claris.

She'd said the same about posture, curtsying, and diction. Any use of local dialect, any weakness of accent, had led to the sting of the birch. Even as a child, Claris had puzzled over it, for her mother had never claimed to be highborn. Now she knew why—her mother had been preparing for the day when Giles Perriam surrendered and married his victim's niece.

She dried the pot and put it on the table. "We have no teacups."

Athena went upstairs and soon returned with a wooden box. She opened it to reveal a tea service. Cups, saucers, a milk jug and sugar dish, along with silver spoons. More evidence of her former life. Athena had arrived with two large trunks. What else did they contain?

As Athena laid out the china, Ellie made tea—just as a lady should, even in a cottage kitchen with boiling water from a kettle black from the open fire.

Claris sat down. "You once enjoyed tea whenever you wished, didn't you?"

"I've been accustomed to many things, good and bad." Athena poured milk into the jug. "I wish the same for you."

"Even the bad? I believe I've had my share of that."

"Then you're entitled to much good. This marriage

will be of importance to the boys, but you won't suffer from it."

"No? Already he's ordering me about. I'm to move to Lord Ashart's house tomorrow, and be married from there within the week!"

Even Athena was startled. "Why there?"

"Because the marquess is Perriam's friend and host. I never had a chance, did I? The marchioness, would you believe, is to advise me about my new station and perhaps even improve my wardrobe. I'm to be pitchforked into the aristocracy!"

"Excellent. I judged Perriam to be a sharp-witted man."

"Sharp enough to cut my throat."

"Claris, if you don't want to remove to Cheynings, refuse. Stay here and marry in the church."

Claris scowled, but she couldn't deny the truth. "I refused that. I won't go through this performance in front of the village."

"Tea," Ellie said, putting the pot on the table and sitting down.

Athena poured the golden liquid into the cups. She put one in front of Claris. "Drink. It will revive and fortify, and we have much to do."

Claris added sugar and milk, stirred, and then cautiously sipped. It was as delicious as she remembered. If it revived and fortified, she'd indulge in a great deal of it.

"You will take my small trunk to Cheynings," Athena said. Yatta meowed. "No, you demanding creature."

Ellie poured milk into her saucer with a little tea, then put it on the floor. The cat set to enjoying it.

Athena sniffed. "You're too softhearted."

"Best someone be," Ellie said with a smile.

"I have Father's trunk," Claris said.

"Black and old," Athena said. "You must arrive with as much dignity as possible."

"Pretend to be a fine lady? With my simple clothing and well-worn shoes?"

"Being a lady is a matter of behavior as much as possessions. There are poor duchesses. Apart from a certain bounce in your walk, you have adequate deportment. Your manners and speech are tolerable. If you act as if you have every right to be there, you'll get by."

While bouncing and behaving almost as she should. Perhaps running the gauntlet of Old Barford might be preferable. But then there'd be Perriam Manor. Claris drank more tea.

"You are wise to consider your clothing," Athena said. "Ellie will inspect the garments you have and see what can be done to improve them."

"You said possessions didn't matter."

Athena waved that away. "Improvement is improvement. Ellie is skilled in such things."

"Ellie does too much work already."

Ellie smiled. "I like to keep busy, dearie, and I do enjoy needlework and fashion."

Claris wanted to grip her spinning head. Ellie and fashion didn't go together at all!

Yet Ellie wouldn't lie, and she too would benefit from this marriage. She might be the most deserving of them all. It would be satisfying to rescue Ellie from scullion work and enable her to stitch away to her heart's content.

"Jewelry," Athena said, standing up. "Alas, I have only trinkets, but some may suit you. Fine handkerchiefs. I will seek other items as I empty the small trunk."

Claris could only say, "Thank you."

Athena went upstairs and Ellie stood too. "That was a lovely cup of tea, dearie. Now, let's have a look at your clothes and see what we can do."

Claris followed, fighting an urge to refuse all improvements and additions because no one had asked her opinion or permission. The whole world seemed set on treating her like a puppet.

When it came to it, however, she couldn't resist Ellie's suggestions and enthusiasm. Ellie had all kinds of ribbon and braid in her trunk, and Athena's produced some lace and silk flowers as well as trinkets and handkerchiefs.

By the time the twins returned home that afternoon, a plain green gown had been trimmed with braid, and Claris's best black hat boasted spring flowers. She'd been put to work and was making love knots from blue ribbon when the boys rushed in.

They stopped and then approached the open basket.

"Oranges!" they exclaimed in unison.

They remembered.

"May we have one?" Peter asked.

They'd have their supper soon, but she gave permission.

They were clumsy with the peel but separated the segments carefully and divided them equally. They took a bite in unison and hummed together in pleasure.

Claris smiled, perhaps truly for the first time that day.

She was doing the right thing.

But then Peter frowned. "Where does all this come from?"

Despite all her efforts, they hadn't escaped the effects of life at the rectory. Beneath good cheer, they always worried about the next blow.

"The basket is a gift from a gentleman called Perriam," she said. "In a way, it's a betrothal gift. I'm to marry him."

"Who is he?" Peter demanded.

Lord above, he was attempting to protect her. She was touched, but she wouldn't allow it. "He's a younger son of the Earl of Hernescroft. He's visited here these past few days."

"But—"

"It is not for you to question my choice."

"But—"

"No, Peter. It does mean that we'll shortly move to Perriam Manor in Berkshire. I'm assured it will provide all necessities and many luxuries."

"What about our lessons?" Tom asked.

That hadn't been discussed, but Perriam had said she

would have everything she wanted. "You'll have a tutor until you're ready for school, and then go to Eton College, which isn't far away."

"I like Reverend Johnson," Tom said. "He's kind."

Poor Tom.

"You'll like your new tutor," Claris promised, but she knew she'd not be able to control his experience at school. She saw that they both were worried, so she brought out the big guns. "Mr. Perriam has said you may have ponies if you wish."

It truly was as if stars lit in their eyes, but then Peter set his face. "Do you want to marry him, Claris? Truly? We do well enough here."

He was such a good boy. "Yes, love, I truly do. And no, we don't do well enough here. It's a scrambling existence at best, and miserable in winter."

They still looked uncertain, and some of their orange was still uneaten.

"Even if you wish to stay here, I confess to selfishly wanting a more comfortable life. I can't have that if you won't come with me. You will, won't you?"

It was shameless manipulation, but it worked. Their tension eased and they looked at each other.

"Ponies . . . ," Peter said.

"Ponies!" Tom echoed.

They jiggled for a moment and then ran outside, orange segments forgotten, their excitement too great to be confined within walls. She heard them running around the garden shouting, "Ponies! Ponies! Ponies!"

Claris fell to laughter and tears.

"I forget that they must be like your children," Athena said. "They were only babes when their mother died."

"There was a nursemaid."

"Could a nursemaid protect them from their father's carelessness? Could one give them a mother's love?"

"That's all in the past." Clarissa rose and grasped one of the bottles by the neck. "Let's open some wine to toast to my betrothal."

"No!" both women cried in unison.

"Why not?"

"After it's been shaken around?" Athena rescued it. "It must stand quietly for days to do it justice."

"Then what purpose to it as a gift?"

"A promise," Athena said.

"A pity he didn't think cognac would tempt you." Ellie looked in the basket to be sure. "Ah well, there's still a meal to do, and we've frittered the day away on furbelows."

Ellie set to work, Athena went off to her stillroom, and Claris took her refurbished clothing upstairs, out of harm's way. When she came back down, she packed Perriam's bribes away in the basket. Soon the room looked as if nothing had happened, as if her life had not been shattered and remade in a whole new pattern.

The basket told the true story, however.

She might end up paying a high price for tea, ginger, and brandied cherries, but looking out at the boys, still so excited, she knew she'd pay anything for ponies.

Chapter 11

Claris endured a poor night's sleep and woke early with a headache. She went downstairs to look at the basket, to prove that she hadn't imagined everything.

A part of her wished she had, that her life was still undisturbed, but most of her feared to find it was a dream. That would be like glimpsing a beautiful garden and then having the door to it slammed shut, locking her out forever.

A knock at the door startled her. It was far too early! She found a groom there, with a letter. "From Mr. Perriam, ma'am."

She turned away to break the seal, concealing her shaking hands. Had he already regretted their agreement and written to take back his offer? No, the letter was simply a plan for the day. He would come at eleven by carriage to collect her. There would be ample space for any trunks and bandboxes.

How many did he think she had?

Once he had escorted her to Cheynings, he would set out for London to obtain the necessary license. Relieving her of his presence, she understood.

He would return in a week and they would marry, after which she and her family would remove to Perriam Manor, which would be ready to receive them.

Complete with ponies? she wondered, unreasonably affronted by this crisp organization. Even with a businesslike marriage, shouldn't there be more?

Her mind turned to Farmer Barnett, so nervous and eager, his skin flushing. That was a proper suitor. Idiot! As if she'd want that, and the idea of sleek Mr. Perriam in such a state was ridiculous. His handwriting expressed him perfectly. It flowed elegantly across the page in straight lines, but with a flourish of fine loops, especially on the capitals.

Ornate, but easily read.

Claris knew her own handwriting was nowhere near so fine, and her writing paper of poorer quality, but she would have to reply. She heard footsteps down the stairs and went into the kitchen, relieved to find Athena.

"Perhaps you should come to Cheynings with me."

"Someone must look after your brothers and deal with vacating this place. We'll have to pack what you want to keep."

"Everything."

"Even the chipped teapot?"

"Yes." Claris knew it was unreasonable, but she couldn't make rational decisions now. "We can sort through everything later. Make sure to pack anything the twins want, no matter how trivial. Oh, I should deal with it. Cheynings can wait a day or two."

"No. You have much to do there."

"It's merely a wedding. Village couples walk to the church without great fuss."

"You are not a village woman. Very well, I promise we'll pack everything, down to the last crumb. Have Perriam arrange baskets and boxes, and a wagon."

"He's already promised that."

"I'm not surprised. A clever man."

"Which makes him a dangerous enemy."

"He's not your enemy, child."

"And I'm not a *child*."

Claris found the paper and sat at the table to write her reply. She hadn't much need for writing and the ink was thick. She watered it down, but too much, so it was faint.

She mended the pen and did her best. She assured him that she'd be ready at eleven, then added, "Please come in a chair or similar simple vehicle, for the lane is narrow and I will have only one small trunk."

The truth was she hoped to escape Old Barford as inconspicuously as possible. A carriage arriving at Lavender Cottage would be like ringing the church bells.

The Mad Rector's daughter was off with that fine gentleman, and in a carriage, no less. What insanity was she up to now?

By eleven Claris was as ready as she'd ever be, dressed in her refurbished green gown, with her least-worn shift and stockings beneath, and her newly trimmed hat on her firmly pinned hair. She wished she were as firm inside. Was she really leaving the place where she'd lived all her life, with a man she hardly knew but was to marry in a week?

At least her sturdy black shoes were familiar, for she owned only the one pair.

As the church clock struck, Athena gave her one last inspection and nodded. "The marchioness will appoint a maid to serve you. Don't let her intimidate you."

"A maid? I can look after myself."

"Only if you wish to be ridiculous. You will be an honored guest at Cheynings, the betrothed of a fine gentleman. Act your future part."

"But I don't know how. I don't know what to expect." She gripped her hands together. "I can't do this. I can marry him, but not all this!"

"Part and parcel. Behave at all times as if you belong. Don't shrink back, don't babble and fumble, and above all don't gawk at the house and its contents."

"Easy enough to say."

"Easy enough to do, if you are resolute."

How could she not babble and fumble when already her heart was pounding? Yatta rubbed against her skirts and she picked him up to cuddle. Perhaps she'd take him with her as guard cat.

"I hear hooves," Athena said.

Claris put the cat down and pulled on her plain cloth gloves. Act as if she belonged when the lowest servant would know at a glance that she didn't?

Rebellion stirred.

Let them look down their noses. She was a decent woman of good birth who'd never shamed herself. She was soon to marry the Honorable Peregrine Perriam, son of the Earl of Hernescroft. The boggle-eyed servants wouldn't know the reason for it, and they could speculate as they willed.

A rap at the door.

Ellie went to open it.

Claris straightened her spine and followed.

When she reached the door, Perriam indicated the plain, open carriage. "I come simply as commanded, but I fear I still stirred speculation in the village."

So he'd guessed her reason. That wasn't difficult when down the row of cottages heads were poking around doorjambs.

"My trunk is in the kitchen."

He'd brought no servant, and it felt odd to order him, but none of them could carry it. She and Athena had brought it down empty. He showed no objection and carried it out without difficulty. He wasn't a large man, and she was disconcerted by such strength.

Sharp enough to cut her throat, and strong enough to throttle her.

Ellie and Athena were at the door to see her off, and Perriam was standing by the chair to hand her up.

This was the moment, then.

This was when everything changed and there could be no return.

Panic still beat inside and everything ahead frightened her, but Claris also had to fight not to run to the gig, not to clamber in and urge Perriam to speed away. This was escape from poverty and hopelessness. However, when she put her hand in his, cloth glove on leather, she was startled by a sense of intimacy as strong as when he'd grasped her wrist. It reminded her of the price she must pay.

It would be a marriage in name only, she reminded herself even as his grip tightened slightly as he assisted her up into the plain wooden seat.

He let go and circled to climb into the driver's seat. She felt the absence of that grip as freedom but also as loss. What a muddled mess she was today! A nervous, apprehensive mess.

The vehicle swayed as he sat. The gray horse took a step forward. Claris clutched at the curved iron that formed an arm of the seat, alarmed by this literally unsteady world. She'd rarely traveled in any sort of vehicle, and she looked back toward the cottage, toward the place she knew and understood, no matter how drab it was.

He picked up the reins and set the horse into action, and the chance was lost.

As they passed the other cottages he nodded to her peering neighbors. She took her cue and inclined her head, trying to look at ease. Would any of them dare to pester Athena with questions?

When they arrived at the village green, Claris saw that an unusual number of people had found business there today. Even the new rector, Reverend Cudlingston, was at his doorway, watching. When he learned that the Mallows were leaving, he'd probably hold a ceremony of gratitude, and it could be well attended.

When they'd left the village and only fields lay to either side, Perriam said, "Wise of you not to want to marry there."

"They're not bad people, but my parents weren't endearing."

"They don't dislike you. I was warned at the inn not to cause you any harm."

"Were you? By whom?"

"The innkeeper and someone called Old Matt."

Claris had to smile. "I doubt the threat had any more teeth than he had."

"Oh, it did. Grannie Mallow would put the evil eye on me."

She put a hand to her face. "And she encourages them for her own amusement. I've been in a constant fret that she'd end up in court."

"Witchcraft isn't a crime anymore."

"That's a blessing, but I'll be glad to see her away from the village. She and Ellie will appreciate the comforts of Perriam Manor."

See, I do this for others, not for myself.

"Ellie is your grandmother's servant?"

"Yes, since they were young women."

"Since your grandmother fled her marriage. What's the story there?"

"I don't know. Only that her husband was intolerable and she left. Left her young son as well."

"It would be unusual that she be allowed to take him. A daughter, perhaps, but not a son. An only son?"

"Yes. She claims she never had tender feelings for my father, but I wonder if that can be true."

"Why not? There are no inevitable emotions, not even for parents."

"None?"

"None. My own parents were rarely at Herne House to see us grow up. For which, I assure you, we were grateful."

"How odd."

"You wouldn't have preferred that your parents be elsewhere?"

"Infinitely. I meant that it's odd to be so careless of children. Poorly raised children become bothersome adults, and then they're less easy to ignore."

"I assure you, my parents took great care over us, especially in the choice of people to guard and guide us. Their visitations to Herne were more in the nature of inspections, and flaws were rigorously corrected."

"You feared them?"

"Enough to curb any wilder impulses, at least. Some others I judged worth the beating."

"Do you calculate everything?"

"Do you not? I recommend it."

Claris realized that again he was conversing to allow her nerves to settle. She resented the efficiency of it but appreciated the effect.

The horse's pace was steady and the day quite pleasant, with only light clouds in the sky. All around colors were shifting from summer green toward autumn gold. They passed a field where hay was being cut, and the sweet smell wafted over. Some of the workers paused to look. Old Barford people observing the departure of the Mad Rector's daughter.

She'd never return. She knew that with certainty.

Her future lay ahead, and also by her side. Their clothes were in contact, and when the gig swayed or jolted, they moved closer, making her simmer with something disturbing. She was unused to being close to a man. In fact, she'd never been so close.

It made her think of intimacies, marital intimacies that weren't going to happen, but she thought of them anyway. She didn't know much, but when not raving about hell's flames, her father had often detailed from the pulpit the sins that might send a person there.

Sinful lustings and burnings.

The devil's fires within.

The brief flame of passion that led to an eternity of pain.

She shifted on the seat, feeling rather hot....

"Are you uncomfortable?"

"No," she said quickly. "Not at all."

His attention was on the road.

He clearly felt no heat.

Of course not.

"As we travel, let me prepare you for what lies ahead," he said. "Ashart comes from a grand line, and his life was all court and the beau monde until recently. Marriage and fatherhood have given him a taste for rural pursuits, but he's still a magnate to the bone."

Claris was glad of a new focus. "I should kiss his feet?" she asked, to show she wasn't overwhelmed.

"Not even his ring. He'll be courteous and perhaps kind, but he can't help his grand manner. Lady Ashart comes from a simpler family. Her father is a naval captain, now retired, and she was born and raised following him on ship and shore. In bloodline she could be less exalted than you."

That could be a comfort, but Claris had seen the marchioness a few times. She was gloriously beautiful and at ease in her role.

"The Asharts have been married less than two years. They have an infant, Calliope, called Callie, and are fond enough parents to sometimes bring her into company. Fortunately, she's a good-natured sprite. Cheynings is a handsome house, but it and the estate were neglected for many years. He's restoring it, but it's a work in progress."

"I'm unlikely to complain of spots of damp."

"You won't find any, but some rooms are scantily furnished and the library lacks books. Mildew and worm," he explained with a smile.

Claris smiled back. She should probably resist his efforts, but she was enjoying a long, rational conversation, especially about something other than her own affairs.

"How was such neglect allowed?" she asked.

"That's too long a story for this short journey, but it means I can't easily research your grandmother's story. Do you know her maiden name?"

"No. Why?"

"Grand connections will be useful at Perriam Manor. The local gentry will be curious about your antecedents."

Claris's comfort dissolved. "Not if I don't meet them."

"You mean to be a recluse?"

She realized that, yes, she'd thought her life would be

the same as at Lavender Cottage, only with more rooms and a lot more comfort. How stupid. Even if the gentry around Old Barford had never accepted her parents, she knew how they lived, constantly visiting and entertaining.

"I won't know how to behave. They'll see that I'm an imposter."

"They will not. You'll be the Honorable Mistress Peregrine Perriam and entitled to respect."

The idea was too much. "I can't do this. I can't!"

He drew the horse to a halt. "You're made of tougher stuff, Claris."

"No, I'm not. You don't understand. I've never mingled with the gentry. My mother complained bitterly about being excluded."

"With reason."

"Why? She wasn't of their sort—her father was a timber merchant—and my father made no attempt to play their games. In fact, he often insulted them from the pulpit. So you see, it won't work."

He took her hand. "A lady takes the station of her husband. If necessary, I'll assert that."

For the first time she saw the Honorable Peregrine Perriam, son of an earl. He frightened her, but there was comfort in his firm grasp and his words.

He would take steps.

If anyone insulted her, he would take steps.

"Trust me?" he said, his blue eyes seeming warm.

"What choice do I have?"

She immediately regretted her tone but wouldn't apologize. She took her hand from his.

"Place no reliance on my grandmother coming from a grand family. If it existed, my mother would have used it for social leverage."

He set the horse to move on. "Your grandmother has the air."

"She puts on airs."

"I've encountered brilliant imposters, but I'd lay

money on your grandmother being exactly as she seems, a highborn but eccentric lady. I'll find out in Town."

"Such a direct way with a puzzle."

"You resent that? You're not slow and timid, Claris, and I hope in time you'll blossom into a true thistle."

"A thistle?"

"Standing tall and armed with prickles."

A laugh escaped. "At my height I can never stand tall."

"Standing tall has little to do with height." He leaned slightly to take something out of a pocket and then offered a purse made of cream cloth embroidered with flowers, its neck held closed with a gold cord. "Some coins for vails."

She took it, feeling its weight. "Vails?"

"Small monetary gifts for the servants, especially when a guest leaves. I'll attend to that when we leave Cheynings, but you may want to reward someone for a particular service whilst there, such as your maid."

That terrifying lady's maid.

Even through her cotton gloves she could feel the quality of the cloth. She was sure it was silk, embroidered silk. It was the prettiest thing she'd ever owned, and he'd given it to her so carelessly. Silk also stirred memories. Memories she couldn't cope with in this fraught situation.

"Thank you," she said, and put it in her right-hand pocket.

The silence felt awkward, so she wasn't surprised when he filled it with a story about a feud between the Marquess of Ashart's family, the Trayces, and the Marquess of Rothgar's, the Mallorens.

Marquesses! How had her life come to this?

It seemed to originate in an unfortunate marriage but had risen to heights from there.

"I've been accustomed to thinking that mine was the only hellish family," she said, "but now I wonder if there are any happy ones."

"I have friends who are making promising beginnings, and two sisters who seem content. You can see Cheynings ahead."

Perhaps a grand house should offer security, but Claris found the enormous pale building with pillars and pediment simply terrifying.

Chapter 12

The house seemed to grow in size as they approached. Its width could encompass Old Barford and all its inhabitants, and the pillared front rose above her, impossibly high. What need had any person of so much space?

The massive front doors at the top of a dozen or more steps stayed resolutely closed. That didn't surprise her at all. They were rejecting the unworthy intruder.

Perriam turned to the side, seeking a more suitable entrance. But then he drew up beneath a portico that had its own grand pillars and where two powdered footmen in blue velvet laced with silver stood ready. The sort of servants who'd see through her pretensions in a moment. Their blank expressions already showed their opinion of the unlikely guest, and they hadn't had a good look at her clothing yet.

She was wearing her best gown, but it wasn't good enough. The green skirt might look sprigged, but the material was only a cheap print. The new braid and embroidery were hasty work. Even her newly trimmed hat seemed laughable, and how could she enter this grand house in her well-worn shoes, which had tramped the roads and fields?

Perriam came himself to hand her down, and she was grateful for that, but as he turned her toward the door, she wanted to mutter, *This is impossible—you must see that.* But she did not. *Act as if you belong here,* she reminded herself and forced her head high. She glanced up once at the high ceiling of the corridor—the height of the entire cottage!—but then remembered not to gawk.

The corridor was quite plain, but even so paintings hung on the wall that she would have liked to study. Then she and Perriam turned into a grander space—the main entrance hall, with a black-and-white tiled floor and yet more paintings on the walls. There were weapons too. The swords and pikes were decoratively arranged but probably real. She looked higher and saw a ceiling painted with gods and goddesses. Half-naked gods and goddesses!

A rank of doors lined the right-hand side, one open to reveal a richly decorated room with red walls and seating covered with golden damask. The brilliance almost stung her eyes. When Perriam led her toward that door she halted, reluctant to walk on the lush carpet. She'd thoroughly cleaned her shoes, but even so . . .

She had to go forward, had to sit on a gold-upholstered chair. *Act as if, act as if . . .*

"This is a lovely room," she said, and thank heavens it didn't sound as strangled as she feared.

"Grander than anything at Perriam Manor," he said, "so don't imagine this is your future. Ah."

Claris quickly rose to curtsy to the Marchioness of Ashart. How elegantly she moved, and her simple blue gown shrieked expense, even to an ignorant eye.

Claris tried to make her curtsy gracious rather than a nervous servant's bob but feared she failed.

Lady Ashart came forward, smiling. "Miss Mallow, I'm very pleased to meet you."

Claris curtsied again, then knew twice was one too many.

Act as if . . .

Act as if . . .

"It's most kind of you to offer me hospitality, my lady."

"I'll enjoy your company, for at the moment I'm trapped with only men apart from my daughter, and she has little conversation. Come upstairs and we can take tea and gossip."

Claris found herself arm linked and steered briskly out of the room.

"I'm sure you've noticed that this is quite an odd house," Lady Ashart said as they climbed wide stairs. "A drawing room on the ground floor? Ashart's grandmother arranged it so, for as she grew older she disliked stairs. We are considering how to create a drawing room upstairs."

She too was talking to put Claris at ease, and Claris appreciated that. Her throat felt tight.

"This is the Grand Saloon," Lady Ashart said as they passed through an elaborate arch into a high, central space illuminated by a glass dome and hung all around with large portraits.

"It certainly is very grand," Claris said, managing not to look up, up, up.

"It was called the Royal Saloon, for a banquet was held here once for a monarch and many of the portraits are of royalty, but Ashart prefers something a little less elevated."

A smile shared the joke in that, and Claris managed to smile back. Not royal, merely grand.

She was steered across one corner of the room, through another arch, partway down a corridor, and into a room.

"This is your bedchamber. Your luggage should already be here. Yes, I see it is. This is Alice," she said, indicating a woman of about thirty, who'd turned from a drawer to curtsy. "She'll be your maid here. When you're ready, come down to the third door on your right. That's my boudoir."

She left, and Claris didn't know if she was relieved or abandoned. The maid returned to the unpacking, which meant she'd be seeing the simple state of everything Claris owned, which meant she'd soon be reporting that to the other servants.

There was nothing to be done about it, and this place wasn't her future, thank heavens. It was far too large and grand.

She took off her gloves, then unpinned her hat and placed it on a gleaming wooden dressing table. She couldn't resist stroking the fine wood, delighting in the silky feel. Even at the rectory they'd had nothing so fine.

This room alone was as big as the ground floor of the cottage. It contained a tester bed, a settee, and two chairs, all upholstered in green. At least, she thought wryly, her clothing matched.

There was also a toilet stand, complete with a china washbowl and tiny pots. White towels hung on rails on either side, and a screen stood ready to be put around for privacy. She hadn't considered that problem before, but would the maid expect to see her in undress, perhaps even naked?

She wouldn't allow that, no matter how inferior it made her seem.

Another piece of furniture was probably a desk, but such a desk! The mellow wood was ornamented with inlays of black, gold, and ivory. A small table sat by the window with a wooden chair tucked in. So she would be expected to eat here. That would be a relief, but it showed how she was considered.

She surveyed the rest of her domain. The floor was of polished wood, with a small carpet on either side of the bed, but richly patterned carpets in jewel-like colors.

Paintings hung on the walls, and ornaments sat on the mantelpiece. One was a ticking clock, its mechanism visible through a glass dome. She longed to inspect it but remembered, *act as if.* She must stop gawking and do something.

"May I have washing water?" she asked, then wondered if she should have commanded it.

"Of course, ma'am." The maid curtsied and hurried away.

Alone at last, Claris sank into a chair, blowing out a

breath, but when she slid her hand along the upholstered arm, her fingers snagged.

The green damask was silk.

You can't make a silk purse out of a sow's ear came to mind and brought back the memories she'd resisted earlier.

Before today, the only silk she'd ever touched had been Aunt Clarrie's silk fichu.

Her mother had treasured the portrait of her dead sister and turned it into a sort of shrine, with several of Aunt Clarrie's possessions hung around. There'd been ribbons, a perfumed sachet that still held a lingering rose perfume, some invitations, and a lovely silk fichu of fine cream silk embroidered with delicate flowers.

Claris hadn't been able to resist, and one day she'd taken it down to wrap around her own shoulders.

She'd been birched fiercely for that.

Seeing a fine thread raised from the damask by her rough finger made her understand her mother's anger. Clearly she should have listened to Athena's complaints about her hands and accepted the lotions offered to improve them.

When her mother died, her father had buried all Aunt Clarrie's belongings with her, even the portrait. Claris had desperately wanted to save that silk fichu. . . .

She stood and went to inspect the marvelous clock. She watched the golden parts moving, backward and forward, backward and forward. They had a simple clock in the cottage, encased in wood, its workings hidden. The tall clock in the rectory hall had also kept its secrets.

So many secrets.

The maid returned with a jug of hot water and poured it into the china basin. She uncovered a china pot to reveal soap. Claris washed her hands and face.

She was drying her hands when the maid came over with a pot. "Where should I put this, Miss?"

Claris recognized one of Athena's pots and took it.

Was it . . . ? It was. The hand cream she'd neglected to use. She quickly smoothed a generous amount into her hands. It wouldn't work an instant miracle, but it gave her hope. Hands could be smoothed, so perhaps a sow's ear could become a silk purse—that is, a lady suited to be the Honorable Mistress Peregrine Perriam.

Whether that was possible or not, she must cease her delay and face the marchioness. She checked her appearance in the mirror—one without a flyspeck anywhere—and left the room.

She found Lady Ashart seated on a settee reading a book, the tea things in front of her on a table.

"I'm sorry for keeping you waiting," Claris said.

She'd been resolved not to gawk but couldn't help looking around in surprise. The marchioness's boudoir was not at all as she'd expected.

"Unusual, I know," Lady Ashart said, putting aside her book, "but to my taste. Some see it as too plain, but I receive such people in the drawing room."

"It's lovely," Claris said, and she was honest. Here, for the first time, she felt comfortable.

The room was little bigger than the kitchen at Lavender Cottage. Even the ceiling was almost as low. It had handsome paneled walls in a honey-colored wood, but the one window was hung with simple blue curtains and the seating was covered in a blue cloth that surely wasn't silk. The floor was carpeted, but instead of one large piece, there were three smaller, mismatched ones.

"I spent years living either on board one of my father's ships or in lodgings ashore. I don't feel comfortable in vast rooms."

Nor do I, Claris thought, but didn't admit it.

"Large chambers can be splendid," Lady Ashart went on, "but I think them impractical for daily living, especially in winter. I had the ceiling here lowered, for in a high room the heat rises. Hot heads and cold feet. Even the king and queen have modest rooms for winter use."

Claris's comfort shattered.

She'd moved from marquesses to royalty!

She knew she should say something, but her tongue seemed stuck.

"Sit, do," Lady Ashart said, indicating a chair. When Claris was settled, her hostess went on, "I wasn't thinking of comfort when I designed this room. I realized later that I was re-creating a captain's cabin on board a ship — except that no captain would allow all these ornaments. They'd be tossed around and broken. Which is perhaps why I like them. They represent my settled life."

It was true that every surface was scattered with something. In addition to china and glass ornaments, Claris saw a number of books, an odd carved wooden statue, a dish of sweetmeats, and some needlework.

Claris forced out some words. "You traveled a great deal, my lady?"

"Constantly." Lady Ashart opened her tea box and spooned leaves into a china pot. "My mother couldn't bear to be far from my father."

"My parents did their best to avoid each other, even within the rectory." Claris wished her tongue had stayed stuck. "I've hardly ever left Old Barford," she hurried on. "And even then I've never gone far."

"Then you'll have much to discover."

"Good and bad."

"Isn't there good and bad everywhere?"

Lady Ashart lifted a kettle from the stand where a flame kept it hot and poured steaming water into the pot. Claris was relieved to see that a marchioness's tea etiquette was similar to the way she'd been trained. One thing she could do right.

Lady Ashart replaced the kettle, put the lid on the pot, and then smiled. "May I call you Claris? I make you free of my name, Genova. I was named for the Italian port where I was born."

"I was named for an aunt."

"The one who laid a curse on a Perriam."

Claris hadn't expected that to be known, but of course Perriam had told his friends. He'd probably told them everything.

"There are no such things as curses," she said.

"No? Ashart scoffs at the very idea, but in my travels I came across strange beliefs and the equally strange effects. I saw one sailor sicken and die after being cursed by a kind of priestess on a West Indian island. He'd raped her daughter."

"Then he deserved it."

"Ah. The case bears some resemblance to that of your aunt, doesn't it? However, I thought the sailor died out of belief, fear, and perhaps even guilt."

"I don't have the impression that Giles Perriam suffered guilt."

"No, and yet his innocent wives and children suffered."

"That had nothing to do with me," Claris protested.

"Did I seem to accuse? My apologies. I simply find such subjects fascinating."

"I don't believe in curses," Claris reiterated, "and still less that my aunt would have attempted one. She was a gentle, virtuous lady. I've seen her well-used prayer book."

"But you must also have seen the curse, written in her own hand."

Claris had no answer to that.

"Resolute of her to have attempted it," Genova said.

"Perhaps," Claris said, hating to be seen as part of a cursing family, "but the apparent results could have been ill fortune and nothing more."

"I'm sure you're right. Do you take milk or cream in your tea?"

"Milk, if you please."

Claris accepted her cup and saucer and added sugar, which here was presented pounded down to a fine powder. It took little stirring, but Claris lingered over the task, awkwardly unable to think of a thing to say.

Lady Ashart sipped her own tea. "Let's talk of your wedding. I expect to enjoy assisting you there, and helping you prepare to be mistress of Perriam Manor. But you mustn't let me harry you if you wish to rest."

She seemed sincere, and in any case, there was no purpose in pretense.

"I'll be grateful for any help. I've lived simply, even when in the rectory, and I wish to arrive at the manor in as suitable a condition as possible."

"Excellent! We'll increase your wardrobe, and of course provide a special gown for your wedding."

"What I'm wearing will do."

"It could," Lady Ashart agreed, "but any lady wishes to have something new for the day."

"There's no time to have a new gown made."

"But time enough to have one altered. You're shorter than I, but a gown of mine might fit in other respects."

"I couldn't take one of your gowns, my lady."

"Genova, please. I have too many, I assure you." But then she turned serious. "First assure me that you're not sacrificing yourself for your brothers. If you need funds to give them a start in life, I will assist you without demands."

Claris stared. "Why? I'm a stranger to you."

"We're women in a man's world. In my eyes marrying Perriam will be greatly to your benefit, but you may not see it that way."

She was serious.

She was offering a way out.

Claris was surprised to realize that she didn't want it. She didn't want to be anyone's pensioner, but more than that, she wanted the prize she'd bargained for—comfort, wealth, and to be mistress of a manorial estate.

"I'm not doing it for my brothers," she said. "I'm not reluctant. Frightened, yes, but not reluctant."

Genova smiled. "It's good to be honest with ourselves.

More tea?" When Claris accepted, she poured, saying, "I helped him to prepare that basket."

"Why?"

"Because of his necessity, but also because I saw the advantages for you and your family. However, I told him that I would stand by your side, and if he mistreated you in any way, he would feel my wrath."

"How?" Claris asked, fascinated.

"I left that unspecified, but I did once shoot a Barbary pirate." Genova's eyes twinkled. "That story seems to give all men pause. I gather you attempted much the same."

Claris put down her cup. "I shudder to think of it! I could have *killed* him. My wretched temper."

"It'll do him no harm to be wary of stirring it."

Claris considered the other woman, who truly seemed friendly. "Will you teach me about pistols? How to load and fire them?"

"You don't know?"

"The pistol belonged to my grandmother. She prepared it, but praise heaven didn't put in a ball."

"An interesting woman. She sounds somewhat like Ashart's oldest great-aunt, though Lady Calliope has never traveled. She and her sisters are not from a common mold either. The common mold is so very common, isn't it? We don't aspire to it."

"We don't?" Claris asked warily. Had the marchioness really meant the two of them?

"We don't," Genova said. "Very well, we need a pistol suitable for a lady, and a number of gowns, one suited for a wedding. Let's move to my dressing room."

The dressing room was larger than the boudoir and contained two clothes presses, a dressing table, and a curtained bath. A maid was summoned and gowns taken from drawers. Even the simplest ones frightened Claris with their grandeur, but she wanted their beauty, by heaven she did.

"Blue," Genova said, holding a gown of blue cloth

sprigged with spring flowers in front of Claris. "No, I don't think so. Pink might suit you, but it's overly sweet on me, so I have none."

The maid offered a sage green one.

Genova rejected it. "Far too dull for a bride."

The maid took a pale dress out of a drawer. "What about this one, then, milady?"

"Too dull," Genova said again, but when the maid held it in front of Claris, she exclaimed, "How clever you are. It's perfect!"

Claris had wanted the sky blue scattered with flowers, and even the sage green with its frills and braid, but see, dull suited her. When Genova turned her to the mirror, however, she sucked in a breath.

The gown had ruffles along the hem and quiet embroidery on the bodice, but it was the color that was magical. By some means, the ivory shade made her sunspoiled complexion look less sallow and her brown hair a little richer.

"With deep pink trimming, perhaps, milady?" the maid suggested.

"The very thing! And truly, Claris, this gown has been hardly worn, for Ashart says it makes me look as if I'm trying to hide. It makes you glow. Undress and put it on and we'll see what needs to be done."

Claris was unhooking her bodice when someone rapped on the boudoir door. The maid hurried to respond and returned to say, "Mr. Perriam asks to speak to Miss Mallow, milady."

Claris hastily refastened herself and went through, her heart thumping. From fear of him? No, she still feared this future being snatched away. She wouldn't return to Lavender Cottage. She wouldn't!

"All is well?" he asked.

"Lady Ashart is being most kind."

"I come to take my farewell . . ."

Her heart thumped harder.

". . . but also to measure your finger for the ring."

Claris had to put a hand on the back of a chair.

"Are you all right?" he asked.

She straightened. "Yes, of course. Everything is moving so quickly."

"I'm sorry for that, but yes, it is and it must."

He produced a piece of string and wrapped it around her ring finger, marking the length. This time his fingers touched hers without the barrier of gloves. Now the rapid beating of her heart wasn't from fear. If he noticed, he didn't comment.

"Is there anything you'd like from Town?" he asked as he tucked away the string.

A pistol, but he'd refuse, given that he was the most likely target.

"I don't think so. . . ."

"Silk stockings," said Genova, entering the room. "A fan or two, for I suspect you have none. Do you, Claris?"

"No. . . ."

"Handkerchiefs."

"I do have some. . . ."

"You'll need more. Do you have pretty shoe buckles?"

"No."

"Enough," Perriam said, and Claris thought he was going to protest at the cost. "I can guess what's wanted and will do my poor best."

He took Claris's hand again, warm on warm, and raised it to his lips for a kiss. The frisson was so powerful she snatched her hand free. "Don't do that!"

His brows rose, but his eyes twinkled. "A mere courtesy from a gentleman to a lady. Adieu, my dear."

Claris watched him go, clutching the hand he'd kissed. Surely their agreement forbade such things.

"Come along," Genova said, "we have work to do."

Her eyes were smiling.

Was she seeing lovebirds? Was Perriam already trying to weaken her with his easy charms? Claris would have none of that. She'd agreed to a practical marriage that would leave her an independent woman of independent means, untroubled by her husband's presence.

To make that clear, Claris led the way back into the dressing room saying, "That's him gone for a week, thank heavens."

Chapter 13

Five days passed in a dizzying whirl. Two local seamstresses shortened and retrimmed the ivory gown and then worked on three other gowns. Some Cheynings maids made new shifts. Genova provided an extra trunk, which began to fill with all Claris's new possessions, including a nightgown of fine lawn trimmed with lace.

Claris wanted to deny the need of that, but she was uncomfortable about revealing details of the arrangement. Let Genova assume there would be a wedding night, but Claris would sleep in her shift, as always.

Around fittings, Genova educated her. One day, as they strolled in the gardens enjoying shrubs, flowers, and pretty vistas, she drilled Claris on titles and the way to address people.

When Claris protested that she'd be living quietly, Genova said, "You never know who will turn up on the doorstep. It's considered polite to pay calls on new neighbors, and people will be particularly curious about you."

"Why?"

"A Perriam marrying an unknown." Genova never minced words.

"Can't I set up as an eccentric recluse?"

"You could, but why?"

"I don't know how to deal with such people."

"Which is why we're having this lesson. How do you address a bishop?"

"A bishop is going to turn up on my doorstep?"

"Unlikely, I admit, but you must know."

There were also lessons in deportment. Genova chose to give them in the Grand Saloon, surrounded by royalty.

"Your deportment is acceptable in general ways, but not for court."

"I won't be going to court."

"You never know. The court curtsy." She demonstrated, sinking down, back straight, and then rising. "You do it. Deeper, deeper, back straight, good . . . Whoops!"

Claris sat on her bottom and glowered.

"Don't despair. You'll have gentlemen nearby to give assistance."

"Why don't they have to do such ridiculous things?"

Genova chuckled. "We should insist on it, shouldn't we? But I'm assured that learning to manage a dress sword is as difficult. Otherwise it rattles people's shins and can even catch on a lady's skirts, revealing more than is wise."

Claris wasn't tied to fittings and lessons, and she gradually relaxed into enjoying life at Cheynings. She wandered the house, feasting on the works of art and becoming accustomed to huge spaces. There was even a glass-walled room full of greenery to be enjoyed in all seasons.

She walked in the gardens, enjoying the lovely vistas of a countryside glowing as the season turned much of the foliage to yellow and gold. This was nature's gift and available all her life, but she'd rarely gone far from the village to appreciate it.

The meals were delicious and appeared as if by magic. The Asharts were gracious hosts and never left an awkward silence, but the greatest pleasure was time alone with Genova—her first friend. She'd never expected such a gift, but it was real. Perhaps Genova's simple background made it possible. She was every inch the marchioness, but she'd been born and raised to ordinary ways.

On the fifth day after Perriam's departure, they were walking through the Grecian Grove, where pale statues stood between old trees.

"I still find it odd that nakedness is acceptable," Claris said. Then she risked the question she'd longed to ask. "Are the male statues accurate? In physique, I mean."

She was blushing even to ask. She'd raised her brothers, but these statues were of men.

"They show the variety," Genova said. "We have our Hercules"—she gestured toward a massive man—"and our Dionysus." She indicated a slender, smiling man holding a wine goblet. "I judge Perriam to be more of his build."

That wasn't what Claris had meant. These statues didn't have leaves obscuring their manly parts. She couldn't pursue it, however.

"Bacchus in Greek," she said, as nonchalantly as she could. "The god of drink and noisy revels."

"You know your classics?"

"I helped my brothers with their lessons."

"Of course. Perriam certainly enjoys festivities. In fact, as I remember, he dressed as Dionysus for the Olympian Revels."

"The Olympian Revels?"

"An annual event when the great and powerful costume themselves from classical times and meet to connive."

"Not to revel?"

Genova chuckled. "That too, but once gathered, they can't help themselves. They connive. The beautiful world, as it's called, is mostly a stew of politics and power beneath the silken trimmings."

"Then I'm glad I'll have no part in it."

"Oh, it can be amusing." But Genova's gaze moved beyond Claris, and the light in her eye said that her husband was in sight.

Claris turned to see two reasons for Genova's delight—Ashart and the infant he was carrying, without sign of a nursemaid. The infant smiled and stretched out her arms to her mother. Genova took her and kissed her cheek. "Good afternoon, darling one. Are you here to explore the gardens?"

Claris was shocked by a stab of something.

Jealousy?

Not precisely that, but envy or longing.

For a child?

She pushed it aside. Hers would not be that sort of marriage.

Ashart was standing close to his wife and child and had given Callie a finger to grasp. Secure in that circle of love, little Callie looked around, taking in everything.

Claris remembered the twins being like that, so full of the wonder of the world, but much of their world had been dark and painful, and she'd not been able to entirely protect them from that.

Callie wouldn't have to learn such lessons—but fate could be cruel to rich as well as poor. Better by far not to have hostages to fortune.

Perriam shocked Claris by arriving that evening, on the fifth day rather than the sixth. She happened to be in the hall when he entered in a surge of energy. He greeted her with a kiss on the hand. When she snatched it free, he merely smiled.

"You look well, Claris, even rested. Cheynings hasn't been too much of a strain?"

He was so pleased with himself that she wanted to claim it had been torture, but he'd know it couldn't be true.

"Lady Ashart has been most kind."

"And Ashart hasn't bitten you? Excellent." He directed that mischievously at the marquess, who was coming downstairs with Genova.

"I save my fangs for worthier prey," Ashart said.

"Are you calling my bride unworthy? Swords at dawn."

Claris gasped, but Genova declared, "Enough! Ignore them, Claris." She steered everyone into the drawing room. "Have you done anything beside create mischief wherever you go, Perriam?"

"Kept the world on its axis and driven away screeching demons, thus saving the realm."

"Make sense, you madman," Ashart said, sitting beside Genova on a settee.

"I wish I could." Perriam steered Claris to the other settee and sat beside her. "I have dispatched a wagon to Lavender Cottage," he told her. "A small one, as requested. Are you sure you don't have a hidden cellar filled to the roof?"

He wasn't close enough to touch, but he was too close, especially with energy sparkling off him like sunlight off silver. Was this what a visit to London did to him?

"A small cart would do, especially as we won't need the beds. I assume Perriam Manor comes equipped with beds?"

"Any number of them, all now being aired and prepared."

"You have been busy," Ashart remarked.

"That was accomplished by letter." Perriam turned back to Claris. "Said wagon has two strong men to load it, and they should already be on their way to Berkshire."

"Already on their way? But the wedding is two days hence."

"I have the license, so there's no need to delay. I stopped on the way here and alerted the vicar."

"Without a word to me?"

"Are you offended? I thought you'd like it done."

She was not so much offended as panicked, but yes, she wanted it done—before fate could snatch it away.

"As you will. I must alert my family."

"I sent a letter with the wagon. They're prepared. Roads permitting, your possessions will arrive at Perriam Manor before you do."

Irritation was overwhelming panic, but Claris managed to be civil. "Then I must thank you."

"Don't feel obliged," he insisted, amusement in his eyes. "I merely do a spouse's duty, my almost wife. Which reminds me . . ."

He took something out of his pocket.

A clear stone sparkled in the sunlight.

A diamond?

She'd never seen one before.

He took her hand and slid on the ring. "Thus I capture you."

Claris pulled free. "The word 'capture' could doom your plan, sir."

"I am captured too."

"I see no shackle on you."

"I should have thought of that. Perhaps I can pacify you with other trinkets. . . ."

"Perriam," Genova protested, "you can't call that ring a trinket, and it would be shameful if it was."

Claris couldn't help looking at the lovely stone, which shot fire as she turned it in the light. She'd thought much the same of him. Beauties were often compared to diamonds. Could beaux also be?

She dragged herself back to the practical. "How will my family come here?"

"A carriage, if Ashart will oblige, can bring them to the church tomorrow." She must have shown a reaction, for he said, "You disapprove?"

"You said we'd marry at Cheynings."

"That is your wish? A special license permits us to marry anywhere, but I assumed a clergyman's daughter would prefer a church."

In normal circumstances she would, for to wed anywhere other than a church would feel wrong. However, talk of a church service reminded her that despite their practical plans, this marriage would be real in the eyes of God. It would be for life, and it would put her in the position of wife, subservient to her lord and master.

That was the truth, however, and should be faced.

"You're correct. I do prefer a church wedding."

He took her at her word and moved on. "After the service, we'll travel to the manor."

"No." That was Genova. "After the wedding everyone will return here for a celebration. A small one," she assured Perriam, "but essential."

"You are most gracious," he said, bowing, teasing. "After which we travel. Without need to stop for a meal en route, it should only take about four hours, roads permitting."

"You're in a vast hurry," Claris said.

"I must return to Town as soon as possible."

He clearly couldn't wait to be away from her. She reminded herself that she couldn't wait to be free of him.

"Are the roads so very chancy?" she asked.

"I forget that you've not ventured far from Old Barford. They can be the very devil. Granite ruts a foot or more high in winter, soupy mud a foot or more deep after heavy rains."

"Can't they be improved?"

"With effort and money, undoubtedly," Ashart said. "Hence the turnpikes."

"Frequently attacked," Perriam said, "because people don't see why they should pay to use a road, even one that is well maintained."

"Why should they?" Claris asked. "Turnpikes are for the convenience of the great."

"Never say you're Farmer Barnett's true companion after all! Most people benefit from the smooth transport of goods."

"Packhorses achieve the same end."

"Not for heavy goods."

"And there we have canals," Ashart said, "which do a

better job than roads. Do we wish to know about Farmer Barnett?"

"No," Claris said, but it clashed with Genova's "Yes!"

Claris frowned but admitted, "He was my worthy suitor, offering me the honor of being wife to a man farming one hundred and fifty acres. Alas, I was compelled to accept another."

"Saved from a life of excessive godliness," Perriam said.

"Is there such a thing? I am a clergyman's daughter."

"All the same, you'd have slipped rat poison into his soup within the year."

"More likely his mother would have slipped some into mine."

Claris realized she was joking, that she'd been tricked into friendly repartee.

She rose. "I must go and attend to my packing."

"By all means." He rose with her. "You have much to pack. When you've inspected my purchases, I hope for applause."

Claris dipped a curtsy and escaped, curious to see what he'd provided, but wary too. He wasn't so much Bacchus as Mercury.

She found her bed strewn with items wrapped in white muslin. Alice was hovering by them, perhaps as curious as she. Claris sent her away. She'd explore this alone. She was remembering the basket Perriam had brought to the cottage and the havoc it had wrought in her.

She first chose a long, narrow package because she knew it must be a fan. Indeed it was, a pretty ivory piece painted with roses. A fan had been among Aunt Clarrie's mementoes, but that one had been of pink lace.

Genova had given some lessons on the handling of a fan, and so Claris turned her wrist. It flowed smoothly open. When she reversed the action it smoothly closed again.

Carefully chosen?

No, the perfection must be from luck.

She opened the fan again, remembering that it could be used in many ways. An open fan could conceal or express emotions. A closed one could be a weapon. She would be permitted to rap an impudent gentleman on the arm or even upon the knuckles.

A weapon in the war between the sexes.

Genova had said that, clearly meaning it lightly, but a truth lay beneath. This was a man's world, and a woman needed all the weapons she could find.

Genova had taught her how to handle a pistol, using her own. It was a pretty little weapon with silver mountings and pearl inlay, but lethal all the same. Claris had practiced with it in the gardens and had once hit the piece of wood set up as target, splintering it.

She didn't have her own pistol yet, but she'd sent off an order to Ashart's London gunsmith for one similar to Genova's. If Perriam kept his promises, she'd have enough money to pay the shockingly high cost. If he didn't, she'd have reason to shoot him.

She returned to the packages, unwrapping each with care. Six pairs of plain cotton stockings and six of wool, for winter wear. Useful but disappointing.

Then she unwrapped three pairs made of silk.

She had been using Athena's cream, so when she tentatively picked one up, her fingers didn't harm it. It was as smooth as Aunt Clarrie's fichu and just as delicate.

She wouldn't dare wear such stockings for fear of ruining them, but they were unbearably pretty, clocked up each ankle with embroidered flowers, one pair even embellished with gold thread that sparkled in the light.

As tempting as sweet ginger.

As seductive.

She carefully rewrapped them in muslin, where they'd probably stay forever.

Gloves of plain white cloth, gloves of lace, and one pair of supple tan leather. Then she noticed something — wear along the seams.

These weren't new.

He'd purchased secondhand goods for her?

Tears threatened, and over such nonsense. Why should he go to the expense of buying new? She was merely the woman he had to marry to secure Perriam Manor. He'd have married Aggie Putbeck, who was short of most of her wits and skew eyed as well, if that had been the price.

She was tempted to hurl the whole lot through the open window, but she wouldn't embarrass herself that way. Instead, she'd open everything.

Another package contained handkerchiefs, some of fine lawn with cutwork design and others plain. At least three of the plain were clearly not new. One even had a darn and wasn't much better than her own. Three cotton fichus, new or not she couldn't tell. One was trimmed with lace so must have cost a fair amount, even from a rag shop.

A larger package revealed a dressing robe in a lovely shade of pink. When she picked it up, she realized it was made of heavy silk. That couldn't have been cheap either.

What was she to make of this mixed collection?

Perhaps that he'd first spent lavishly and then regretted it?

It was a lovely garment, however, designed for a lady to wear over her nightgown, or over her undergarments if she paused in dressing.

She draped the robe over a chair and reached for another package—a very light one. She opened it and discovered a fichu of silk.

Claris let it fall to the bed.

How had he known?

How could he have known about Aunt Clarrie's fichu?

She inhaled and carefully picked it up. She spread it over her hands, as light as air, so fine that she could see her fingers through it, beautifully embroidered.

It wasn't the same exactly, for the embroidery was of

curlicues, not flowers, but when she put it around her shoulders, she shivered with awareness that it was forbidden. Now, however, it was allowed.

She sat at the dressing table and considered herself.

In the portrait, Aunt Clarrie had worn her fichu with a low-necked gown so that it covered, or rather veiled, the upper half of her breasts. Claris's gown was modest, but the silk whispered against her neck like sin.

She snatched the cloth off and wrapped it up again.

At Perriam Manor she'd have no more occasion to wear the fichu than to wear silk stockings, and it was better so. Silk was dangerous. It could enchant the mind. She would be a sturdy countrywoman, just as she'd been at the rectory and at Lavender Cottage, only in more comfort.

All the same, she knew she would take the fichu out of its wrapping to admire now and then without fear of a birching. She'd think of poor Aunt Clarrie and hope she'd found solace in her niece's marriage, in her niece achieving the place at Perriam Manor she'd believed would be her own.

Perhaps even her mother's shade would garner some ease from that.

Despite the curse, it was easy to think of Aunt Clarrie in heaven, but impossible to imagine her angry, bitter mother there, despite her piety.

She quickly went through the rest of Perriam's purchases, not checking to see if the items were new or used. A needlework case, a delicate hand mirror, a set of perfumed sachets, a silver-backed hairbrush and a bone comb.

She'd left the largest item to the last. It was a dome-topped tapestry-covered box with a lock, and she feared she knew what it contained.

Trinkets.

When she opened it, she gasped at the array of jewels in the upper tray but then realized they probably were trinkets in his mind. She touched a string of green beads, a silver bangle, and a brooch of translucent purple stones.

Trinkets to him, but she'd never possessed any ornament other than her silver cross and chain—and now a diamond ring.

Her mother had owned some jewelry, some of which had been inherited from Aunt Clarrie. When she'd died, Father had sold them and given the money toward the building of almshouses.

Claris lifted out the top tray to find compartments below, each containing a treasure. She picked up a ring with a clear blue stone surrounded by tiny pearls. It fit her middle finger, pretty and glittering, as tempting as sweet ginger and oranges. He probably intended the jewelry as additional persuasion in case her resolve was wavering, but she was delighted to have such things in her life.

She added the silver bangle and a silver filigree brooch to her bodice. There were earrings, but she'd never had her ears pierced. Then she saw that they didn't have a loop of wire, but instead wires that formed a sort of clip.

Did he notice *everything*?

Slowly she took off the jewelry and put it back in its place. She'd not give him the satisfaction. She'd wait to wear it until he'd taken her to Perriam Manor and gone on his way.

A knock on the door and Genova came in.

"I'm longing to know what he brought."

Claris gestured to the bed, where most items were still unwrapped. "All that a lady might be expected to own. Not a grand lady, but one of modest origins and fortune such as I."

"How clever!" Genova either had not noticed or chose to ignore Claris's tone. "When the servants at Perriam Manor see your possessions, they won't wrinkle their nose at signs of poverty, but they'll not be made suspicious by new luxury, either."

So that was why some were used. He *did* think of everything.

"Pestilential Perriam," Claris muttered.

"A clever husband isn't a bad thing."

That rather depended, Claris thought, on whether the husband was ally or enemy. Perriam was intent on securing Perriam Manor for his family, and her own needs would always be secondary to that.

Chapter 14

The next morning Claris prepared for her wedding. She'd become comfortable at Cheynings but must leave for the unknown. Perriam had described the manor as modest and comfortable. She didn't think he'd lied, but that left much undescribed, in particular the servants.

Whatever the servants at Cheynings thought, they were restrained by the presence of the Asharts. At the manor, she would be on her own. She'd have Athena, but even Athena wouldn't be able to awe and quell disdainful domestics.

At least Alice had agreed to come with her for a while.

Perhaps she would stay, and there'd be Ellie as ally among the servants. Or would there? What would Ellie's position be at Perriam Manor? It didn't seem right that she be a servant. She was part of the family. But could she be comfortable in the drawing room and dining room?

Ellie, she decided, would do just as she wished.

She was already in her shift—one of the new ones—and put her arms into her new stays so Alice could lace up the back.

She'd never owned boned stays before, and she'd been reluctant to make the change, but Genova had been forceful. "Your unboned ones are acceptable for everyday, but beneath a formal gown, you must wear proper stays."

She'd commanded a stay maker to Cheynings to make a first pair and instructed Claris to have at least one more pair made as soon as possible. Because of Perriam's impetuosity, they'd almost arrived too late. This was the first time she'd been laced into them, and she was struggling to adjust to the fit and feel.

"Not too tight."

"Of course not, ma'am. Don't want you fainting at the altar."

Lord above, absolutely not.

Claris checked that she could breathe deeply. She could, but she was aware of the stiffness encasing her. A prediction for her future life?

Nonsense. She would be mistress at Perriam Manor and wear unboned stays at all times if she wished, style and fashion be damned.

She bit her lip on that mild curse. Genova was somewhat free in her language and had infected her. Well, if she wanted to say "damnation" or "devil take it," she would.

Genova came in, her eyes bright. "May I attend the bride?"

"Of course. You see the changes begin. I'm appropriately confined in whalebone."

"And looking well. Do they pinch or squeeze?"

Claris had to admit that they didn't. "They're very well made, but I won't be able to work in them."

"Which is why you have the others. You'll see the benefit when we put on your gown. Petticoat first."

Claris stepped into it and then tied the laces at the waist. It would show beneath the open front of the gown's skirt, so the white cloth was prettily embroidered with pink flowers.

"Stockings," Genova said, but then protested, "You must wear a silk pair."

"Be sensible. I'm to travel in my wedding clothes, and I'll not have those stockings ruined."

"They can be mended. Alice knows how. Don't you?"

"Yes, milady, but I'm not as skilled at it as some."

"Then you must practice. Which means," Genova said to Claris, "that you must damage some to give her cause."

Claris ignored that and sat to put on the pair of cotton stockings. "These are much more suitable, and they're new, without mark or mend."

"If they weren't, I'd tear them off you. Such plain garters . . ."

"Will they shock the Perriam Manor servants? I'd think they'd be pleased that their new mistress was frugal."

Genova rolled her eyes but shrugged. "As you will, you prickly thing."

Thistle, Claris remembered.

That had seemed like a compliment in an odd sort of way, but clearly it wasn't.

"Now the gown," Genova commanded.

Claris hadn't put on the ivory gown since the final trimming, and she had to smile at how pretty it was with its ruched pink ribbons down the front of the bodice, fixed in place with bunches of tiny pink rosebuds.

She put her arms into the sleeves and drew it to the center to fasten, watching in the mirror. The alterations had been skillful, and it fit her perfectly in every way.

Perhaps too much so now that the stays pushed up her breasts. The bodice rose only an inch or so above her nipples.

She put a hand there. "I can't go to church like this."

"No, though it's lovely for other occasions. You need a fichu."

"There's one laid out, milady," Alice said, picking up the one of fine lawn.

Claris made an impulsive decision.

"Wait. There's a silk one."

"That's packed, ma'am."

"Can you find it, Alice? It would be perfect."

The maid knelt by the open trunk, which was almost ready to go. She poked around and then triumphantly produced the muslin package. She unwrapped it and gave it to Claris.

"Oh, that's lovely," Genova said. "Perriam?"

"Of course."

"Such excellent taste. Let me arrange it." Genova took it and put it around Claris's shoulders. That whisper on the skin again, sending a shiver down her back as Genova carefully tucked it there, and then beneath the shoulders of the bodice. "You do the front."

Claris looked down as she slipped the silk between stays and bodice; then she turned to check in the mirror.

"Claris, what is it?"

She smiled for Genova and said, "Nothing. Only that it looks so well."

For a moment, however, it had been as if Aunt Clarrie had looked out at her. Only for a moment, for Aunt Clarrie had been pretty and sweet, and she was neither, but in that painting she'd been wearing a gown of similar color, and a silk fichu so very like this one.

Clarrie Dunsworth had laid down the path to this day, first by allowing herself to be seduced and duped by Giles Perriam, and then by directing that vengeful curse. Surely she must be satisfied now.

Three dead wives and four dead babies . . .

"You've turned pale," Genova said. "Do you want some wine?"

Claris turned away from the mirror. "A bride is supposed to have some tremors. I'm anxious that everything go as it should."

"Of course it will. You need a bride gift. I have the very thing."

Genova hurried away and soon returned with a pretty pearl bar brooch. "It will keep the fichu in place," she said, carefully fixing it. "Don't worry, I'm not puncturing the silk."

"You're very kind."

"You're kind to provide this opportunity. I've enjoyed the past week."

"As have I. Oh, I'm not going to cry. I never cry. . . ." Claris found her handkerchief and dabbed her eyes.

"Never?"

"No, never."

It seemed Genova would say something serious, but then she gave her a hug. "I hope you never have cause to. Shoes."

Claris had new shoes for her wedding, ones made from the ivory cloth cut from the hem of the gown. They really weren't suitable for traveling, but she wouldn't commit the sin of putting on dark leather ones.

She had a new pair of sturdy brown leather shoes that had never tramped over fields and down muddy lanes. She'd kept her old pair, however, for she'd be tramping again, she was sure.

She had a wedding hat, also made from the trimmings, decorated with more pink ribbon and rosebuds. It was too small to be practical, but when it was fixed on top of her pinned-up hair, she knew she looked as well as possible.

Perhaps here stood the Honorable Mistress Peregrine Perriam.

She was brown haired and ordinary, but for today, at least, she looked her part.

"Lovely," Genova declared, "though it's a pity that lotion didn't fade your freckles."

Claris wrinkled her nose at her. "They're indelible."

"And will continue so if you keep forgetting a hat."

"I'm sure I was born with them."

"No baby is born with freckles. Hat, parasol, and lotion will eradicate them. We must go down. The carriage will be waiting."

Claris walked toward the door but then froze in a sudden panic.

Why now? She'd made her decision a week ago, and again when Genova had offered her a way out. This marriage was sensible, rational, and in truth the only decision possible.

Why balk now?

For no reason on earth.

She made herself walk out of the room and even found a smile of sorts.

The marquess stood ready at the bottom of the stairs to escort her out to the carriage.

"Perriam's gone ahead to be sure all's in order at the church," he said and led her outside. Before handing her into the carriage, he kissed her hand. "You look charming, my dear."

She smiled her thanks, but as she settled on the seat, she was aware that Ashart's lips on her knuckles hadn't created the same frisson Perriam's had. That was as well, given that he was another woman's husband, a friend's husband, but it was also worrying.

Perriam was all too beguiling when he cared to be, and Claris accepted that she was susceptible. Probably he'd make no attempt to charm her, but she must be on guard. Otherwise, the clever man would roll her up and do with her as he wished.

Genova climbed in and sat beside Claris, and Ashart took the backward-facing seat. The carriage moved forward.

It didn't take long to reach the village and the church, where the vicar stood outside awaiting them. Claris had come here last Sunday, so there was no excuse for panic now. When Ashart offered his hand, she took it and climbed out.

Then she did halt. People were hurrying toward them, whispering, chattering, speculating. . . .

"Just village curiosity," Ashart said. "Because of the license there's been no announcement, but they must guess."

Just curiosity, but Claris felt as if every eager eye was on her. She needed no encouragement to hurry into the cool privacy of the church.

Her family was already present at the front. The boys, polished to a shine, stared at her, their eyes widening.

Was she so changed?

She smiled and wiggled her fingers in greeting.

They grinned back.

Then Claris noticed Athena, or rather what Athena was wearing. Claris had never seen the dark blue sacque gown trimmed with lace. It wasn't ostentatious, but it blared high style and cost like a trumpet, and Athena wore it with ease.

Even Ellie was different. Her gown was gray but almost as stylish as Athena's and trimmed with silver embroidery. She wore a very fetching hat over a cap, and a necklace of silver and pearls. Athena, Claris now noted, wore amethysts.

She did falter for just one step, feeling severed from all that had so recently been solid and true. She'd expected changes, but she'd thought she'd known what form they'd take.

And there was the cause of all this turmoil, moving into place by the vicar, showing no sign of uncertainty. She was very tempted to turn and walk away simply to upset his plans.

Even he was changed.

Instead of the familiar riding clothes, today he wore a suit of plum-colored cloth, richly embroidered down the front edges and around the cuffs. Cuffs and neckcloth frothed with precious lace. Here was a fine gentleman, suited to the grandest houses, and even for court. Far above her, and only marrying her to secure a manor house for his family.

When she arrived by his side, he bowed, smiling. "You look lovely, Claris."

She dipped a curtsy. "As do you, sir."

"Too grand for a country wedding? A marriage should be celebrated with some distinction, don't you think?"

"I have taken some pains."

"Was it so very uncomfortable?" he murmured, eyes teasing her.

"Yes. I'm wearing stays."

Amusement sparkled in his eyes, and perhaps something more as he glanced at her bodice. "They become you. Very much indeed."

The vicar cleared his throat, and they both turned to him. Claris's cheeks were burning. What had driven her to mention stays—in church? And how dared he ... ?

The man could drive her mad.

The vicar moved briskly through the service, and the time for vows rushed upon her. The vows Athena had once spoken and then had to fight to escape. Claris had prepared herself for this moment, however, and her nerve didn't fail her. She repeated the words firmly, even the one about obedience, accepting as compensation the gift of all his worldly goods.

Perriam Manor, its lands and income.

Her prize.

He slid the golden ring onto her finger, and then all was done save signatures in the register. Once that was completed, her husband linked arms with her and they walked out of the church.

The villagers were still there, even more of them now. They knew nothing of practicalities and cheered the bride and groom. Some had grain and flowers, symbols of fertility, and tossed them along with good wishes.

Why, she wondered, were people always so sure a wedding was cause for joy? Experience should teach them better.

Perriam produced a bag of small coins and scattered them, especially toward the children.

Always prepared, always appropriate.

She could detest him for it.

Then they were back in the carriage, with Perriam beside Ashart. Her family followed in the carriage that had brought them from the cottage.

"That went off perfectly," Genova said. "I'm glad the villagers came out to celebrate." Even she was determined to make a delight out of this.

Claris had thought the worst was over, but when they arrived back at Cheynings, the senior servants were lined up outside the door to cheer them and throw yet more grain and blossoms. She'd have thought that they, at least, would have sensed the truth. Perhaps people preferred mindless tradition to truth.

Once inside, she brushed off petals.

Perriam said, "Allow me."

His hands brushed across her shoulders and down her back.

She stepped away. "There's no need."

"True, the blossoms are pretty on you, wife."

Gloating over his triumph?

She turned to him. "We know our terms. I trust you'll keep them."

"As well you might. Ah, here is your family."

The twins came over almost shyly, so she drew them in for a hug. "It's so lovely to see you again."

"You're different," Tom said.

"It's just trimming. We're to have a meal here and then we'll be traveling on to our new home."

"Perriam Manor," said Peter.

"Ponies," said Tom anxiously.

They didn't truly believe. Hardly surprising. They'd known so many disappointments.

Not this time.

"Ponies," she agreed. "And a fine home with all we need and more. I promise."

They relaxed, trusting her completely.

Pray God she never betrayed that trust.

Once relaxed, they began to gawk, especially at the display of weapons on the walls. Thank heavens they were out of reach.

Athena wasn't gawking. Instead she was surveying Cheynings as if making an inspection. Ellie had Yatta in her arms and was keeping an eye on the boys but seemed equally at ease. Clearly she wasn't to be a servant here, but what precisely was she?

Athena settled that by introducing Miss Gable to the Asharts as her companion. Ellie went comfortably into the dining room for the celebratory meal. Claris could hardly believe that she'd spent the past year scrubbing, laundering, and cooking.

In all her worries, she'd never thought about the etiquette of cats. Ellie put Yatta on the floor, and Yatta slipped under the table as if trained to it.

The twins were awed by the rich array of food, but that didn't stop them from eating with relish. Claris kept an eye on them to be sure they didn't stuff themselves to sickness. She found it hard to eat more than morsels.

When Ashart rose to propose a toast, she was glad the ordeal was nearly over. The speech was brief, elegant, and unspecific. Perriam responded in witty style, delicately avoiding anything that might imply fond togetherness.

Claris thumbed the gold ring that now sat beneath the diamond. Genova had told her to move the diamond there, that the queen had started the fashion. A diamond was the hardest stone and impossible to damage, so placing it above the wedding band guarded and protected the ring and all it symbolized.

Despite cheers, grain, and even vows, all this ring symbolized was a pact to secure an old manor house for the family of the Earl of Hernescroft.

No, it sealed more than that. The marriage brought justice for Aunt Clarrie and a future of comfort and independence for herself, the twins, and even Athena and Ellie, if they wanted it.

She had to fight an unseemly grin.

She'd done it!

She took another sip of wine in a private toast to herself.

Chapter 15

Claris wasn't aware of having formed an image of Perriam Manor, but she certainly hadn't expected to pass between monsters to get to it. There was no gate, but two stone pillars each held an odd creature.

"Gryphons," said Athena. "Head and wings of an eagle and a lion's body. Said to be especially good at guarding hidden treasure."

"They're probably part of the ridiculous feud over the house," Claris said.

They'd completed the journey in the predicted four hours, she, Athena, and Ellie in one carriage, with Yatta in attendance, the boys and Alice in the other. Perriam had ridden alongside on a fine black horse.

She took comfort from that.

Already he was keeping to their agreement of separation.

By that agreement, she had command of this place.

"I suppose I can get rid of them," she said.

"Not always wise to get rid of well-established guardians."

"Those creatures didn't deflect a curse, nor the tragedies it brought."

"So you believe in that now, do you?"

"I don't know, but I could do without gryphons." As the house came into sight, she inspected it for more monsters. "All that ivy could hide an army of them."

She supposed she had formed a vague expectation

from Perriam's words, and it had been of a mellow, welcoming place. Instead the carriage was drawing up in front of an ominous mass of dark green ivy, through which she could glimpse only small areas of brick and glints from latticed windows.

Ellie said, "It must be gloomy inside with the windows overhung like that."

Claris made her first decision. "The ivy will have to go."

"It's said to protect against drunkenness," Athena said.

"Moderation protects against drunkenness, though perhaps this place could drive a Puritan to drink."

The carriage door opened and her husband came to hand her down. "Welcome to Perriam Manor," he said, as if the place were heaven.

Claris climbed down. "You didn't warn me about the ivy. Or the gryphons."

"It wasn't in my interests to warn you of anything, but I promise they're the worst of it."

He let go of her hand at the first possible moment and turned to assist Athena and Ellie. *He's as unwilling as you,* she reminded herself. *He'll be off at any moment, riding on to London.*

The twins were scrambling out of the other carriage, taking in everything. They ran over.

Tom said, "Did you see the gryphons, Claris? Tremendously grand! Are there more?"

"I sincerely hope not." She could almost see the boys twitching with excitement. "You may explore if you wish, but be careful."

Such a vague command. She had no idea what perils the place might hold.

Perriam arrived at her side. "If you go to the stables, don't attempt to ride anything. Your word on it?"

They solemnly gave it but, inspired by the word "stables," raced off around the right side of the house.

"Wrong direction," Perriam said, "but it won't do them any harm to have a long run."

"Thank you for forbidding them the horses. I'd not have thought that they might attempt to ride one."

"I was a boy once too. There are grooms who might have the sense to stop them, but your brothers are now the young masters of the house."

"Oh, my heavens! That strikes terror into my heart."

"Yours to deal with. You'll also need to decide what to do about the horses. . . . Ah, I see the principal servants have come out to greet you. *En avant.*"

Claris braced for the next challenge but was reassured by the way he spoke.

Yours to deal with.

He was keeping his promise.

Perriam Manor was hers, and that included a number of servants. Even in the rectory they'd had only a cook-housekeeper and a maid of all work.

Perriam introduced a slender middle-aged lady in black as Mistress Eavesham, the housekeeper. An equally thin man, also in black, was Mr. Eavesham, the butler. Both welcomed Claris to Perriam Manor, but in a distant manner.

Here was a problem she hadn't anticipated. All these servants might know about the feud and the curse and thus the reason for this marriage.

A younger woman in a green striped dress and a white apron and cap was the upper maid, Deborah. She smiled as she curtsied, but Claris thought her sly. A man in his thirties was Charles, the footman. He looked rather grim. The Cheynings footmen had worn livery, but Charles was in plain dress. That must be the difference between the aristocracy and lesser mortals.

There were only two shallow steps up to the large door, which stood open to show a distressingly dark interior—dark wooden floor and dark wooden paneling. She went inside and was excessively relieved to see a white plaster ceiling.

But what a ceiling.

She was gawking but couldn't help it. The swathes of

plaster were thick and occasionally lowered into spikes.

"A Tudor fashion," Perriam said. "Extraordinary, isn't it? Too much so to rip down, even if it does feel as if it might sag at any moment and crush all beneath."

Claris turned to him. "Are you saying I may not have it ripped down?"

"Ah. I did give you the freedom of the place, didn't I? As you wish, but it'll make a grand mess, and there's more like it. Most of the ground floor, in fact."

Athena and Ellie had entered and the servants were hovering.

Yatta leapt out of Ellie's arms and scampered off to explore. Claris prayed he wouldn't get into trouble, but she needed to take command of this situation.

She addressed the housekeeper. "Please take my grandmother, Mistress Mallow, and her companion, Miss Gable, to their rooms."

"Room," Athena corrected. "I prefer to have Miss Gable at hand. We will have tea there as soon as may be."

Claris saw Mistress Eavesham snap to attention. Oh, to have the way of it.

"Do you want tea?" Perriam asked. "Or shall I give you the tour?"

So that was why he was lingering instead of riding on his way. She was tempted to refuse the tour, but she needed one and preferred him to the chilly housekeeper.

"First," he said, taking her to a door on the left, "the reception room." This was small, also paneled, and also with a white plaster ceiling, though not quite such an excessive one. "A place to put unexpected visitors, especially those not completely welcome."

"We had a similar room at the vicarage," she said, reminding him that she hadn't always lived in a laborer's cottage.

He inclined his head in acknowledgment.

"The dining room," he said, moving back into the hall and into the next room. "There's a parlor of sorts beyond. As it's east facing, it can serve as a breakfast room for anyone who chooses not to eat in their bedchamber."

She'd grown used to breakfast in the cottage kitchen, but in the rectory everyone had breakfasted in their rooms, even though it had been a task for poor Lottie, the maid.

He took her across the hall. "Library, not well stocked, but with another plainish ceiling, you'll be pleased to see."

The room had two windows and might be bright once the ivy was removed. The shelves were half-empty, but one slim volume stood on a stand on the long dark table that filled the center of the room.

"There's an office at the back of the house, but unless you wish to see that now, we can progress upstairs."

"By all means, upstairs," she said, keen to have this done.

She'd seen paintings in the dining room and library, and some other items she wanted to inspect, but she'd wait until he'd left. Portraits hung on the walls above the massive wooden staircase. It was as wide as the one at Cheynings, but not so elegant, being hewn out of dark oak. It rose one story in three stages, each with a square landing, and took them to a corridor that seemed to run the width of the house.

Perriam directed her ahead. "The drawing room."

The room startled her. There was no dark paneling here, but instead pale walls divided into sections by white moldings and decorated with images of urns of flowers.

"Clearly done over not long ago," Perriam said. "By one of Giles Perriam's wives."

She'd forgotten them, but they'd each been mistress here for a while.

Three dead wives and four dead babies.

Perhaps the mournful ivy was deliberate.

She was the start of a new regime, however, and she would assert it.

She went to one of the windows and peered out. "This could be a bright room if the sun could penetrate. I intend to have the ivy stripped as soon as possible."

She stated it as a challenge, but he said, "An excellent idea. Shall we move on?" He led the way back to the corridor. "The other rooms up here are all bedchambers. This is the mistress's chamber." He opened a door. "I've had it prepared for you, but if you wish to choose another, you may, of course."

The room had probably been decorated by the same wife who had decorated the drawing room, for the walls were in the same light, elegant style. It could even be called luxurious. A carpet nearly covered the floor, and the curtains and bed hangings were of a bright, flowered material. It all spoke of good cheer and hope, but here, too, ivy overhung the window.

Claris pushed that thought aside for fear of falling into a morbid depression.

"It's lovely," she said.

He went to a door in a side wall. Did she have a dressing room, as Genova had?

"Here, of course, we have the master's bedchamber."

Claris went through to find a room in keeping with the darker side of this house. The walls were white above wainscoting, and the bed was of heavy dark oak with crimson hangings. Then she saw some papers on a desk, a book, and a hairbrush.

She turned to him. "You are not staying."

His brows went up. "Of course I am. This is our wedding night."

"Oh, no . . . ." She backed away.

He raised his hand. "I didn't mean it in that sense, Claris. But to ride away now would give a very odd appearance."

"I don't care about appearances. You *promised*!"

"I promised to give you free rein here and to rarely intrude, but do you truly want to be the subject of gossip and speculation?"

"I don't care about gossip and speculation!"

"Of course you do. This is your home now. You can make it a bed of thorns or a bed of roses."

"Roses have thorns," she pointed out.

He stared and then laughed. "Keen as always. Then let's say a bed of rose petals. Or even of downy feathers. We need to talk about this. Sit, please, and converse."

Panic still pounded in her. He could seem so *reasonable* in his unreasonableness. She returned to the mistress's bedchamber and sat in a chair, straight backed, hands in lap, prepared to fight.

He took the settee, completely at his ease.

She wanted to throw him out for that alone.

"Perhaps I should have explained in detail," he said, "but as I confessed, it wasn't in my interests to tell you anything that might deter you."

"Go on."

"Cousin Giles explained the situation to me on his deathbed, and there were a number of people present. Some, such as the doctor and vicar, might be discreet, but I'd not stake my life on it. Giles's valet probably tattled to the other servants here before he left. Thus it must be known that we have married to secure the estate."

Her nails dug into her palm. "I suspected as much."

"It's no great scandal. Practical marriages are common enough and there's no shame to them. It's less common for a couple to largely live apart, but it happens, and we have an explanation. You have a strong preference for country living and I am strongly committed to Town."

She studied him. "There truly are couples who live like that?"

"On my honor. It's more common later in a marriage, but when a marriage is known to be practical, it won't cause a furor. However, to separate virtually at the altar . . ."

". . . would cause talk," she completed, but warily. Was this was another attempt at manipulation? "What do you propose?"

"To stay for a day or two, that's all."

And a night or two, but she didn't raise that. He had no more interest in the marriage bed than she.

"A day or two only. You promise?"

"On my honor."

Claris nodded, but she'd be sure of one thing. She rose and went to that adjoining door. She closed it, locked it, and put the key in her pocket.

"That too could cause talk," he pointed out. "And if I'm bent on mischief, there is another door."

Claris glared and realized she'd actually growled. "You are the most *infuriating* man!"

"So many say."

"Perhaps one of them will shoot you. I'd rather like to be a widow."

"A return to your favorite color." He rose and came to her. "We have no cause to be enemies over this. We're allies, and we both have what we want. We can, if we choose, be smug together."

For some reason that forced a laugh from her, even though she knew she was being manipulated. She unlocked the door and left the key it in.

"There. We will preserve the facade. Is there anything more to discuss?"

"A great many practicalities, such as stables and estate administration, but that can wait until tomorrow. I assure you, I'm as eager to leave as you are to see me gone, but we must be practical in all ways. It's possible, even likely, that neighbors might call tomorrow to pay their respects. I should greet them by your side, and won't you be more comfortable that way?"

"Tomorrow?" she echoed, appalled.

"Sped on by the unusual stories surrounding us."

Claris sat down again. "I could claim to be ill."

"Spare my reputation! They'll think the worst of your wedding night."

Cheeks flaming, Claris glared at him again. "I'm not sure I believe any of this. What are your plans?"

"Completely as stated. On the subject of visitors, ask your grandmother."

She rose. "I'd forgotten her. Is their room adequate?"

"I'm sure she'll complain if it's not. There are only three good bedchambers, so your brothers have a lesser one. Do you wish to see it?"

"Yes," she said, and he took her there.

It was half the size of her own bedchamber, but many times the size of the one the boys had shared in the cottage. They'd probably use the tester bed as a castle, a ship, and even a coach drawn by imaginary horses.

"I assume it will do for the night at least," he said. "You will know best if they'd want separate rooms."

"No."

"Or separate beds."

"No. But there must be a children's area here? Nurseries, schoolroom, small bedchambers?"

"There is, but it's long unused except for infants."

"I should at least look."

"I advise against," he said.

Ah, the dead babies.

"After all," he said, "nurseries are unlikely to see use in our time."

Why she should feel a touch of sorrow over that, she didn't know.

"I should show you something else," he said. "Something outside."

His tone disturbed her, but whatever it was had best be faced.

Chapter 16

They left the house by a side door near the kitchens. As best she could tell, the kitchens, storerooms, and such were clean and in good repair. The door took them into an area of herbs that would interest Athena.

"The walls over there enclose the kitchen garden. It seems in reasonable condition but could be improved. Giles only visited here occasionally, which is why there's some neglect. This way."

A graveled path led along the side of the house, and ahead stood a dense green hedge.

"Yew?" she guessed, but was puzzled. It was six feet high, but not very long. "A maze?"

"I wish it were."

When they passed the hedge, she found it was one of three walls around a grassed area containing five stone plinths. On each plinth lay a white marble shape—the shape of a small, sleeping child entirely covered by a sheet.

No, not sleeping.

"Five?" she said, but then wondered why she'd asked that particular question.

"There was a daughter, never mentioned."

She went toward the nearest one and saw the name engraved on the stone. "Giles Perriam," with dates. He'd been two months old.

On the next, "Giles Perriam."

And on the next.

"Was he mad?"

"This isn't his work, though the naming probably was. The last boy is Charles because when he was born his older brother still lived, though not for long. The girl was Beatrice. They are all the children of Giles's first wife, Louisa Forbes, and this is her work."

"Poor, poor lady. Are they actually buried here?"

"No, they lie in the churchyard. I'm told Louisa created this after the last child died, Giles number three. She followed him the next year."

"Heartbroken. But I thought there were two more wives."

"As soon as it was decent Giles married again. That wife, Amelia Shaw-Cobham, had the good fortune to be barren but the bad fortune to succumb to the smallpox after six years. His third wife conceived but never brought a babe to life. After a series of miscarriages and two still-births, she went mad. She took her own life, here among these memorials, just over a year ago."

"More things you didn't tell me."

He spread his hands. "I had my own necessities, and none of this affects you."

"No? Isn't the curse supposed to be passed on with the manor?"

"If you believe in the curse, then believe that our marriage has appeased your aunt. That's what your mother promised."

Claris opened her mouth but closed it, unable to think what to say. Her mother had been obsessed, and she'd have said anything, but Aunt Clarrie and the curse? That had never seemed possible.

"As there will be no children of our marriage," he said, "these memorials need not disturb you."

She laughed, entirely without humor. "They're macabre! And remember, one wife died of smallpox."

"You could be inoculated."

"That's far too dangerous, and beside the point."

"We can debate the danger some other time. I have no

belief in that curse, Claris, or I would never have married you or any woman, Perriam obsessions be damned."

Struck by his sincerity, she turned back to the sad display and approached the one for Beatrice, who'd survived for three years. Old enough to walk and talk. Had that made her loss even worse?

"Is Perriam Manor haunted?" she asked.

"If any place deserves to be, this does, but I've heard nothing of it."

She touched the marble sheet, irrationally surprised to find it cold. "I want to tear this back to let the poor child breathe." She curled her fingers at one edge as if it might be possible.

He pulled her back. "It's only stone. Solid stone."

She turned to him, into his chest, fighting tears. Those poor, poor infants, and their poor mother, whose heart had been shattered five times. She only slowly realized where she was, what she was doing, and pushed away. "I'm sorry."

He let her go. "No need to apologize."

His arms had been around her, and they had warmed and comforted her in a way she'd never experienced before.

He touched her shoulder. "We know the boundaries of this marriage, Claris, but they don't have to deny us comfort, or even friendship."

She took another step back. "With you in London and me here? That wouldn't be practical at all." She briskly led the way out of the shadow of yews. "Thank you for showing me that. It would have been worse to come across it alone. Something must be done. The boys . . ."

"Will delight in the horrid."

"Oh dear, you're probably right. There was a tomb in the church in Old Barford that showed a skeleton with worms weaving through it. That was their favorite."

"I'm sorry to have missed it. We males are warped in that way. We can continue around the house to the front door. There are no more grim surprises."

She followed his lead, seeking something prosaic to speak of. "How big is the estate?"

"A little over six hundred acres, including the home farm. I should introduce you there tomorrow. A great deal is productive woodland. No one seems to have attempted much with the area close to the house."

"At least it's tidy."

"Because I told them to tidy it. I look forward to seeing what you do with it."

She paused to look at him. "You expect to return frequently?"

"No, but there is one other thing I didn't tell you. By the terms of the very exacting will, I must reside here for thirty days in every calendar year or lose the estate."

"Thirty days! You said you'd stay only a day or two."

"And spoke the truth. The days need not necessarily be consecutive. A few days a month will do."

She managed not to echo the words "a few days a month."

"We're late in September. Does that mean you have to be here for thirty days between now and January?"

"'Struth, I'd not thought of that. That's about ten days a month."

He spoke as if it were a prison sentence. She felt so torn about everything. She was determined to have this place to herself, but it hurt that he'd happily never return.

"Can the clause not be contested?" she asked.

"It might be possible to reduce it in proportion, but the way lawyers and courts work, it wouldn't be settled before the year was over and their bills could eat a year's income from the manor. We'll have to cope as best we can."

"If what you say is true."

"I will always speak the truth to you."

"But not the whole truth." Her unruly temper was simmering.

"But not the whole truth."

"Only what suits you."

"Of course, and you will do the same, I'm sure."

"I have nothing to hide!"

"Don't you?" he asked.

Affirming words stuck in her throat. "Nothing that affects you or us." When he smiled, she said, "Oh, I wish I had a pistol with me!"

"Temper, temper."

She truly, deeply wanted to hurl something at him, but the memory of firing that pistol was leash enough.

"It won't be so bad," he soothed. "We can avoid each other most of the time. I'll hide in my bedchamber and work on a book I've thought to write."

"On how to irritate people?"

He laughed. "On court etiquette for the provincial gentleman."

"Are you joking?"

"Not at all. So many come to Town for a momentous visit, then bumble around in anxious confusion."

"Such a book might be a kindness."

"You don't think me capable of kindness?"

"Only when it suits you. Enough of this. Now I do want tea, and food as well. I'd have thought the twins were starving. Will it be seen as scandalous if they eat in the dining room?"

"They're of an age for it outside of any formal entertainment."

"Which I won't be holding."

"Best not to be rigid. You may make friends in the area. If you wish, have your brothers eat with you at all times. You can set up as an eccentric."

"I may well do that. It comes in the blood on both sides of my family, and the Perriams aren't clear of peculiarities." With that, she led the way across the threshold, going from sunshine into gloom.

When her eyes adjusted, she saw the footman and asked him if he knew where her brothers were.

"I believe they're in the kitchen, ma'am."

Perriam said, "If you will permit, I have matters to attend to in my room."

Claris permitted, wondering if he were giving her a free hand with the kitchen or he was involved in something more devious.

She found the twins seated at a long table eating bread and cheese and chattering to an attentive group of servants. She'd never given a thought to what they might say. As well write her business on the walls!

At sight of her, the servants hurried back to their work with many a wary glance.

"You're not to bother the servants here," she told the twins.

"We were hungry and couldn't find you! Mistress Wilcock doesn't mind."

They smiled at a plump, aproned woman who must be the cook, and she beamed at them. "Lovely to have healthy appetites to feed, ma'am."

"You're very kind, but I must apologize for the disorder. It will take a day or two for my family to settle here." She thought of something. "Have you seen our cat?"

"The black one, ma'am? He had a bit of an argument with our mouser, Mog, but no blood spilled."

"Oh dear."

"They seemed to come to an understanding, ma'am."

Claris couldn't think of anything useful to do about the cat world. "Mr. Perriam and I would like a light meal in the dining room as soon as may be." To the twins, she said, "You may share it if you still have room."

Bright eyes implied vast chasms yet to be filled.

"Something simple will do," Claris added, hinting, "We too are hungry after a long day."

The cook curtsied. "I had that in mind, ma'am, and can have a cold repast on the table in a trice."

Claris thanked her for her thoughtfulness and took her brothers away. No point berating them for chatter. Truth will out.

"So what do you think of our new home?" she asked as they returned to the front hall.

"It's splendid!" Peter said.

"But there aren't any weapons," Tom complained.

"A very good thing too." There was another problem. There might be weapons somewhere in the house. As Perriam was still here, she'd set him the task of finding and securing them. The twins were generally very well behaved, but it would be folly to take chances.

"Did you find the stables?" she asked.

The boys stopped and stared at her, eyes wide. "The ponies are already here!"

"Castor and Pollux," Peter said.

"But we're not sure whose is whose," Tom said. "We didn't try to ride them."

"Because we'd promised."

"That was very noble of you," Claris said, loving them for it. "I look forward to meeting the ponies, and I promise that tomorrow Mr. Perriam will arrange matters for you. Whose is whose, and any lessons you need."

She realized she was granting him some authority, but as with the weapons, he was the best person for the task. What was more, he'd kept his promise about the ponies, and more generously than she'd expected. It couldn't have been easy to buy them in such a short, busy period, and he'd named them after a famous pair of twins.

She would not sink to surliness, so she admitted to herself that he'd been correct about the benefit of him staying for a day or two. Only for a day or two, however. If he showed any inclination to linger . . .

He wouldn't of course. He itched to return to his beloved Town.

She took her brothers up to see their room. It satisfied them, but it couldn't begin to compete with ponies in their starry minds.

"Castor has a white blaze," Peter said.

"And Pollux has white socks," Tom said. "We'll need riding crops."

"If we can afford them," Peter said.

It was so delightful to be able to say, "Of course we can, darlings. And perhaps leather breeches."

In unison they said, "Really?"

"And books for your studies," she reminded them. "You'll have a new tutor soon." Something else to discuss with Perriam. "Don't forget you'll be going away to school soon."

They'd always looked forward to school, but now they frowned.

"Will we be able to take the ponies?" Tom asked.

"That seems unlikely, but you'll be able to return here for holidays, because your school isn't far away." When they both scowled, she used the old saying. "Count your blessings. And don't go in search of troubles, for they'll come quickly enough to find you. Now, I see your boxes are here, so you'd best unpack them before the meal."

Another question arose.

Perriam had said they were now the young masters of the house. Should they have a servant to take care of their clothing, bring up their water, and such? Probably they should, but what they'd make of it she couldn't imagine.

She suddenly wanted to grip her head for fear it would spin off her neck.

"Are you all right, Claris?" Tom asked.

She smiled for them. "Of course, but this has been a momentous day, with many changes. There's much to do to make this our home, and I confess I don't know quite how to do some of it."

"Mr. Perriam will know," Peter said.

"We like him," Tom said.

"That's excellent, but he must soon leave here because he has great responsibilities in London."

"You'll be going with him?" Peter asked, alarmed.

"Heavens, no."

"But you're his wife."

"And would dislike London enormously, so he is kind enough to leave me in the country. Besides, I'd never abandon you. Unpack quickly and then come down. The meal will be ready soon."

Claris left them and went to her bedchamber to wash with cold water and try to ease away tension. She'd won what she'd wanted—a comfortable home and a promising future for her brothers. Her head was spinning only from so many new ways and uncertainty. But Peter was right; Mr. Perriam would know.

She dried her hands, braced herself, and then knocked on the adjoining door.

He opened it, coatless, hair loose of its ribbon, an unfolded letter in his hand.

The moment seemed shockingly intimate.

"I . . . I've interrupted you. I'm sorry."

He smiled. "In the case of some correspondence, interruptions are welcome. I may help you?"

Practical matters flew out of Claris's head. "Only to say that food will be in the dining room shortly."

"A very welcome interruption. I'll join you there momentarily."

He turned away and Claris closed the door, needing to steady herself on it with one hand.

She'd seen men without coats before!

And with unconfined hair.

But never a gentleman, and it had made him seem completely unconfined in all kinds of ways.

His hair waved in a way she envied, and a bit of sun glinting through the ivy had caught those hints of flame and copper there—as on that first day. It seemed so long since she'd studied an invader through the open kitchen window, knowing he brought trouble to her haven of content.

She pushed off from the door. Lavender Cottage had been a haven of the meanest sort, and the invader had made this improvement possible. She was grateful and would show it, but she couldn't afford to find him attractive. That way lay weakness, which he would exploit in a trice.

Athena and Ellie. She'd forgotten them.

She went down the corridor and knocked.

Ellie opened the door wide, just as she'd always opened the door to Lavender Cottage, welcoming all. "Come in, dearie. All in order?"

"As much as could be expected."

The room was as handsome as her own, though still in an old-fashioned style, with white walls and dark wood. Athena was at home in it. She was seated in a comfortable chair, her feet raised on a padded stool, spectacles on her nose, reading a book. Yatta was curled nearby, as if he'd never contested anything here.

Ellie, in her handsome gray, settled in another chair and picked up some needlework. Not simple mending, but embroidery.

A new and different world.

She'd always known that her father and grandmother came from the gentry and that Athena might be nobly born, but she'd never *felt* that noble connection until today. Athena had volunteered little about her life, and Claris hadn't been sure she wanted to know, but perhaps it was time. For now, she had advisers.

"I've ordered a hasty meal in the dining room if you're hungry."

"We grew tired of waiting," Athena said, "and had a meal brought here."

Completely at home.

Unreasonable to resent that.

"Perriam was showing me around the house and grounds. There's an adequate herb garden."

Athena looked up over her spectacles. "I am not devoted to herbs, Claris. My knowledge merely proved useful for a while. I have yet to decide what I will do here."

"Advise me, I hope."

"Of course, but Perriam is better suited to that."

"He'll be leaving soon, and that's all to the good. I will be mistress here."

"Excellent, but pick his brains dry before he goes."

"I'd rather pick yours. I need to know about a servant

for the twins. They will be supposed to have one, won't they?"

"Of course. Consult the housekeeper. She's assigned us a maid. The footman will do for the boys for now, but she'll probably have to hire someone new. Instruct her to hire an older man, not one young enough to encourage them in mischief."

"Thank you." Claris turned to the new Ellie. "You're comfortable here?"

"As long as I have something to keep me busy, dearie. Not a bad house, this, once the light's let in. Thanks for acquiring it."

Trust Ellie to remember to thank her. No one else had.

Claris said, "Be free to command anything you need or want," and retreated back to her bedchamber to try to sort out her tangled emotions. She felt as if she'd been caught in a fairy circle and spun off into another world.

Her grandmother had become a grand lady and was acting as if she were mistress here. Claris was surprised to discover how much she resented that.

Ellie was now a well-dressed lady's companion, as comfortable in one of the manor's finest bedchambers as anyone could be. Claris didn't resent that, but it would take time to grow used to it.

Her husband would be sleeping in a bedchamber separated from hers by only a door. An unlocked door. He was so comfortable with the situation that he'd answered the door in disarray. He might open it next in his nightshirt!

At least the twins were still the twins, for better or worse.

As she went downstairs, she considered the paintings hanging there. Some were landscapes, but there were three portraits.

The first was a full-length painting of a handsome young man in country clothing leaning against a tree, a hound at his feet. His hair was dark, but his complexion fair. His features were a little blunt but still well put together, and his slight smile was both arrogant and tantalizing.

Giles Perriam himself? Most likely, but if so he'd been more handsome than she'd thought. Because he'd been vile she'd assumed he'd look it, but that made no sense. Aunt Clarrie wouldn't have succumbed to a monster.

A warning there about the appeal of unscrupulous, handsome Perriams.

The other two portraits were of ladies, and by the style of their gowns the paintings weren't old. Two of Giles Perriam's wives?

One was of a young woman in a simple white gown with flowers in her hair. A bridal portrait? She wasn't a beauty, having a round face, thin lips and mousy hair, but she looked pleased with herself, presumably anticipating a pleasant future.

The woman in the other portrait was a bit older and bolder—a handsome brunette in a red dress.

Brides one and two, Claris suspected. The first had been an heiress, but also the one to suffer the death of all five children. The one who'd constructed that ghastly grove.

The second Mistress Giles Perriam had been the one with the good fortune to be barren, but fate had struck her down anyway. Was there a portrait anywhere of the third, the one driven to madness and suicide?

At that moment, in the dark and gloomy hall, looking up at two tragic Perriam brides, the curse seemed all too real.

Claris looked higher, in the direction of heaven.

Here I am, Aunt Clarrie, the Perriam bride you should have been.

Be appeased!

Chapter 17

Perry arrived at the dining room prepared for any-thing. Foolish not to realize that Claris would expect him to leave her at the doorstep, but foolish of her to imagine such a thing. Perhaps he should have told her about the thirty days earlier, but as he'd said, there'd been no sense in telling her more than he must until everything was settled.

Hardly surprising, however, if she was as twitchy as a burned cat, ready to scratch at anything.

He found only her and her brothers at the table, which was too large for four. They'd have been more comfort-able at the small table in the anteroom, but he didn't sug-gest a move. That might be taken as a criticism.

There was no need to strain for conversation, for the boys assailed him with thanks for the ponies, questions about the ponies, and their expectations for future ad-ventures on the ponies. He didn't mind. They were good lads.

When they paused to eat, he looked down the table at Claris. "Would you like to learn to ride?"

Her eyes widened. "No! Thank you, but it looks un-comfortable."

"It needn't be, but if you don't wish to ride, you need to learn to drive."

"Why?"

"To get around."

"I have legs."

"You may wish to travel farther afield."

"Isn't there a coach?"

"Why would there be when Giles was rarely here? If one's needed it's hired from Maidenhead."

She cut into a slice of ham. "I see. But I don't expect to travel far. I will be content at home."

He reminded himself that this life was new to her. "You may wish to visit the village."

"That's not far from the gates."

"Or visit local families."

"Unlikely."

She was making a battle of this when he only wanted to help. He really should stay here for weeks to ease her into the way of things, but he couldn't, and she'd probably shoot him if he tried.

"I suspect your grandmother knows how to drive," he said, "so there should be a chair for her use."

That seemed to make an impression. She frowned but said, "Perhaps I would like to learn."

"Excellent. I'll purchase a chair and a suitable horse. Which reminds me, unless your grandmother or her companion wants to ride, we should sell Giles's horses." He regretted the "we" as soon as it escaped, and quickly said, "But that is for you to decide."

She relaxed a little, but she was definitely en garde.

"Why don't you learn to ride?" Peter asked her. "Then you could ride out with us."

Instantly she was softer, gentler. "I'm sorry, darling, but there are some sacrifices I will not make, even for you."

She made it a joke and they took it as such, smiling and turning to him.

"Are there fishing rods, sir?" Tom said. "Jake—he's one of the grooms, sir—said there are fish in the river."

"I have no idea. You and your sister must sort that out."

Peter said, "There are plenty of rabbits too. Too many."

Perry understood where that was going. "You're too young for guns, but you may trap them if you want. If," he added, "your sister approves."

"Oh, she won't mind. We caught dinner many a time."

She looked embarrassed, and indeed, the footman had come in with the coffee tray. He didn't see any way to stop the twins from chattering about their former life.

Their hunger seemed appeased, for they asked permission to leave. Claris gave it but seemed anxious as she watched them go.

"They're good lads," Perry said. "No need to fret."

As she poured the coffee, Perry moved to a seat beside her and sent the footman away. If she objected to that, she could choke on it.

She seemed preoccupied by her brothers. "They are good but adventurous."

"As they should be."

"But up till now they've adventured within a familiar world where they knew the hazards and the rules. It's different here. Are there weapons in the house?"

A reasonable concern.

"I have my sword and pistols, but you mean others."

"Yes."

"Very likely. You think they'll meddle with them?"

"They've never been trained not to. That's my point."

"Don't worry. If you permit, I'll find out if there are any and secure them."

He was braced for objection, but she said, "Thank you. However, I thought of that danger, but what ones have I not thought of? This is a complex new world."

"You can't leash them to your apron strings, Claris. If you wanted to try, you shouldn't have permitted the ponies. Once they're at ease with them, they'll roam all over."

"Within the estate."

"Perhaps."

"They'll do as they are told!"

How would she react to advice?

"But best, perhaps, not to make the rules too tight. They're nearly twelve years old. They might still seem children to you, but they'll soon be youths, and soon after that men, completely beyond your control. In the end their welfare will depend on good sense and good luck. I judge them to have both."

Her fingers tightened on her coffee cup. "I only want to keep them safe."

He realized something.

"You've as good as raised them, haven't you? You were, what, twelve when your mother died?"

"Almost thirteen, but they had a nursery maid."

"One maid, two babes. You took your mother's place."

An emotion flickered over her face.

"A penny for that," he said.

"What?"

"The thought you didn't speak."

She shook her head. "It was of no importance. Yes, I played the part of mother to the twins and will continue to do so. A mother has authority over her sons, even as they grow."

He'd like to offer to be a father to the boys, but thirty days a year wasn't enough time for that. "I'll advise them when I can. If you permit."

She thanked him but was inscrutable. He found that interesting. He rarely failed to read and understand people.

She put down her coffee cup. "I saw the portraits on the staircase. Are they the first two wives?"

"Yes." Anticipating her next question, he said, "I asked. Giles destroyed the only portrait of the third, of Lydia Helmcock. Perhaps even his hard heart couldn't bear her looking down at him."

"He didn't marry again," she pointed out.

"Don't give him credit there. I've learned he was negotiating for a local girl, as good as buying her, when his illness began to destroy him."

"Thank heavens she escaped."

"Amen."

She looked at him. "Are we safe?"

She meant, *Am I safe?*

The sun was setting, and even through the ivy the ruddy light lay grimly on the darkly paneled walls.

He covered one of her tense hands. "If there was a curse, we've done our best to end it."

"I suppose so. But . . ."

"My dear, why would your aunt want to harm you?"

He saw her react to the phrase "my dear" and wasn't surprised when she slid her hand from under his. How very careless he was becoming.

"Indeed, why would she?" She rose. "We should go elsewhere and discuss the many things I need to know."

He rose too but shook his head. "Are you so redoubtable? Pity the weaker male. It's been a long day and I still have correspondence to deal with. Wouldn't you like some peaceful time to yourself?"

"Maybe later," she said. "I should see what the twins are up to."

"Stables. I'll lay odds on it."

"They can't spend their lives there."

"They'll try. Go and rest, Claris. Your day's labors are done."

He meant it kindly, but again he was clumsy. She took it as an order.

She dipped an ironic curtsy, said, "As you command, sir!" and marched out, head high.

Perry blew out a breath.

Perhaps there *was* a curse on this place. He was making wretched work of this.

Claris was heading for the stairs when she thought of the library and went there instead. She'd never had access to a wide range of books. There had been some in the rectory, but mostly of a religious nature. Her father had a few other books he used in teaching the twins, but most were in Latin and Greek. Her mother had owned a copy of *Pilgrim's Progress* and a volume of sermons by a Dr. Burton. She'd taught Claris to read from those, and from the Bible.

After her mother died, her father had done his best to prevent her reading anything, always ranting that books were time wasters for a woman with duties to attend to. He'd ensured her duties by dismissing the nursery maid when the twins were only six months old.

Despite that, she'd managed to enjoy a history of Britain and a book that described the nations of the world. She'd delighted in the occasional illustrations of strangely dressed people. She'd taught the twins their letters from those books, not the religious ones. She'd probably go to hell for it, but her parents had given her a deep dislike of religion.

The library was even gloomier than the dining room, for the sun had long left this side of the house, and the ivy blocked what little light there was. A tinderbox sat by a branch of candles, so she made a flame and lit them, then carried them around. Perriam had said it was poorly stocked, and he'd been right, but the shelves held more volumes than she'd ever seen before.

The spines of large books indicated subjects such as the laws of Britain and the duties of magistrates. Here, too, were volumes in Latin and Greek, and others in French. She wanted something lighter and in English.

She found a book that listed racehorses and their pedigrees, and another that listed women in London. Dear Lord, it was a list of whores with details of their charms and skills! She shoved it back on the shelf, then reconsidered and hid it behind some other volumes. She doubted the twins would explore the library, but she certainly didn't want them finding that!

She turned to the bookstand on the central table.

The History of the Perriam Family.

She opened it to find an engraved picture of a grim lady in a spiky Tudor ruff. A scroll beneath declared her to be the Lady Beatrice Perriam Stakeleigh.

One of the feuding sisters, originator of the Beatrician line, who'd taken possession of this manor house. Claris flipped through the heavy pages, but there were no more illustrations. Certainly none of Cecily, the older sister and originator of the Cecilian line, which was now headed by the Earl of Hernescroft, Perriam's father.

Her father-in-law.

Now, there was a terrifying thought!

Claris extinguished the candles and took the book up to her room. She found the beginning interesting, though it told the story of the original division from a very biased angle. Nothing about Cecily was good, whereas Beatrice was a saint who had been bullied into signing away most of her birthright.

A glance at the engraved portrait suggested that was unlikely.

Claris put the book aside. It was nothing but a continuation of a vicious feud that had lasted to the present day, when Giles Perriam had done his best to make the inheritance a poisoned cup. She saw no dark emotions in her husband, but what of his family? She hoped never to have to meet any of them and find out.

She yawned and acknowledged that Perriam had been correct. It had been a long day involving momentous events. She glanced at the door. Was he steadily working through his letters, or was he too yawning and thinking of bed?

Separate beds.

She suddenly remembered the twins and hurried to their room. It was dark, but she could see them safely in bed and on the edge of sleep.

"Good night, my dears."

"Good night, Claris," they said in unison.

"This is a grand place," Peter added.

"Yes, it is, isn't it?"

She returned to her room smiling. This would be a grand place for them, and worth any sacrifice.

Because of the stays, she needed Alice to undress, but

how to summon her? Cheynings had bell wires that fed down to the servants' area. At the rectory, if they'd needed service they'd opened a door and called, "Lottie!"

Claris opened the door but couldn't believe that a shout from here would reach the servants' hall. She certainly couldn't bring herself to yell loudly enough. She went down the corridor to the top of the stairs, hoping someone was in the hall, but it was deserted. She was certain that going to the servants' hall to summon her maid would make her a figure of fun.

She'd have to ask Perriam.

No, Athena would advise her.

Ellie opened the door more cautiously this time, for she was in her nightgown and robe. "Oh, come in, dearie. We're just going to bed."

Athena was in the big bed, nightcap on her head. "What's amiss?"

Claris shut the door behind her. "I don't know how to summon my maid."

"Why are you whispering?"

Claris blushed. "I don't want to appear the fool."

"Then don't whisper. I use Ellie to summon others, but she can't oblige in her nightclothes. In a house like this, your maid should mostly be in your room ready to serve."

"That sounds tedious for her."

"Her pleasure is not the issue. She can occupy herself with mending or other stitchery. Or she can accompany you, especially if you go out walking."

"I don't want Alice trailing after me everywhere I go. I'm not sure I even need a lady's maid, but Lady Ashart insisted."

"It gives a good appearance. Simply, Claris, if you want your maid now you must call for her, and call loudly. It will not be considered strange."

As if in confirmation, a male voice bellowed, "Auguste!"

Claris knew she couldn't do that. But . . .

She hurried out, and when a neatly dressed manservant ran upstairs, she was ready to say to Perriam, "How convenient. Your man can summon my lady's maid when he returns downstairs."

Twitching lips said that he saw right through her, but he gave the order, along with his own for washing water.

The valet hurried away, but Claris lingered.

He was even more undressed.

He'd shed his neckcloth and waistcoat.

The open placket of his shirt revealed a vee of chest.

She raised her eyes from that, saw his smile, and fled into her room. Once there she was strongly tempted to lock the adjoining door, but as he'd pointed out, she couldn't lock both, or how would Alice get in the next morning? She could only trust his word.

And pray for good sense.

He'd always had the ability to set strange sensations churning within her, sensations that revealed human urges, sinful urges that must be controlled. Except that the morning's vows meant that to succumb would not be a sin. It might even be her holy duty.

It would change their agreement and give him dominion over her.

This was a practical marriage with clear rules and boundaries. Her very sanity depended on maintaining them at all times.

It would be complete folly do otherwise. It truly would.

Chapter 18

Claris didn't sleep well. She tried to block thoughts of the man next door by focusing on the many decisions to be made, but questions turned into dilemmas, and dilemmas threatened to be abysses of failure.

No abyss could be deeper than succumbing to the seductive powers of her husband.

Who'd never tried to seduce her.

Who surely didn't want to.

He'd married her only under great compulsion, and she would not be a fool over that. . . .

When Alice wakened her by bringing up hot water, Claris groaned. "What time is it?"

"Nearly ten, ma'am."

Alice's eyes held a glint, and Claris realized the maid thought her exhausted by a wedding night.

Heaven help her, what should she do?

What impression did she want to make? That of a true wife or a practical, untouched one?

Instantly, she knew. A true wife. Perriam had been right there—she didn't want the house and then the neighborhood to know that her husband wasn't interested in her.

"Ma'am?"

She realized Alice had said something.

"Yes?"

"Chocolate and a sweet roll as usual, ma'am?"

"Yes, thank you."

As soon as Alice had left, Claris sat up, fretting about details. Should her husband have been found in her bed this morning, or would it be normal for him to return to his own bed after ... after whatever took place?

She looked at the two pillows on top of the bolster. She'd had such a restless night that both looked used.

What else?

Blood.

She'd heard enough village comments to know there was often blood involved in a wedding night. In fact, it was seen as proof that a bride had been a maid.

Should her sheets be marked with blood?

How much blood?

Claris found her needle case, pricked her finger, and squeezed a dome of blood. She smeared it on her bottom sheet, hoping it was enough. Surely the act couldn't be so violent as to cause more.

She went behind the screen to wash, but halfway through she was struck by another thought. Had the twins washed last night? Would they this morning? She must definitely arrange a manservant for them.

She was in her shift when Alice returned with her breakfast. She put on the pink silk robe and sat to eat, wondering what to wear. Something simple, for she expected to be busy.

"The blue skirt and caraco jacket, Alice. And I'll wear my unboned stays and old shoes."

When she was dressed, she studied herself in the mirror. She looked sensible and ready to work, and that was as it should be. She pinned her hair up herself.

"Do you want a cap, ma'am, now you're married?"

"No, but I suppose I should. Do I have any?"

"Oh!" Alice bit her lip.

Claris broke into laughter and the maid joined her and then clapped a hand over her mouth.

"By all means laugh. So much careful preparation, but one lack. I confess wearing a cap at all times seems a bother, but I should acquire some for formal occasions."

She remembered Perriam's prediction that neighbors might visit, even as early as today. "Go and ask if my grandmother can see me."

Alice returned, Athena behind her.

Athena waved away the maid and shut the door. "How are you?"

There was an implied question, but Claris decided it was none of her grandmother's business. "Well enough considering the many challenges. I don't have any caps."

"Improvident. Come to my room. We will provide."

Once there, Athena opened drawers herself.

"Where's Ellie?"

"Exploring. This one will do." She produced a small, shallow mobcap with an English lace trim. "It would be better with ribbons behind—flightily suitable for a bride—but that will have to wait."

Claris put it on top of her head. "It serves no useful purpose."

"Few things do. Will you be content here, do you think?"

Was she deliberately referring back to that so recent day when Claris had insisted that she was content with Lavender Cottage?

"I believe I can be," Claris said as she pinned the cap in place. "The manor is larger than I expected and in a less pleasant state, but in time it can be my home."

"And your husband?"

Claris turned to face her. "Is keeping to our agreement. He will leave tomorrow."

The twitch on Athena's face was impossible to interpret.

"What of you?" Claris asked. "Can you be content here?"

"I'm never content, child. I'm a restless soul. However, Perriam Manor is a vast improvement on that cottage."

Claris asked a question that puzzled her. "Why did you stay there with me?"

"I decided to do my duty for once."

"The boys and I are well situated now. If you wish to travel again, you must do so."

"I'm too old for interesting travel. There, that's an admission that's hard for me to make. And Ellie would prefer a more settled life, though she never complains."

"Perhaps you'll tend the herb garden after all," Claris said, and was rewarded by something between a laugh and a snort.

"You'd be well served, you hussy, if I set up as the local witch in truth. Begone. I'm consumed by a very biased account of the Commonwealth. I'm old enough to have known many who lived through that."

Claris escaped, realizing that was true. The monarchy had been restored a century ago, so the rule of Cromwell would have been living memory in Athena's youth. She wondered how the Perriam family had managed in the civil war. Had the two sides split in allegiance then? Perhaps she would read that family history and find out.

She returned to her room and asked Alice to find some ribbons to trim the cap. She rather liked the idea of being flighty.

Then she went to find her husband. They had much to discuss about the running of the manor, and the sooner that was done, the sooner he'd be gone. The footman told her that he'd gone to the stables with the twins, so she went outside, startled by the brightness of the day. The ivy would definitely have to go.

She walked around the house, choosing the direction that avoided the memorials. Something else that needed to be attended to, but how could they be removed with respect?

A gardener and a lad were pruning back dying growth. It was that time of year, with winter on the far horizon. She paused to speak to them, but again, they seemed uneasy, even surly.

They'd come to know her in time. She carried on toward the brick buildings that must be the stable. As she came close she saw the twins in the field alongside.

They were on their ponies, a groom alongside each. Perriam was giving a steady stream of instructions. Postures changed, hands moved. Her brothers were intent on his every word, so she halted before she distracted them. He was allowing them only to walk their ponies in a circle. She'd feared they'd be racing at a gallop from the first.

He is a good man.

The thought startled her and she resisted it, but she forced herself to be fair. There'd been no need for him to be so quick to provide the ponies, nor any need for him to begin the boys' lessons today. He was doing his best by them, and probably meant the same by her.

For the first time she imagined her situation if the Perriam involved had been a man like Giles. All very well to feel that she'd have rejected the bargain, even with the advantages to her brothers. A man like Giles Perriam might have found ways to force her.

But then, her husband might have done the same if she'd not been persuadable. He'd been determined to secure Perriam Manor.

She must remember that. Beneath the complex curlicues, his writing was straight and clear. Beneath his airy nature lay steely determination.

Thus, she must match him in steel. She turned and headed back to the house to take up her duties. The kitchen garden wall lay to her left, and she decided to enter and inspect.

She had her hand on the gate latch when she heard running footsteps. She turned to see Perriam running toward her, loose hair flying in the wind, waistcoat unbuttoned, but at least with his coat on. He ran with boy-like ease and stopped at her side, scarcely out of breath. "You wanted something?"

"Shouldn't you be with the twins?"

"I believe I've impressed good behavior on them. The grooms can do the rest. You intend to inspect the kitchen garden?"

"I did, but that can wait. We have many matters to discuss, I think."

"You're determined to drag me back inside the gloomy horror?"

"You so desperately wanted Perriam Manor."

"Not for myself. Harvest's in, so if we spread the word we could have men here ripping away ivy by this afternoon."

Claris noted the "we," but she heartily approved the plan. "By all means."

"There's an estate steward and I've summoned him. He should be here shortly."

"Every moment a new surprise. What is he responsible for?"

"Running the estate, but he oversees the maintenance of the house as well. Parminter's a reasonable enough man. Lives with his family on the edge of the estate by the village."

As they entered the house she asked, "Do I have any other servants I don't know of?"

"I don't think so, but there's a firm of lawyers in Slough and a bank there too. Come to the office and I'll try to lay it out, but bear in mind that my knowledge is scant. I'd never been here until a few weeks ago, and my actual nights beneath this roof number eight."

"But you've been trained to this life."

"Devil a bit! I'm the youngest son of four and was firmly encouraged to interest myself elsewhere. I've never taken even an idle interest in estate management. You're the answer to a prayer in all ways."

"If you'd inherited the manor without hindrance, you'd have left it in the hands of the steward?"

"And rented it out. It's never good to leave an estate without a family, and preferably one that spends a considerable time there."

"Ma'am . . . ?"

Claris turned to one side. They were passing the kitchen and the cook was curtsying.

"I was wondering if you had requests for the meals today, ma'am."

Another responsibility she'd forgotten.

"Of course. Do you have any favorites, Mr. Perriam?"

"Mistress Wilcock knows them and does them very well," he said, charming as always.

"Then why not follow my husband's preferences for today," Claris said. "I'll draw up some suggestions for the future."

The cook curtsied again. "Very well, ma'am. And may I say again what a pleasure it is to be cooking for young gentlemen with eager appetites."

Claris chuckled. "My brothers will certainly satisfy you in that respect, but don't let them pester you. Feel free to send them on their way."

"Thank you, ma'am, but they're such good lads."

As they walked on, Perriam said, "They are. They're a credit to you. It can't have been easy."

He was being charming again, but Claris couldn't deny a warm sense of pride. "Not always, no, but my father's flaws lay mostly in neglect rather than action."

When they entered the office, she said, "The very depths of gloominess!"

"It is rather, isn't it? The window's small and almost entirely covered, but even bright sunlight wouldn't make it pleasant."

The floor was bare wood in the familiar dark oak, and the shelves and cupboards were similar. Unlike the rest of the house, however, they seemed uncared for.

"The Beatrician line despised business?" Claris asked. At his look, she said, "I've been reading the family history."

"Bizarre, isn't it? I don't believe my line has a similar volume, but I must check." He was tidying himself, buttoning his waistcoat and tying back his hair. "As for this room, Cousin Giles left matters mostly in the hands of Parminter and his predecessor. Like me, he was a Town man."

He took down a ledger and put it on one of the two

plain desks. "This contains the recent household accounts. I glanced at them and they seem in order, but you'll know better."

He was neat, but still without a neckcloth. Deliberate? She was sure he'd seen the effect he could have on her. *Deal with business and get rid of him.*

She sat at the desk. "I know nothing of the running of a house like this, but I'll learn. I'll learn about the running of the estate too."

"Going to take complete command, are you?" When she looked sharply at him, he added, "I have no objection."

Claris folded her hands on the ledger. "May I ask about financial arrangements?"

"You may ask about anything."

"How much of the estate income will you want?"

"None. My income is more than adequate for my life. I only ask that you don't fall into deficit and want some of mine."

Could he be serious?

He'd promised not to lie to her.

"Does the estate provide enough income to support itself?"

"I devoutly hope so. Ah, Parminter. Good day to you. My dear, this is the estate steward. Parminter, my wife."

The stocky, gray-haired man bowed. "Welcome to Perriam Manor, ma'am."

Claris inclined her head, assessing him. He seemed all solid worthiness, but she'd hold judgment. "I look forward to working with you, Mr. Parminter. I also look forward to gaining a thorough understanding of the manor, house, and estate."

A definite twitch at that, but only to be expected. The sliding glance at Perriam was more worrying. Parminter was checking the husband's opinion, and perhaps even looking for amused condescension.

"My business will mostly be in Town," Perriam said, "so my wife will have the responsibility here. As a first

action, she wants the ivy stripped from the walls. Will it
serve to simply put out a call?"

"As well as anything, sir."

Parminter didn't so much as glance at her.

"Do we have ladders?" Claris asked, forcing him to
look her way.

"There are three or four in an outbuilding, ma'am."
He looked back to Perriam to ask, "You wish this done
immediately, sir? I could ride around and set it going."

"If you agree, my dear?" Perriam asked.

She gave him credit for including her, but as she
agreed to the plan she recognized another reason to get
rid of her husband. She'd not be true mistress of Perriam
Manor until then.

Once Parminter left, Claris dismissed her husband
and explored the ledgers and documents for herself.
There were papers here covering centuries, but she studied only the recent ones. She wished she had something
with which to compare the figures.

Was ninety-eight pounds a reasonable annual amount
for the sale of excess produce from the home farm? Was
seventy pounds a year an appropriate salary for Mr. Parminter? He also received sixpence a pound on timber
sold from the estate's woodlands. Was that fair? Was it
too much?

Wood seemed to form a good part of the estate's income, but it varied, with some years having a large felling
and others small. Rents from tenant farmers came to
nearly five hundred pounds a year, which seemed a huge
amount, but she also saw from other entries how much
it cost to maintain the house and estate.

Claris rested her tired eyes, remembering Perriam's
discussion with Farmer Barnett. Barnett had been correct in one way, for it seemed Giles Perriam had left
most of the management of the manor to others and
pocketed the profits. Perriam had been right too, however. Landowning was complex, and anyone who wanted
to have the oversight of it would work hard.

The details choked her brain and the amounts of money involved frightened her, but she would be a responsible landowner.

For now, she'd leave further reading until the ivy was cleared to let in more light. Given the one small window, she might need better light even then.

One of her father's few indulgences had been a branch of candles with a polished reflector to focus the light. That had been left at the rectory, but she could acquire a new one. No, a number of them. There should be one or more in the library, and she'd like one in her bedchamber. Old habits made her bite her lip at such indulgence, but she could afford it now.

She searched drawers until she found writing paper, then laid a sheet on the desk. She found a pen, mended it, dipped it in an inkpot and began a list.

Reflecting candles.

Requested foods from Athena and Ellie.

Riding clothes for the twins.

A valet for the twins.

A tutor for the twins.

She brushed the end of the quill against her lips, wondering where they would take their lessons. They could use the library, but that would prevent others from enjoying it much of the time.

There might be a schoolroom in the unexplored children's area of the house. She didn't like the thought of going there, but she couldn't leave a part of the house untouched forever like a mausoleum.

She must do something about the smothered babes.

She added "schoolroom" to her list and underlined it. That was the most urgent need.

She capped the ink and stood.

What better time than now?

Chapter 19

She asked the footman for directions to the children's area of the house but refused his escort. When she stood before the door, she almost felt as if she should knock, but she pressed down the handle and pushed it open. She was braced for it to be stiff, for hinges to squeal, but it opened smoothly.

Perhaps she should have delayed until the ivy had been cleared, for the gloom seemed particularly thick here, but she walked forward into a corridor. No dust. Clearly this area was regularly swept and dusted, as it should be.

She opened a door to her left and found a plain and empty room. It was modest in size but had a fireplace. Perhaps a governess's room, or a senior maid's, or an infant nursery, able to be kept warm in the coldest weather.

The next room was similar but without a fireplace. And the next. Had the whole place been stripped of furniture? Why?

"The last child died of a purulent fever."

She turned to find Perriam behind her.

"Two of them, in fact. A Giles and the daughter, Beatrice. This part of the house was thoroughly cleaned and fumigated, and all that they'd had contact with was burned. As there were no more children, it was left as is."

"Perhaps that's why there are no ghosts."

"Is ghost detection another family skill?" She must

have reacted, for he said, "That was a joke, not a taunt, Claris. You have a purpose in coming here?"

"Am I not permitted?"

"My dear thistle," he murmured. "I merely wondered if I could assist you."

Impossible to demand that he cease to use meaning-less endearments, but each usage was like a jab, or a spark, or something.

"I'm looking for a schoolroom, or somewhere that will serve that purpose."

"This, I suspect." He opened a door on the opposite side. "It's the largest room and has two windows. There are shelves in the alcove, which implies books. You'll make bedchambers up here for the boys as well?"

"Not unless they wish it. Where should a tutor's room be?"

"Here. As we have a tabula rasa and no expectation of babies, he could have two good rooms and privacy. You want me to find a suitable tutor?"

"Yes, please. Make it clear that it will be only for a year or so. I want the twins to go to school and make friends as soon as possible."

"Then there are other things they should learn. You should bring in a dancing master."

"Dancing?"

"It will be in their future, but such a man would also teach deportment."

Claris stiffened. "There's something amiss with their deportment?"

"Not for general use, but I doubt they know the finer styles."

In some subtle way he adjusted his stance, standing a little taller, head cocked in a certain way. Despite his un-ruly hair and clothing, he was suddenly grand. Smiling at her oh so slightly, he executed a smoothly elegant bow that involved three full circles of a graceful hand. Then he was himself again.

"I can't imagine the twins ever doing that."

"Yet the sort of friends you want them to make will have been trained to it from a young age. In fact . . ."

He was so rarely hesitant that she was alarmed.

"What?"

"With your permission, and in due course, they should visit Town."

"Why?"

"So I can introduce them to all its wonders, including some places where the grand style is used. You don't want them to seem country bumpkins."

She didn't, but she resented the implication that they were.

"You expect me to send them off to you?"

"You could accompany them."

"To London?"

"To *Town.* Town is the fashionable part, the court and political part. There is also the City, the oldest part, which is now the heart of commerce. The boys should experience London as a whole, but I was mainly speaking of St. James's, Westminster, and Mayfair."

Claris used the mealymouthed escape of "We'll see."

That was his world, where she'd be terrified of making mistakes, but she couldn't let the twins go there without her.

She turned to immediate matters. "I'll need to order furniture for these rooms."

"We could see what's in the attics."

"I thought you said everything was burned."

"The infected children were both too young for a schoolroom. Come on," he said, leading the way out. "Such fun to explore attics! With luck there are things there from centuries ago."

"Of use now?" she demanded, pursuing the gadfly.

She'd thought of him becoming himself again, but what was his true self?

He led the way down to a door that opened onto a staircase up to the higher floor. She followed him up, feeling rather like a rat following the Piper of Hamelin—without the ability to resist.

"There are probably maids' rooms up here," she warned. "Perhaps we should ask Mistress Eavesham. . . ."

He ignored her, opening and shutting doors until he said, "Aha! The accumulation of centuries."

She followed him into a huge space that seemed to be one end of the house, open to the rafters. There were stacked furniture covered by cloths, wooden chests that could contain treasures, and small items stuck up from open-topped boxes.

"Fishing rods," he said, touching a cane, "and doubtless poles and perches too. Aha! A bird cage." He pulled the metal object free. "Would you like a linnet? Or perhaps your grandmother would like a crow."

"She's not a witch. She's not even interested in the herb garden here."

Claris wasn't looking at him, however, but at a shape beneath its own white shroud. She removed the cloth and found, as she expected, a cradle.

It was as dark as the oak elsewhere in the house, but beautifully carved with vines and flowers, which were picked out in colored paint and in some places gilded.

He came to hunker down by it. "Thank God this survived the cleansing inferno. It's old, perhaps as old as the feud."

"Used through the generations."

He glanced up at her. "If my father learns about this, he'll want it for Millicent's baby. My sister-in-law," he explained, "expecting her third soon."

"Do I have to surrender it?"

"Feel free to contest it, but the wiser course would be not to let him know." He touched it and it rocked. "Though it would be a shame for it to linger unused."

Was he implying . . . ?

"Perhaps not," Claris said, "when one considers its recent history."

He rose. "Don't blame the cradle. Let's look for desks or tables suitable for learning."

Claris carefully replaced the cover before joining in the search. They soon found two desks, plus wooden blocks with letters carved into them, a counting frame, and a globe richly painted to show land and sea.

"Giles's children never achieved an age for this," Perriam said, gently turning it. "These things show that there have been happy families here, with children who grew to schoolroom age and then to adulthood."

Again she wondered if there was a meaning beneath his words. After all, they were married, for life. He might want an heir, and she . . .

She heard a noise outside and hurried to a window. "Is it possible?"

He joined her. "The ivy massacre commences?"

With some effort, he forced open the latticed window so he could lean out. "Yes. Let there be light!"

He stepped back and Claris leaned out to see men climbing ladders, armed with knives and hooks. In moments they were ripping long vines of ivy from the walls and throwing them down. On the ground, women picked them up and tossed them into one of two carts. Other men were hacking at the thick bases of the ivy.

"It looks as if everyone in the area has come to help," she said.

"Work's always appreciated, but I'm sure they also want to get a look at the new owners."

"Objects of curiosity, are we?"

"You in particular. They know me a little. They'll need refreshment at some point."

They were standing too close, in contact.

Warm contact.

Claris moved away. "I hope Mistress Wilcock can cope."

"Ale, bread, and cheese will do. I should go and supervise."

His eyes were as bright as the twins' thinking of ponies.

"Or assist?" she said.

He grinned. "You're coming to know me!"

That was true.

Dangerously true.

Then he spotted something behind her and darted over. "Swords!"

She whirled, alarmed, but saw that the finely detailed medieval swords were toys.

He tossed one to her and she caught the hilt by instinct. It was made of wood and quite light.

"Have at you!" he said, taking a stance and poking the sword toward her.

"Stop it, you madman!"

His eyes were brilliant with laughter. "Defend yourself, wench."

Claris gripped the hilt and poked her sword at him, but he circled his weapon, driving hers to one side.

"Unfair! You're trained at this."

She saw something behind.

Tentatively jabbing at him, she edged around until their positions were reversed. Then she dropped the sword. "I'll chop off your head, varlet!" she cried and grabbed the battle-axe she'd spotted.

She instantly dropped it with a mighty clatter. "My stars, it's real!"

He picked it up. "So it is, though not very sharp. Murder of a husband is petit treason, my bloodthirsty wench, so have a care."

"What is going on up here?" Eavesham came to a shocked halt. "Sir, ma'am, your pardon!"

"No, ours," said Perriam, unabashed. "We came in search of furniture and were reduced to play. Later I'll instruct the footman which items to take down to the schoolroom."

"Very good, sir. Is there anything I can assist with?"

Before she could be ignored again, Claris said, "Please ask Mistress Wilcock to prepare some refreshments for the workers who are clearing the ivy. To serve in a few hours, I mean."

"She already has it in hand, ma'am, and may I say how pleasant it will be to have the ivy gone."

"You may. The windows will need a thorough cleaning, but soon we will be able to enjoy sunlight again."

He bowed and left.

Perriam put the battle-axe away in a corner. "May I abandon you? To ivy I must go."

"Of course."

Alone, Claris looked around the room, but she was really surveying herself, aware of changes though not entirely sure what form they took.

She gathered the two swords and fishing poles to give to the twins, but then she changed her mind and pushed them back into the box. The twins would enjoy exploring up here themselves. Under her careful supervision, she thought, shuddering at the axe.

She looked once more at the cradle, strangely tempted to carry it down to her bedchamber. It seemed smothered and abandoned up here, but it had rocked five ill-fated babies and was best left beneath its shroud.

Chapter 20

When she returned to her room she found her window already cleared and sunlight streaming in. She laughed with the pure pleasure of it. When she opened the window she heard chatter and laughter outside.

Perriam Manor was coming to life.

She too wanted to be down there.

She hurried downstairs and out through the front doors. At the moment the workers were all on the side of the house. As soon as she reached there she saw Perriam up a ladder, hacking at ivy with a will and tossing down hanks of it with saucy quips. The village women responded with laughter and quips of their own, be they young or old.

"Irresponsible scamp."

Claris turned and found Athena by her side. "Only when it suits him. He was very responsible in teaching the twins to ride."

"Then he should exert responsibility now," Athena said, pointing.

The twins were each beginning to climb a ladder, blade in hand.

Claris raced over. "Come back down now."

"But . . ."

"Now!"

They obeyed, but sullenly. "Perry's doing it."

"He's a grown man, and he's Mr. Perriam."

"He told us to call him Perry. He's our brother now."

She supposed he was.

"A very much older brother. I'm sorry, darlings, but it's dangerous, and you could hurt others. You could help load the carts."

"That's women's work!"

"Please, Claris," Peter begged. "There are boys our age helping."

When she looked around, she had to admit it was true. Country lads worked from a young age, often at difficult and dangerous jobs. Her brothers had never been country lads of that sort, and she wouldn't have them thinking of themselves that way, but this was a unique occasion.

"Very well," she said, "but be careful."

They began to climb again, and Claris watched as if that could keep them safe.

"They twist you around their fingers," Athena said.

"One reason I want them to go to school." Claris remembered the other thing. "Perriam wants to take them to London. No, to Town, as he insists in calling it."

"He sometimes has sense. Will you accompany them?"

"Of course."

"Apron strings," Athena said, but added, "When the time comes, Ellie and I will go as well. It's too long since I visited Town, and there are places I can show you."

"I'd much prefer to stay here. Why is nothing turning out as I expected?"

"How tedious if it did. Be open to experience, Claris. It will reward you."

"I've had more than enough experience for a lifetime."

Claris tore her gaze off the boys but then couldn't help seeking Perriam.

Still up a ladder.

Still working like a laborer.

Like the other laborers he was down to breeches and shirt, his sleeves rolled up. His hair had lost its ribbon again, and the sun struck fire in it.

His arse was firm. . . .

Claris turned away, hot faced. "Food!" she said to no one in particular and rushed back into the house.

Once in the dark-paneled hall she paused, hand on the back of a carved chair. She'd never paid attention to a man's behind before, never. They were probably all the same, all as muscular. . . .

She hurried on to the kitchen.

Mistress Wilcock had everything in hand and was clearly enjoying feeding a multitude.

"And soon we'll have light in here again, ma'am. That'll be grand."

"The ivy hasn't always cut off the light?"

"Bless you, no, ma'am," the cook said, hands still busily cutting cheese. "The third wife . . . I mean, Mr. Giles Perriam's last wife, poor lady, she wouldn't have it cut. Then when she died Mr. Giles forbade anyone to touch it. It could be cleared, he said, when he had a son."

Mistress Wilcock's hands stilled and shot Claris a wary look.

"I understand that he was planning a fourth marriage," Claris said.

"Yes, ma'am. But then he began to fail. Likely it was all his fault, ma'am. Some men can't sire healthy children. Bad seed."

Claris realized the woman was trying to reassure her, and perhaps herself.

"Right, then," Mistress Wilcock said to her minions. "Let's get all this into the baskets and outside. Would it be all right if they eat and drink with the others, ma'am? They're all family."

"Of course," Claris said, and carried a heavy jug of cider herself.

A man with a strong voice declared the halt, and everyone gathered around the baskets and jugs. Claris helped to distribute the food and readily answered any questions, though in general terms.

She was a clergyman's daughter from Surrey.

Her parents were dead.

Yes, she intended to live here.

That clearly pleased everyone. The manor would provide work and buy from local people. It would bring prosperity. She would ensure that. It was a new thought, but these were her people, hers to take care of.

She saw Perriam eating and drinking with a group of men, laughing and creating laughter, completely at his ease. She was less so, because of her lifetime's experience in Old Barford. These people didn't know about the Mad Rector, however, and hadn't experienced her mother's harsh tongue. If she sometimes caught their eyes on her, or heard a whispered comment, it was only curiosity about someone who would be important in their lives.

She took a piece of bread and cheese and a pottery mug of ale and joined a group of young women who were sitting on the ground, some with babes in arms. Ancients seemed to have care of the children too young to work. Some were charming in their excitement and curiosity, while others were imps.

A nearby baby set up a howl, demanding to be fed. Its mother undid her bodice without interrupting her conversation and put the baby to her breast. The infant clutched, attached, and suckled in such expert seriousness that Claris had to smile. She quickly looked away, but no one seemed to have noticed or minded.

A toddler in a smock staggered over to present her with a buttercup. There was little more to it than the head, but Claris put down her food and drink to take it. "Thank you, poppet."

She held it beneath the child's chin so the sun reflected yellow off it. "I see you like butter."

The child chuckled, perhaps knowing the game, or perhaps simply from joy. Was it so easy to be joyous?

The child toddled off to a woman, presumably its mother, for she smiled shyly at Claris. Claris smiled back but looked away when the toddler climbed into its mother's lap and found a breast for itself.

The woman on Claris's right also had a babe, but hers

was asleep on a blanket on the grass, another blanket over it. So like the memorials, but so not.

"A boy or a girl?" Claris asked.

"A boy, ma'am."

"How old?"

"Two months, ma'am."

"Do you have other children?"

"Two, ma'am. But we've lost two."

There was sadness in the words, but acceptance too. Children died so easily in their early years. Giles Perriam's first wife had simply been more unfortunate than most.

"I'm sorry if I upset you, ma'am."

Claris wanted to deny any discomfort, but she wouldn't be believed. Instead, she tackled the subject. "I was thinking of the babies who died in this house recently."

The woman nodded. "Right sad it's been. Me mam says it was bad seed."

The same explanation Mistress Wilcock had given.

"That's what comes of sin," the woman went on. "As you sow, so shall you reap."

But then she looked alarmed.

She'd just insulted a Perriam.

"Giles Perriam was a bad man," Claris agreed. "My husband is a very distant relative."

The woman relaxed again. "That's what I heard, ma'am." Her baby stirred and so she picked it up, but she glanced at Claris. "He's a fine-looking man."

Claris felt herself blush. "Handsome is as handsome does," she said, then heard how that sounded. "And he always does most handsomely."

The woman grinned. "I'm not surprised, ma'am. Men like that, they have a way with them. A woman can always tell."

Men like what? Claris wondered, but she feared she knew. Lusty men who had a wicked way with women.

"Lawks! There's Billy running off!" The woman

looked around and then dumped her baby in Claris's arms before racing after a young lad who was heading for one of the cart horses.

Claris looked down at the baby, who looked up at her, its mouth working as if suckling. Its swaddling was damp, so she held it away from her skirts.

It was darling, though, reminding her of the twins at such a young age. She'd used to talk to whichever twin was in her arms, babbling whatever came to mind. They'd seemed to like it.

"You're a treasure," she said to the wide-eyed baby. "And your mother's a fine woman. You're going to grow up strong and happy in Perriam Green. Nothing will ever harm you...."

She realized she was trying to cast a spell of her own, one that would keep this little innocent safe. She could feel how painful the child's death would be, and she wasn't its mother.

Those haunting memorials.

What was she to do with them?

Impossible to destroy them, but if she had them moved to the churchyard, she'd expose more people to their disturbing design.

"I beg your pardon, ma'am," the young mother gasped as she sat down and retrieved her baby. "I shouldn't have taken advantage of you like that."

"That's all right. He's behaved perfectly."

The baby was beaming with delight at its mother, so happy to see her again, but without a trace of anxiety. Claris was sure her own mother had never felt like a secure haven.

"I've taken Billy to his father. He's only three, but he's a terror for venturing." She picked up the remains of her food, jiggling the baby on her knees. "It's grand to have a family here again. My granddad talks of how it was in his younger days. Plenty of work and always help in hard times. Feast days too."

Claris suspected she was being nudged toward extravagant benevolence, but she smiled. She'd do her best.

"This was when Giles Perriam's father was alive?"

"They've all been Giles, ma'am, as long as anyone can remember, but before him was his grandfather. His father died young. Racing a horse, or so they say. His father was one of four, but the others were all girls and married away. Him dying so young, Mr. Giles was the only child."

Claris disentangled this to mean that Giles had been the only child of a Giles who'd died young, before his own father had died. He'd have been raised by his grandparents, and probably inherited at a young age. That could spoil a man, and he'd been very spoiled to ruin Aunt Clarrie.

The strong voice bellowed again, and everyone scrambled up to set back to work. The young mother carried her baby over to a toothless old man and went to a cart.

Claris stood and surveyed the progress with satisfaction.

She couldn't rip the shrouds off those poor dead infants, but she was ripping the shroud off the house. Now she could see mellow red brick and massive exposed wooden beams. It was an old house and not straight in all its lines, but it had its own beauty.

And it was hers.

Hers to delight in, hers to care for.

The windows were dirty, but soon their lozenge-shaped panes would gleam and there would indeed be light in every room. The light would spread throughout the area. There would be work, and she'd provide assistance in hard times. If there truly were traditional feast days, she'd revive them.

She set to work, helping the servants to collect the debris. She was adding pottery mugs to a tray when she saw a carriage coming up the drive.

Visitors?

And here she was with her skirt kirtled up, no cap on her hair, which was escaping its pins as usual. All the servants were out here. Would there be anyone in the hall to open the door?

Claris frantically looked for Athena or Perriam. Where were they?

Lord help her, someone had to greet their guests, and it seemed it must be her. She unpinned her skirt and ran toward the front, only slowing as she approached the corner, where she'd be in sight.

A portly gentleman in a white wig and fine suit of green cloth had descended and was assisting a lady dressed in a hooped gown, who was wearing a very fine cap under a three-cornered hat decorated with a bold green feather.

Grand visitors!

Claris thought of retreat, but that wasn't possible. She took a breath and went over, pushing one long tendril back under a pin. With a curtsy, she said, "Welcome to Perriam Manor. I'm Mistress Perriam."

The middle-aged couple were looking around in amazement, but the lady smiled. "You're having the ivy stripped. Excellent idea."

"It seemed of first importance, ma'am. You must excuse my state of clothing."

"Of course, of course. You must excuse our impetuosity."

"And our manners," said the man with a warm smile. "Sir Ernest and Lady Fosse, of Pilch House, a few miles to the east. We were keen to welcome you to the area, but perhaps too keen."

She immediately liked them and hoped she wasn't deceived.

"Not at all. I'm delighted to make your acquaintance. Won't you come in? I could enjoy a cup of tea."

Thank heavens she'd been so busy talking that she'd eaten and drunk little.

As they turned toward the doors, Perriam came over, easy in his manner despite his undress. He carried his waistcoat and coat slung over one shoulder.

"Fosse. Lady Fosse. How kind of you to call. You find us in complete disarray, but in a good cause."

"We were just saying as much," said Lady Fosse, smiling at him. "Mistress Perriam has kindly offered us tea."

"I'll join you," he said, offering an arm.

Despite the arm being half-exposed and somewhat grimy, Lady Fosse took it and went into the house with him, saying, "I do hope this means you intend to reside here."

Claris took Sir Ernest's arm, hearing her husband say, "My wife does . . ."

She felt compelled to explain. "I prefer country living."

"I'm the same myself, ma'am. Reason I gave up my seat in Parliament years ago. Pity Perriam's so much obliged in Town." At least he didn't seem to find this odd. "With or without him, you must come and dine with us when you will. You might also enjoy the company of our daughter, Jane. Mistress Jordan now, but living not far away. She's about your age, and also a young wife."

"That would be lovely," Claris said, and a part of her meant it. Another part, the old part, shrank from all this sunny conviviality and wanted to fade back into the shadows.

Claris settled the Fosses in the drawing room and ordered the tea, and then hurried to her room to tidy herself. Her husband came with her, bellowing down to the hall, "Auguste!" He glanced at her. "Maid's name?"

"Alice."

"And Alice!" he shouted.

Claris made it to her room only a minute before her maid. She would have to gather the nerve to shout like that. Or acquire loud bells. Yes, that was it. A large bell in each room. There could even be a different tone or pattern for each member of the family.

"Tidy me. Quickly. Change? No, it would look odd. Do I have dirt or grass on me?"

Alice brushed her down. "Perhaps clean stockings, ma'am?"

Claris saw hers were muddy. "And my new shoes."

While Alice found them, Claris brushed out her hair and pinned it up. "The new cap! Oh, you've trimmed it already. Thank you."

Claris didn't know if the ribbons hanging down the back would make her flighty or not, but she'd use any improvement she could.

When she returned to the drawing room, the requirements for tea had arrived and Athena was preparing it. Claris was shocked by a spurt of annoyance. Her grandmother was usurping her place. She hid that behind a smile and sat down, looking forward to learning more about the area and the local families.

Athena had charge of that too, however, and the talk was about Town delights. When Perriam came in, restored to neatness, he joined in. Excluded, Claris did the only thing possible and paid attention so as to learn. She was going to have to go to fashionable London with the boys one day.

Yet again, however, a situation was being twisted away from her expectations. Something would have to be done.

When the Fosses left, Athena said, "We dine at two?"

Claris hadn't given a thought to normal daily patterns.

"With everything at sixes and sevens, I think it best if we each eat in our rooms when we will."

"The workers don't need constant supervision. Or assistance."

Perriam had left, probably to rejoin the merry throng outside. Claris envied him.

"It's good to be at ease with the local people," she said.

"Pandering will make them idle. Dinner at two. It is necessary to maintain good order, especially in disordered times. I shall tell the cook."

She left before Claris could find an argument. She'd thought her husband the biggest threat to her status here, but perhaps she'd been wrong.

Had Athena ruled the roost in the cottage?

Perhaps she had. When she'd arrived, she'd been the one with worldly knowledge, while Claris had been deeply ignorant.

Her grandmother liked to be in command, but so, Claris realized, did she.

Perhaps if Athena decided she could now abandon her grandchildren it would be no bad thing. Claris would miss Ellie, but no one was going to usurp her hard-won authority over Perriam Manor.

Chapter 21

However, when they gathered for dinner, Claris accepted that Athena might have been right. This was her family's first proper meal at Perriam Manor, and it would set a pattern.

Perriam was at the head of the table. She was seated opposite him. The twins, scrubbed and neat, sat on her left side. Athena and Ellie sat on her right. The first course of dishes was laid on the table and they all began to help themselves and one another.

The twins were bright-eyed at the selection and needed to be nudged to serve others as they should. They'd never eaten like this before.

"Cook has done wonders to prepare this as well as the food for the workers," Claris said.

"She might be enjoying the challenge," Perriam said.

"I think you're right. I gather your cousin rarely came here."

"Not until his last months."

"According to one of the village women, the manor was lively in his grandfather's time." She related what she'd heard. "I hope to restore that way of life."

"Easy enough," Perriam said. "Merely living here will do it."

"My sympathies are with your cousin Giles," Athena said, "and his love of the beau monde. Such a pleasure today to speak of important matters with people of fashion."

"Sir Ernest and Lady Fosse rarely travel," Perriam said drily. "Their knowledge comes from *The Gentleman's Magazine.*"

Athena's brows rose. "It must be a most informative publication."

"It is. Shall I subscribe to it for you?"

Claris sensed a clash but couldn't understand it.

"Claris might benefit from it," Athena said and then turned to Claris. "You were somewhat tongue-tied, child."

Oh, that word "child"!

"I was bored. I would have much preferred to learn more about local affairs."

"Of course you would," Ellie said, peacemaking. "It's wise to understand the ways of where you live. We've always made a point of it, haven't we, Thenie?"

Claris had never heard Ellie use that name before, or challenge Athena. To her surprise, it seemed to work.

Athena returned her attention to her plate. "Why anyone would want to live the year round in the country if they didn't have to, I cannot imagine. But if one does . . ."

"Even a person who lives only part of the year in the countryside should understand its ways." Perriam winked at the twins. "Note the lesson, lads."

"We like the countryside," Tom said.

"It's all you've known," Athena said.

"I hope you always like it," Claris said. "But Mr. Perriam thinks you should visit London at some point and learn its ways."

She was surprised when their eyes lit, until Peter said, "There are wild beasts in the Tower!"

"There are wild beasts everywhere in London," Perriam said. When the twins stared, he added, "I'm speaking of the human kind. That's why you should learn its ways—to know beasts from men. But it has many delights."

He went on to relate some, choosing just the things to appeal to eleven-year-old boys—displays of weaponry, dungeons at the Tower, and military parades at Horse Guards. There was even a swimming area called the Peerless Pool, but it would be too late in the year for that.

Claris rang for the next course, considering what she was learning, not about London's pleasures, but about herself and her family.

Athena did not want to live here all the year round. Perhaps she didn't want to live here at all. In some ways that might be good.

But if Athena and Ellie left, when the twins went to school she would be alone in this big house. . . .

"Do you not agree, Claris?"

She started and looked down the table. "I'm sorry, I was woolgathering."

"Were we boring you again?" Athena asked in a tone that made Claris grit her teeth.

"I was considering when it would be best for us to visit London," Claris lied. "My brothers must first become settled into their studies. Can you acquire a tutor for them as soon as may be, Perriam?"

"Of course. A stern one, I think, with a heavy rod and dour manner." But again, he winked at the twins and they grinned.

They liked him.

They'd said as much.

Perhaps in a way, more than they liked her.

It was only natural, for she was more like a mother than a sister, and they were of an age to want male company. Also, he charmed as easily as he breathed. Even so, their defection hurt.

She was relieved when the meal was over and used the workers as an excuse to avoid the after-dinner tea. She went to her room to change her shoes, remembering that she must acquire a broad-brimmed hat to try to discourage freckles.

She laughed at that impossible ambition and sat at her desk to add to the list of things she could achieve.

Bells.

Hat.

How? Where? When?

She scribbled through that line but rested her head on her hand. She felt overwhelmed, but that wasn't surprising. It was her nagging dissatisfaction that disturbed her. She had what she wanted, didn't she? She'd won a comfortable home and had independent charge of it. She could spend her life making it exactly as she wanted.

A little voice said, *Is that all?*

She went to the window, a window free of ivy so that light poured in and she could look over her domain. When she looked down, however, she realized it overlooked the yew-guarded memorials. Of course the first wife would have constructed it where she could easily see it, but the smothered babes made her shudder.

She turned away. Was her destiny to live alone amid ghastly memorials and ghostly nurseries, haunted by an empty cradle that must wait for another generation to be filled?

What generation?

If Perriam died, she'd inherit the manor from him, but after her?

She could leave it to one of the twins, but that created a new thorny thicket. Which one? Peter because he was the older, or Tom because he was less likely to make a brilliant career?

An impossible choice.

That was far in the future! For now, she would be grateful for all she had, for how much improved life was for herself and her family.

She went outside to find that two sides of the house were clear. The brickwork was still marked where the ivy had clung, but the mellow beauty made her resolution easy. Perriam Manor would be her perfect home.

Perriam came over to her. "Much improved."

"It's lovely."

He looked at her. "Do you truly think so?"

"Do you truly prefer the straight and modern?"

"I confess, yes."

They were different in so many ways, perhaps in all ways. She must remember that.

"Not climbing ladders?" she asked.

"I've forgone pleasure for duty and am at your disposal."

"If you speak so rudely, sir, I might dispose of you in the river!"

"My sincerest apologies! Clearly rude labor has infected me. Of your kindness, sweet lady, accompany me on a tour of the estate?"

That charm again.

"Why?"

"You must want me to introduce you to the Moores at the home farm . . ."

Oh, must I?

". . . and you will want to survey your domain."

She twitched at another command beneath his fancy phrasing but had no argument to make.

"Very well, but as we go, tell me about the village. How many live there?"

"About one hundred."

As they turned to walk away from the house, he touched her lightly on the back, as if she needed urging forward. It worked, because she felt that touch through cloth and stays.

"Smaller than Old Barford, then, but with a church. I saw it as we drove through."

"Dedicated to Saint Beatrice, though as you'll guess that only dates from the sixteenth century."

"Your family is obsessed!"

"Not mine. We never renamed a church after Cecilia. I'm not sure there is a Saint Beatrice, whereas there is a Saint Cecilia."

"There you go again, scoring points."

"Trained to it from the cradle," he agreed cheerfully, "but by our marriage we've put an end to all that. Rename the church if you want."

They'd reached the end of the house and turned along the path to the kitchen garden, walking between low hedges splashed with golden celandine, blue toadflax, and scarlet poppies.

"Wouldn't I need consent from the bishop?" she asked.

"Probably, but it shouldn't be difficult to obtain."

There spoke the man with generations of rank and power behind him.

"If I do change the dedication, it won't be to Saint Cecilia."

"Father will be disappointed."

"He'll have to endure it."

"All very well as long as you don't have to face him."

"Is he really so terrifying?"

"Imagine a vengeful god. The sort that wields thunderbolts and breathes fire."

"Then keep him away from here. You promised."

"Did I?" he asked, looking alarmed.

"Do you truly fear him?" She found it hard to believe that Perriam feared anything or anyone.

"On my honor. Mostly because he's irrational. My mother is as formidable, but icy reason flows in her veins."

It was an oddly disturbing description. Claris had grown up amid passions and had thought she'd like calm, but icy was a different matter.

"I shall rename the church Saint Placid's," she said.

"Is there such a saint?"

"Yes." She looked around. "Where are we going? The home farm is off to our left."

"At a distance. If we're to see the whole estate we'll need to ride."

Claris stopped. "I don't ride, and I've no desire to."

"You'll be safe riding on a pillion behind me."

"I'd rather we walk."

"Have sense, Claris. I'll keep you safe. We'll only be ambling around."

"Ambling means at walking pace," she pointed out. "So what advantage?"

"Endurance. On horseback we can explore longer."

"I'm able to walk for many miles, having never had the luxury of horses."

"Then pity the pampered one. In any case, on horseback we'll cross rough ground more easily. Trust me, it's the better way."

He was charming her again, seeking his own way, but his points seemed reasonable.

"Oh, very well. But if I break my neck I'll hold you responsible."

"And you'll send down a curse?" But then he raised a hand. "I'm sorry. Not a subject for humor."

"No." She halted to look back at the tall yew hedge, still visible at a distance. "What am I to do with those memorials?"

"I don't know."

She saw he was serious. "I can't destroy them."

"No."

"It would feel wrong to hide them away in the attics."

"Yes."

"I could have them placed in the church, but they'd take up a lot of space, and they're . . ."

". . . unsettling. In the extreme," he completed.

"Yes."

"I trust your judgment."

"Why?" she asked, genuinely bewildered.

"Because you're you. You've survived a difficult life and kept your sanity and good humor."

"You described me as a thistle!"

He smiled. "A good-humored one. Despite your parents, you raised your brothers to be happy, healthy lads. You can solve the problem of the ghastly memorials."

Claris wished she had his faith. She was tempted to admit her other problems to him, but he mustn't know that the curse bothered her, no matter how she reasoned against it, and she felt guilty about her resentment of Athena.

They entered the stables and found the twins putting saddles on their ponies under the watchful eye of a groom.

"We're just going to ride around the paddock again," Peter told Perriam.

"See you do. I'm taking your sister for a ride."

"But she's never ridden," Peter protested, protective again, dear boy.

"Which is why she'll be riding on a pillion behind me. I'll keep her safe—my word on it."

That instantly satisfied the boys, who went back to their work, but Claris was aware again of the manly circle being formed, one that excluded her. He gave the order to another groom and went over to chat with the twins.

The groom soon brought out a brown horse that seemed huge in comparison to the ponies. It was fitted with a pillion saddle, which consisted of the main saddle and a flat pad behind that had a raised back, a side bar, and a footrest beneath.

A chair, in effect.

She'd seen women riding this way, and they'd seemed relaxed, but the horse was big and the chair high.

Perriam mounted and rode the horse to the mounting block. A groom assisted her into her seat. She gripped the side bar. When he set the horse into motion, she gripped harder. Perhaps she made a sound, for he said, "Put your right arm around me if you wish."

The thought didn't relax her one bit, but she needed to hold on to something substantial. She put her arm around him and clutched his jacket at the front.

"Better?"

"A little."

"You'll get used to it."

That seemed highly unlikely. Her arm curved around his strong torso and she was pressed tight against him.

They went slowly out of the stable yard and were soon crossing open land, following a shallow slope across a sheep-cropped meadow surrounded by trees. It was a pleasant day, with only a few clouds in the sky, and a sweet freshness in the air.

Perhaps this wasn't too bad.

But she'd rather be walking.

He pointed right with his crop. "That stand is walnut, I'm told. Remember, I'm almost as ignorant about such things as you. Parminter's your man."

She had to twist to see. "Then perhaps he should be giving me this tour."

"I'm sure he will, and pass on greater wisdom. However, it will be best if I introduce you at the home farm and at the mill. We can probably circle back through the village and call at the parsonage. Very suitably, the parson is Reverend Rightworthy, and very fortunately he's not as starchy as that sounds."

"Good. It's a name for a Puritan."

"He's definitely not a Puritan. Better now?"

Claris realized she'd relaxed her grip on his coat and was growing accustomed to the gentle rocking movement of the horse. She wasn't yet at ease with his hard warmth.

"It's still a long way to the ground," she said.

"Trust me. That section ahead is called Chelsy Coppice and thus is used for coppicing. Ash, used for stakes, poles, handles, and such. It will soon be time to harvest it."

"Parminter will manage that?"

"Yes. There are a number of other sections producing regular crops, but most of the woodland is timber plantations, such as the walnut and oak."

"Why is there so much woodland and so little pasture or arable land?"

"Easier to manage, I suspect, plus the nature of the land here. To the west, where the home farm lies, the land is better for arable."

She frowned at one dense area of tall trees. "Are the woodlands safe?"

"Full of bears and wolves."

"What?"

"I'm teasing."

"I know that. There are no bears and wolves in England. But there are other hazards."

"You cosset the boys too much."

"I can't help it."

"Give them the freedom of the estate. They'll only come to harm through stupidity."

"They'd still be harmed."

"And learn by it."

"Or die."

"That's in the lap of the gods."

"You wouldn't say that if they were your brothers."

"Oh, yes, I would, and wish them to the devil to boot."

"You can't mean that."

"Still with illusions of happy families? My oldest brother's a weak fool, Rupert is a bully, and Arthur can't resist temptation, especially that of the gaming tables. The only blessing is that most of the time I can ignore all three. That area ahead was felled a couple of years ago and has been replanted with elm. Good for bridge timbers, quays, and coffins."

Claris considered the area of very young trees. They wouldn't come to harvest for decades.

Woodlands were planned over decades rather than seasons, and she liked that. She'd see those trees grow tall and be harvested, and could make decisions on plantings that would come to fruition after her death.

Her gaze on the trees had been idle, but now she blinked. "I see smoke rising. Are there homes in the woods?"

"Charcoal burners. With permission and paying a rent. There's the home farm ahead."

Claris looked over his shoulder and down below,

through a break in the trees, she saw the sort of house she'd imagined Perriam Manor would be.

It was built of brick like the manor, but about a quarter of the size. It too was shrouded by plants, but only up to the first story, and many carried flowers. They certainly hadn't been allowed to cover windows. There were other brick buildings behind the house, forming a sort of courtyard. There was also a large barn, already well filled with hay.

If she'd married Gideon Barnett, she could have lived in such a place. She had to fight a laugh at the temptation. She'd make a terrible farmer's wife, for she'd no taste for making cheese and sausages, not to mention slaughtering chickens and making blood pudding.

They met a wide lane, cut with cart tracks, and followed it. The horse made easy work of it, but it would have been difficult on foot. What was more, from horseback she could see over the hedges. On their right lay good pasture grazed by cows. On their left lay the stubble of wheat or barley. A flock of starlings rose, alarmed by their passing.

"Farmer Moore should pay his rent in kind," Perriam said, "but with so little being needed at the manor in Giles's time, he's been selling the produce and paying in cash. You should settle with them for the products you want and strike a fair balance."

"It won't be so very different once the boys go to school. I'm not sure Athena and Ellie will stay."

"No?"

She'd opened up the subject without meaning to. "I think my grandmother pines for adventure, despite her age. She certainly pines for company. She intends to accompany us when we visit London. She may not return."

"You could hire a companion."

"Why would I want such a person?"

"Companionship?"

"Pleasant if congenial," she said, "but hellish if not."

"In that case you dismiss your employee."

"I fear I'd not have the heart. Aren't companions usually ladies who've fallen on hard times? I'll simply keep busy. I intend to turn Perriam Manor into a delightful home and a prosperous estate. I'll even manage the kitchen garden."

"And hoe the weeds? As you will, my dear, as you will."

The problem with pillion riding was that she couldn't see his face and attempt to read his expression, but she feared he thought her ridiculous.

She'd prove him wrong.

Perry was a little concerned about this visit to the home farm, which was why he'd wanted to accompany Claris here. The Moores would know all the gossip and might resent their new mistress. They certainly assessed her over tea and cake, and did seem a little distant. Claris behaved perfectly. She didn't attempt fine airs but treated them as equals.

She asked about the animals raised and the crops grown, not hiding any ignorance or inexperience. She knew a great deal, however, because she'd lived in the countryside all her life.

After the tea, she asked to borrow a pair of Mistress Moore's pattens so she could stroll around the muddy farmyard. Perry knew Auguste would be distressed by the damage to his boots, but he went with her.

She paused to look over a fence at a new litter of piglets, lined up to suckle at their mother's teats. "No wonder she looks exhausted."

"Especially as they'll soon be like that lot," Perry said, as some older piglets ran by squealing.

"Let them run," Claris said. "They'll soon be bacon."

"What a morbid mind you have. In time we'll all be dust, but before that we'll be food for worms."

She laughed. "To speak of morbid!"

He smiled back, enjoying her relaxed pleasure in this setting. "The common fate is reason to enjoy life whilst we have it."

"To run and squeal?"

"At times."

She looked around and beyond and said, "I like it here."

"In the mud and dung?"

She smiled at him. "Yes. But all of it. Thank you."

"For bringing you here?"

"For persuading me to marry you."

Her eyes were bright, the hazel color warm, and her open smile approached beauty. Shockingly, he wanted to kiss her, there and then, quite desperately.

"It has been my pleasure," he said, "and I grant you, the estate is in good heart. Some small credit to Giles, I suppose. He kept good managers."

"Yet for you London has greater charms."

Did she sound a little wistful?

He didn't want her to build expectations. He knew his limitations.

"Greater stimulation," he said lightly. "You've seen how I am. A day of rural calm and I'm climbing ladders, knife in hand."

She shook her head at him, but still smiling. "We'd best head back. The sun's low in the sky."

"Perhaps that's why you're singing the praises of a farmyard—the golden glow." It was touching her face, warming her delightful freckles. Before he could stop himself, he touched them.

She flinched but didn't step away. "They won't rub off," she said, smiling, blushing.

Who would have thought a farmyard so dangerous?

"Come along," he said, taking her hand.

He'd merely meant to make sure she came, that they escaped this unexpected intimacy, but they'd touched so rarely, and now, hand to hand, warmth flowed between then. A warmth that in other circumstances could lead to delights.

Perry reminded himself of the promises he'd made. As soon as they reached the farmhouse, he let go of her hand.

They said their farewells and Farmer Moore brought out their horse. Perry checked everything and tightened the girth himself. There was no mounting block, so he bent one knee slightly and had her put a foot there. He put his hands on her waist and boosted her up, keeping his hands in place until she was steady.

An even more intimate touch, especially as she wasn't wearing boned stays. She smiled down at him, clearly wondering at the lingering moment.

She was his wife.

Why had he agreed that it would be in name only?

But he had.

He mounted in front of her and they rode away.

"Where's the mill?" she asked. "Won't it be dark when we arrive there?"

"Yes. We've dawdled too much even to visit the village. Parminter can take you to those places. If we ride to the right here we'll be back at the house soon."

He turned the horse that way, hastening toward sanity.

Even so, by the time they left the horse at the stables the sun had set, turning trees to dark silhouettes against the peach-pearly sky. A few clouds drifted by, touched by the pink light, and a night bird sang. So intoxicating and she so warm and pretty . . .

"I'd like to look at the house now the work is completed," she said, not appearing to be affected at all.

"Better done tomorrow in good light."

"I'll look tomorrow as well."

So they walked all around the house, somehow hand in hand again.

"There are more windows than I thought."

"Blinking, like a man whose eyes have been bandaged."

"Not in this light," she pointed out, but smiling at his whimsy.

"I'm imagining their state tomorrow, hit by morning sun."

"They'll welcome it."

"Yes, they probably will. As I'll welcome the light shining inside."

He'd strolled with many women, and sometimes in the fading light of day, but it had never felt like this.

She was unaffected. "I intend to have trellises put up so some flowering plants can climb, as at the farm. And perhaps flower beds here at the front."

"Including lavender?"

"Why not? It gives a sweet aroma that soothes the soul."

"Then definitely lavender," he said.

Irresistibly, the thought came that he could seduce her. He knew the ways of it and he sensed her susceptibility. She was sensual. He knew that from the ginger and cherries. She was warm and giving, lively and spirited, and her temper promised fire. Wouldn't that all continue into a bed?

It wouldn't be wicked to seduce his wife.

It would be wicked to break a promise, however, and unfair to use tricks and arts to seduce her into breaking her resolve.

Thank God he was leaving tomorrow.

This sunset madness would fade with the light and he'd soon be sane again.

Chapter 22

As they went inside, Claris was reluctant to slip her hand from his, but she did it.

"My shoes are muddy," she said as an excuse. "I must take them off here." She didn't quite dare to order him to take off his boots, but she looked at them. When he continued toward the stairs, she said, "What purpose in tramping mud all over the place?"

He seemed startled by the notion, but he sat on the lower stairs. "What purpose indeed?"

He began to pull off his boots, but the footman hurried over to assist him.

Claris hadn't noticed the servant, and now she blushed at her tart question.

"Shall I take the boots to the scullery, sir?"

"And my wife's shoes," Perriam said, standing. "We require washing water in our rooms. Come, my dear."

Claris put down her shoes and joined him to go up to their rooms. "I'm sorry. I was rude."

"But to the point. Of course, we'd normally have entered by the back, where leaving our footwear would be more natural."

"My fault."

"There's no fault in any of this, Claris."

He said it gently, but as if there was greater meaning. What else had she done that might be faulted?

He opened the door to her room and for some reason her heart began to pitter-patter, as if he might enter with her. He merely guided her inside with another light touch on her back—merely!—and left.

Claris closed the door and leaned against it, trying to shake nonsense out of her head. It had to arise from the magic of the evening light.

Would she really have let him enter with her?

Why not? asked reason.

Because it would cross the boundaries they'd established. It would imply something.

Had he wanted to come in?

She pushed away to go to the window, to look out at the darkening sky. She couldn't stop herself from glancing down. The memorial enclave was deeply shadowed and yet some trace of light touched the five marbles, making them even more ghostly.

Alice came in with warm water and Claris turned, smiling, probably too brightly.

"My shoes need a good clean. I've been visiting the home farm."

Alice poured hot water into the basin. "Yes, ma'am."

"The estate is very interesting."

Alice uncovered the pot of soap, then took the towel and stood ready. "Yes, ma'am. Do you want the candles lit, ma'am?"

Claris realized that she'd been conversing with a servant, which probably wasn't appropriate. Certainly Alice showed no sign of interest in her day, and why should she?

"Yes, please."

A companion would have to at least feign interest. It seemed such a dismal relationship, however, with one side obliged to be pleasing, no matter how she felt. Ellie wasn't like that, but Claris wasn't sure what Ellie was, and Athena was certainly no conventional lady.

As Claris washed her face, she remembered that Alice was only on loan from Cheynings. She too might want to leave.

"Do you think you'll want to stay here, Alice, or will you prefer to return to Cheynings?"

"I'll stay as long as you need me, ma'am, but my family's there, you see."

"It's your home. I understand." Claris dried her face and hands. "I'll find a new lady's maid as soon as possible. Are there any maids here who would be suitable?"

"I don't think so, ma'am. None have any experience in such work. The last Mistress Perriam had no need of a lady's maid for many years, or so I'm told."

Because she'd been mad.

"I don't mind staying here for a while, ma'am. It's interesting to see a new place."

"Do you find the other servants friendly?"

The maid's eyes shifted. "They're a bit somber, ma'am."

Claris realized that she too had that impression. "More so than at Cheynings?"

"Oh, yes, ma'am. We had merry times there."

"This house has known a lot of sadness. It will take time for change, but I hope daylight will begin the repair."

"Likely it will, ma'am," Alice said, but she didn't sound hopeful.

She poured the used water into the slop bucket and took it away. Claris sat on the chaise longue, fighting the dismals again. She wanted this to be a happy house, but was she going to have to dismiss the servants and hire new to have a fresh start?

No, it would simply take time.

Time. Her idle gaze was resting on the clock on the mantelpiece. It wasn't as fascinating as the clear one at Cheynings, but it was still pretty, with gilt ornamentation and flowers painted on the face. She contrasted it with the simple clock in the cottage. She hadn't unpacked the boxes from Lavender Cottage and had no urge to do so. Athena had been correct, and most of the contents would be discarded, but even unpacking them would prove the poverty of her former life.

She certainly didn't want anything of her mother's in her new life. She hadn't liked her mother and hadn't been able to love her, perhaps because her mother hadn't loved her. It was as if her adoration of her younger sister and her need for revenge had used up all her emotions.

She hadn't mourned her mother. She'd been too absorbed by her baby brothers. Even so young, she'd known they were hers to protect.

A thought tickled at the back of her mind.

Ah. For the first time she wondered how they'd come to be. The normal way, people would say, but after her own arrival there'd been no more children. In theory her parents had shared a bed, but her father had often, perhaps always, slept on a daybed in his study. She wasn't precisely sure what was required to make children, but it happened in the marital bed. Whatever the process was, her parents must have done it in order to conceive the twins.

Why, after so long?

She glanced at the adjoining door and realized why this subject had suddenly occurred to her, and where her mind was wandering. . . .

After only the briefest knock, the twins burst in. "Supper's served, Claris!"

She held up both hands. "Stop. You knock and then wait. What if I'd been washing?"

They both looked doubtful. Did they not think she washed?

But they both apologized.

She felt guilty for chastising them, for their arrival and chatter had cleared her mind as effectively as stripping the ivy had cleared the windows. What folly she'd been contemplating.

"Apology accepted," she said, rising. "Now we can go down."

"Did you enjoy your ride?" Peter asked.

In so many ways. "It was terrifying at first."

"You'll get used to it."

"And soon you'll be riding alone," Tom said.

"No, I won't. My legs turn limp at the thought. I'm sorry if that gives you a disgust of me, but there it is."

"Never a disgust, Claris," Peter said, but clearly she was now a subject of eternal pity.

"I wonder what's for supper," she said, which distracted them. To them, meals were now a cornucopia of wonders.

Claris was nervous about facing Perriam again, but the moment passed easily and the meal went well. Everyone had something to say about their day. Ellie and Athena had conducted a thorough review of the library in search of interesting books.

Athena gave her judgment. "You should throw out most and restock."

"That will have to wait," Claris said. "There are more important improvements."

When Athena sniffed, Claris suspected she'd been hoping for new books to her taste. If she wanted them, she could buy them herself.

When they went to the drawing room, Perriam suggested the boys come with them. Once there, he produced a pack of cards.

Both boys stared.

"Cards are the devil's work," Tom said, looking as if he feared flames would spurt.

"They're merely pieces of card," Perriam said, riffling them. "We make them what we will."

"Perhaps I object," Claris said to remind him who was in charge here.

"I propose a very undevilish game," he said. "Casino."

Athena sniffed and retreated to a chair with a book, but Ellie said, "Oh, I enjoy casino," undermining Claris's objection.

"It's a harmless game," Perriam said to her, "and your brothers should learn to play."

Despite misgivings, Claris gave in and took part. Once she understood the rules, she enjoyed it. Ellie was skilled at it, making clever matches and pointing out good ones to the twins. Claris suspected that Perriam was underplaying so as to let the boys win.

After a while he gathered the cards in and shuffled them. He gave them to Peter. "You try."

The result was cards all over the floor. Both twins worked at learning how to shuffle a deck of cards. Claris watched, sufficiently influenced by her father's rants to still feel as if the devil hovered in the room.

She hadn't noticed Perriam leave the table, but he returned with a wooden box prettily inlaid with ivory. When he opened it she saw small wooden disks marked with numbers.

"Counters. We can play brag."

It took a moment for Claris to understand. "A *gambling* game? That *is* the devil's work!"

The dark room, lit only by two stands of candles, took on the ambience of hell.

He ignored her and spilled the counters onto the table. "Better they learn here than in a corner at school." He pushed the counters toward the boys. "Share those evenly between us. I can't tempt you to brag, Mistress Mallow?"

Athena gave him a look. "If you progress to something interesting such as quadrille or basset, perhaps."

"Like playing deep, do you?"

Athena did not reply, but Ellie said, "She does. And she generally wins."

"I'm sure she does, but there's no need to teach the lads beau monde games yet, especially as our monarch disapproves of gambling."

"Which is to his credit," Claris said, still very uneasy.

"I so easily forget that you're a clergyman's daughter."

He made it sound a deplorable state, and she glared at him.

Secretly she disliked feeling her father's disapproval

like a weight on her shoulders, but there it was. She truly did think gaming evil. Hadn't Perriam disapproved of one of his brothers for play? She should forbid this, or at least leave the table, but she noted what Perriam had said. Better the boys learn here than at school. She was going to have to send them into the world and she didn't want them in danger through ignorance.

She accepted her counters and arranged them by amount. "If these were guineas, I'd be rich."

"By most people's reckoning, you are rich," Perriam said.

She looked at him in surprise. "I suppose I am."

"Everyone ready?" he asked.

The twins were bright eyed and eager, and she could almost feel her father's fearsome breath on her neck. No. She'd not allowed him to ruin everything in life, so she certainly wouldn't let him do it from the grave.

"You'll be dealt three cards," Perriam said. "To win, you need the best combination. We'll play the simplest version tonight, only counting pairs and threes. So the very best combination is three aces, then three kings and so on. Easy enough, yes?"

The twins nodded, following with more rapt attention than they'd ever paid to worthy lessons.

"In addition we have the braggers—the ace of clubs, the knave of spades, and the nine of diamonds. These can substitute for any card, so if you have two tens and the nine of diamonds, you can claim three tens. Yes?"

They nodded.

"If you have two braggers, you can claim a three of the other card, so the king of spades along with the nine of diamonds and the ace of clubs is three kings. However, if someone else has the three other kings, they win."

"We understand," Peter said, speaking for them both as he often did. "Can we try now?"

"Don't you want to know how to lay a bet?"

"Can't we play without betting?" Claris asked.

"That would make the game pointless."

"There's no harm to it, dearie," Ellie said. "Or at least, not if they're sensible. And if they're not, it's best they understand the risks."

"If you truly object . . . ," Perriam said, but he'd already hooked her brothers and knew it.

"Continue," she said, but with a look that should have shriveled his soul.

It had no obvious effect. "I'll deal three cards to each, but first I'll lay down a stake." He looked at the twins. "Always limit the stake, or you can be tempted into losing far more than you can afford. You understand?"

They both nodded.

"Do you agree to a limit of two counters?"

The twins looked at each other as if debating it; then both nodded.

"Two counters it is." Perriam picked one up. "These have numbers on them, but we'll count each as one. One penny? One shilling? One guinea?"

"Guinea!" the twins said in unison.

"But then how would you pay?"

"With the counters," Tom said.

"But they must represent real money, or where's the point? How much can you afford to lose?"

Both twins slumped. "Nothing," Peter said. "We have no money."

Claris saw Perriam about to give them some and spoke first. "I should be providing a small allowance for you, shouldn't I? We'll discuss what it should be, but for now, I promise you two shillings each to celebrate our wedding, yours to game with or not, as you wish."

She hoped they'd retreat from risking real money, and she saw their hesitation, but then Peter looked at his counters. "We each have twenty. If they're worth a penny, that's one shilling and eight pence." Again he hesitated, glancing at Tom. Tom nodded. "We'll play for pennies and stop if we lose a shilling."

A shilling would seem like riches to them, but they were willing to risk it. That worried Claris, but she adored

SEDUCTION IN SILK   221

them for their careful consideration and caution. She also understood Perriam's purpose. He was going to teach them about real consequences.

She hoped they lost.

Perriam put a counter in the center of the table. "I bet one penny. Now I deal three cards to each of you and you decide whether to match my stake or not. If not, you're out of the game at no loss."

"We have to decide our chances of winning?" Peter said. "How can we know?"

"Unless you're holding three aces, you can't. You can estimate the probabilities, but that takes practice. For now, you guess. You should also watch your opponents, for some show their hand in their expression."

"But some put on expressions in order to deceive," Ellie warned.

"They do indeed." Perriam deftly dealt three cards to each of them.

Claris picked hers up, acknowledging the tingle of excitement when she found two fives. Only fives, but two of them. What was the probability of getting a pair? Surely it couldn't be high.

"Fan them like this," Perriam said, and she imitated him. "It doesn't matter in handling three cards, but with more it's essential."

"I'm not likely to make a habit of card playing, sir."

"As your husband, I approve." He turned to Ellie on his left. "Miss Gable, do you wish to match my stake, or even raise it?" To the boys he said, "Raising the stake is a means to frighten off other players and can sometimes have a weak hand win."

Ellie said, "I'll merely match your stake, sir," and put a counter in the middle.

The twins each did the same. Claris considered her fives and put in two counters.

"Aha! Does she have a strong hand, or is she bluffing? Now we'll have to add two pennies to stay in the game." He matched her two pennies.

Ellie put down her hand. "I retire."

The twins looked at each other and at the counters in the middle. There was eight pence there now, a very tempting sum.

It was Peter's turn next and he looked at Perriam. "I don't like competing with my brother. Can we play together?"

"No."

Peter frowned, but he added two counters.

Frowning just as much, Tom put down his hand and copied Ellie. "I retire."

That left only Claris, Perriam, and Peter.

"What now?" she asked.

"We continue until only two remain."

Claris didn't want to compete with her brother, so she put down her cards. "I retire."

"But you raised the stake," Peter protested. "You can't give up so easily."

"I didn't know what I was doing." Perriam raised a brow at her, however, and she saw the message. This should be real. "Oh, very well." She picked up her cards and put two more counters in the middle.

Perriam put down his cards. "I retire."

"Do we get to see what you held?" Claris challenged.

"No. Now you and Peter can continue to bet until one of you runs out of money or loses your nerve, or one of you can put in double to see the other's cards. Then the best hand wins. Peter?"

Watching her, Peter put in two more pennies. The clever lad knew she'd pay the double to put an end to this.

She did. "Show me your cards."

When he put down the ten of hearts, the nine of diamonds, and the ace of clubs, she didn't know whether to be delighted that he'd won or terrified that he'd get a taste for this.

She showed him her pair of fives. "You win."

He whooped and gathered in the money, but then he happily shared his winnings with his brother.

"Can we play again?" Tom asked, arranging his wealth in lines of five.

Claris agreed, praying that the play go against the boys and teach them a lesson. It did. They continued to play, and luck wandered evenly around. Claris suspected that Perriam and Ellie sometimes retired good hands, for she certainly did, but the twins lost as often as they won.

When she finally called a halt, they were down three-pence from their original twenty. She thought that about right for a lesson but could only hope they hadn't been infected with a mad taste for gambling.

They went off to bed and Claris gathered the counters back into the box. "I'm not sure that was wise."

"It's played everywhere, and the ignorant can be sucked into a game with stakes too high and honesty too low. I'm sure you can impress upon them the folly of wagering large amounts. Unless it runs in the blood."

"My parents never touched cards or dice."

"What of your family?" he asked Athena.

"My husband's vices were other."

"And your parents? Lord and Lady Littlehampton, I gather."

So Athena was from the nobility, Claris thought. How odd, especially when it meant she was too, after a fashion. No wonder her mother had been so bitter about Father not "taking his place" in local society.

Athena gave him a cool look. "Been digging into it, have you? My mother ruined us all with her gaming, which is why I was sold off to Mallow. I, however, have no addiction to the tables."

"Quadrille? Basset?"

"Can amuse and even be profitable. A clear mind and a keen eye can reap rewards."

"That's true." Perriam turned to Claris. "Teach the

boys never to play drunk, especially if anyone at the table is sober."

She was to teach. He was leaving tomorrow, and that caused an ache in her chest. He'd been such a pleasant companion and he was very good with the boys.

He turned to Athena. "The current Lord Littlehampton is your nephew, I believe. He seems steady enough. Your family could be a useful connection for Claris and her brothers."

Athena smiled drily. "Make it if you can, you busy boy. I was consigned to darkness for fleeing the blessings of marriage."

"I accept the challenge." He rose. "My apologies, but I must prepare to leave. I bid you all good night."

Claris watched him go. She would not fall into misery over the man.

"As you said, sharp enough to cut," Athena said.

"You had no problem with that until the blade was turned on you."

"Of course not."

"There's nothing amiss with being clever."

"That depends on where the blade is pointed. If my husband had been clever, I'd not have won adequate support from him. He actually bargained to keep Henry, as if I wanted him."

"You must have," Claris protested. "Just a little."

"Rid yourself of this notion of maternal destiny. I felt no more for my son than for any other child, which was little, and I'm not the only mother to feel that way."

"I find that hard to believe. What if he'd died? Would you have felt nothing?"

"I'd have regretted the wasted effort, and especially that my husband would have wanted to try for another." She rose. "Believe what you want. I bid you good night."

Ellie lingered long enough to say, "It's true, dearie. I don't think it's common, but she never gave him a thought as best I could tell."

Alone in the drawing room, Claris put away the cards

and counters. It made no sense to her that a woman could bear a child and feel nothing for it. She'd been entranced by the twins from the first. If someone had tried to take them from her . . . she didn't know what she would have done, but she would have fought with every weapon possible. She'd have bargained away her soul.

She'd even felt fondness for the baby she'd held so briefly today, and for the little boy who'd run to the horses and been captured to safety. Rescued by Perriam, who'd seemed at ease with the lad.

She wanted to think of him as Perry.

Her brothers called him that, so why not?

Because it would be a perilous weakening of the defenses between them.

Did she want to maintain those defenses?

She extinguished most of the candles, keeping one to light the way to her bedchamber. Alice was waiting for her, attending to some needlework. Bells. She must see about bells.

Alice hurried away to get hot water, and Claris undressed herself, her mind still circling, circling. Once she had the water, she sent Alice off to bed.

Then she found the nightgown, the lovely impractical one that Genova had provided, which she'd never worn as yet. She put it on and considered herself in the mirror. It didn't transform her into a siren.

In some way when she was with Perriam—with Perry—she didn't feel so lacking in charms. She rubbed at the freckles across her nose, but they weren't going to come off. She'd not yet plaited her hair and decided to leave it loose. There were no bright threads in it, but it was thick and glossy.

Alice had left out her robe, the pretty mass of pink silk. Claris put it on and tied the ribbon that held it together at the top. She looked in the mirror again.

Better. The warm shade suited her, though she feared it emphasized her freckles as if shining a light on them.

She extinguished the candles except for one and then

sat on the bed's edge, on the side facing the adjoining door.

She knew what she wanted, and thus what she had to do.

Foolish or not, she knew.

It was only a matter of courage.

Chapter 23

He might have already gone to bed, but that seemed unlikely. He had too much energy for an early bedtime.

He probably was dealing with papers, making plans, drawing up lists.

She shouldn't distract him.

But he would leave tomorrow.

The thirty days might bring him back soon, but it might not. Even if he returned in a week this wouldn't be any easier.

She slid down off the bed, rubbed her hands together for a moment, and then walked to the door and rapped her knuckles on it.

The seconds seemed eons, but then it opened.

"You need something?"

He was in shirt and breeches again, the shirt open at the neck and down a few inches. He was in stocking feet. "Claris?"

"Yes," she managed. "Yes, I need something. . . ."

Behind him, she could see papers on his bed and table.

He seemed at a loss, which wasn't surprising. "We can't speak across a threshold like negotiating armies. Your room or mine?"

She backed away and he came in. Why had she imagined she could simply ask, that it could be a practical matter?

"Has something upset you?" he asked. "Would you like some wine, or brandy?"

"No. I'm sorry. I shouldn't have interrupted you. . . . You have ink on your finger."

Why on earth had she said that?

He looked at it and pulled a wry face. "The perils of hasty writing. You haven't interrupted me. The important stuff is done." He took her hand with his ink-stained right one. "So tell me what you need."

She looked into his eyes and blurted out the words. "A baby."

But then she pulled free and turned away, hands over her face. "Oh, I shouldn't ask. I shouldn't. You didn't bargain for that!"

Hands on her shoulders, he turned her to him, then pulled down her screening hands. She squeezed her eyes shut.

"You can't imagine me unwilling."

"Why should you be willing? You agreed to a practical marriage."

"What could be more practical than a baby?"

She risked a look at him.

He didn't seem distressed.

He seemed, perhaps, amused.

"Don't laugh at me!"

"On my honor, I'm not."

"It was never mentioned. I never thought of it, I promise. Until today . . ."

He was holding both her hands now, gently, warmly, firmly. "The cradle?" he asked.

"And other things. Mothers with babies. Athena. She claims not to have loved my father at all."

"You wouldn't be like that."

"I know. I loved the twins from the first. But soon they'll leave. . . . It's unfair to you. You can't want . . ." She tried to pull free, but he tightened his grip.

"What you saw as amusement, Claris, was delight. May I kiss you? I've wanted to kiss you for quite some time."

She stared up at him. "Why?"

"Freckles."

He slid a hand behind her head and drew her to him, pressed his lips to hers.

Claris's heart pounded with sudden anxiety, but with something else—something that came from firm, warm lips on hers. His lips encouraged hers to part, and their breath mingled.

He drew back.

"I hope that shows that I'm more than willing to consummate our marriage, my dear. If you're sure."

If you're sure.

"You said the curse was dead, but is it?"

"There's no surety of anything, but we can't live in fear. I'm certain we face no more risk than any other couple." When she hesitated, he said, "It need not be now. I'll return from Town as soon as possible."

No surety. Life was chancy, and not only for infants. Her healthy mother had died of a sudden fever. Her father had been struck down mid-rant. The thought of Perriam dying made her want to clutch him close, to lock him safely here.

"Is your London life dangerous?" she asked.

"No more than any other man's. The chances of my returning are excellent, Claris."

He was speaking sense and she wasn't, but Claris had come to a realization, enlightened by a kiss. She didn't want only a baby; she wanted the marriage bed. Parts of her had been warmed to growth during this pleasant day and were now unfurling, demanding. . . .

"I want a baby," she said, because it was the only excuse she could speak. "I want to try now."

His smile turned warm. "Thank you." He sobered to say, "I must warn you of one thing, however."

The horrors of the marriage bed.

The pain and mess that her mother had mentioned.

"In other times, in other spheres, I might like to be a true father, but my plans remain the same. I will mostly be in Town and in other places where I am required, even abroad. You will have to raise the child alone."

That hurt, but she found a light tone. "Except for thirty days a year."

"Which are beginning to seem a gift. I do hope hell allows the residents to witness what goes on here. Cousin Giles will be exploding with fury."

It made Claris laugh, but she shook her head at the same time. "You're being kind."

"Not to Cousin Giles."

"To me! About this," she said, gesturing toward the bed.

"My dear, I'm restraining myself from wild enthusiasm for fear of frightening you."

"I know it will be unpleasant."

"Do you?"

"My mother told me, and Athena. . . ."

"Disregard both." He took her hands and kissed them. "It will be pleasant, my word on it. I aspire to more but won't risk breaking my word."

He unfastened the ribbon that held her silk robe together at the front. "I chose this for you because it was pretty, but I had no hope then of enjoying it, on and off."

He eased it off her shoulders and it slithered down her arms, down her body, to the floor, whispering promises.

"Your nightgown is pretty too, and not of my choosing."

With hardly any breath to speak, Claris managed, "Genova."

"Has excellent taste." He led her to the bed, which Alice had already drawn down, then lifted her in his arms and laid her gently there. Her head swam with a sense of weightlessness. "I can go and put on my nightshirt and probably should, but you're an unpredictable woman, my wife. I daren't risk you locking the door. Would you object to nakedness?"

Claris felt extremely odd, lying here in her nightgown,

conversing with a man about nakedness, and she carefully considered her response.

"I'm sure I should, but I'm very curious."

He laughed. "You are a dear delight." He unfastened his cuffs and drew his shirt off over his head.

His look asked a teasing question, and Claris responded in kind. "I've seen no other man's chest, husband, so cannot evaluate."

He laughed again and sat to remove his stockings. When he tossed them aside he sent the same teasing question.

"Your feet seem adequate."

"They get me from place to place." He undid the buckles at the bottom of his breeches and then stood to unfasten the front.

Claris found she'd half-closed her eyes and forced them open as he lowered them and revealed the manly secrets.

A soft swelling and a long thickness.

She'd heard the term "rod."

That sounded painful.

Remember, you want this, she told herself. *You want a baby, and this is the only way.*

He joined her in the bed, pulling the clothes up over both of them. "You're thinking unpleasant thoughts again."

"Please don't worry. I won't mind."

"Idiot," he said and drew her in for another kiss.

Drew her against his nakedness. Thank heavens for her nightgown.

One of his hands cradled her head again, but the other . . . the other wandered. As their breath melded, he stroked down her back, then over her hip, then down her thigh, making her squirm.

His tongue.

Touching hers, teasing hers. Hand touching, teasing. Brain spinning between the two and all places in between. He'd captured her mouth completely now, exploring as his hand pulled up cloth and stroked her thigh. . . .

She tensed, resisted. He broke the kiss. "We're married, remember. This is permitted, even blessed." He rolled her back and his hand slid from thigh to between, to touch.

She flinched.

His hand drew back and worked its way up, up her belly, fingers teasing, the heel of his hand pressing as he scattered light kisses on her chin, her cheeks, her lowered eyelids.

She was bewildered by sensations.

Dazzled.

Then he cradled her breast, brushing her nipple with his thumb.

This time she jerked.

She couldn't help it.

"I'm sorry."

"I'm not. My dear, sweet wife, you're ripe for this. Such a delight. I really do think you should join me in nakedness. You permit?"

"Is it necessary?"

"To be honest, no. But I would like it, very much."

The warmth in his eyes allowed only one answer. "Then as you will."

He sat her up, worked off her nightgown, and tossed it to the floor. Then he lowered the hands she'd raised to cover her breasts. She'd expected to be beneath the covers again, but he kept her there, looking at her.

"Closing your eyes doesn't mean I can't see, you know."

She opened them, glowering, but the teasing warmth in his eyes thawed her and she couldn't help smiling back through her blushes. "This feels wicked." But her heart wasn't in the protest, not with such an expression on his face.

"This feels delicious," he said, looking at her left breast, which was cradled in his hand. "Round, firm, perfect. If you permit . . ."

Without waiting for her consent, he lowered his head

and kissed the top of her breast and then her nipple. Her very sensitive nipple.

She'd felt that sensitivity before sometimes and found it irritating, especially when it joined with a stabbing ache between her thighs. She'd never connected it with this, with the marriage bed. This wasn't irritating. It was ... ecstasy.

He kissed, he licked, he sucked, and that ache between her thighs made her squirm. He laid her back and continued to torment her with pleasure. He put a leg over hers so that her surges of movement met resistance, which seemed to make them worse.

Or better.

She clutched.

His hair.

His hip.

Whatever part she could.

His hand between her thighs again, stroking, pressing, feeding the ache so it spread throughout her body, building, coiling, tighter and tighter.

"You said it wouldn't hurt," she gasped.

"It doesn't," he murmured. "Surrender to it, my lovely. Fly with it."

"How?" she demanded, the ache tightening, her body tense with it. But then it happened. A spasm that tipped pain into pleasure, into pleasure so intense she cried out with it, pressing into his hand, into the whole of him, especially his commanding mouth.

She sank into pure sensation as her body, her wild, unruly body, rippled down from the peak, stroked and pressed by his hand, back into something that could be normality, except that nothing would be normal ever again.

Her heart was still pounding, her breathing passionate, and every bit of her was hot and sweaty. Strangely, she knew how her mother could think such mess and passion unpleasant.

The word "wanton" came to mind.

Yes, indeed, that had been the epitome of wanton.

He was nudging her legs apart, moving over her.

It wasn't done?

No, for she remembered the rod. She could feel it now, as hard as wood pressing against her, where she was still so very sensitive. An ache inside welcomed it, but the sensitive parts shrank back.

He kissed her again and pushed inside her. She felt a sharp pain and then fullness. She opened her legs wider to try to accommodate him, but the fullness pushed deep inside, where the ache had been, was, the ache that wanted this so much.

He pulled out and she thought it done.

Regretted that it was done.

But then he pushed in again, a hand beneath her hip moving her with him, and the knowing ache commanded. She moved with him, finding the rhythm, celebrating the rhythm with fierce necessity. Like a drumbeat it carried her up, up into that ache again, and beyond into red-hot darkness.

She came back slowly, reluctantly, aware of him stroking her hair and murmuring things, sweet things she was sure, but understanding was too much effort.

He was looking at her, a smile in his eyes.

He kissed her again. "What a perfect wife you are."

"Perfect?"

"Hardworking, practical, and passionate. Oh, Giles, how tormented you must be."

She pushed at his chest. "Don't bring him into this."

"My apologies. Very maladroit. You are passionate, my wife, and lovely, and I am a lucky man."

"You don't have to flatter me."

He turned onto his back, taking her with him to lie on top.

"I will flatter you all I wish, but that was pure truth." He tucked her head down on his shoulder and cradled her. "It would be flattery to call you a beauty. Nor are you stylish, elegant, or sophisticated. But you are lovely.

You are also spirited, strong, and courageous. I first admired you for firing that pistol."

She stirred to look up at him. "I could have killed you."

"Precisely." He tucked her back down against his shoulder. "You're kind, generous, and very, very passionate, and those are jewels to me." After a moment he said, "You could perhaps not flatter me in turn?"

Claris smiled. "You too are kind—and sharp enough to cut your own throat."

"Pity me!"

She chuckled. "You have a dozen aspects, but once accustomed, I like each well enough." She stroked his chest, which was more muscled than she'd expected, though she should have known. "Above all, husband, I have come to trust you. That is a jewel to me."

He stroked her hair—such a magical sensation. "You can always trust me, Claris."

He shifted so they could kiss, perhaps their first kiss of that sort—of tender togetherness. But then he moved away from her and climbed out of bed. She felt the chill of his absence but didn't complain. Despite sweet words, theirs was still a practical marriage. Of course he'd return to his bed once they were done.

"I've realized I left my candles burning. A shame to burn the manor down. I'll return if I may? I would like to sleep with you."

Claris knew she was blushing and showing too much pleasure but had no control over it. "Of course."

He soon returned and extinguished the one candle in her room. Then he joined her in the dark, taking her once more in his arms, where she drifted into sleep.

She hadn't expected to share passion again, but they did, deep in the night, then again fell back to sleep entwined.

When she woke to morning light, she was alone. She stroked the pillow still dented from his head, aware of smells that reminded her of what they'd done. Smells that would tell Alice what had happened here. That made her blush, but they were married, after all. As he'd said, their wantonness was blessed.

She put a hand low on her body, wondering if a baby was beginning there. Missing her courses would be the first sign, but she had no idea how likely a baby was after just one night. Some people married and had a child in nine months. Others had to wait longer.

She wanted a baby, but she couldn't help thinking that having to try again and again and again might not be a bitter penance.

Chapter 24

Perhaps she drifted back to sleep. When she next opened her eyes the sunlight seemed brighter. She rolled to look at the mantel clock and sat up sharply.

Gone nine!

The adjoining door was closed.

Had he already left for Town? Surely he wouldn't do that.

She ran to the door, stuck out her head and yelled, "Alice!"

As soon as her maid arrived, bearing a jug of steaming water, Claris demanded, "Has my husband left yet?"

"No, ma'am. I think he's with the steward in the office."

Relief was followed by a spurt of alarm.

Without her?

What to wear? Nothing too showy, but she wanted to look her best. "The green," she said, hurrying to wash.

She was sticky between her legs, and when she washed there, a little blood stained the cloth. She remembered the brief pain forgotten among much pleasure, then wondered what the servants would make of two blood-stained sheets.

She didn't care.

She hurried into her clothes, had her hair simply pinned beneath the cap, and hurried to find her husband. She must see him before he left, but she must also be sure he wasn't usurping her authority now that he was her husband in every way.

He was indeed in the office with Parminter going over some maps.

"Good morning, my dear." His smiling eyes spoke of the night, making her hot all over. "Parminter is seeking instructions about an area needing better drainage. I happily hand all decisions on to you."

The steward's tight face told the story. He'd come here early because he'd heard the lord and master was to leave, and he'd hoped to have the decision made by him. This would be a battle, but she was ready for it.

"Of course I'll take care of the matter, but it must wait until I've attended to your departure. My apologies, Mr. Parminter."

"I am at your disposal, ma'am," the man said, looking more unhappy than angry. She hoped to win his approval, but if not, he'd have to go.

"When must you set out?" she asked her husband as they left the room.

"Soon." He took her hand, and it was the sweetest sensation. "I've sent for a chaise. I'll leave Othello here but send my groom for him. He's a proud Town horse and will pine if left too long in the country."

Like you, she thought. "You rode him here from Cheynings. Why not ride him today?"

"I like to ride, but the chaise will be faster."

In such a hurry to return to his real life. She twined her fingers with his, but knew she'd never hold him here.

"I've written to the bank and lawyers giving you the necessary powers, and asking them to call on you here at their earliest convenience. Remember, they are yours to command, but they're good men, so you should heed their advice."

This was the authority he'd promised, but now it frightened her. She wouldn't admit it, as much for his sake as hers. He needed to return to his life in London.

She wouldn't tie him here. She was handling Parminter, so she could deal with the rest.

They'd arrived in the hall and the footman stood ready. That didn't deter Perriam from raising her hand and kissing it. "I truly regret having to leave so soon."

He seemed sincere. True or not, she welcomed the words and hoped they were true, at least a little.

"I regret it too. I hope your journey is smooth and your Town business prospers...." She took the risk. "Perry."

"I like that." The warmth in his eyes seemed so real. Could she send him on his way with a kiss?

"Your chaise arrives, sir."

Devil take the footman, chaise, horses, and all.

They went outside and she saw a light chaise drawing up, harnessed with four horses—an extravagance needed to race him to Town.

He'd made no pretense, she reminded herself. She wouldn't complain.

His valet was organizing the disposition of two trunks and a leather bag.

"Will you write?"

Claris looked at him. She'd been afraid to ask the same of him. "Of course. You'll want to know about the estate."

"I'll want to know about you."

The baby. Even though he'd have little to do with it, it would be his, perhaps a boy and thus his heir.

"And about the twins," he said. "I haven't forgotten the matter of a tutor. I'll attend to that immediately. I'll even welcome news of your grandmother and Miss Gable—will they go adventuring again and such."

The loading was complete and the valet was entering the chaise.

"You won't have time to read such long letters."

"I'll find time. Adieu, my dear." She thought he might kiss her as she longed to be kissed, but his lips only brushed her cheek. Then he walked to the chaise with that light, energetic step that made her think *gadfly* but also *spring steel*.

As soon as he was inside and the door closed, the postilions set the horses into motion. Claris watched until the chaise was out of sight, and might have lingered, watching the place where she'd last seen it, had she been so foolish.

She made herself turn back toward the house.

She wouldn't mope over his leaving. She wouldn't.

She had work to do here, good work, and with God's blessing she'd soon have a child to pass Perriam Manor to in due course. She would build a future for her family and for the whole area.

That should be enough to satisfy any woman.

Chapter 25

Perry generally read on coach journeys, but his mind wouldn't attend to his book, and really, did he care about the history of the Carolingians? He couldn't imagine why he'd purchased it.

He should apply his mind to some matters that awaited him in Town, but it lingered at Perriam Manor, on his wife and her inexperience in estate management, on Parminter's hostility. In truth he couldn't stop thinking about her.

Especially about their extraordinary night.

He knew the skills and tricks of making love to a woman, but he'd never had a wife before—an inexperienced and even naive wife. He'd been cautious and gentle. He'd not expected flaring passion.

Perhaps her aunt Clarrie hadn't been a duped innocent, but a woman driven by passion into folly. Hard to imagine Giles as such a lure, but he'd been a handsome gallant decades ago.

He wondered where the affair had taken place and whether he could find people who remembered it. The curse raised questions too, especially now that he knew Clarrie was supposed to have been so good.

He smiled wryly, acknowledging his addiction to solving puzzles. He was skilled at it, which made him useful to others, but he sometimes pursued a mystery for his own amusement. He generally kept any results to himself, for puzzles often covered scandals.

The scandal in Claris's family seemed obvious, but the pieces didn't quite fit.

Henry Mallow, once Giles's associate in sin, ending his days as a ranting rector who'd married the least likely wife.

Harpy Mallow—the bitter, angry woman who'd tried to blackmail Giles into marrying her young daughter. Mad and bad, but there was more to it, he was sure.

Good sense said that these matters were all in the past, but Claris worried about the curse. Now there was the possibility of a child, the curse troubled him too. His logical mind scoffed, but those marble memorials were haunting.

Devil take it, if he was going to busy himself with this, he should have questioned Claris about her childhood and her parents. Did she still have anything that held a clue? He'd do that next time he visited the manor.

An excuse . . .

He didn't need one. Giles's will compelled him. *Thank you, Giles.*

He forced his mind to the problems ahead. The sooner they were dealt with, the sooner he'd be free to return.

Before Giles's summons, he and Cyn had been yoked together to investigate leaks of military information from both the Admiralty and Horse Guards. They hadn't made much progress, largely because of his absences, but discovering the traitors must have priority on his return.

The peace with France was only two years old, yet threat of a new war hung like warning clouds. There'd recently been French naval activity off Canada, Africa, and the West Indies. As the British government had unwisely reduced funding once the war was over, the navy was vulnerable. It was highly undesirable that the French learned how much so. The army had also suffered, and the French were interfering again in Canada and the American colonies.

Despite the problems, or perhaps because of them, he smiled. His blood ran faster when in pursuit of solutions at the very heart of power in the greatest city in the world.

Pleasant days at Perriam Manor and even the passionate night with his wife faded as his mind focused ahead.

He'd always known how it must be.

Claris would not let herself mope, not least because Athena would notice and make a caustic comment. She returned to Parminter and let him educate her about drainage. She approved some of the work he recommended but put other suggestions aside for consideration.

Now Perry had left, the man seemed to have accepted defeat. His manner wasn't warm and he sometimes spoke as if she were ignorant, but she knew she was.

She also knew her abilities.

She could and would learn.

Next she settled to establishing the manor's income and expenses. She needed to know how much she could spend on the improvements she wanted to make. When she was satisfied with the numbers, the excess income seemed huge, but she knew it wouldn't be. She would have to manage carefully.

She was keen to get to work on the future, but first she must deal with the past—with the belongings brought from Lavender Cottage. She discovered that the boxes and bundles had been put in an unused bedroom. When her brothers returned from the stables, she insisted that they assist her.

"In case there's anything you particularly want."

"There won't be," Peter said. "It's all rubbish."

That hurt, even though it was probably true.

When it came to it, he was mostly correct. For some reason Tom wanted a three-legged stool. Perhaps simply to balance that, Peter asked for their father's Bible. It was a large, leather-bound volume, much worn with use.

Claris would have preferred to have nothing of her

parents' in her new life, but she'd said the boys could keep what they wanted, and what was she to do with it otherwise? To give or throw away such a thing would be peculiar, especially when her father had recorded his children's dates of birth in it. To burn it might be sacrilegious.

Her brothers left and she considered the remainder. She wished she could wave her hand and make it disappear, for most of it shrieked of their poverty, but in the end she sent for the housekeeper.

"We have no further use for all this, Mistress Eavesham, so kindly dispose of it. There are a few items that might be of use to the servants or people in the village. A clock, a tea service, some glassware."

With that, she left and hoped never to see any of it again. There were many things to be done, but first she wanted to learn more about her new home, so she prowled the manor, growing more familiar with it, noting facilities and problems, trying not to think about the man who was no longer here.

That was hard to do when his place was empty when they dined. Peter and Tom asked when Perry would return. Claris made no false promises. She said she didn't know.

Work was the thing. After dinner she summoned the Eaveshams to the drawing room to discuss her observations of the house. They took suggestions of improvements as criticism.

To appease them, she said, "I know Mr. Giles Perriam was rarely here and cared little for Perriam Manor."

"That's true, ma'am," Eavesham said.

"There are modern parts. My bedchamber and this room."

"That's the first wife's work, ma'am," Mistress Eavesham said. "The second liked Town as much as the master. And the third . . ."

It was as if shadows seeped into the room.

The poor, tragic third.

"It's time to correct any problems," Claris said firmly. "I've seen some damp on the ceiling of one of the bed-chambers, and I don't like the feel of the floorboards near the storage attic." She saw the butler stiffen and the housekeeper bridle, but she wouldn't apologize. "I'm sure you've done your best, but it must have been difficult when no one would spend enough money."

They both relaxed a little, and Eavesham spoke. "That's true, ma'am. We did try, but ..." He shook his head, perhaps unwilling to put the complaint into words. "The most serious concern is the possibility of beetle in an attic joist. I told Mr. Parminter, who told the master—"

"Mr. Giles," Claris corrected. She wasn't sure if that was the proper term, but she wanted no confusion.

"Yes, ma'am. He didn't care."

"He was dying."

"Yes, ma'am. But he never cared."

"I care. This is now my home and I intend that it be a pleasant one. I'll authorize Parminter to see to the beetle and have the damp and floorboards investigated. Do you know of anything else?"

After a moment, Mistress Eavesham said, "A number of the hangings are moth-eaten, ma'am. We do our best, but ..."

"I understand. Unused rooms are hard to maintain. Now the ivy's gone, the windows must be cleaned, inside and out, and inspected at the same time—the leading and the wooden frames. The brickwork should also be checked."

"Very wise, ma'am," Eavesham said, "but Mr. Parminter must put that in hand."

Delineation of duties. She'd rather deal with the Eaveshams than with Parminter, but she wouldn't be frightened of anything.

"Very well. You must let me know of any other improvements you think necessary, even if they're only to make life here more pleasant. Also, we must hire a man to act as valet to my brothers. A man over thirty, of a steady nature. Is there anyone local? He need not be skilled in the valeting part."

"I will inquire, ma'am," Eavesham said, and they left.

Claris blew out a breath. They were still reserved, but that's how it must be, mistress to servants. In any case, the Eaveshams were too old to be friends. The maids of an age with her were Deborah and Alice. She'd frequently caught the housemaid looking at her oddly, and Alice would soon return to Cheynings.

She went to her room and added to her list.

Find lady's maid.

She'd rather do without, but her dignity demanded it. She noted down the discussion with the Eaveshams and then recapped her inkpot. She'd taken the first steps. Soon Perriam Manor would be a comfortable home, for herself and for the child she was determined to have.

Perry arrived at his home near St. James's at three in the afternoon, feeling all the usual satisfaction. His rooms were spacious, elegantly furnished, and staffed by a footman, a man-cook, and two lads of all work, so that his every need was catered to.

The building, officially called the Lyceum, was for gentlemen only and colloquially known as the Knaves' Palace. In part this was because it sat next to an excellent inn called the Knave of Spades, which served as a club for the inhabitants, but the reputation of the inhabitants added to it.

Women weren't allowed in the Lyceum, but pretty wenches were plentiful in the Knave, along with good food and drink.

Normally when Perry arrived home without warning he went to the Knave for a beefsteak or chops. He'd often meet other Palace residents and catch up on the latest on-dits. He'd no mind for chattering company now, however, and a number of letters and invitations to deal with, so he sent his footman to bring food in.

His principal correspondents had known to send letters to the manor, so he wrote three quick letters to announce his return to Town and dispatched them by his lads. That done, he glanced through a pile of invitations, sorting them according to importance and promise of entertainment.

Lastly he looked through the letters. One was from his sister, Georgia, so when his food arrived he sat to read it as he ate.

Georgie's style was lively, and her unlikely adventures as a country wife always amused. He laughed at her description of being chased by geese that seemed to think it their job to guard the orchard. She still seemed content with her rural life. He hoped her idyll lasted, but he had some doubts. Georgia had delighted in Town as much as he.

In fact she concluded the letter with a threat to flee back to Town, but he knew she wouldn't unless her beloved Dracy came with her. As Genova had said, love was the very devil, and frequently drove people mad. Oddly, lovers seemed to revel in the insanity. Cyn could be idiotic about his Chastity. Even the haughty Lord Rothgar was besotted with his wife, and she with him.

He finished the letter and put it aside. Georgia had made her choice and must live with it, especially now that she was expecting a child.

He remembered that Athena Mallow had borne a child and then fled the marriage. Georgia was of a different stamp, thank God. She'd be a loving mother.

If she survived.

He pushed that aside. Most women survived the ordeal.

Even Giles's wives had escaped death in childbed. Infants were less robust, but with good care . . .

Presumably Queen Anne's offspring had had the best care, but only one had lived long enough to be hopeful, and he'd died, leaving her childless at death.

As antidote, he thought of the Earl of Royland. He had thirteen children and never one lost. The king and queen were also producing healthy children at a good rate, as was his brother's shrewish wife.

Claris would do as well, and she had everything else she wanted for a happy life.

He rang for the food to be taken away and coffee brought, and then read the other letters.

Richard Protherby could be depended upon for amusing Oxford gossip. Jeanne de Lely chattered about Versailles. Silly stuff—nearly everything about Versailles was—but her delicious charm came through. Perhaps it was time for a visit to Versailles.

He was a married man now.

It was a practical marriage, but even so.

Mark Killmore's pages from Ireland were mostly complaints about the weather. Cate Burgoyne's from Yorkshire were too much about sheep rearing, though it was pleasant to see that he was still happy in his marriage—especially as his bride was as unlikely as Claris and also found in poverty. Prudence had risen to the challenge of becoming a countess, so Claris should be able to cope with a smaller transformation.

A rapping on the door brought him out of his thoughts. Who?

Then he recognized the voice. Devil take it. He'd hoped to escape a face-to-face discussion with his father for a while.

The Earl of Hernescroft stalked in, impeded in dignity by fat thighs, above which his belly swelled. His jowly face was red with anger, as it often was.

"What do you mean by it, sir? What do you mean?"

"Perriam Manor?" Perry said, hoping a calm manner would pour oil on stormy seas. "Won't you be seated, Father? May I offer you wine, brandy, tea?"

"*Tea?*" his father bellowed, as Perry knew he would. "Women's pap. Brandy, and I hope it's good."

Perry ignored that. No one had cause to doubt the quality of all he selected. He poured the brandy into a fine glass and took it to his father, who'd sat wide legged

in the center of the settee with the demeanor of a monarch on a throne.

The earl sipped the brandy and nodded, but he still
scowled. "Explain yourself, sir! Perriam Manor was to
have come to me or to Pranksworth."

His father probably expected him to stand like a
naughty schoolboy, but Perry sat back at the table and
crossed his legs, hoping to look at ease.

"Have you read the original pact, Father?"

"What?"

"From 1541."

"Course not. Damned scribble."

"I read the copy at the manor. Assuming it to be accurate, it was carelessly phrased, at least on our side. It
doesn't specify that the manor must pass to the head of
our line, only to the line. Giles Perriam was within his
rights to will it to me."

"Was he, by gad? Underhanded, as anyone would
expect. It can be amended, however. You now pass it
on to me."

"As I explained in my letter, sir, his will specifically
forbids that."

"The legal men will sort that out." But then his father's eyes narrowed. "Fancy it for yourself? Can't see
why, since you've always moaned about the countryside."

"No, I don't fancy it for myself, Father, but legal pro-
ceedings are expensive."

His father grunted, but that would have hit home. The
earldom was wealthy, but it was the wealth of land and
possessions that couldn't easily be sold. Ready money
was scarce at the moment, in part because his father had
indulged in some unwise lawsuits, and also because of
Arthur's gaming debts.

"There's no need to go to that expense," Perry said.
"Nothing in Giles's will bars me from leaving Perriam
Manor to you."

"I expected to see it in my lifetime." Did his slit-eyed
look anticipate Perry's early death, or even wish that

he'd take out a pistol and conveniently shoot himself? "It must be done immediately," his father stated. "Knowing your feckless ways, I'll take care of it. Babcock will bring your new will here tomorrow. Be sure you sign it!"

Perry hoped he kept his anger concealed, and his alarm.

Claris.

She expected the manor to be hers, and he'd promised her that. If he predeceased her, his father would be able to throw her out and was capable of doing so.

As if picking up on his thoughts, his father said, "So you married a nobody. In keeping, in keeping."

"Am I to be chastised for that too? It was the only way."

"Mallow. Mallow. Who's heard of Mallows?"

"A respectable gentry family," Perry said, and played a trump. "Her grandmother is a Littlehampton."

His father did straighten at that. "Is she, begad?"

"Though estranged from her family."

"Never say it's Athena Littlehampton!"

"Bad as that?" Perry said, but with a deliberate smile to lighten the atmosphere. "I'd like to hear your account of her in her younger days. She's a formidable presence now. She's in residence at the manor, along with my wife."

"I've a mind to visit the place."

'Struth, had his father and Athena had a relationship in the past? That was only one of many reasons to prevent the visit.

"I'll willingly take you there, Father, as soon as I'm able."

"Why not now?"

"Have pity, sir. I've only just arrived and am much in demand."

"Your wenching and gaming can wait."

Perry bit back anger and played a trump. "I'm summoned to the king." That wasn't strictly true, but Perry expected it to be as soon as Rothgar heard he was back.

"Why?"

His father was not a stupid man, but he disliked using his brain. He chose to believe that Perry's life was given to pleasure apart from the occasional matters he handled for the earldom. Perry riffled through possible explanations and chose one that had the virtue of being mostly true.

"Among my sinecures is a position in the Admiralty. There are some irregularities there and it's thought I might have insight."

"Never say you're under suspicion!"

Perry sighed. "No, Father. In fact, I'm considered particularly trustworthy."

Did every son feel a slight desire for parental approval, no matter how unlikely that might be?

"Odd," his father said. "How trustworthy is your effort to block that canal, I ask you?"

"The canal is supported by men as powerful as you, Father. I can't work miracles."

"Can't work at all; that's the problem. Idle flibbertigibbet, and if you've a mind to keeping Perriam Manor for yourself . . ."

A tap on the door saved Perry from a sharp retort.

The footman entered with a letter.

Rothgar's seal.

"If I may . . . ?" Perry said, and his father grunted permission.

Perry snapped the seal, unfolded the paper, and read. He was to report to Malloren House with all speed.

He refolded it, saying, "I must go out soon, Father. I have a copy of Giles's will if you care to read it. He went to lengths to make our way difficult."

"I'll go odds he did! Do we have Perriam Manor now, I ask you? Beyond all question?"

"We do, sir. I've made the required marriage. The only other condition is that I spend thirty days and nights there a year. You see that Giles knew how much I would dislike that."

"See you keep that condition or I'll have you flayed." The earl drained his glass and stood. "There would have been better ways to handle it, but what's done is done. When you receive your new will tomorrow, sign it immediately. I don't want to lose the manor through you falling in with ruffians on one of your adventures."

Once he'd gone, Perry blew out a breath. Any interview with his father was an ordeal, but that had been the worst.

And what about Claris?

He could defy his father over the will, but that way lay ruin. His father couldn't take away the money that had come to him at twenty-one, but that was a small part of the whole. The rest was at his father's will, and he wouldn't hesitate to stop the allowance if displeased. Even the sinecure positions had been arranged by his father and could be as easily disarranged.

It wasn't only that. The need to restore Perriam Manor to the earldom ran in his blood. It should be so.

But Claris . . .

He shook his head. He'd find a way to untangle that Gordian knot, but later.

For now, he must make haste to Malloren House.

Chapter 26

He should have changed out of his traveling clothes as soon as he arrived. Now he weighed the delay of changing against the effect of presenting himself at Malloren House in country wear. Neither he nor Rothgar would consider his clothing significant as long as he wore some, but he might in truth be carried on to an audience with the king. It would not be a formal audience, but all the same, there were requirements.

"Auguste! The light blue with braid."

He hurried to his bedchamber to strip and wash, and then dressed in clean linen and shirt. He added a neck-cloth trimmed with particularly fine lace and fixed it in place with a sapphire-headed pin. Auguste, with his excellent instinct, had selected clocked stockings rather than plain, but simple black shoes with silver buckles.

The suit was made of fine wool rather than silk or velvet, and only trimmed with bronze braid, but the style was elegant and the waistcoat embroidered with bronze flowers finished it off perfectly.

Perry chose a lace-trimmed handkerchief and a braided three-cornered hat and approved the whole. He didn't have only Rothgar and the king to consider. In his journey to Malloren House he could encounter any number of people and he had a reputation to uphold.

He left the Lyceum and walked briskly on his way. The midsummer heat was only a memory, so the stink of Town was lessened to a level a true Londoner scarcely noticed. Odd that he noticed it now. The perils of country living.

Countrymen deplored the crowds and noise, but the bustle and crowds lightened Perry's step. He was frequently hailed by both men and women. Every encounter promised good company by day or night, but he exchanged only the briefest words, promising more later.

Much of fashionable London consisted of modern terraced houses, but Malloren House was a mansion from the previous century, set in a square built by one of Lord Rothgar's ancestors. Malloren House stood apart from the terraces on either side and was in the old style. It had a front courtyard protected by high, spiked railings, and was entered through guarded gates, one for carriages, one for pedestrians and sedan chairs.

Old-fashioned, but such protection could have been useful in the summer riots when the mob had rampaged, particularly enjoying smashing the windows of noblemen they thought offensive. Some had even sought to invade the grand houses, and a few had succeeded.

He entered through the smaller gate and crossed the courtyard to the steps. The porter who sat in an alcove there alerted those inside, and the door opened to admit him.

He was taken to Rothgar's private study, which lay in what Perry thought of as the business part of the house. Most of the work done here concerned the administration of the marquessate, but a considerable part involved matters of state.

The king of France had a secret ministry to do his bidding, which the official ministry did not. Perry didn't think Rothgar's work was on that scale, but he knew the king relied on him for independent information and advice.

The marquess was a tall, dark-haired man in his thirties. He could dress magnificently when necessary but today wore a plain dark blue suit, discreetly ornamented.

"Your country business went well?" It could be seen as courteous, but there was a mild reproach in it.

"Very well, and very essentially," Perry said, taking the chair to which he was waved.

A twitch of the marquess's lips acknowledged the correction.

"It involved marriage?"

"Which won't interfere with my work."

"I wish you well of that," said Rothgar drily, "but if you are free, that is all to the good."

"We still don't know who's responsible for the leaks?"

"No. I've had spurious information fed into both Horse Guards and the Admiralty. It emerged into French hands, but the channel remains unclear. Your position in the Admiralty should enable you to detect likely suspects there."

"My position? I go there a few times a year. Won't daily dabblings raise questions?"

"If the guilty parties are alarmed, they'll make mistakes."

"I'll be cast out of the best clubs for actually applying myself to a sinecure." Perry was only half joking.

"Perhaps you'll set a mode. Too many live idly."

"Are you turning leveler?"

Rothgar smiled. "I enjoy my eminence too much. If anyone questions your attention to duty, claim it to be a wager."

Perry laughed. "Anything's accepted on those terms. Even Casper Fanshaw spending a week playing hostler at the Swan with Two Necks."

"At least that young idiot gained a taste of real work. Now we must go to the king. For some reason he's taking an interest in our inquiries, and he's particularly requested your complete application."

"I'm honored," Perry said, insincerely. That way lay a dense bramble thicket.

King George was behaving oddly these days, and with the heir a young child, monarchical derangement could be ruinous. In the spring, the drawing up of a Regency Act had led to the fall of a ministry and deep divisions.

Thank heavens that wasn't a problem anyone expected him to solve.

"You shouldn't have been so proficient," Rothgar said.

Perry spread his hands. "My failing."

A few weeks ago the king had summoned him to a private audience and ordered him to find the person who was making screeching noises in St. James's Palace.

"Trying to rattle me," he'd said, his rather bulbous eyes twitching. "Factions. I know what they're about."

He was right about the factions. A number of powerful men were secretly forming possible regency administrations, and it might suit some to drive the king mad. Unfortunately, the king had been the only one hearing the noises.

By sheer chance, Perry had presented an elaborate explanation of cats and mice just as the king ceased hearing the shrieks and whines. He'd been hailed as hero, and now, it seemed, was expected to achieve miracles at every turn.

"His majesty is in good health?" he asked delicately.

Rothgar was inscrutable. "The birth of a new son has greatly cheered him, but he's rationally determined that France gain no advantage through espionage. Cyn will accompany us."

Rothgar rang a bell. When a footman entered, he was sent to alert Cyn.

"I assume he's having no more success at Horse Guards?"

"He has a list of suspects, but it's too long."

Cyn soon arrived, dressed in the full glory of his military uniform. He gave Perry a wry smile. "Are you sure you prefer Town life to rural simplicity?"

"I'm having my doubts."

They traveled to St. James's Palace in a coach. The king lived in the Queen's House, which had once been Buckingham House, but he attended to state business elsewhere. He was oddly domestic, preferring a quiet life with his wife and children to fashionable revels.

That would be admirable in an ordinary man, but it was less so in a monarch. King Louis might have the better idea—keep the rich and powerful under close scrutiny in the magnificence of Versailles, and busy them with protocol and pleasure.

Perry certainly didn't blame the king for not wanting to live in St. James's Palace, which dated back as far as Perriam Manor but was even more of a dusty warren. The king received them in a paneled room that managed to be chilly despite being small and having a fire in the hearth.

"Married, eh?" the king asked Perry, clearly attempting to be jovial.

Perry bowed again. "Yes, Your Majesty."

"Excellent, excellent. We would wish all our young men safely within domestic life."

"May I congratulate you, sir, on the recent safe arrival of a son?"

"You may, you may! I wish you the same satisfaction, in good time, of course, eh?"

Not inside nine months, in other words.

With Cyn, the king went straight to business. "How go things at Horse Guards, eh?"

"As before, sir."

The king pouted, but he must be in control of his wits, for he simply turned to Perry. "I hope for better from you, Perriam."

Was he supposed to produce the traitor out of thin air? If he didn't would the king's wits be turned? Sadly there was something a little odd about him, even now.

"I will do my best, sir."

"Indeed, indeed, but with care, eh? Need to find the right man or men. Can't have innocent men cast under a shadow, eh?"

"Assuredly not, sir."

"Excellent, excellent! Find the true culprits, gentlemen, and we'll gladly see them hang."

Perry and Cyn were dismissed, but Rothgar was kept behind.

"Not even for our ears," Cyn murmured as they passed the guards and made their way out of the palace. "I need to bring you up to date. Your place or Malloren House?"

"Mine's closest," Perry said. Once they were out of earshot of anyone, he said, "He's not well."

Dangerous to say whom, but Cyn would understand.

"No. Often says odd things, such as that babble about innocent men."

"A perfectly reasonable sentiment, but it worries me."

"Why?"

"Perhaps he has a particular man in mind, one he wants to be innocent."

"Oh, devil take it."

"Quite. I can bear losing His Majesty's favor, but I don't want to be the one who brings him news bad enough to turn his wits."

Chapter 27

Claris flung herself into work and didn't think of her husband more than once or twice a day.

The nights were different. She often lay awake remembering, and not just their lovemaking. That mad sword fight in the attic. His kind firmness with the boys. His arms around her amid the smothered babes.

She still hadn't thought of a solution there.

She received the first letter two days after his departure and took it to her room to read in privacy. Athena protested, demanding news of Town, so later Claris shared those parts. Perhaps Perry understood how it would be, for he'd included gossip and mention of titled people Claris could not know.

She wrote back, wishing she could make her letters as amusing. He couldn't be the slightest bit interested in drainage and treatment for the beetle, but that seemed all she had to say. She had the boys write short letters to include. That should lighten the whole.

His reply came a few days later, with a separate note for each twin. Of course he would realize that a letter each would thrill them.

Four days after Perry's departure, a one-horse chair came up the drive. Claris thought it brought a guest, but it was driven by a groom who announced it was for the use of Mistress Perriam. The contraption made her very nervous, but she set to learn to drive.

Chestnut, the horse, was very well mannered, and

driving proved much less frightening than riding. Soon she could drive herself confidently to the village and back. Then, accompanied by the groom, she drove over to visit the Fosses, arriving flushed with triumph.

After that she could take Athena and Ellie on visits. There were a number to make as local families came to call. Claris did find the Fosses' daughter, Jane Jordan, particularly congenial and began to tentatively hope for a friendship there.

Each letter from Perry became a precious moment, but she wished they sometimes contained something personal. He never wrote about his family or about special friends. In truth, she could have read the letters to Athena and Ellie as soon as she broke the seal, for they contained nothing personal at all.

The letters were probably an onerous duty, but she wouldn't let him off the hook. She replied to each one, thus demanding one in return.

Then a letter told her to expect Lionel Lovell, who would tutor the twins, subject to her approval. Perry listed impressive qualifications, adding that Lovell was well suited to a temporary post because in a few months he was to be secretary to the new ambassador to Poland.

Lovell was only twenty-two, and Claris hoped he'd be able to manage her brothers. Their new freedom and status were making them unruly, and they wrapped their valet, Matthew Greenwell, around their fingers despite his being nearly forty.

She'd been insisting that they sit at desks in their newly prepared schoolroom with some books gleaned from the library, but she couldn't force them to learn. She certainly couldn't test them on Latin and Greek.

When Lovell arrived, she knew he'd been chosen with care. He was a stocky man, very robust and active, but also with bright-eyed intelligence. He came armed with a box of carefully chosen texts and insisted on immediately testing the twins. Claris saw that they longed to rebel but knew they'd met their match. No, their master.

Claris wrote to thank Perry.

"The twins were disgruntled at first, but Mr. Lovell has won them over by interspersing study with outdoor activities. He takes them riding but insists they speak Greek all the way. He's teaching them about a game called cricket, but only if they both produce a perfect Latin exercise. I thank you for finding him."

She added some details of estate management before signing it, as always, *"Your affectionate wife, Claris."*

It would be more conventional to write "your loving wife," but she couldn't do that. She liked her husband, and she'd liked their marriage bed, very much indeed, but to claim love, no matter how conventionally, would be untrue. How could she love someone she'd known for so few days? Affection, however—that she could honestly claim.

She wished that he'd sign a little more warmly than *"Your servant."* They'd made an agreement, however, and he was doing his part and more, so she must be content.

He seemed to pick up on any little thing she said. When she wrote about a particular sort of fire iron she'd admired at Jane Jordan's, a similar set arrived within days. It had been only a passing comment. Her main purpose had been to tell him that she was visiting neighbors and finding congenial companions. In other words, that she was perfectly content without him.

It was a lie. She pinned her hopes on his having to spend some days here to fulfill the terms of the will.

That requirement was one thing to lay to Giles Perriam's credit. She'd found nothing else. He'd been a careless owner of the manor and a more than careless husband. By now the servants had relaxed enough to sometimes mention his flaws.

Until his last illness, he'd visited the manor only in the company of cronies—disreputable cronies who drank till they puked, assaulted the servants, and broke things for amusement. His poor last wife, Lydia, had been terrified by his visits, and the servants had concealed her to keep her safe.

Apparently Giles had never even asked after her except to once say, "Still alive, is she, the bitch?"

She wished he were still alive to be beaten till bloody. And there was a silly thought all around!

When not indulging in foolish thoughts about Perriams, she was making good progress on the house. The beetle problem had been corrected. The damp had been caused by deteriorating leading, so that had been repaired. New hangings and curtains were being made for one room, but elsewhere a thorough cleaning and some darning had done the job.

Athena disdained such economy.

Claris retorted that she'd not waste money. She wished her grandmother would find some occupation other than observing and criticizing.

At Lavender Cottage, Athena had worked hard at her herbs and potions, but she showed no interest in such work here. She read books and wrote letters. She received replies and sometimes shared gossip from them. Apart from an occasional walk around the grounds, she took no exercise.

Claris reminded herself that for all her briskness, her grandmother was an old woman. If she wanted to sit with her feet up for most of the day, she must be allowed to do so.

Ellie certainly didn't want to. As at the cottage, Claris hardly ever saw her sitting down. She accompanied Athena on her strolls but also took brisk walks alone. She seemed to move easily between the servants' hall and the main house and was liked by all.

When Claris decided to conduct a thorough inventory of the attic in order to find anything of use, Ellie plunged in with enthusiasm. They found a number of pieces of furniture that could be used with only cleaning or minor repairs. Each was a triumph, but by agreement, they didn't share that with Athena. There were a number of chests full of this and that, and they left those for later.

Next they attacked the great number of narrow cupboards around the house and found them all packed with linens.

When confronted, the housekeeper was defensive. "We were never given instructions about whether to mend or discard, ma'am, so we put things away."

Claris assured her that she held no blame, but later Ellie wasn't so forgiving.

"A housekeeper should make such decisions. What's happened is that no one fancied mending when they've been allowed to buy new. They sit idle in the servants' hall when they could be mending."

"A little rest is allowed," Claris said, "but I want to sort out what we have. And yes, I will expect some mending. Let's go and explore that one at the end of the west corridor. I think it's the oldest."

They unloaded all the shelves of sheets, pillowcases, shifts, and nightgowns.

"So much," Claris said. "But at least everything was stored with herbs. We'll test each for thin places. If any are sturdy, we might find a use for them."

She took a sheet, shook it open, and saw only a tear. "With a patch this would be good as new."

Ellie took it from her. "But not good enough for the house, dearie. The servants would appreciate such things. They all have families locally who'd make good use of them."

A lifetime of frugality made Claris reluctant, but she saw the sense of it. There was no need for family or guests to sleep on a patched sheet.

"Make a pile for the servants, then, and another for rags. I still haven't quite the knack of being the lady of the manor, Ellie. It's as if I'm acting a part, a part I don't really know."

"Then you're acting it well, dearie."

Claris picked up a pillowcase. "I should be more like Athena."

"Not a bit of it. This isn't a grand place, and there's no

call for grand airs. Anyway, there's never any point in trying to deceive servants. To them you're a respectable clergyman's daughter who fell on hard times but has always been a lady through and through."

Claris lowered her voice. "It's as well no one here knew the respectable clergyman!"

Ellie chuckled. "I certainly thank the Lord I never had the pleasure."

Claris decided to ask a question that had been troubling her. "Ellie, why are the servants here so cold with me?"

"Cold?"

"Perhaps reserved. They don't smile. They seem afraid of me. I've given them no cause."

"A new mistress, that's all. Are you putting that on the rag pile?"

Claris looked at the pillowcase, which she'd just ripped with ease because it was so thin. "It would be an insult to imply this was of value."

"The ends are still sound, and embroidered. They could make a child's cap."

Claris put it on the servants' pile. "I thought I'd known poverty, but I haven't."

"Rags are riches to some, and what are you to do with the rags? Burn them?"

"You see more clearly than I. Very well, two piles only. Good enough for the house as they are, and the rest. The servants can sort through those and use as they wish. It'll have to be done fairly, though."

"See, I'd not thought of that. I can supervise that if you want."

"If you don't mind. They'll be more comfortable with you."

"It'll all sort out in time, dearie."

Claris wasn't so sure, but she let the matter drop, embarrassed by her own neediness. She picked up another piece of cloth. "A sheet, but small."

"For a child's bed. Well used."

By which child or children? One of Giles's? No, these

linens probably predated Giles, but she wondered what eerie memories the other cupboards might hold. She could never entirely avoid the smothered babes, even though she avoided that side of the house and rarely looked out from her window.

She cocked her head. "Wheels?"

She hurried to a front-facing window and looked out. "An elegant carriage," she called back to Ellie, "with a liveried footman behind. Not the Fosses. Someone new."

Perhaps the carriage was bringing someone else to be a friend, and here she was in one of her plainer dresses, probably dusty to boot. She shouted for Alice and fled to her room. There was still water in the jug and she washed her face and hands. Her hair was untidy. Her maid rushed in.

"A cap. My best!"

She took off her apron and inspected her gown for marks. All was well. She grabbed the cap and pinned it in place.

"Jewelry box!"

She added earrings and a seed pearl bracelet.

"The silk fichu!"

Her gown wasn't low, but the fichu would lend elegance. She fixed it carefully with the bar brooch Genova had given her, took a deep breath, and hurried out. She made it to the middle landing of the staircase as the door opened.

The guests' liveried footman entered first and announced, "Lady Bigelow, Miss Youngman, and Mistress Foxell-Smith!"

Claris had to bite her lips. It was as if they were an embassy from the East!

As she went down the stairs, she remembered some comments Lady Fosse had made about Lady Bigelow. Lady Fosse didn't stoop to criticism, but Claris had gained the impression that Lady Bigelow had airs above her station. She was the wife of a sugar merchant who had purchased their estate, Esham Court, only three years previously.

Claris reminded herself that she had no reason to look down on people for their origins and that it was very unchristian to do so. Lady Bigelow might be a comfortable companion.

She greeted her guests and took them up to the drawing room, ordering that tea be brought there. She already doubted Lady Bigelow would become a friend. She was young and round faced and could have been pretty but for a downturned mouth. Miss Youngman was a better prospect, for she had a ready smile. From the resemblance, she was Lady Bigelow's sister so probably was only visiting.

Mistress Foxell-Smith was a creature from another world. She was obviously a Lady of Fashion. Claris felt capitals were essential. Her green silk gown spread over wide hoops that must have been inconvenient in the carriage. Her glossy dark hair was piled high and crowned by a large hat with a bold red feather. She was painted as well.

When they arrived at the drawing room, Athena was already there and ready to be amused. She adored guests. Ellie often absented herself, as now. Claris didn't think it was a matter of social standing but that Ellie had considered the party and decided they would be boring. She was probably continuing to sort linen, and Claris wished she were with her.

She introduced Athena. Miss Youngman was pleasant, but the other two ladies showed no interest in an elderly Mallow. Claris disliked them already, but she set to be polite, asking about Esham Court and Lady Bigelow's family.

"I have a son," Lady Bigelow said, showing at least one positive emotion—smug satisfaction. Her mouth drooped again. "But I'm now with child again, much to my inconvenience."

"Inconvenience?" Claris asked, relieved that the tea makings were being brought in. The sooner they'd drunk, the sooner they'd leave.

"Of course I'm delighted to be able to present my

husband with another little gem, but he is insisting I remain in the countryside throughout!"

"Positively barbarous," said Mistress Foxell-Smith. "I've come to keep Anabelle company for a little while, but already I pine for Town."

Claris poured boiling water on the tea leaves. "And you, Miss Youngman? Do you dislike country life?"

"Not when the weather's fine. London was dreadful in the summer heat."

Mistress Foxell-Smith tittered, but from all Claris knew, Miss Youngman was correct. It had been a shockingly hot summer, and that had spread contagion in the city.

"I'm surprised you put up with such barbarity," Athena said to Lady Bigelow. "A husband should not be a dictator."

"Alas, he has every right, ma'am, as you know. I assure you that no argument, no plea, no tears, will move him. I have tried. After all, did not the queen remove from Richmond to London for her confinement?"

Claris said, "I'm surprised that makes no point with your husband, ma'am."

"He is obdurate. I even pointed out to him that country living had not served the ladies of Perriam Manor well. To no avail."

Miss Youngman looked uncomfortable at that, but Anabelle Bigelow was oblivious.

"Bigelow is a brute!" Mistress Foxell-Smith exclaimed. "Only think, poor Anabelle's babe will arrive in January. January in the wilderness!" She gave an exaggerated shudder.

"This is not exactly a wilderness," Claris objected.

Another titter from Foxell-Smith. "My dear! Clearly you have nothing with which to compare it. All countryside is barbaric, especially in winter."

Miss Youngman spoke up. "It's not so bad as that, especially at Christmas."

The Fox, as Claris was calling her in her mind, looked

down her thin nose. "We were speaking of January, my dear. Perhaps even February." Another shudder. "Roads so hard with ice that travel is torture, even between estates. Houses impossible to keep warm. I assure you, Mistress Perriam, that even a modest house such as this will have icicles inside."

Claris ignored that exaggeration and poured the tea, summoning the maid to pass around the cups. Duty done, she attacked.

"Lady Ashart said much the same, ma'am, but the Asharts enjoy winter at Cheynings because they have created small private rooms for cold weather. Fortunately, some of the rooms here are quite small so will serve that same purpose."

Possibly Lady Bigelow and her sister didn't catch the reference, but the Fox did. Her eyes narrowed. "You are intimately acquainted with the marquess and his wife?"

Claris sipped her tea. "Not intimately, no, but my husband is well acquainted with them and I visited Cheynings recently. In fact, my wedding took place from there."

The Fox was taken aback but rallied. "Instead of from your own home, ma'am?"

Claris saw she'd created a trap for herself.

"My parents are dead. It was thought more suitable." She turned to Lady Bigelow. "Were you married in Town, ma'am, or from a country home?"

"In Town. My family lives in Town."

A flush showed Claris that she'd made another misstep. A family who lived permanently in Town was not of the upper class.

"I hope to visit Town," she said brightly. "I've heard much of its delights."

"Including your husband," said the Fox, "though I gather he hasn't changed his residence."

Claris knew that was another trap—why was the Fox

so hostile?—but she didn't understand how. For a fatal moment, she couldn't think what to say or do, and the Fox filled the silence.

"You must know that Perriam lives in the Knaves' Palace. Perhaps you only know it by its correct name, the Lyceum. An exclusive and elegant establishment of bachelor rooms. You must know the rules?"

Claris's temper simmered. "Clearly I don't, ma'am. Please enlighten me."

The tone took the woman aback, but not for long. "No women are allowed, ma'am. None at all. Not maid or female cook, and certainly not wife."

"No mistresses either?" asked Athena.

The Fox flushed at the lewd reference. "No mistresses either."

"There are always other places for that," said Athena. "And you, ma'am, do you have a country house?"

Claris saw the glint in her grandmother's eye.

At daggers drawn.

Why?

The Fox's nose pinched. "I had. When my husband died it went to his brother. I content myself with a small house in Town and can only visit the country by the kindness of friends."

"My condolences, ma'am," Claris said and offered more tea to everyone.

They all took some, alas. She couldn't tell what Lady Bigelow was thinking, but Miss Youngman's eyes met hers brightly. All very well for her to be enjoying the sparks.

The Fox took aim at Athena. "And you, ma'am? You are also a widow, I assume?"

Did she know Athena's story, or was that a shot at random?

Athena smiled and sipped her tea. "I separated from my husband so long ago, ma'am, that to claim widowhood might be improper."

"Separated!" gasped Lady Bigelow. "How can that be?"

"Very simply. A wife merely needs to prove severe cruelty for the courts to take pity on her."

"Severe cruelty?" Lady Bigelow repeated, her cup actually rattling. "What could that be?"

"The details would be distasteful to you," Athena said, though it was clear that all the ladies would be willing to tolerate that. "However, being obliged to live in the country during your pregnancy would not count."

"I ... You ..." Lady Bigelow ceased spluttering, put down her cup and saucer, and rose. "Thank you, Mistress Perriam," she said and swept out.

Wide-eyed, Miss Youngman dipped a curtsy and gave her thanks before hurrying after.

The Fox took her time. "Well routed, ma'am, if that was your intent."

Athena said, "I generally intend what I do, as I'm sure do you."

The woman turned her gaze on Claris. "You're an odd wife for Perry Perriam. But then, I understand you were the requirement of a will."

Claris was shocked by such overt discourtesy but answered calmly. "I was, ma'am."

Her admission disappointed the woman.

"He dislikes the countryside, you know."

"He seemed to enjoy it well enough whilst here."

The Fox tittered again. "He does have exquisite manners."

"Yes, he mingled very well with the local people," Claris fired back. "He even climbed a ladder to help with the removal of the ivy."

"You were able to compel him to that?" The woman drawled the words, but her narrowed eyes showed a hit.

"Not at all. He was eager. Perhaps he has more facets than you are familiar with."

Mistress Foxell-Smith chuckled. "I very much doubt that, Mistress Perriam. Very much."

She swept out, and Claris felt obliged to follow to see

her guests out. It was as well she didn't have a pistol to hand. The woman's silken back was a very tempting target.

As soon as the door closed, she marched back to the drawing room. "What was all that about?" she demanded of Athena.

"My dear girl, that woman had hopes of Perriam. She foisted herself on the silly Bigelow to have an excuse to verify the stories and to see the woman who'd stolen him."

"I didn't steal anyone! What's more, I can't imagine him admiring a woman like that."

"Don't be ridiculous. I strongly suspect she's been his mistress, to put the polite word on it."

"His . . . ?"

"You can't expect that he's been celibate."

"I . . ."

Claris had never thought about that, but of course he hadn't.

Athena raised her brows. "Have I upset you? I forget how naive you are."

"No, I didn't think he'd been celibate. But that woman . . ."

"Is beautiful beneath the ornamentation, and many would admire the ornamentation itself, especially in his world."

"He did enjoy himself here," Claris protested. "With the ivy, with the twins . . ."

"He has many facets, as you said, but most are fleeting. Don't imagine you know him, Claris, or he'll break your heart."

"I—"

"The Foxell-Smith woman is exactly the sort he'd dally with. A sophisticated, expert lover who wouldn't be too demanding. Unlike your namesake."

"Aunt Clarrie? How does she come into this? She believed she was married."

"Perhaps there was some ceremony, a Fleet marriage

or such, but one way or another, Giles Perriam cheated her, doubtless with Henry's connivance."

"Father's great sin," Claris said, finally understanding. No wonder he'd been in anguish when the victim had killed herself. "How shocking."

"Such stories were two a penny before the law was reformed, and your aunt was a fool to believe that a man like Giles Perriam would marry beneath him. Open your eyes, Claris. The world is not kind to foolish women."

"Which includes Mistress Foxell-Smith, it would seem, as you think she had hopes."

"I grant you that point. Is there a sensible woman in the world when it comes to men?"

"You, it would seem."

"Oh, child, I've had my follies. Perhaps I'm a fool to try to teach you how to go on."

"I appreciate your advice."

"No, you don't. You'd prefer to drift in pleasant unrealities, but you're part of the wider world now. Even if you hide here, the world will come to you, as you have seen. Learn to live well in it, or it will destroy you."

Athena then put on her spectacles, picked up her book, opened it, and settled to read.

Claris left, stung by her grandmother's words and still disturbed by her father's wickedness. How could he have played a part in a woman's ruin? Yet it must have been so. It explained so much.

That was in the past, however, and Mistress Foxell-Smith was very much in the present. She was from Perry's world—that of the beau monde, the royal court, and wicked, glittering Town. Even in the countryside, simply dressed and enjoying country pastimes, he'd carried that aura with him.

At this very moment, he was probably dressed in silk and lace and dallying with Fox-like ladies in a royal park or an elegant salon. He'd have no thought in his head for his country wife or the country estate he'd never wanted, and which he'd given over to her entirely without regret.

She was tempted to take refuge in her room, but that would be far too revealing, so she headed back to the linen cupboard. Ripping things would suit her mood.

There was one good aspect. Whatever the sleekly vicious Fox had been to her husband, Perry was now married to her.

Two good aspects. He was in London and the Fox was here.

She took comfort from that until she realized that Town must be full of wicked women. Her husband had certainly not been celibate before their marriage. Would he see any reason to be so now?

Chapter 28

Perry was with Cyn in Malloren House, reviewing progress thus far. Cyn's wife, Chastity, had been with him when Perry had arrived but had discreetly left them in private.

Progress was slow, even after three weeks.

They'd reduced their suspects to four—Farringay and Pierrepoint in the Admiralty, and Browne and Ryder at Horse Guards.

Lieutenant Farringay was a war hero who'd lost the use of his left arm in battle, but he was also a rake with too much fondness for drink and dice. Debt might have driven him to treason, and he seemed suspicious of Perry's frequent visits to the Admiralty.

Pierrepoint was Farringay's opposite. His nerve had broken during his first naval encounter and he'd been found a desk job by influential friends. Perry couldn't believe he'd the guts for treason, but he could be a dupe. The main count against him was his behavior. He jumped at his own shadow.

Captain Browne, late of the infantry, was an older man, in his forties, frustrated by lack of advancement. He hadn't the money to buy a higher rank, so he'd married a wealthy wife. She, however, hadn't wanted him posted abroad, and her family had desk-tied him at Horse Guards, procuring uniforms. His surly anger over that marked him a suspect. By selling secrets he could earn the money to buy advancement.

Abraham Ryder was the least likely suspect. He was a stiff-rumped civilian clerk of the strictest moral principles. However, he, like Pierrepoint, was marked by anxiety and dread. In his case it took the form of deep gloom and occasional mutterings about damnation, but it was as powerful.

Perry and Cyn had each tried to spend time with their two in order to learn more about them. Perry had found it easy, though unpleasant, to join Farringay in his haunts but had learned nothing new from it. Pierrepoint had oscillated between gratification at Perry's interest and terror of every encounter made.

Cyn had the greatest challenge because Browne was so much older and Ryder so very moral. He'd hardly managed to spend time with them at all.

They needed to make progress. Thus far the leaked information had been on minor matters, but that could change. However, the powers that be didn't want only the culprits but the means, and if possible proof that the Comte de Guerchy, the French ambassador, was behind it all. It would, apparently, suit both the kings of Britain and France to have him disgraced and removed. Perry and Cyn had twice been summoned to St. James's Palace to make a further report on their progress.

Last night they'd tried a new device—a gentlemen's card party in Perry's rooms. Get the suspects relaxed and drunk, and who knew what might be revealed.

Not enough, they now agreed.

Ryder hadn't attended, but they'd expected that.

"Cards being tools of the devil," Cyn said. "But he's the least likely. His fear of damnation is probably because he looked at a woman's ankles."

"I thought he was to wed."

"He is, but he's probably not looked at her ankles yet. Will he ever? I ask."

"The mating habits of the Puritan species are of no interest here." Perry shifted papers to find the report on Ryder prepared by Rothgar's people. "Nephew to Lord

Rothermere, who got him the post. That whole family's never moved far from Puritan times. What could push him into sinful treason?"

"Hard to come up with," Cyn admitted. "What of Farringay? He held his drink well but was far enough under the hatches to become indiscreet. He joked about the risk of a sponging house, but it probably wasn't a joke."

"He's living hand to mouth and he's a rascal, but is he a villain? He was a true hero and his hatred of the French rang true."

"Clever of you to steer the conversation that way. But I didn't detect any shilly-shallying on that from any of them."

"I didn't expect any, but I hoped to detect insincerity or ambivalence. Pierrepoint was uncomfortable with the topic, but he's constantly in a twitch over everything, poor man."

"Poor man? He's an outright coward."

"Not everyone can be brave. I've never been tested under fire."

"You'd do your duty."

"I hope so, but even if it seems cowardly, I hope never to have to."

"Are we no further forward?" Cyn asked impatiently. "You rule out both Farringay and Pierrepoint?"

"No. It has to be one or the other. I pick Pierrepoint. Farringay's shiftiness is explained by the extent of his debt, but we've uncovered no reason for Pierrepoint to be in such a state. I've talked to men who've known him a while and he's definitely worse now. Which do you pick?"

"Damned if I know. I was surprised Browne attended, but I suppose he was pleased to escape his wife for an evening. He didn't reveal anything new that I could tell." He looked a question at Perry.

"Nor I. Surly by nature and miserable by circumstances. To go from there to treason is a giant step, and would he earn enough to buy advancement?"

"Not quickly, but *Ryder*? He drinks only tea and small beer and calls God to witness every second word. I'd have thought he'd go to the lions before committing a sin."

Perry considered the matter. "What if he saw his actions as supporting a godly cause?"

"But what? A plot to return to a Puritan commonwealth? There was an insane sect in Yorkshire called the Cotterites. . . ."

"Thoroughly dispersed, and who, by Zeus, would think the French more godly than us?"

"That would need insanity. Perhaps that's it. Both men are mad."

"But then they wouldn't be sick over what they've done, what they are still doing. Pierrepoint is."

"Ryder too. Very well, I pick him, but I hope to learn what instrument of torture has driven him to act so completely against his conscience."

"As do I. There's something deviously unpleasant beneath this affair." Perry tossed down his papers. "We'll have Ryder and Pierrepoint followed and hope to catch them in contact."

"It will only be with a minion," Cyn said.

"With luck, a minion who'll tell all under pressure. Guerchy's notorious for underpaying and underappreciating those who work for him. That's how his attempt to murder a rival with poison came out."

"The devil he did!"

"Opium in wine. Almost dragged into court over it. The point is, if we can catch his underling, we might have the proof that's required."

"And two men go to the gallows," Cyn said. "They're traitors, but I could feel pity for Ryder. And his family."

"And I for Pierrepoint. A damnably unpleasant business."

"Give me direct action and a clear enemy anytime."

"I'm not averse to direct action myself," Perry said, "but opportunity rarely comes my way. Which brings to mind . . . would you care for a bout at the new fencing academy nearby? Francesco's."

"You're skilled with the sword?" Cyn asked.

"Tolerably."

"Then yes, but why now? You expect danger?"

"From Ryder and Pierrepoint?" Perry laughed. "I merely want stimulating exercise to clear the dregs from my mind."

"Then by all means let me stimulate you."

"You're too confident, my friend. *En avant.*"

As they left Malloren House, Perry realized that Tom and Peter should have some training with a sword. What would Claris think about that? She hadn't minded them having toy swords, but she'd not wanted them near real weapons. Wise, but they must be prepared for the world.

How was she? She'd written to thank him for the chair and fire irons, and in other letters she'd described some outings to visit neighbors. She seemed satisfied with Lovell and his way with the twins. The twins had each written to him, most recently in Greek, which must have been at their tutor's insistence. They'd reported on their progress with the ponies and described their angling successes.

Peter's Greek was good, but Tom's still needed work.

He worried about their differing abilities. They were deeply attached, but their lives might not flow evenly together. How would they handle that? Claris must have the same concerns. He could discuss it with her when he found time to put in some of his obligatory days at Perriam Manor.

Where was she now?

Hoeing vegetables?

That made him smile, but he knew it was unlikely. Her letters showed she was engaged in learning to be mistress of her new property.

Which, by the will he'd signed, would pass on his death to his oldest brother. He'd made that amendment because his brother would be more kindhearted than his father. To be sure, he'd made Pranks promise that she be allowed to live out her life at Perriam Manor. Even so, it wouldn't be hers, and it wouldn't pass to their child, if there was one. He could regret that too, but there was no way around it. Perhaps he could accumulate enough wealth to buy some other estate.

Was Claris with child?

If she wasn't . . .

"Penny for them?" Cyn said.

Perry realized they were already crossing Marlborough Square. He came up with an excuse for his abstraction.

"I was considering my wife's brothers. Twins, nearly twelve. It's time they learned sword work."

"Indeed. Rothgar had us all trained to the highest standard. He said he wouldn't lose us to a bullying swordsman."

"A wise decision. If my sister's husband had been trained that way, he wouldn't have been murdered in a duel."

"I heard the tale. A man paid to call him out and kill him. How is the lady now?"

"In a new marriage, which is apparently happy, despite immuring her in muddy Devon."

"It can't always be muddy!" Cyn said with a laugh.

"My mother's account of visiting there is vivid. Georgia was such a Town butterfly."

"You worry about her. It's the way with families. I worry about my twin, even though she seems happy. And she worries about me."

"I'd forgotten you're a twin. I'd ask advice, but male and female twins must be different to two boys, and identical at that."

"When we were young we didn't allow the differences to rule us, but in time we were each pushed onto a different path. I didn't mind, but Elf did, a lady's path being much less adventurous. It was hard for her when I joined the army."

"Envy or worry?" Perry asked.

"Both, but mostly the latter. She'd have had me in a drawing room stitching samplers."

"It's not unreasonable to worry about a soldier."

"That's what she says. I tell her it comes down to luck, but that never seems to reassure her."

"She wishes to control destiny, as do I."

"A fool's game," Cyn said. "Life's too chancy."

"I refuse to believe that."

"Then why are you married?"

"A point, damn you, but the marriage was caused by Cousin Giles's malice, not chance."

"Unless the curse was behind it."

"I don't believe in curses," Perry said, but he knew that deep inside that curse still worried him. He wished there was a way to prove it to be nonsense.

"One's shaped your life, even so. And your wife's life, with less blame on her side."

"I carry no blame for Giles Perriam's sins."

"It came through your blood."

"I'll be damned if I accept blame for everything a Perriam's done through the ages. Do you accept every Malloren sin?"

"No, but I don't believe we can control life. We can only do the best with what comes and pray for good fortune when the balls whistle around our heads."

They had reached the fencing academy and paused by the steps.

"Shall we fight on the point?" Perry said. "Can life be steered aright with enough sense and application, or are we feathers on the wind of fate?"

"Agreed," Cyn said, and they went in.

When a long hour of fencing resulted in a draw, Perry found that rather ominous.

Chapter 29

Claris tried to put the Fox out of her mind but failed. Her marriage might be a practical one, but Perry was her husband and she burned with outrage.

She wasn't in the mood for tedious linens, so she suggested to Ellie that they explore some wooden chests in the attics. "Even a glimpse the other day showed much grander discards."

"A good idea," Ellie said. "We might find pieces that could be used to trim our clothing."

"I thought we were above mending and patching."

"Trimming's different, dearie. If they were as careless about fine discards, there could be some lovely silks, velvets, and lace."

There were, but mostly well used and past repair.

All the same, ripping a silken bodice that had decayed beneath the arms felt more satisfying than ripping a sheet.

Ellie chuckled. "Now, who would you like that to be? Can I guess?" She was sitting on a chair by the chest, inspecting a long embroidered flounce.

"Mistress Foxell-Smith."

"And who's she to raise your temper?"

"Athena thinks she's my husband's mistress." Claris told the story. "Perhaps she did have hopes that he'd marry her."

"Very likely." Ellie put the flounce on their good pile.

"He's only a younger son, but the younger son of an earl. Not to be sniffed at."

"She can hope no longer. He's married—to me."

"That might make her your enemy, dearie. So be careful."

"Our paths won't cross again. She won't return here to face Athena." Claris considered the ripped bodice. "The front and back are still strong, and it's lovely silk. It could be used for a purse, shoes. . . ."

Ellie took it. "Not for you, dearie. Servants' pile."

"Will they really have use of silk?"

"Of course they will. A pretty purse, a pair of shoes."

Claris shook her head. "I'm stupid about so many things."

"No, you're not. You just haven't experienced much yet."

"Certainly not the right things."

Ellie pulled out a long piece of lace. "The Foxy woman will probably hurry back to Town."

"For fear of Athena?"

"Perhaps."

Or to rush back to Perry. Claris tugged at a blue velvet jacket, but it didn't give her the satisfaction of parting. "Still sturdy, but sadly faded in places."

"One of the servants will make a treasure out of it."

Claris put it on that pile. "Perhaps I should give them the entire chest. As you say, I don't need patched and mended finery."

"Worth checking," Ellie said. "Look at this." She spread a gown of lilac brocade over a nearby table, where the weave caught the sunlight. "There's nothing wrong with it except where it's singed on the hem here. Some woman was lucky not to be burned."

"Indeed." Claris went over to touch the skirt. "It is lovely."

"And not so old as to be out of style. The color would suit you."

"But where would I wear it?"

"You spoke of going to Town with the twins."

"Oh, yes."

Claris fingered the skirt, loving the feel of the silk, which always connected in her mind with her silk robe, how it had slithered to the floor, and what had followed. . . .

"We won't be attending balls."

"You never know. Best to be prepared."

Claris didn't want to disappoint Perry.

"With luck it's a bit long," Ellie said. "It'll be easy to cut off the burn."

Attending a ball, dressed in this gorgeous lilac gown.

"You should at least try it on," Ellie said. "Even if it's the right length, we can find some other way to conceal the damage. Careless to have discarded it over such a blemish."

"Perhaps the memory frightened the owner," Claris said.

"More likely it belonged to the second wife. According to all I hear, she was one to discard anything without a thought and buy new. Of course, she was failing to conceive. Turns some women odd, that does, and turns many to buying, buying, buying, as if to fill the hole."

"I hope I don't become that way, if . . ."

"Still not sure, dearie?"

There'd been no way to conceal the consummation from Alice, and so no way to hide the fact from Athena and Ellie. Athena hadn't commented, but Ellie was excited at the possibility of a baby.

"My courses are a little late," Claris confessed.

"Well, then," Ellie said with a beaming smile. "You'd best wear that lilac whilst you can." She returned to the chest and pulled out a brown bodice. She tossed it on the servants' pile. "It'll be grand to have a baby here."

"Athena won't think so."

"It's a big enough place to keep them apart."

Claris inspected a long gauze shawl, seeing a lot of pulled threads. "Does she truly dislike children?"

"Not to want to murder them, but she's not drawn to babies like most women are."

"Did you never want children?" Claris asked.

"I suppose most women do now and then, dearie, but not without a husband if they have sense. I never met a man who tempted me from Thenie and her exciting ways. Let me see that."

Claris passed over the shawl, recognizing an opening to a subject she wanted to discuss. "She doesn't seem content here."

"She's not one for country living any more than your husband is. This could be mended, but it wasn't fine stuff when new."

"Then put it for the servants."

"But there's not much money left."

It took a moment for Claris to see the context. Athena. Money.

"What happened?" she asked. "Didn't she receive an allowance when she separated?"

"Heavens no. That would have meant a connection, and neither of them would have tolerated that. She won a lump sum and he had to sell land to pay it. She managed it well enough, but in her prime she never thought she'd live to an old age."

Claris tugged at a woolen caraco and it held, but moths had worked on it in places. It could be mended. . . . But that was her old ways speaking. She put it in the pile for the servants and picked up a pair of silk stockings, knotted together. As she untied them she pondered her grandmother's finances. Had she come to their rescue not because she cared but because her money was running out?

Did no one want her without a selfish motive?

That was pitiful thinking. Both Athena and Perry had benefited her, no matter what their motives.

She put her hand into one of the delicate stockings, gently stretching it so she could search for flaws. It was embroidered up the side.

"Ivy," she said with a laugh. "I wonder if that had some meaning. A thread's given here and caused a run, but I gather stockings can be mended."

"So well that no one would ever know. No servant would have a use for those."

"Though a servant could wish she had."

"Not wise to wish too high, dearie. Reach for what's in reach. Ask your maid if she can mend those. If not, take them to London when you go. There are people there who make it their trade."

Claris folded the stockings carefully. "I'm of a mind to go to London soon."

"That'd be nice."

Claris took out a petticoat. "My husband said the boys should visit London before they go to school."

"Are they off to school soon, then?" Ellie asked, putting a stomacher on the good pile.

"No, but we can still go to London."

"You want to guard the chicken house from the Fox," said Ellie. "You're his wife, dearie, not her."

"But . . ." Claris huffed out a breath. "I know I have no right to object, but I can't bear the thought of him and her."

Ellie just gave her a look.

"I know," Claris sighed. "It's a practical marriage and we'll mostly be living apart, so of course he'll want other women."

"Some men can do without."

"I doubt he's one, and why should he? He married me to oblige his family."

"Some men take their vows seriously, no matter how made."

"But why should he?" Claris repeated. "I don't mind," she added, knowing it was a lie and that Ellie would know it too. "I want to see his world. I want to see him in his world."

So I'll understand how far apart we are and always will be.

So I can accept that he'll never spend more time here than he must.

So I can make my life good here without him.

"In that case," Ellie said, standing up with a bit of a wince, "we'd best see to the lilac gown. We can improve your wardrobe, as well. There are a couple of maids here who are competent with a needle, and a seamstress in the village who's reputed to have some skill. We already have the makings in this pile of rescues."

Ellie gathered up the pile, but Claris carried the lilac silk downstairs. It was a more delicate silk than her wedding gown and it rustled and slithered in her arms. Once in her room she hurried to try it on.

"You'll need hoops beneath that," Ellie said. "Athena has some she hardly ever uses."

The color did suit her, and it fit perfectly except for being too long. Even when Ellie returned with the hoops and Claris put them on, spreading the skirt wide, three inches trailed on the ground. When that was cut off, the blemish would be gone.

Alice hurried in. "You should have called for me, ma'am."

"Miss Gable assisted, but this gown must be shortened and soon, for I intend to take my brothers to London. I hope you'll accompany me."

The maid's eyes sparkled. "Yes, ma'am!"

Claris turned back to the mirror, loving the way the skirt swayed with the hoops and the soft whisper of the silk.

She could be a fine lady in this gown.

Perhaps she could even show her husband that she might belong in his world.

Perry read his wife's letter with a grimace. He'd suggested that her brothers visit Town and would have made arrangements in good time. But not yet.

Not now, when he was entangled in politics and diplomacy and ready to shoot someone, many someones, to cut through it all. Ryder and Pierrepoint were clearly guilty, but the link to Guerchy eluded them. The men were being followed at all times, and he and Cyn sometimes took part.

They'd discovered nothing and feared Guerchy had discovered their suspicions. He might have stopped the espionage, or turned to some other, as yet undetected tools. With the rumblings of war growing louder, that was intolerable.

There were frequent meetings with Rothgar, often attended by the secretaries of state, the Duke of Grafton and Mr. Conway; the first lord of the Admiralty, Lord Hawke; and the new commander in chief of the army, Lord Granby.

Too many cooks, came to Perry's mind.

As he'd always known, he had no time for a wife.

She was coming, however. She wasn't requesting permission but announcing the date. He could exert his authority and command her to stay at Perriam Manor, but that went against his nature and their agreement. If he tried, she might well travel to Town anyway, pistol in hand.

He smiled at the image, which made him accept that he'd be happy to see her again. He looked forward to showing her the many aspects of London and hearing her opinions. She'd probably disapprove of much, but he hoped she'd enjoy the better parts.

He looked forward to sharing a bed with her again, but would they? She didn't say whether she was with child or not. It had been nearly four weeks, so she might know. If she was . . . ? She'd been enthusiastic and passionate, so surely she'd want to enjoy more bed play.

He refolded the letter, stroking the folds that she had made. His wife's arrival would be a damned nuisance, but it could also be pure delight.

As the departure for London drew near, Claris became more and more sure she was with child. Her courses were now nearly three weeks overdue.

Should she write to Perry with the news or wait to tell him upon her arrival? Perhaps she should write. If she told him in person, he might not show the pleasure she wanted to see. By letter, he'd say all that was appropriate.

But ... perhaps she needn't tell him at all.

Raw desire played a part in her urgent need to go to Town. If she was pregnant, he might feel no need to join her in bed.

Could she keep it secret?

Athena and Ellie were coming to London, and they might mention it.

Athena was seething with plans, and letters flew in and out daily. She frequently mentioned Lady This and Mistress That, and a woman known only as Sappho.

Claris had asked Lovell the origin of the name Sappho. He'd blushed and avoided answering, so she'd dug around in the library until she'd found a book about the ancient Greeks, which included a reference to the lady as a poetess. One of her poems was included, but unfortunately in Greek. She thought of Lovell's blush and decided not to ask him to translate it.

Perhaps she'd ask Perry about Sappho. Every time she thought about their reconnection, she couldn't help but smile.

By the day before departure, she still hadn't decided whether to tell Perry about the child. She wasn't even sure. Common knowledge said that women with child vomited, especially in the morning, but she hadn't. Folklore said that cats acted strangely around pregnant women, but Yatta was his arrogant self.

She summoned Mistress Eavesham and asked if there was a local midwife.

The woman's glance was sharp, but she answered. "Yes, ma'am. Becky Green in the village. She lives in a cottage hard by the Perriam Arms. She has an excellent reputation."

Claris walked there, upset by the housekeeper's reaction. Did she, like Athena, think babies too much trouble?

Mistress Green was gray and stooped, but her eyes were sharp. She accepted Claris's gift of tea but turned grim when asked for advice. She asked a number of questions and then said, "Aye, ma'am, it's likely you're carrying. If you miss another bleeding, you can be sure."

"Is there anything I should do?"

"Do?"

"To ensure a healthy child."

"No one can ensure that, ma'am. It's in God's hands."

Claris didn't care for the surly tone, so she left, thinking she might seek another midwife when her time came. On her way home, however, she came to a possible understanding.

When she summoned the housekeeper again and asked, "Did Giles Perriam's wives use Mistress Green for their deliveries?"

"Yes, ma'am. She's the only midwife locally."

"Does she also tend to the dead?"

"When called upon, ma'am."

Claris sat for a moment in thought, and then went out to the smothered babes. Becky Green would have delivered all five and also laid out their corpses.

The second wife might have asked for the midwife's advice on her lack of a child.

The poor third . . . .

Mistress Green had spoken grimly of God's will because she feared more tragedies for a Perriam wife. Perhaps everyone here did. That could be why they were reserved, why Mistress Eavesham had seemed upset to be asked about a midwife.

Some of the servants could have been here when these children died, one after another over a short period of time. When these eerie memorials had been created and installed. Most of them would have known the poor third wife, haunting the ivy-shrouded house even while alive.

"We've killed the curse," Claris said, as if arguing with the infants. "My child won't end up here."

She turned and hurried away. Even if something happened to her child, she would never add to the marble ghosts.

Nothing would happen to her child.

Why should it?

She wished it were a brighter day. Brilliant sunshine would burn away shadowy fears, but the sky hung low and gray and a touch of mist veiled the distant trees.

If there had been a true curse, Aunt Clarrie should have been appeased by her marriage.

Yet that curse, the one Perry had brought to her at Lavender Cottage, had been intended to last for generations, and it had contained nothing about a way to end it. The solution had been her mother's device, created solely in an attempt to marry her daughter to Giles Perriam.

Why should her mother know anything of curses and their removal?

But then, why should Aunt Clarrie?

Perhaps they'd both been ardent members of a coven of witches.

She entered the house wishing she knew more about her mother's and aunt's origins and early lives. Her mother had mentioned growing up near London, and that her grandfather Dunsworth had been a timber merchant for the shipping trade. Perhaps she could find out more about her mother's younger life during their visit. But where near London had they lived?

She remembered something and asked the footman where her brothers were.

"Out with Mr. Lovell, ma'am."

Good. She hurried upstairs and went to the boys' room. She didn't have to search, for her father's leather-bound Bible sat on the mantelpiece. It was quite large, so she took it to the side table before opening it to the early page. As she'd remembered, he'd recorded life events there, as many did.

He'd written down the date and location of his marriage to Eleanora Anne Dunsworth. As she'd hoped, he'd noted her mother's prior residence. *"Of Wellsted, near Deptford."*

A gazetteer in the library told her Deptford was on the Thames near London. If she could go there, she might discover that her mother and aunt had been thoroughly conventional Christian ladies. Then she'd know Aunt Clarrie could never have cast a true curse, and she'd have nothing to fear for her baby.

She put her hand low on her belly.

She must prove that curse to be merely the spewing of a deranged mind.

Chapter 30

They set off for Town in grand style.

They required two carriages, which had been hired for the whole journey, along with four horses each. The distance was only twenty miles and the road was said to be good, so they should arrive within four hours.

They were to stay in a house. She'd remembered the Fox's comment that Perry lived in a bachelor building, so she'd asked him to recommend an inn. He'd written back to say that he'd hired a house for them for a week.

That was the period she'd specified, and she hoped she could survive that long. She looked forward to seeing him, but everything else worried her. Town would be full of perils, including people like the Fox, and she wouldn't know how to go on, especially if Perry wasn't by her side.

He'd hired a house but not said he'd live there with them.

Surely he must, but he had a home elsewhere.

He'd promised to supervise the twins' introduction to London but also warned he'd have to leave much of it to Lovell. He'd also warned he wouldn't be able to attend her as much as he'd wish.

She would not feel unwanted, she told herself as her carriage rolled through the village, watched by the villagers.

She was traveling in the first coach with Athena and Alice, while the twins traveled in the second with Lovell and Ellie. That allowed her, Athena, and Ellie forward-facing seats, and Ellie seemed to genuinely enjoy the twins' company.

The twins were torn between the excitement of London, including the wild beasts at the Tower, and the misery of missing their ponies.

Claris put a hand on her front, for it truly felt as if butterflies were rioting in there.

"I hope you're not going to be carriage sick," Athena said.

"Of course not. My busk is a little uncomfortable."

"I told you to wear a simpler gown for travel."

"You were right, but I want to make a good impression."

Especially if Perry is waiting at the house to greet us.

Her gown was a brown-striped one from Genova, made grander with trimmings rescued from the trunk of finery. It now had an embroidered stomacher above the waist and she was wearing her ivory petticoat below—her wedding one, but now stripped of the pink bows. Her cap was a ridiculous froth of lace topped by a small brown hat trimmed with gold braid.

When Parminter had heard of the visit to London, he'd informed her that there was some jewelry locked away. All three wives had willed most of their jewels to family, friends, and faithful servants, but some was left. Claris had expressed her displeasure at not being told before, but she'd enjoyed going through the treasure trove, and now Alice had charge of a box that contained more than trinkets.

She was as ready as possible to face both Town and Foxes.

On arrival in Goodwin Street, she climbed out of the carriage, surprised. She'd assumed a house would be a house—that was, separate from others, like the rectory. This one was tall, narrow, and part of a row of identical houses.

"Don't gawk," Athena said, pushing her toward the

single step and the glossy black door that was already being opened.

Claris pulled herself together and went in, to find a very narrow hall with a room to the right and a staircase to the left. Was this all Perry thought her worthy of? It was clean, she allowed, and quite handsomely furnished, but it was so narrow, as if squeezed by the houses on either side.

And where was he?

A black-gowned woman was curtsying. "Welcome, ma'am. I'm Mistress Crowbury, your housekeeper. Mr. Perriam left a letter for you."

Claris took it and broke the seal, hoping no one could see her trembling hand. He couldn't even be bothered to greet her? That clear but elegant writing again, but in this case used in greater haste, so the lines wandered a little upward.

> *My dear, my humblest apologies, but I am called away by imperative duty. I believe all is in order for your comfort and I will attend you at the earliest possible moment.*

"Earliest possible" could be next week!

Very well, if that was how it was to be.

"May I take you to your room, ma'am?" the housekeeper asked.

Claris said she could, then made her way up the narrow stairs, her skirts brushing either side. The stairs wound up another level, but her room was on the first floor they reached, and at the back of the house. Was that another insult?

It was small, but her spirits rose a little when she saw clear evidence of male occupation. Perry was living here and using this room! A small house had advantages if it meant that husband and wife shared the same room and the same bed.

"Charming," she said to the housekeeper, and meant it.

She allowed that this room, too, was quite handsomely furnished, even including a thick carpet that covered most of the floor.

"The drawing room is at the front on this floor ma'am," Mistress Crowbury said. "If you and your family would wish for tea, it could be served there, or a simple dinner is available should you want that."

"Dinner, thank you. Can it be ready in half an hour?"

"Certainly, ma'am." The housekeeper curtsied and left.

A manservant came in carrying her trunk, followed by Alice, who set to unpacking it. Claris took off her silly hat with a sigh. Traveling in finery had been a wasted effort.

All very well to rejoice in Perry's hairbrush on the dressing table, and a pair of his boots standing by the fireplace, but was his work truly so urgent? Or had he grasped an excuse not to be here? Fretting about that served no purpose, so she went to check on the other accommodations.

Athena and Ellie had the second bedchamber on this floor, and it was as well furnished as her own. The twins and Mr. Lovell had two rooms on the next one. Lovell was to valet the boys when necessary. Above that was an attic floor, where apparently the female servants slept. The one male servant slept in the basement, which also held the kitchens and accommodation for Mistress Crowbury, who was both cook and housekeeper.

All was provided for, but such a tall, narrow house still astonished her.

While waiting for the meal, she went to inspect the drawing room. It stretched the width of the house, with two windows that looked out onto the street. The walls were painted a pale green and trimmed with white panels and cornice. A settee and three chairs were upholstered in straw-colored brocade, and the wood was a pale golden color.

"A fine town house," Athena said, entering. "Perriam has done well."

"It seems quite small, and in a row of many."

"Few have mansions anymore, child, and terraces are the latest style. Land is expensive in the fashionable parts of Town."

"Very well, but it feels cramped after the manor. It's almost as confined as Lavender Cottage."

"Don't be foolish. This is completely appropriate, and when in Town, who wishes to stay at home? The wonders of the world are all around you!"

"All I saw around me was more terraces," Claris retorted, but then she smiled. "I'll complain no more. I can't wait to see the parks, and the Queen's House, not to mention Westminster Abbey."

"And the Tower," said Peter as the twins came in, shepherded by Lovell. "They have an execution block there still stained with blood."

Claris rolled her eyes at them. She'd sent for a guide book to London and they'd been poring over it. She'd noted a few things to be avoided, including executions and the madhouse called Bedlam.

"Where's Perry?" Peter asked. "You said he'd be here."

"He was called away. He promises to return soon." Remembering the wording, she added, "If he can. You know he has many obligations."

"He can't be busy all the time," Peter said. "I want to tell him about that trout I caught."

"And about the way Pollux takes the jumps now," Tom said.

"He won't be busy all the time," Claris said, praying it was true. "We're to eat soon. I'm sure you're hungry."

That could always be guaranteed to distract them, and they were soon happily tucking into their dinner.

Claris could honestly compliment Mistress Crowbury, for it was a tasty meal well chosen to be ready whenever they arrived. There was an excellent soup along with cold pies and the sorts of vegetable dishes that could be quickly heated. For dessert, they had fruit tarts and custard.

She took her tea afterward, determined to be in good

humor with her husband over the arrangements he'd made for them.

When he returned to be thanked.

Perry was wearing scruffy clothing as disguise, because today he was following Pierrepoint himself. They'd triggered action by giving Pierrepoint access to significant, though spurious, financial records. He'd taken the bait and stolen them to copy, so Perry hoped he was now on his way to pass on the document.

Pierrepoint was a damned traitor, but Perry felt pity as he watched the man hesitate yet again, and even turn back as if to give up his purpose. Even though that would ruin the plan, Perry hoped he would. Alas, he reversed and continued on his way.

Cyn was also following. He didn't need a disguise as Pierrepoint didn't know him well, so he was strolling along at a distance, accompanied by a trusted fellow officer. They both seemed absorbed in their conversation. There were enough people of all stations going about their business to mask their purpose.

But where was Pierrepoint going?

Too much to hope that he'd take them to the French ambassador's residence, and they weren't going in that direction.

The next best result would be a meeting with one of Guerchy's known minions. If he met with an unknown party, they'd have to decide whether to arrest both and take them for questioning. That would reveal that the espionage was known, and if the contact didn't provide the link to Guerchy, all chance would be gone.

Perry wondered why Pierrepoint had been chosen for this task. His nervous, shifty manner must have even idle passersby wondering what he was up to. *Look at him now, at a halt, eyes sliding furtively in search of . . . what?* Perry was sure he didn't know he was being followed. Whatever the fear, Pierrepoint almost ran into the Merry Maid Tavern.

Perry followed, not hurrying enough to attract attention. By the time he arrived at the door, Cyn was with him, his friend having taken his leave. They entered together, but inside, halted.

"It's a molly house," Perry said quietly, recalculating everything.

This room looked like any tavern, and men were sitting at tables drinking. The barmaids, however, were also men—in women's clothing. Some made an attempt to look feminine, but others didn't bother. One had a beard.

One of them came over, frankly ogling Cyn. "Welcome, gentlemen. You want a room?"

"Perhaps," Cyn said. "I thought I saw a particular naval friend of mine enter."

"He's in a private meeting, sir, but perhaps if you wait?"

Cyn pouted. "Missed my chance, have I? I wanted my friend here to meet him. I'll arrange another time."

As they left, Perry muttered, "Damnation."

"Indeed. A clever way to arrange a meeting, though."

"Unless Pierrepoint really is a molly boy. That could be reason enough for his nervousness when he could hang for it."

"A point, but I don't think so."

"Why not?"

"Don't you remember at the card party," Cyn said, "when he was too drunk to sit straight? He started up a bawdy song that was definitely all about the charms of a woman. I doubt he has the wits to put that on, and he was too drunk to try."

"*In vino veritas.* We'll watch to see who leaves and pray Pierrepoint leaves with someone, but I should go to my wife. Can you observe for a while? I'll send substitutes."

Cyn agreed and Perry hurried off.

He would have liked to go directly to Goodwin Street, but to present himself in these clothes would lead to questions. He'd go to the Lyceum first, re-create himself in good order, and send a message to Rothgar about watching the Merry Maid. He had people skilled at such work.

As Auguste produced washing water and fresh clothing, Perry flipped through the day's delivery of post. He saw nothing of interest until his father's seal caught his eye. He snapped it and unfolded the sheet, braced for trouble. No, a blessing instead. His parents were off to Paris and Versailles, but Perry was to continue to press the canal matter in his absence.

His father could whistle for that, but at least his parents wouldn't turn up on Claris's doorstep to inspect her. More important, they wouldn't reveal the terms of the new will.

He'd have to tell her himself, but not yet.

Chapter 31

Claris had lingered over tea as long as was reasonable, but she had to surrender to her brothers' demands to explore. She could have sent them out with Lovell, but she would not sit at home waiting, waiting, waiting.

She was apparently to be left to manage for herself. This was what she'd wanted, she reminded herself—to be independent, and especially not to be dependent on any man, especially a husband, for anything.

Athena and Ellie had already left to call on friends.

Her brothers wanted to go to the Tower, but Lovell explained that to do so would be a long journey, so they settled for walking to St. James's Park to see the pelicans.

"And then to Horse Guards?" Tom begged. "There might be soldiers on parade."

Claris consulted the map. "That's a reasonable way to return. This evening we can make plans for other outings."

Pelicans and Horse Guards satisfied the twins as a first effort, even though the adventure took little over an hour. Once home again, they planned longer adventures. Perry still hadn't come.

Claris allowed her brothers to teach her a new card game, and she was too absorbed by it to hear noises, so his entry into the drawing room startled her.

In truth, it caught her breath, and he almost seemed a stranger. She could only be grateful that the twins were greeting him with wild enthusiasm, competing to tell him all their news in a moment. She had time to compose herself before having to face him.

She rose to curtsy. "Good evening, sir."

"So formal. Cross with me?"

"Very well, yes. I enjoy being mistress of my own estate, but you abandoned us in strange territory."

All the same, she couldn't suppress a smile. Despite the elegant blue suit, the silver-buckled shoes with a high heel, and the expensive lace at neck and wrists, he was still Perry.

"I'm sure you've managed splendidly. Lovell not here?"

"I gave him the evening off."

"Kindhearted as well." He looked at the counters on the table. "Brag again?"

"Matrimony, which Lovell seems to have taught my brothers. Another gambling game."

He pulled up an extra chair. "Let's resume. But I need to fortify myself. Tom, of your kindness, run down to command wine for me. A glass for your sister as well."

Tom hurried off, proud to be put to use, and soon the upstairs maid came in with a decanter of wine and two glasses.

Claris resolved to be as carelessly demanding.

Of her husband as well as her servants.

They settled to the simple game, which required no skill at all. She preferred it to brag because she thought the illusion of skill in that game was too appealing to her brothers, especially to Peter.

Was Perry truly more handsome than she remembered?

Did being here in his Town brighten him so much?

That only emphasized the differences between them, for despite her silken finery, she already longed for the simple life at Perriam Manor. All the same, she began to resent her brothers. She was unsettled by her husband, but she wanted to be alone with him. Very much.

The clock struck eight, and Perry gathered the cards.

"Off to bed," he said to the twins, "if you want to be fit for a visit to Westminster Abbey tomorrow."

Tom plucked up courage to say, "We'd rather go to the Tower."

Perry laughed. "When William the Conqueror built the place, he could never have imagined its appeal to the young."

"Will you take us?" Peter asked.

"I must decline. The appeal of the wild beasts faded sometime back. They smell."

Both twins shook their heads at this paltry attitude, but they went off without further protest. Tom even yawned.

Claris suddenly felt tongue-tied.

"Your grandmother and Miss Gable?" he asked.

"They went out after dinner and haven't yet returned."

"I doubt they've come to harm. They're wise to the ways of the world. How are you, Claris? You look well."

"I am," she said, wondering if he was asking about a child.

She should tell him.

But if she did, he might not . . .

They were to share a bed. . . .

"Something disturbs you?"

"It would be pleasant to be able to conceal my emotions!"

"Then practice. What bothers you? 'Tis a husband's duty to smooth your path."

To bed?

She seized on her only other need. "Then you may smooth my path to Deptford."

He blinked. "You intend to take ship, or build one?"

Claris shook her head. "I'm sorry. I'm not making sense."

"Why Deptford?" he asked gently.

"My mother and Aunt Clarrie were born and raised in a village nearby, a place called Wellsted. I want to go there and find out about them."

"It's decades ago."

"There must still be people who knew them, who knew their family."

"True, but why? Why now?"

"When before have I had the opportunity?" she snapped. Then she took a deep, steadying breath. "I apologize again. I know it's foolish, but the curse still weighs on me. At Perriam Manor there are so many reminders of the tragedies."

"Such as the smothered babes." He took her hands. "Claris, if there was a curse, we've negated it with our marriage."

"I know, I know, but ..." She clutched on to him. "*Have* we? The curse was to last through the generations. It was my mother who claimed it could be ended by my marriage to a Perriam, but that could have been pure invention. Why would she know anything of curses?"

"Why should your aunt?"

"Exactly! I need to know more about them."

"You want to discover that they were good Christian ladies, true to the bone. What if you discover they were both witches from a long-established coven?"

"They both had prayer books."

"Perhaps witches can pretend to be Christians. This is an unhealthy obsession, my dear."

"You don't worry about it?"

"No."

She studied him. "Truly?"

He grimaced. "Not since leaving Perriam Manor. Perhaps you need to avoid the place."

"It's my home."

Was that another grimace?

"You truly want to visit this Wellsted?" he asked.

"Yes."

He raised her left hand and kissed her fingers. "Then I'll take you there as soon as possible."

That proviso again. "When?" she demanded.

"I can't be specific. A particular matter I'm involved

with is coming to a head. Any old truths aren't going to evaporate. Wellsted will wait."

"I'm only here for a week."

"Ah, true. Then I promise to take you within the week."

She squeezed his hands. "Thank you." With great daring, she drew their joined hands toward her and kissed his fingers.

His eyes rested on hers, darkening with promise. She met his gaze and smiled, hoping that made an invitation, an agreement....

Athena and Ellie entered.

"So delightful to be in Town!" Athena exclaimed, oblivious to any mood. "We've enjoyed the company of a number of old friends. Sappho is holding a philosophical assembly the night after tomorrow. You should come with us."

"Sappho?" Claris queried, wishing her grandmother to the devil. She and Perry had separated hands and she felt the loss.

Perry answered her. "A poetess among other attributes. Her gatherings are always entertaining—as long as one isn't of the most conventional disposition."

"I probably am."

"Then you should overcome the flaw. If I'm free, I'll escort you."

"We need no escort," Athena said, settling on the settee, "but Claris would probably be more comfortable. I have news that might interest you, Perriam. I encountered my nephew's wife at Lady Collarby's. She almost choked on her cake and then tried to pretend that I didn't exist."

"She was worried about her husband's reaction," Ellie pointed out, sitting beside her. She sent Claris a look that might have been apologetic.

"Indubitably," Athena said, "but only a mouse worries about such things."

"As a husband, should I object?" Perry asked.

"You're not such a fool, and Littlehampton is hardly dangerous. I've had encounters with him from time to time. When put out he merely sulks."

"He might be otherwise with a wife," Claris said. "When at home and private."

"Then she shouldn't tolerate it. Speaking of ladies who tolerate no nonsense, I gather Theresa Cornelys still reigns in Town despite her debts. So wickedly delightful . . ."

She continued in this vein, and Claris couldn't bear it. She rose.

"You must excuse me, but I'm tired. Good night."

This house had bellpulls, so once in her bedchamber, she rang for hot water.

She was somewhat tired. Today she'd moved from a country manor to fashionable Town; from countryside to groomed parks. She'd expected St. James's Park to be the exclusive preserve of the rich, but elegant men and women had strolled amid ordinary folk, and some who looked very disreputable.

She'd seen an urchin snitch a man's handkerchief and flee nimbly through grasping hands to make his escape. She'd been glad, for he could have faced the hangman for it, despite his age. All the same, it pointed out the dangers of this world.

London was also noisy, sometimes chaotically so. Wheels jangled on cobblestones, and street sellers cried their wares, selling everything from pies to pins. Even here, on what should be a quiet street, there seemed to be endless comings and goings. Perhaps that was why the bedchambers were at the back of the house. It was quieter here.

She rubbed her head.

Oh, for the peace of the countryside.

But Perry wasn't in the countryside. He was here. His blue silk robe was draped over the end of the bed, side by side with her pink.

Alice brought hot water and helped her out of her gown.

"Are you comfortable here?" Claris asked.

"Well enough, ma'am. The other servants are pleasant, and interested to know I'm from Lord Ashart's household."

In other words, Alice had established her high status in the basement realm. That could serve Claris as well. Had Alice known that? Probably. The maid was experienced in such matters.

Claris went behind the screen to wash. "Do you have friends or relations in Town, Alice?"

"My brother is footman to Lord Hertford, ma'am, but I don't know if he's here."

"If he is, we must arrange a time for you to visit him, or he could come here."

"Thank you, ma'am."

Alice had put the fine nightgown to hand, so Claris put it on, but when the maid left she considered a daring idea. She could imagine the heavy silk sliding off her naked body. . . .

It seemed wicked in the extreme, but she took off the nightgown and put on the robe. Usually she tied only the ribbon at the neck, but now she tied all four. Alas the lowest one was at thigh level. When she walked, her legs showed.

She swallowed and looked at the nightdress, tempted to put in back on.

But she wouldn't.

Alice had plaited her hair, but now she unraveled it and brushed it out. She turned her head to see the effect in the candlelight. On Ellie's advice, she'd been rinsing it in beer, and perhaps it had brought out some lights. Her hands were smooth now, thanks to the cream and to remembering to wear gloves when she puttered in the garden.

She used a cream on her face as well, and it might have conquered the effect of the sun, but it hadn't erased her freckles. She leaned closer to the mirror. If she painted, she could cover them up. . . .

"Have you found a blemish?"

Claris turned on the seat, heart pounding. "How can you be so quiet?"

Perry looked at her and smiled. "I came in quietly in case you were already asleep." His gaze moved down to her legs, her exposed legs. "I'm so very pleased that you aren't. That is the perfect garment for you."

Claris blushed, pulling the front together. "I . . . I . . ."

"You hoped to please your husband, and you do. Very much."

He captured her clutching hands to free them and drew her to her feet. Smiling into her eyes, he said, "I've missed you."

That made it possible for her to say, "I've missed you too. I'm sure I shouldn't. . . ."

"Why not?" He kissed her lips.

"You bullied me into this marriage!"

"I persuaded you into it. And wasn't I right?"

She looked into his eyes, his darkened eyes. "Maybe."

"Tut-tut. You'd rather be at Lavender Cottage?"

"Irritating man. Very well, you were right. Despite the curse."

He kissed her again, more firmly. "There'll be no more mention of that curse tonight."

"Or?"

"Or I'll have to kiss you all the time."

"Curse, curse, curse . . ."

He kissed her for a long time, picking her up, sitting on the bench with her on his knee. She twined around him, reveled in him, in them, together, at last. When the kiss ended, she rested her dazed head on his shoulder, aware of his fingers in her hair, against her scalp. His lips across her shoulder.

Her robe was falling off.

He'd untied some of the ribbons!

She tried to pull it together again.

He stopped her.

He rose and put her back down on the bench, untying

the last two ribbons. "If you will be so kind, my wife, sit there like that while I undress."

Claris felt the heat rise through her and the ache deepen inside. She desperately wanted to pull the robe closed, but he'd asked, and she wanted above all to be kind.

He looked at her, smiling, as he took off his clothes. Shoes, coat, waistcoat, breeches, stockings, drawers. Then he pulled off his shirt over his head and was naked before her. Her mouth was dry, her breathing rapid, and she was now leaning back against the dressing table simply because she couldn't stay upright any longer.

He picked up his own robe, the one of heavy blue silk woven through with gold, and put it on, leaving it open at the front as he came to her.

He pulled her to her feet and into his arms, hot flesh to hot flesh, surrounded by coolly slithering silk. The kiss was even deeper, the effect even more devastating.

Claris was in the bed without knowing how, still on silk, him over her, still in silk, lost in the heat and smell of him, reveling in his clever hands and mouth as he slid slowly into her.

Even in the kiss he made a sound of satisfaction, and she echoed it. She'd wanted this so much for so long, to be like this again, perfectly matched, deeply one.

It was as if they'd done this many times before rather than just twice, for she knew him and knew the rhythm of it. She knew the peak of it now and could enjoy the slow winding tension and explosive release, and the deep, deepest contentment that came in its wake.

She snuggled up to him, holding him tight. "Thank you."

He kissed her ear. "You are most welcome, my dear, especially as my pleasure has to have been greater than yours. I'll hear no contradiction on that."

"Shall we fight over it?" she asked, smiling as she traced a pattern on his chest with her nail.

"We shall never fight over anything."

"Impossible. I'm a willful woman."

"Then we'll make peace most delightfully." He shifted to hold her closer. "Dear, dear Cousin Giles must be howling."

"No mention of Giles. Neither Giles, nor the curse."

"That word again." He kissed her, a long, soft, gentle kiss, unlike any they'd shared before. When they separated, he kissed her nose. "Freckles must be a sign of wisdom. Good night, my wise wife."

"Good night," Claris said.

He went to sleep, but she stayed awake for a while, smiling. All was well between them. Perfect, in fact. There had to be a way for them to make a true marriage, one that had them together most of the time, kissing most of the time.

Curse, curse, curse . . .

No, for all he'd made a game of it, it wasn't amusing. She'd never rid her mind of worry until she'd settled the matter in her mind. Settled that neither her mother nor her aunt had known how to cast a curse.

The next morning, Perry woke to the delight of his wife at his side, so soft and desirable in sleep. He shouldn't wake her, but he did, with a kiss, delighting in her bright smile and ready blush.

He kissed her cheeks. "I think I love your blushes as much as your freckles."

"You're insane."

"Aren't all lovers?" He kissed her and made love to her, finding his deepest pleasure in hers. He slid out of her, sighing with satisfaction. "In a just world we could spend the day in bed, but you have brothers."

"Westminster Abbey," she said, perhaps looking as wistful as he felt.

"We could send them with Lovell."

"You promised. You shouldn't break promises to a child."

"Alack and alas. Then we must prepare for the day."

He got out of bed, drew the curtains around it, and

rang for washing water. Auguste brought it with a rather pinched expression.

Auguste was not best pleased to be here instead of the Knaves' Palace, where valets had their own club and company. He'd be even less pleased to spend more time in the countryside. Another problem, but it must be so. Perry knew he was going to spend as much time at the manor as possible, even though it would be difficult to arrange.

He could shed his work for Rothgar. He wasn't irreplaceable there, only convenient.

The king was another matter. Monarchs liked their useful subjects to be at hand and could be dangerous if disappointed. The king could order his sinecures taken away on the very reasonable basis that he wasn't in Town to perform his duties. That would severely reduce his income.

Then there was his father. The earl couldn't take back the lump sum that had come to him at twenty-one and which provided a modest income from investments. However, he could cease the generous extra income given so he'd serve the earldom's interests in London.

There was nothing to be done now, so Perry dressed. He smiled when he noticed that Claris had parted the curtains a little so she could watch him.

"I'm tempted to do the same," he said, kissing her, "but I'll go down to breakfast."

As he ate, a report arrived from Rothgar. It listed all the men who'd left the Merry Maid, including Pierrepoint. None of the names meant anything to him. Two were French, but Guerchy didn't use only French agents. One seemed Irish, and they were often in league with the French.

Rothgar was investigating all of them, and Ryder and Pierrepoint would be followed today by Rothgar's people. In other words, he could keep his promise and take Claris and her brothers to the abbey. What was more, once away from here, he couldn't be found and dragged back into harness.

He remembered Rothgar's unofficial motto: "With a Malloren, all things are possible." Not that, he hoped. He was looking forward to his day.

Chapter 32

Claris set out for the expedition in anticipation of a
lovely day. She searched her memory for another
such day and could think only of the two that Perry had
spent at the manor.

Lovell was accompanying them, so Claris could link
arms with her husband and leave her brothers to him.
They walked along terraced streets similar to Godwin
Street and past the palace of St. James. They crossed the
park toward the river and soon saw the ancient abbey,
where kings were crowned. As they approached the
magnificent front with its two tall, square towers, she
halted to take in the view.

"It's much larger than I expected. An abbey, after all."

"It was a cathedral for a brief period," Perry said, "to
protect it from harm during the dissolution of the mon-
asteries."

He took her inside, into cool dimness, but what light
entered came through beautiful stained glass windows. She
couldn't help but gawk. Ranks of fluted pillars marched
toward a distant altar, stretching high above to meet at
carved points.

A guide hurried forward. "The pillars and arches rise
to above a hundred feet. They are said to re-create God's
wonder of nature, an avenue of trees. This wonder dates
from the thirteenth century...."

As the guide went on, Claris smiled at Perry and murmured, "Thank you."

"For bringing you here?"

"For persuading me to marry you. Otherwise I might never have seen anything so wondrous."

He smiled into her eyes. "There are so many wonders. A lifetime of them."

The guide cleared his throat and they turned to pay attention.

"We see before us the monument to Captain James Cornewall, a noble sea captain killed at Toulon. . . ."

Perhaps the abbey wouldn't be a poor substitute for the wild beasts at the Tower. The twins were transfixed by the huge work of marble, which was carved with fossils, shells, and sea plants, but also with cannons, anchors, and flags.

As the abbey seemed to be encrusted with tombs and memorials, they should be well satisfied. Certainly the one of an old knight who'd cut off a Moor's head—the head being depicted—was a success. For her own part, she enjoyed the magnificence and beauty of the building. In such a place, prayer came easily, so she offered sincere thanks.

"And here we have the most recent addition to the wonders of the abbey," the guide said.

Claris glanced and was fixed in place. Though the life-sized figures were adult, the monument strongly reminded her of the smothered babes. A man was supporting his dying wife while trying to fend off a spear launched at her by a lower figure.

"Here we see the work of the late Monsieur Roubiliac, whose genius graces the abbey in many places, but this is held to be his supreme achievement. Behold Sir Joseph Nightingale and his wife, Lady Elizabeth, come to term too early through a strike of lightning, and killed thereby. In vain the devoted husband tries to defend her from the fatal dart."

As with the memorials at Perriam Manor, the marble figures seemed so real, their garments flowing like real cloth.

"Does it distress you?"

She turned to Perry. "What? Oh, you mean another wife dying young. It happens too often, but then, we've passed many memorials to men killed young in battle."

"My practical wife. But still . . . Never mind. It is very well executed."

"Did the guide say he was dead? The sculptor."

"Yes, I think so." Perry asked the man, who confirmed it.

Claris asked, "Was he considered the best sculptor to work here?"

The guide pursed his mouth. "Not quite, ma'am. Sir Henry Cheere holds that palm, as is shown by his being knighted for his talents. In fact he trained Monsieur Roubiliac at one time."

Claris thanked him. Perry said, "You have another memorial in mind?"

"I was only curious." That wasn't strictly true, but she hadn't yet thought through her plan. "We'd better catch up, or I'll miss more anecdotes."

The tour was long and tiring, so when they eventually emerged, she was ready for home and dinner. Even Peter and Tom were showing signs of needing a rest before new adventures.

All the same, Peter said, "That was splendid, Perry. Thank you for bringing us."

"I've enjoyed your appreciation. I assume you're now ready for a test on the kings and queens of England and their memorials?" At their expressions, he laughed. "I leave that to Lovell. Behold a hackney stand. Wheels can carry us home."

Home, Claris thought, smiling.

Anywhere where they were together was home.

Perry had hoped to spend the whole day with Claris, but on his return he found a note from Rothgar asking for his attendance at three. At least he could enjoy dinner with his family. Yes, his family. Didn't the Bible command a husband to leave the family of his birth and cleave only to his wife, and she to him?

With pleasure, especially as Claris's grandmother was out again. He rather liked Ellie, but in his estimation Athena was selfish to the bone. She'd served Claris well for a while, but he feared she'd serve her ill if it suited her purpose. She'd alerted him to the usefulness of the twins when she couldn't have been sure he'd be a good husband.

Claris had a letter too. "Perry, it's from Genova. She and Ashart are in Town, and she asks if we can visit them this evening for a small salon. She warns the talk will probably be dominated by astronomy."

"Ashart's passion. You want to attend?"

"I want to see Genova again."

"Then we will." He drew her to him and kissed her lips. "Until later, my dear."

After he'd left, Tom said, "You're becoming soppy, Claris."

"Then Perry is too." When he looked appalled, she laughed. "I'm afraid it's sometimes to be expected from husbands and wives. You may enjoy that one day. Now, however, I believe Lovell has an educational exploit for you."

It was a tribute to their tutor that the announcement didn't cast them into gloom. They went off cheerfully enough, and Claris found herself alone for a while.

It felt very strange.

Alone in a strange place where she knew no one.

Except Genova. It would be delightful to see her again.

She and Alice must choose a gown for the evening, but first she asked Mistress Crowbury to find out where Sir Henry Cheere did his work. She soon reported that Cheere was retired but still had workshops—one at Hyde Park Corner and another hard by Westminster Abbey. "I'm told that's where they do the marble work, ma'am."

So near to where she'd been! At least that meant she knew where to go. Tomorrow, if possible.

For now, she decided on the lilac silk gown for the evening because all her other fine gowns were made over from Genova's. She should purchase more, but her frugal side rebelled. Most of her time would be spent at Perriam Manor, where she had little need of silken finery.

She had her hair dressed in plaits so it wouldn't slither free, and then Alice fixed in hairpins topped with flowers made from the silk of the dress. Ellie had made those, and she'd stitched silver beads at the heart of each.

The jewels that Parminter had given her included an amethyst necklace. The ones Perry had provided, oh so long ago so she'd have suitable possessions on arrival at the manor, contained pretty amethyst and silver earrings.

One day she must get her ears pierced, but for now, the wire clips worked.

When Perry returned she asked for his assessment.

"You're lovely."

Claris blushed at the implication. "I mean of my clothes."

"You look very grand, which is doubtless the effect you want, but it's only the Asharts."

"A marquis and marchioness, and whatever guests they've invited?"

"A great many will be scientists, mathematicians, and such."

Claris didn't entirely believe him, especially when they arrived at the marquess's town house. It was also in a terrace, but it was double fronted, and they entered a spacious hall from which an elegant staircase took them up to a series of rooms that had been opened up to make the evening's salon. It was already half-full, and Genova was by the door to greet them.

"Claris, my dear!" she exclaimed, kissing her cheek. "How magnificent you look. And happy too." She allowed Perry to kiss her hand. "Perhaps you're treating her well enough, sir. I shall have all the details soon. The Raymores are here, and Lady Raymore particularly wants to meet Claris."

As they walked into the room, Claris asked, "Raymores?"

"Lord Raymore's a friend of mine. He's perhaps told his wife about you. He's the youngest brother of the Marquess of Rothgar and she's the youngest sister of the Earl of Walgrave. 'Struth, Walgrave's here too. Quite a family gathering. His wife is Raymore's twin sister."

"That makes me feel a complete outsider."

"Then I'd better take you inside." He led her over to a slender man in regimentals beside a very pretty woman with a mass of honey-colored hair. They were talking to an older couple and a singleton officer. The talk was about Canada, where the Raymores had been stationed until recently. Claris thought she'd dislike dense forests, bears, and wolves, but she enjoyed hearing about them.

The older couple moved away. Their place was taken by another couple—the Earl and Countess of Walgrave. She couldn't help thinking how delighted her mother would have been to see her in such grand company.

The earl was tall and dark, with a touch of the same haughtiness that marked Ashart, but the countess sparkled. She had reddish hair, and her resemblance to her brother, Lord Raymore, was striking. Twins, she remembered. Their easy fondness touched her, and she hoped for the same for Peter and Tom as adults.

The company was soon commanded to the chairs set out. Claris braced herself for a lecture on stars and planets, but a string quartet came out to play a piece specially commissioned by Ashart on the subject of Venus.

Claris became lost in the beautiful music, and when it ended, she sighed and whispered to Perry, "That was the most magical thing I've ever heard."

He traced a kiss by her ear. "I must feed you magic morn to night. We could have musicians at the manor."

"That would be a wild extravagance."

"For magic? Then perhaps we should become musicians and encourage the servants to the art." Claris wondered about that "we," but before she could comment, he said, "Ah, the lecture."

Claris turned to pay attention, fearing she would be bored.

Lord Ashart stepped forward, and she thought he was to give the lecture, but he introduced a gentleman called James Ferguson, and in admiring terms. The long-faced, gray-haired Scot had apparently been born to a simple family and received only three months of formal education in his life, and that at the age of seven.

"When he was set to shepherding at the age of ten, he very naturally studied the stars, but he also passed the time in making ingenious machines. When taken ill, he amused himself by making a clock, and in time he became one of our most skillful inventors of devices and most excellent speakers on the subject. You will, I am sure, enjoy his explanation of the upcoming transit of Venus, especially as it is accompanied by illustrations in two and three dimensions."

Servants carried out large charts and diagrams and propped them up in the places provided. Then they wheeled out a complex machine made of gleaming brass, touched with copper, silver, and gold.

Another form of entrancement. Claris was bewildered at times, but she began to understand the movements of the planets and principal stars, especially when Mr. Ferguson turned handles on his machine and the beautiful representations of the planets moved around the lamp that took the place of the sun.

In August there'd been a partial eclipse of the sun, but she'd not really understood what that meant. Now she did. How ignorant she'd been, and how much learning was available here, in London Town.

She remembered Farmer Barnett arguing with Perry about the idle rich. This was another aspect—the intel-

ligently curious rich who were active in the natural philosophies and appreciative patrons of all ranks.

"You're looking dazzled again," Perry said when Ashart put an end to the questions and supper was announced.

"I am. I want to look more closely at that machine."

"Because it glitters prettily?"

"Because it fascinates me. I wish the boys had been
here."

"Ferguson often gives public lectures. I'll let you
know when one is scheduled and you can bring them to
Town."

Another excuse to be together.

He led her to the machine and deftly cleared a way
for her to go close. A tall, dark-haired man stepped back
to make way.

Perry said, "Allow me to introduce my wife, sir. My
dear, this is the Marquess of Rothgar."

Claris curtsied but blurted out, "I'm surrounded by
peers."

"To which you are equal," said the marquess, smiling.

Peers. Equals. All the same she was mortified. "I do
apologize, my lord."

"Unnecessarily. We are all truly equal before knowledge. You are interested in Mr. Ferguson's machine?"

There was nothing for it but honesty. "Fascinated."

"Then turn it," he said, guiding her around to one of
the handles.

"It won't break?"

"No."

She gently turned the handle and the parts began to
move with silent ease. "How wonderfully it's made."

"Ah," said Lord Rothgar. "People rarely appreciate
that. Perriam, I would enjoy showing your wife my toys."

He moved away, and Claris stepped back, uncomfortable with being the center of attention. "Toys?"

"Automata and other clockwork devices. A particular
interest of his."

As they walked toward the supper, she said, "Are all these grand people mechanics at heart?"

He laughed. "Definitely not, though Ashart will have invited those who'd appreciate Ferguson. The beau monde has its share of fools and wastrels, but it also has many with the time and money to explore the universe. Or who make money that way. That gentleman in pale green is the Duke of Bridgwater. He's repairing his fortunes by building canals and shipping coal cheaply."

"A poor duke?"

"Not reduced to a Lavender Cottage, but yes. Lady Walgrave takes an active interest in silk manufacture here in Britain. Sir Barton Crowe over there has twelve ships trading on the high seas."

"I think I have the tapestry of the world fixed, and then someone—usually you, sir—unravels parts of it and remakes it in a different design."

"How boring if it were otherwise. I see Genova directing us to our seats." He settled her in hers and went to select food. Genova took a chair at the same table. "I think all is in order, so I can demand details of your adventures at your manor house."

Claris laughed. "Adventures? Most of my days have involved the exploration of forgotten cupboards and the correction of neglect."

Genova wrinkled her nose at that, but she couldn't ask more questions, for the Raymores joined them, bringing along a man in sober, dark dress. Claris thought he must be a clergyman, but he was introduced as Mr. Ryder, of Horse Guards. She knew that was the army administration.

He seemed a fish out of water here, but he had an interest in astronomy and mechanics and made some sensible remarks on the subjects. Everyone else at the table was lively and interesting, and soon Claris was relaxed enough to take part in the fast-moving talk. She realized only later that the food had been delicious. She also realized that Ryder had left, unnoticed.

As they rose to return to the performances, she turned to Perry to comment, "I felt sorry for that man. He seemed out of place."

"He's a dull dog. Almost a Puritan."

"That must be it, I suppose. But he seemed . . . I have it. He reminded me of my father. Weighed down by something, even to the edge of reason."

"Mad? I didn't see that."

"I probably imagined it, but my father could appear normal—if it is normal to be sullen and morose—even when the demons churned inside. Then they would explode."

He took her hand and squeezed it. "All that is past."

"Yes, thank God."

For the new entertainment, a couple performed some pieces from opera and then a man did clever tricks, making items appear and disappear, even animals at times.

Claris whispered to Perry. "Does magic truly exist?"

"Only clever tricks, love."

"But I don't see how it's done."

"That's his genius. Are you worrying about the curse again? Such things don't exist."

At the end of the performance, Ashart asked the man to reveal the secret of one of his tricks and he did so. His skill was magical in its own right.

As they traveled home in a carriage, Claris thanked Perry again. "Though now I'm not sure what's real or not."

"A good thing to remember, and often the key to uncovering truth. As are kisses."

He began to kiss her, there in the carriage, as it rolled through the night streets, doing nothing more than kiss if she didn't count his fingers on her shoulders and neck, and teasing at the edges of her hair.

Only kisses, but when the carriage halted in Godwin Street, she wasn't sure she could walk. She managed, with his help, and when she arrived in their bedchamber, Alice was waiting.

Nothing for it. She must undress. She must have her hair undressed and brushed out. As soon as possible she sent her maid to bed, and then she considered her options. This time she slid naked into bed and pulled the covers up to her chin.

Then, breathing deeply with anticipation, she lowered them so they only just covered her nipples. Her tingling nipples.

He came in and smiled. A lusty, hungry smile that made her laugh with pleasure. She seemed to have no restraint left in her. She stretched her arms wide and said, "Come bed me, husband."

"You deliciously wicked wench."

He extinguished the candles, all except one, which he moved to his side of the bed. Then he undressed quickly and joined her, and loved her just as she'd wanted and more.

They lay together afterward.

"This is almost as lovely. Not as fierce, but longer lasting."

"Sometime we truly must find an excuse to spend a day in bed."

"A whole day?"

"And a whole night. Loving, teasing, embracing, talking . . ."

"It sounds magical — and impossible."

"We'll see." He kissed her hair. "I've enjoyed today."

"So have I. And we have a lifetime of them." She instantly regretted that, for they didn't. "Whenever we want," she added.

"Encounters are made more wondrous by separations."

"Yes." She stroked his chest. "I've arranged to go to some shops with Genova tomorrow. Lady Walgrave will probably come. Is she really called Elf?"

"Short for Elfled, the Lady of Mercia."

"You said she was interested in silk, and she wants to take me to silk works and warehouses."

"Beware of the obsessed, but buy all you want, love."

She poked him with her nail. "I don't need your permission."

"True enough. But if you beggar yourself, by our agreement, I can't save you."

"So be it. I am independent."

"Except for this," he said, and kissed her, his clever hands already stirring her passions.

Except for that.

Chapter 33

Perry went to a meeting at Malloren House, hoping to see the end of the mess.

The council the day before had laid out the plans. In addition to the marquess and Cyn, in attendance again had been the high officials of the Admiralty and Horse Guards and the secretaries of state. It had become clear that Rothgar was representing the king's interest in the case. In that capacity, he had suggested that Pierrepoint and Ryder be offered immunity from prosecution if they would reveal all.

Perry had remembered the king's concern about innocent men, which he'd suspected meant a personal concern. Pierrepoint or Ryder?

Pierrepoint, he decided, so easily removed from active service. Pierrepoint and the king were close in age but not on intimate terms, so it was probably pressure from the king's mother, perhaps on behalf of a friend of hers. Irrelevant here, but he'd find out.

The politicians caught the way the wind was blowing and agreed to the plan. The military men were more reluctant and were persuaded only when promised that the traitors would be punished. Pierrepoint must return to active service, and Ryder must never hold public office again. A mild punishment, but he was ambitious, so it would sting.

Today they were separately presented with their guilt and their options. Pierrepoint's nerve broke almost immediately, and indeed he'd seemed relieved that it was over. He admitted taking or copying documents and passing them on at the Merry Maid. He said the person he'd met there had given the name Harrison.

No connection to France other than there being a well-known family there by the name Harrison.

No matter how pressed, he wouldn't say why he'd done such things. He claimed to have been bribed, but his demeanor shrieked that a lie. Never had eyes so wildly avoided contact. Threat of prosecution and hanging had reduced him to tears, but he hadn't changed his story.

Ryder had been harder to crack, but Perry had been struck by the accuracy of Claris's insight. Beneath the stony exterior dwelled a tortured soul.

In the end he'd used that. The questioning had all been about duty to his office and the Crown. Though Perry was supposed to be an observer, he'd put it to Ryder that his immortal soul depended on his speaking the truth.

Ryder had covered his face with one hand and perhaps even sobbed. "Alas, alas, I have put myself in danger of damnation. I admit my sins. I admit them and beg for your forgiveness on earth, and Almighty God's in the hereafter!"

"All very well," Lord Hawke had snapped, "but our forgiveness is conditional upon you revealing the whole truth, sir!"

Ryder's tale had been similar to Pierrepoint's. He'd passed on information to a man called Harrison in a private room at the Merry Maid.

"A disgusting stew," he'd added.

When asked why, he'd not even tried an excuse. He'd refused to answer with all the stoicism of a martyr. When pressed, he'd retreated into prayer. Eventually he'd said, "Hang me if you must, sirs. I deserve it. I will say no more."

Afterward, Perry, Cyn, and Rothgar had been at a loss.

"What terrifies them more than hanging?" Cyn demanded. "Torture? They believe the French are going to torture them before the hangman gets them?"

"Torture by means other than physical?" Rothgar asked. "What could Guerchy reveal about them that seems worse than hanging?"

"They're such different men," Perry said. "There's no commonality between them at all. It's damned frustrating to be missing the last key. What worked once could work again."

"We've done our best for now," Rothgar said. "We'll pressure them some more."

As Cyn accompanied Perry to the door, he said, "Chastity would like a closer acquaintance with your wife. She was universally admired."

"Thank you. I wasn't sure how she'd cope with the *haute volée*."

"She has adequate wings, mostly by natural honesty and intelligence."

"The natural philosophies, yes. I believe we're to go to a gathering at Sappho's tonight. Will you and Chastity be there?"

"The theater, I believe."

Perry left, thinking he must take Claris to the theater. For another kind of magic, he visited a jeweler on his way home.

Claris was in an emporium, overwhelmed, though in a most delightful way, by waterfalls of silk. The room was lined with shelves, each holding a roll or bale, and some were loosed to fall down and display their wonders.

As soon as she or Genova showed interest in any, an assistant spilled some and invited them to feel its quality. If it was a high bale, he would climb nimbly up a ladder. It reminded Claris of the men clearing the ivy off the manor walls, which reminded her of Perry. . . .

He was never far from her mind, but she still enjoyed the silks. Perhaps she would buy some lengths simply to play with.

Genova soon chose three lengths. "You should buy some, Claris. The prices are excellent. So much less than from a shop or through a mantua-maker."

"A mantua-maker would still make up a gown?" Claris asked.

"Of course."

So she succumbed to the figured silk that had first caught her attention. Though lighter in weight, it was the exact shade of her pink silk robe. She knew it would make Perry think of bed, even in the middle of a ball.

She also bought a long shawl in pale lilac to go with her lilac gown. It was woven as a piece and had been enhanced with embroidery and fringing. Discarding frugality, she purchased two more, one blue and one green, for Athena and Ellie, and then enough of a heavy brown and gold brocade to make a waistcoat for Perry. He doubtless had more than enough waistcoats, but she wanted to buy him something.

They accepted an invitation to dine with the manager of the silk warehouse and his family, and then it was a long journey back to Mayfair, so Claris put aside any idea of visiting Sir Henry Cheere's workshop today. But when she saw how close they came to Westminster Abbey, she asked if they could pause.

"I have in mind some marble work at the manor, and I admired his statues in the abbey. He's retired now, but his workshop continues."

"Do let's explore," Elf said. "I know nothing of the sculptor's business."

Claris smiled at Elf's constant interest in business.

She could hear noise from the work yard, and blocks of marble were being unloaded from a wagon, but there was also a neat shop, and they went in there. The first thing she wanted to establish was that the work produced was as fluid and natural as the examples she'd seen. It was. She admired a bust of a man with flowing hair and vague draperies at his neck that gave the illusion of soft linen.

A middle-aged man came to her side. "An excellent piece, is it not, ma'am?"

"It is. Is this Sir Henry's work? I understand he's retired."

"He is, ma'am, though he still takes an interest. This is by Mr. Crane, trained by Sir Henry, as I'm sure you'll detect."

"Of course. How long does such a piece take to make?"

"I could guarantee delivery in three weeks, ma'am, and sooner if there was urgency."

"Is it suitable to be placed outside?"

"Certainly, ma'am, though such busts are usually displayed indoors. And on a plinth. We have a number of designs to choose from." He gestured toward a rank of them against one wall.

"I suppose a more normal outside piece would be a statue. Or a tomb."

The assistant put on a solemn face. "We execute a great many tombs and memorials, ma'am, all to the commissioner's express design. May I direct your attention to this headpiece for a stone, with mourning cupids?"

Claris turned and was struck by how real the marble cupids looked, with their sturdy legs and round cheeks. A pity they were eternally sad. She couldn't resist stroking one smooth cheek, as if to console the creature.

Cold, of course.

"What happens if a piece is damaged? Chipped, perhaps."

"A chip is easily repaired, ma'am. Sir Henry has developed his own formulation of powdered marble and other ingredients, which can restore a piece to perfection. Even a badly broken one can be restored."

"What if I didn't quite like the finished result? Could it be altered?"

She could see he thought her a difficult customer, but he preserved his amiable manner. "That rarely happens, ma'am, but some correction can be made. Most easily if material is to be removed, but in the case of a lack, the marble paste can be built up."

She had the information she needed.

"I want some work done for my house, Perriam Manor, near Windsor. Would it be possible for someone to visit there to consult with me?"

"Certainly, ma'am."

"Then I shall write when I return home."

Claris settled back in the carriage, thinking of those cherubs. They were cold, but at least they weren't smothered.

She hadn't told Genova and Elf that she was with child, but her baby's presence became more real every day. It would be born in the spring.

A good time, surely.

And by then, there'd be no smothered babes to haunt Perriam Manor.

Perry was home when she returned and listened with amusement to her description of the silk warehouse. She didn't mention the visit to the sculptor's because she wanted to be sure her plan would work before sharing it, even with Perry.

"Are you sure you want to attend Sappho's soiree?" he asked. "You must be tired."

"Only a little. A rest and some tea will restore me. I'm only here for a week and want to experience all I can." She glanced at him. "You haven't forgotten about Wellsted?"

"No. I believe we can go tomorrow."

She thanked him with a kiss, delighting that kisses were as natural as breathing to them. Tomorrow, she'd rid her mind of the curse entirely. She was sure of it.

The lady poetess was as unconventional as promised. Her skin was the color of coffee with cream, and her dark eyes slanted over high cheekbones. She wore her long, dark hair in a plait woven with ribbons, and her gown was a loose robe of opulent fabric. To Claris, she seemed magnificent and extremely foreign.

Her company was as unconventional as she was. Claris was introduced to a poetical duke, a female mathematician, and a hunchbacked mapmaker in shabby black.

The event, alas, was not to her taste. She used fatigue as an excuse to leave early.

When she and Perry were in the carriage, he asked, "Bored?"

She had to confess it. "I'm sure I should have been interested in sonnet forms or whether animals have souls, but I wasn't."

"Nor I. London is a rich banquet. We don't have to eat every dish." He looked at her in a way she'd come to recognize. "A benefit of leaving early is a longer night at home. You could display some of your silken purchases."

"I could wear the shawl, but the length of silk isn't made up."

"All the better to play with," he said.

"Exactly what I thought when I purchased it."

Play with it they did, until she protested that she wouldn't have it ruined. They made love on white linen sheets, the shawl and length of silk draped over the bed rail like a rainbow waterfall.

Chapter 34

Perry hired a chair for their journey to Wellsted and suggested they both dress simply. Claris chose her blue skirt and caraco jacket, and he wore the same riding clothes he'd worn when they'd first met.

"We could almost be back at Lavender Cottage," she said as he gave the sturdy brown horse the order to go.

"Or at least en route to Cheynings. Instead of an old married couple."

She chuckled at the idea, but it caught at her heart. They looked like the sort of couple who could live contentedly in a place like Perriam Manor.

She put such foolishness aside. Blessing enough that they suited each other in a surprising number of ways.

She was interested to see a different part of London as they traveled toward the river and crossed by a bridge. It gave a unique view of the mighty river.

"So many boats, from tiny to grand."

"The big ones are barges," he said. "Beyond London Bridge there are sailing ships that cross the oceans, and all the services and warehouses that involves. We could have made our journey by boat, but we'd be at the mercy of the tides, and the water's still low from the summer heat. People have been stranded on stinking mud banks."

"Then I'm very glad we're driving."

When they left the bridge, they drove along a street between buildings but were soon in the countryside.

"Ah, this is pleasant," she said.

He shook his head. "Who can converse with trees and fields?"

She thought back to Sappho's. "Poets, it would seem."

Though the weather was cooler than it had been in summer, it was still warm for autumn. Claris wore a hat with a brim wide enough to shade her face and with a veil to be let down if they encountered dust.

The roads here were lightly used, but that left them rough in places so that it took more than an hour to travel the few miles to Wellsted. After a while the view to their left, toward the river, included the tall masts of ships, some of them substantial.

"Greenwich, Woolwich, and such places," Perry said. "Shipbuilding and repair, chandleries, customhouses."

"My grandfather Dunsworth made his fortune by supplying timber for shipbuilding and repair. Better for his daughters if he'd been less successful."

"Why?"

"Then they'd never have taken the notion of venturing into fashionable life in search of a fine husband for Aunt Clarrie."

But in that case she would never have met Perry.

"It could have been in their natures."

"I'm not sure it was ever in Aunt Clarrie's. It's strange, but I feel I know her. I spent a lot of time as a child looking at her portrait and at the mementoes my mother treasured."

"She wrote that curse."

"In anguish and despair."

"Do people alter so completely?"

"If they go mad," she said.

"True, we speak of the insane as deranged, which means altered. Ah, nearly there."

He turned the carriage as directed by a fingerpost that read "Wellsted, 1 mile." Ahead the tip of a spire rose above trees. Claris's heart was beating faster than was reasonable. She'd probably learn nothing of significance here.

"How shall we go about this?" she asked.

"Churchyard first, seeking your grandparents' graves."

"But I don't care about them."

"It gives a purpose to our visit and an excuse for your curiosity. We probably won't find out much," he warned.

Claris realized that her fingers were clasped. She relaxed them. "I know that. But I have to try."

They passed between farmhouses, complete with yards and animals. Perry had to rein in the horse when some hens wandered into the road. A narrow bridge took them over a stream and into the center of the village. She saw two inns, a shop, the church, and a nearby house that was probably the clergyman's residence. There were three other houses of modest grandeur on the opposite side of the green.

"Your mother and aunt probably grew up in one of those," Perry said, halting in front of the Ship in Full Sail.

A hostler ran out to take charge of the chair and horse, and Perry helped Claris down. She wanted to begin questions immediately, and Perry must have guessed, for he shook his head.

He'd said that solving puzzles was his talent, so she'd trust him in this. In any case, the hostler couldn't be more than thirty. He'd know nothing of Aunt Clarrie's time.

They strolled over to the low wall around the churchyard and surveyed the graves.

"This could take some time," Perry said.

"We could inquire at the vicarage. I remember people doing that now and then."

"An excellent suggestion." He led the way to the lychgate and opened it. "With luck the vicar is ancient and can answer all our questions."

Alas, slender Reverend Thurstow was not much older than the hostler, but he clearly recognized Perry's quality and became embarrassingly eager to help.

"Dunsworth, Dunsworth. I'm sure I've heard the name. We must consult Bowerbridge. The sexton, you see. He knows all these things. Let me take you to his cottage."

At the cottage behind the church, Mistress Bower-bridge informed them that the sexton was "out and about somewhere." She was quite elderly, and Claris would have questioned her, but she was very deaf. She hoped the woman's husband had better hearing.

However, when they found the sexton, ripping out invasive weeds in a shady corner of the churchyard, it was clear the strapping young man must be her son, or possibly her grandson. At least he was open faced and ready to talk.

"Dunsworth, sir? Aye, I know the grave."

He led them across the grass. Claris noticed one marble headstone surmounted by cherubs because it reminded her of the one at Cheere's. There was no other like it here.

"Here we are," the sexton said, stopping at a plain rectangle on which the writing was still clear.

Here lies Samuel Dunsworth, merchant,
1665–1730
And Mary, his wife, 1690–1736
Those who labor with a good heart will
reap their reward.

Also,

Samuel 1714–1717
John 1716–1724
George 1721–1724
Marianne 1724 aged 6 months

Claris read that sorry tally and shivered. "So many little ones lost, and all at once."

Another curse?

But the curse that haunted her had been created by a Dunsworth, not directed at one.

"There were many burials that year," Reverend Thurstow said. "Wellsted was afflicted by a virulent fever. The incumbent at the time recorded details. Fully a half of the village caught the pestilence, and a quarter of the afflicted died. It fell hardest on the young, as you see, but it carried away others, leaving some families in dire straits."

"That's the truth, Reverend," said the sexton. "Carried off m'father and his brother, it did. M'grandfather had to return to the job, despite his years, till I was old enough to take on the work. Another daughter's buried alongside."

It took Claris a moment to understand, but then she turned to the right, to the stone with the grieving cherubs.

Aunt Clarrie's grave!

Here lies Claris Maria Dunsworth, 1719–1739
daughter of Samuel Dunsworth of this parish.
Gone too soon, but she is with the angels now.

"An impressive memorial," Perry said.

"Aye, m'grandfather often spoke of it, sir. Thought it was out of place, he did, but still a credit to the devotion of Miss Claris's sister, who commissioned it. There was only the two of them survived, you see, sir. They got all the money and went off to live in London Town." He shook his head. "Nasty place, London Town. We can see the bad air over it in wintertime."

Eager Reverend Thurstow broke in. "May we help you in any other way, sir?"

"My wife is curious to know more of her family. Is there anyone in the village who might remember the Dunsworth sisters?"

"Alas, sir, I'm too recently here to know."

The sexton answered. "There's any number old enough, sir, and in a place like Wellsted, everyone knows everyone. I'd say your best chance is Miss Pellew over at Read

House. She'd be of an age with Miss Claris and her sister, and being a gentle lady, likely a friend."

Perry thanked him and gave him a coin, then managed to avoid an invitation to the vicarage without giving offense. Soon they were crossing the village green toward a gabled house. Read House wasn't large except in a village context. Here it was substantial.

"That implies the Dunsworths were also a gentle family," Claris said. "No hint of scandal."

"The vicar might not know, and the sexton might be discreet, but I agree." He paused. "What do you hope for here, Claris?"

He hadn't challenged her curiosity so directly before.

"I want to believe that Aunt Clarrie knew nothing of curses. That whatever drove her to create one was nothing to do with witchcraft."

"She's buried in hallowed ground with angels on her stone."

"Perhaps witches can be. But there's another thing." She looked at him. "If Aunt Clarrie committed suicide, how can she be buried in hallowed ground?"

"A clever insight! Though sometimes a pitiable suicide is masked out of kindness to the family."

"Ah yes, that's true." Claris glanced back. "All those dead children . . ."

"From an illness. Clarrie was five years old when the illness visited here. Are you imagining she cast a curse to bring it?"

"No, no . . . But if there was a coven here . . . Oh, madness must be in my blood. Let's talk to Miss Pellew. Read House doesn't look like a likely home for witches."

"Perhaps witches disguise themselves as ordinary people. I would if I were one." He rapped on the door and it was opened by a neat young maid. "Yes, sir?"

"Is Miss Pellew at home? We are Mr. and Mrs. Perriam, but my wife's mother was Nora Dunsworth."

A very slim lady came into the hall. Though not old, she looked frail and supported herself with a cane, but her eyes were bright and her smile warm. "Nora's child? Heavens above, I'd no idea she married."

Then she looked a bit alarmed.

"Yes indeed," Claris said quickly. "To a clergyman, the Reverend Henry Mallow."

"My gracious, what a lot you must have to tell me. Do, please come in. May I offer you tea?"

They were ushered into a front parlor and tea was ordered.

"Do please excuse my not taking you up to the drawing room," Miss Pellew said as she eased herself into a chair. "I have an affliction of the hip and prefer not to use the stairs any more than I must. Now, tell me about Nora."

Claris obliged until the tea arrived, already made in the pot.

As Miss Pellew poured, she said, "Nora married. I never would have thought it. She wasn't *giving*, you see. She always wanted her own way, always thought her own way best."

"She didn't change," Claris admitted.

"Her husband must have been a saint. Oh dear, I shouldn't have said that, should I?"

Yet Miss Pellew wasn't repentant. Twinkling eyes showed she was enjoying herself, and Claris hoped she'd share more indiscreet thoughts.

The lady sipped her tea. "Truth to tell, my dear, your mother and I never rubbed along well. Clarrie was my friend. Chalk and cheese they were. Clarrie was the most giving person in the world. Sometimes to her own pain. Do please have a piece of cake."

Claris took a piece of ginger cake, wondering what to ask. She'd like Perry to take the lead, but he seemed to be leaving this to her.

"What sort of pain?"

"Oh, only small things. She was pretty, you see, and more charming than she was pretty. No, that's not quite right, for charming implies effort. People were attracted to Clarrie's natural sweetness, and young men lost their hearts. She was too sweet to discourage them."

"Perhaps some of them appealed to her."

Miss Pellew nodded. "Perhaps some of them did, but Nora would have none of the local men. She had her eye on the gentry."

"For Clarrie?"

"Oh, never for herself, dear! She knew she didn't have the looks or the appeal, and she had a low opinion of men and marriage. That's why I was surprised . . . But enough of that. I hope her marriage was happy."

Claris didn't want to lie. "No, it wasn't happy," she admitted. "In fairness, my father was a difficult man."

"Oh dear." But Miss Pellew shrugged. "Enough of that. How can I help you, dear?"

"I simply want to know more about my mother's family, ma'am. Where did they live here?"

"Two houses to the right. It's still called Dunsworth House, though the Buckhams live there now. Your grandfather spent a great deal of time by the river for his business, but your grandmother didn't want to live there, so he built the house here."

"I saw in the churchyard that they lost a number of children."

"In 1724. Such a terrible time. The sickness spread so quickly there was no chance to flee, even for those who had the means. Came and went like a fire, and then burned out."

"No one knew the cause?"

"Many thought it was a sailor returning from abroad. Jethro West's son, Saul. Came home sick but was so keen to meet his old friends he'd been everywhere before he took to his bed."

Perry entered the conversation. "No one spoke of evil causes, ma'am? In such times, some will whisper of spells and witches."

Miss Pellew hesitated and then lowered her voice. "There were some such, sir, or so I was told. I was a young child myself at the time. There was an old woman called Betty Stoker whom some blamed, but the vicar of the time defended her. Perhaps the feelings lingered, for I can remember him preaching on the subject for years afterward."

"On unjust suspicions?" Perry asked.

"On that, and that it was a sin to believe in superstitions such as witches and the evil eye. I must confess that as a girl I found such sermons more exciting than the ones on thrift or forbearance."

"I'm sure I would too," Claris said. She decided to invent a story. "There was a parish not far from where I grew up with a tradition of witchcraft. Not in the present, but the past. There was even a place called Coven Close—a dip in the ground where some said witches used to gather."

"How exciting!" Miss Pellew said. "Did you ever visit it?"

"I was far too nervous."

"Oh, I would have. You might not believe it, but I was quite venturesome as a girl. Clarrie remonstrated with me many a time, but in time I could remonstrate with her, when she related her adventures in London." She paused, then said, "Would you like her letters, dear?"

Claris stared. "Aunt Clarrie's letters?"

"Yes. She wrote to me a few times when she was in London. I still have them, for it didn't seem right to burn them once she was dead, though I'm sure that doesn't make sense. . . ."

"It does to me."

Miss Pellew smiled. "You're more like Clarrie than Nora, you know. Though not much like either."

"I think I take after my father."

"Except for the freckles."

"My mother didn't have freckles."

"Clarrie did. Nora made her cover them with paint." Miss Pellew sighed. "If only Clarrie had stayed here and married a local man. But what's done is done. I would be grateful if you'd take the letters. I don't read them now, but in a sense they haunt me. I sometimes wonder if there was anything I could have done to prevent her going to London."

"I'm sure there wasn't, ma'am. My mother was a forceful woman."

"She was, and they had all their father's money. He left it to them without restraint. Clarrie was not yet twenty-one, but Nora was. Oh dear, oh dear."

"I'm sorry if our visit has upset you."

"It's stirred some old aches, I admit, but enlivened my day. I shall enjoy gossiping all around the village about Nora Dunsworth's marriage and her happily married daughter. We so rarely have news."

Claris had to chuckle. "I understand, ma'am. I can add more news. I have brothers—twins, aged eleven."

"Eleven. Does that difference in age indicate lost children?"

Claris could only say, "No."

She should have remembered that village spinsters were not always naive. "I see," Miss Pellew said, clearly speculating. Then she smiled. "The letters."

She rang the bell on the table and the maid came in. "There are some letters in the bottom drawer of my dressing table, Annie. Please bring them down, and the box that's beside them."

The maid soon returned with the letters, which were tied with a pink ribbon, and a small cardboard box.

Miss Pellew passed over the letters and then opened the box.

"Clarrie made a will. She left nearly everything to Nora, of course, but she asked to be buried here and she specified some legacies to her old friends. I received this necklace. I've worn it now and then over the years, but it's not a style suitable for an older lady. I believe she would like you to have it, my dear."

Claris took the delicate necklace. It was a silver chain set with small ovals of amber.

"Freckles," Perry said.

"I see what you mean. Are you sure, Miss Pellew? About this and the letters?"

"Completely, my dear. I have good friends, but no close female relatives to leave that necklace to. And as I said, I think Clarrie would like you to have it. I do believe it was given her by Jeremy Knightly. A local man. A good man."

Her sigh spoke of might-have-beens.

"I will treasure it," Claris said, "and the letters."

"How pleasant this has been. Might you be so kind as to write to me now and then? I'd like to know how you go on."

"Then I will."

Claris thanked the woman again and they took their leave.

As they walked back to the inn, she said, "It's hard to believe that Miss Pellew's Clarrie wrote that curse, even if deranged."

"And impossible that she created a true curse. You have nothing to fear."

Claris paused to look at the church, the well-tended graveyard, and the tranquil green. Such a wholesome place to grow up. But it had once been blighted by a pestilence.

"Perhaps I'll come to believe that soon."

"Is it the infant memorials? I'll have them taken away and destroyed—"

"No!" Claris exclaimed. "No. That would be horrible."

"They're marble, Claris. The infants themselves are buried far away."

"It wouldn't be right. That really would curse us."

"There are no such things as curses!"

"Don't shout at me."

"My apologies, but I dislike seeing you afraid. I wish I'd rid the manor of the things before you saw them."

"Perhaps I do too, but we can't turn back the clock. Thank you for bringing me here. It has helped. Before, I only had the portrait of Aunt Clarrie and my mother's praise of her, but now I know her better. I'm sure she could never truly ill-wish anyone, but I'm equally sure that Giles Perriam deserved it. How foul he must have been to treat such a sweet lady so cruelly."

"You'll hear no argument on that from me. Come. Let's go home."

As they went to the inn, Claris was aware of the letters in her pocket, wishing she could read them now.

"We could take refreshment here," Perry said.

"We just had tea."

"There might be gossip to confirm what Miss Pellew told you."

Claris was desperate to get home and read the letters, but he had a point, so she agreed.

The keeper of the Ship in Full Sail was a Mistress Greenberry, very round, very short, and very jolly. She quickly provided coffee and cakes for them but then hovered, clearly as keen to know about them as they were to know about the Dunsworths.

"A pleasant village, ma'am," Claris said, sipping her coffee. "My husband brought me here to seek news of my mother's family, the Dunsworths."

"The Dunsworths!" exclaimed Mistress Greenberry. "Fancy that. Hasn't been a Dunsworth here for many a year, and they were newcomers before then."

Claris had forgotten that aspect—that most of the families here would go back centuries.

"We visited Miss Pellew and she told us about my grandfather building a house here."

"That he did, back when I was a girl."

"What sort of man was he?" Claris asked.

"Hearty, ma'am. A bit blustery, but warmhearted."

"And my grandmother?"

"A kindly lady, though a bit reserved. Of course, after the 'twenty-four she became more so, poor lady. And he less hearty. But many were hereabouts."

"It must have been a terrible time."

"Took two of my brothers, ma'am, which is why I have the inn now."

Claris had the impression that in that regard the '24 hadn't been a complete disaster. She could understand. There were few opportunities for a woman to be independent in this world.

"These are delicious cakes, ma'am. Are they your own work?"

"They are, ma'am."

Having dished out praise, Claris continued her questions.

"Miss Pellew described my Aunt Clarrie as a heartbreaker."

"That she was, but not by intent, poor dear. I'd tell her she must be colder to her swains, but she'd say she couldn't be. There were many lasses around here who were glad when her sister took her off to London, God rest her soul."

Claris hadn't thought of that—of the jealousy of the other young women. She also noted that in youth Clarrie had been on good terms with the innkeeper's daughter, even though they would have been of different status in the village. Had that been her kind heart again, or had they been true friends?

"So sad that she died," Claris said. "My mother grieved for her most deeply."

The innkeeper stared. "Never say you're Nora Dunsworth's daughter? I hadn't thought how you came to be, but *Nora*? She had no time for men at all."

"People change. She married my father, the rector of Old Barford in Surrey."

"Well, I never." The woman subsided into a chair. "Well, I never. When she came back here to bury Clarrie, she spewed her hatred of all men, but especially the one responsible for Clarrie's death. She never said who or how, but he must have broken Clarrie's heart. She was too gentle for this life. I always worried about her."

Claris tried to find a way to introduce the subject of

covens but failed. She didn't want the whole village wondering why those Perriams had been asking about witches.

As Perry said, the whole idea was ridiculous.

But then why and how had that virulent curse come from sweet, gentle Clarrie Dunsworth?

Chapter 35

Soon they were on their way back to London. Claris resented the journey, for she desperately wanted to read Aunt Clarrie's letters. Perhaps Perry felt the same. As they left the village, he said, "Why don't you read those letters aloud as we go."

"What a good idea." Claris dug them out of her pocket and untied the ribbon. She caught a faint perfume and put them to her nose.

"Any scent could as well be from Miss Pellew as your aunt," Perry said.

"I know, but I think it's the same. Yes, it's the one I remember from Aunt Clarrie's fichu and handkerchief. It brings back so many memories. And it's sweet and gentle, as she is said to have been."

"Read the letters," he said. "And start from the first."

She sifted through them. "The date of handling is written on the front, so this one."

The address was written in careful, upright writing, with each loop flourished. It was light, as if Clarrie had barely touched the pen to the paper. Sweet and gentle, like the lady herself.

"*My dear Olivia* ... How odd. I would never have thought Miss Pellew an Olivia."

"Don't be distracted by incidentals."

Claris stuck her tongue out at him, even though his eyes were on the road and he wouldn't see. Perhaps because of that.

*My dear Olivia, so here we are in London. I must
confess that I find it noisy and the air not good,
though I'm told it is much worse in the height of
summer, and in winter when everyone is burning
coal for heat.*

"What's the date on the letter?" Perry asked.

"May twelfth. It doesn't say the year."

"It's 1739, I assume. The year she died, unless this mis-
adventure lasted over a twelvemonth. Is there an address?"

"At the sign of the dove, Dun Street."

"When I said to read the letters, I meant the entire
contents."

Claris stuck out her tongue again, and this time he
saw it. He grinned.

"I'd tell you to read the letters," she said, "except that
I don't want to drive. Shall I continue?"

"By all means. But every word."

Claris found her place.

*Our rooms are pleasant. We have two bedchambers
and a parlor in which we also eat. It has an outlook
over a field. Our landlady, Mistress Stallycombe, is
very respectable. She provides breakfast daily and
clean bed linen once a week. She will also provide a
dinner if requested, at extra cost. I suppose we are
comfortable, and there are parks nearby, but it is not
at all like village life.*

*I must not repine! We attended a play last night.
So magical, my dear Olivia, and so dramatic. I wish
you were here to share such excitements. There were
some parts that I felt not quite proper, but Nora
commanded me not to be a bumpkin, and most of
the company was amused, ladies as well as gentlemen. Your dear friend, Clarrie.*

Poor Aunt Clarrie," Claris said, folding the letter.

"She would have been much happier marrying a local man."

Something was teasing at her mind.

"The next?" Perry prompted.

"Did anything in there strike you as significant?"

He glanced at her. "No. You?"

"I feel there's something."

"Did you read every word?"

"Yes."

"It will come to you later. Read the next."

She unfolded the single sheet and read it out, beginning with the same address and the date, May 25. It related a trip to St. James's Park, and paying a call on a Lady Steventon.

"She seems to expect Miss Pellew to know the name," Claris said, "so she was probably a local lady. We could go back...."

"Not today. I can find out about Lady Steventon in Town. They would have been hoping the lady would be their entree into better circles. We'll find out if that worked in the next."

Claris refolded the second and went on to the third. "A trip to Ranelagh Gardens." After she'd read to the end, she said, "Clarrie thoroughly enjoyed that. Would I?"

"Illuminations, music, and fireworks?" he said with a smile. "I assume you would, and I will enjoy taking you there."

Claris reflected his smile, no longer regretting the length of their journey. They were alone together with a shared purpose, in harmony. It seemed so easy to be in harmony with him, despite her prickly nature.

"The next?"

She unfolded and read it. "Ah, here we are. *'At Ranelagh I met a particular gentleman. He is an acquaintance of Lady Steventon's and very fine. He has such charming manners and a delightful smile....'*" She looked at Perry. "Giles? I'd never have thought him charming. I suppose his portrait shows good looks."

"As Miss Pellew said, charm requires some effort. A rake finds it worthwhile to make the effort. Does Clarrie name him?"

"Not in this letter." Claris read an account of an assembly where a certain gentleman paid marked attentions and went on quickly to the next.

"They won't disappear if you don't read them fast enough," Perry said. "Attention to detail is key."

"I've read you every word. If only she named her admirer."

"Let's assume it was Giles. Do you think she was completely pleased with him?"

Claris read over the letter in her hand. "I don't know. She remarks on how pleased Mother was with him." She frowned at the decorative lines of Clarrie's writing as if they could reveal more than the words. "Mother was in control of this. She was pushing Clarrie toward Giles as much for her own sake . . ."

And then it came.

The point she'd missed all along.

"Perry, look at this!"

He drew the horse to a stand. "At what?"

Claris thrust the letter at him. "The writing! It's nothing at all like the writing on the curse."

He whistled. "It isn't, is it? When you first saw the curse, you said the writing was similar to your mother's, only smaller."

Everything fell into place.

"Mother wrote it. Oh, yes, I can believe she could invent such vitriol. But, Perry, I can also believe that she could create a curse that would have effect!"

He rescued the letter from her clutching hand. "How could your mother know how to do that? Even if a curse is possible."

"Perhaps hating fiercely enough makes it possible. I know I'm unreasonable about this, but it matters."

"Only if you believe in it."

"Don't you? Not at all?"

His hand tightened on hers. "Occasionally. In the dark of the night, and only because it would be just if betrayed innocents could wreak vengeance. But then I see that there's no justice in the workings of this. The innocents suffered the most."

"I'm sure my mother rejoiced in each death."

"But didn't cause them. They were ill luck as much as the pestilence that visited Wellsted. Please try to believe that."

"I'll try."

He kissed her gloved hand and released it. "There's one more letter."

He set the horse in motion again as Claris unfolded Aunt Clarrie's last letter. She expected dark drama, but it was another light recounting of London entertainments. The only hint came at the end. " *'I will soon have exciting news to share with you, my dear friend....'* I wonder how it played out. Wouldn't you think she'd have written to Miss Pellew after the spurious marriage?"

"She was probably told not to. That it must be secret for some reason. Giles was still quite young, so perhaps he warned of trustees who would object. Hers wasn't a unique story back then. Only the vows were necessary, and rakes exploited that with false clergymen and cronies as witnesses who'd later deny the vows were ever said."

Claris put the letters neatly together and retied the ribbon around them. It was now thinning and weakening with age.

"Poor Aunt Clarrie. It would be a sin, but I could hate my mother for what she did to her."

"She was probably convinced that she was doing the best thing for her sister. That's the worst about people like that. They are sure of their own righteousness."

Claris thought back. "Yes, that's the word. Even when doing vile things, she was sure she was righteous. She never, ever made a person happy, and when she saw happiness she sought to destroy it. She made Father ban the maypole."

"It does have pagan, and even vulgar, connotations."

"I'm sure that was her argument. When she died, he reversed the ban and a number of other petty restrictions she'd insisted on."

"Because he wanted to wipe her influence away," he said. "I could almost be sorry for Henry Mallow. If there's truth to the notion that suffering on earth reduces suffering in the afterlife, he might now be in heaven."

"He certainly tried." Claris tucked away the letters and revealed something she'd never told anyone. "He whipped himself."

"What?"

"I came upon him once, in the church late in the evening. . . ."

Perry took her hand and halted the horse again.

"Peter had fallen and banged his head. It swelled and I went in search of my father. He was kneeling before the altar, bare from the waist up, with only the light of the setting sun upon him, swinging a many-stranded whip, muttering prayers for mercy."

"That must have shocked you. Could he have been the clergyman at the supposed wedding?"

"No, he became one shortly before moving to Old Barford."

"A false witness, then. How old were you when you came across him?"

"Fifteen, I think."

"You are a remarkable woman to have survived all you have."

"I had no choice. I had the twins to care for."

"And now I will care for you and your brothers. Let your burdens pass to me."

She looked at him, absorbing his words. He was offering true support, and she could trust him as she'd never felt able to trust anyone before.

She squeezed his hand. "Thank you. You can't know what that means to me. Together we can make Perriam Manor a happy home for our children and our children's children."

She instantly regretted the implications of that and wasn't surprised when his lips twisted a little, nor when he said, "I will always do my best."

He was still devoted to his London life, and she must count her blessings. Her many, many blessings.

They were home just in time for dinner. Claris would have preferred a peaceful time to think over many things, but Athena and Ellie were in the drawing room and Athena demanded to know what she'd learned. Claris regretted telling her the purpose of the expedition.

She told them, but not about the revelation of the handwriting.

"On that curse," Athena said, "was there any mark that could be blood?"

"I don't think so." Claris looked to Perry for confirmation.

"Not even a blob of ink. Very neat, all in all. Why?"

"As you are still fretting about it, I consulted someone who interests herself in superstitions. I'm told that a curse requires blood, preferably used as ink, but if that's not possible, a drop."

"Thank you for asking," Claris said. She'd thought her grandmother entirely wrapped in her own affairs.

"I hope you are now reassured that Giles Perriam was unfortunate by chance."

"That points to an unjust God," Claris protested.

"So do the deaths at Wellsted, and the families killed by fire in Whitechapel not long ago. We live in an unjust world, Claris, and must survive as best we can. The meek do not inherit the earth, and indeed, what would they do with such responsibility?"

That made Claris laugh. "You should write a commentary on the Beatitudes."

"That would get me whipped at the cart's tail. I'm more interested in commentaries about the injustices perpetrated against women. You left last night before Miss Sprott read Sarah Fyge's 'The Emulation.' An excellent piece. 'Say, Tyrant Custom, why must we obey / The impositions of thy haughty Sway; / From the first dawn of Life, unto the Grave, / Poor Womankind's in every State, a Slave.'"

"Not Empress Catherine of Russia," Perry pointed out, "nor Maria Theresa, Holy Roman Empress."

"And much good they've done for the women in their dominions."

"A woman's fault, not man's."

The debate shot backward and forward. Claris met Ellie's eyes and saw the same resigned amusement.

Claris agreed with Athena in principle, but she couldn't become passionate about it. Her passions flowed into Perriam Manor and the child within her.

And the man who'd given her both.

The man who was enjoying the spirited debate as much as Athena.

The man who loved the rich tapestry of London life.

In bed that night, sweetly in his arms, she finally told him. "I believe I'm carrying a child."

"You know so soon?"

"I've known for some weeks."

"Why didn't you tell me sooner? I'm pleased, of course. I know you want a child."

How to answer his question? Not with the truth, that she'd been afraid he wouldn't want to pleasure her in this bed if there was no purpose.

"I'm not sure," she lied. "Something to do with the curse."

He shifted to hold her closer. "No wonder it's weighed on you with a child already on the way. I truly believe it's hollow, my dear. You have nothing to fear beyond life's normal hazards. *We* have nothing to fear."

She turned to kiss him. "I like 'we.' Our home, our child, even if you must often be away."

"I will do my best to be a good father," he said, but she heard the underlying tone, that he doubted how good that could be.

She snuggled closer.

She'd find a way.

He would visit Perriam Manor for at least the thirty days a year, and in between she would visit London. There was the problem of his male-only rooms, but perhaps they could afford to rent a house like this frequently.

She would find a way to have this sweet togetherness most of the time.

Chapter 36

In the morning, they fell out.

Over breakfast Claris said, "Today, Dun Street."

"I'll take you, but not today. I have matters to attend to."

"I can go alone. I'll take Alice."

"It's not safe, and nor is this obsession. Put any thought of a curse out of mind and think of our baby."

Claris put down her cup. "We know Aunt Clarrie didn't cast a curse, but my mother might have done. I need to understand, and explanations could lie in Dun Street. I can't bear delay."

"But you must. I forbid it."

"What?" She stared at him. "So you turn tyrant now? Exerting your husbandly authority?"

"In this case, yes. I'll try to find the time—"

Claris thumped the table so that crockery rattled. "And if you can't, I'm to forgo this opportunity?"

"Yes!" He rose. "There's nothing more to discover, and you need to put it out of mind."

He left before she could make a retort. She grabbed the sugar bowl and hurled it to shatter on the door. And then burst into tears.

Ellie hurried in and gathered her in her arms. "Dearie, dearie, what is it?"

Claris sniffed. "I don't know! Perry. The curse. Aunt Clarrie . . ."

"There, there; there, there. It's likely the child. Makes for funny moods."

Claris blew her nose. "Do you think so?"

"Even Thenie was weepy at times."

"That's hard to imagine."

"True, though. You need to avoid things that upset you."

"Like the curse."

"That's right. There's nothing to it, dearie, and if there was, what could you do?"

"My marriage was supposed to end its power." She still hadn't told Ellie and Athena that the curse was her mother's work, and she didn't want to. It brought it too close to home.

"There, then," Ellie said.

"Yet it haunts me all the same. And Perry forbade it!"

"Forbade what?"

"My going to Dun Street to learn more."

"What's at Dun Street?"

"It's where Mother and Aunt Clarrie lived when in London."

"That was a long time ago."

"We found people in Wellsted who remembered them, so why not there?"

"What do you hope to learn?" Ellie asked.

"Something. Anything. How Aunt Clarrie was when there. How she died. Perhaps then I can put her shade to rest. Yes, that's it. I feel as if I owe something to Aunt Clarrie."

"Well, then, why don't we go?"

"We?"

"You and me. Your grandmother's gone off to a meeting about the rights of women. I excused myself. I find it all a bit silly."

"I'm sure it's not. Husbands can be cruel oppressors and are supported by the law."

"Talking isn't going to change that. It'll need bloody war."

"I hope you're wrong."

"So do I, but I prefer to do things that can be done.

We need to know how to get to Dun Street. Do you have an address?"

"At the sign of the dove, and there's the landlady's name. Stally-something. I'll reread the letters and find out." She hugged Ellie. "Thank you! I'm sure I'll feel at ease when I've followed this last thread."

Claris hurried upstairs and took out the letters.

But then she hesitated.

Perry had been so firm on the subject.

She shook that away. *Say, Tyrant Custom, why must we obey / The impositions of thy haughty Sway.*

She would *not* be ruled by a husband. That had been clear in their agreement. She was to be independent. Just because they'd consummated the marriage, just because that was so sweet, just because she loved him . . .

Oh, she did, she did.

But that couldn't be allowed to weaken her.

She found the right letter. Mistress Stallycombe. An unusual name that would be remembered. When she returned the letters to the drawer, she saw her pistol case.

She opened it and took out the gun. It was still loaded from the journey, but she'd emptied the firing pan for safety. She poured new powder there and carefully settled the pin.

How to carry it, though?

It would fit in one of her pockets, but she didn't like the thought of it there. What if by some mischance it went off? It wasn't cocked, but accidents could happen.

She found the cardboard box in which the mended stockings had been delivered, lined it with handkerchiefs, and nestled the pistol there.

When she went downstairs, Ellie said, "What's that?"

"An excuse. More stockings to be mended."

Ellie shrugged, but when they were outside she said, "You don't need an excuse to leave the house, Claris."

"I know, but it's done now."

"Let me carry it."

"No. Did you get directions?"

"Yes, but the stocking mender doesn't lie that way."

"I've heard of a better one. How far is it? Should we take a hackney?"

"Not unless you've lost the use of your legs. We can go most of the way across the park and I could do with a good walk. I've sat around too many fancy salons in the past few days."

Chapter 37

Perry regretted the argument as soon as he was out of the house. He'd return except for that smash of china. He'd give her time to calm down. In any case, he was expected at Malloren House to review the situation. Claris should understand that he couldn't devote every moment to her whims and fancies.

Clocks began to strike around Town. Nine o'clock. Too early for Malloren House. He went to Porter's coffeehouse, a fashionable place, which meant there would be few customers at this hour. He needed to think.

There were only two other gentlemen in the establishment and he knew neither. One was reading a book, the other a newspaper. He picked up one of the other newspapers provided by the proprietor and carried it to a table, where he ordered coffee. He opened the paper but turned his thoughts to the two spies.

He wanted the matter tied up so he could devote the next few days to Claris. There were so many London treats she hadn't tasted. The theater, Ranelagh . . .

Concentrate. The one remaining puzzle was why Ryder and Pierrepoint refused to explain their actions. What pressure had been fierce enough to make them act against their natures, and why wouldn't they reveal what it was, even when promised immunity?

At this point, no one wanted to prosecute them. If their acts were made public, they would reveal vulnerability in the two military offices. Did they guess that?

There was also the matter of the king not wanting Pierrepoint prosecuted, but Perry didn't think the man had the wit or nerve to exploit that.

So what did they gain by keeping silent?

Why didn't they want those who'd tormented them to suffer for it?

He went round and round it but made no progress, so he looked over the newspaper to clear his mind.

The destruction of the bastions at Dunkirk had begun at last. It had been agreed on in the peace treaty, but France had been delaying. That would make a French invasion less likely, but another article reported that French boats were fishing on the Grand Banks. Deliberate provocation.

Had the French learned anything useful from Pierrepoint and Ryder?

Did Guerchy have other spies as yet undetected?

He flipped a page. Trouble at home, and not caused by the French. Miners were refusing their labor in the north and the military had been ordered in. Cate Burgoyne had written him a letter about that. Pure greed on the mine owner's part, according to Cate, but then, he'd always taken the side of the persecuted.

He turned to lighter news. The Duke and Duchess of York were making merry in Brunswick. Soon they'd return with the Prince and Princess of Brunswick and Town would be afire with levees and celebrations. A pity Claris would have left by then.

One small item caught his eye. A gentleman of comfortable means and excellent reputation who was soon to have been married had shot himself in his rooms in Jethro Street.

Jethro Street.

He rose, put a coin on the table for the newspaper, and left. Soon he was at Malloren House, where he asked for Cyn. After a short delay he was taken up to a parlor, which must be part of Cyn's rooms here. Cyn was alone, wearing a dressing gown over shirt and breeches. A table held the remains of breakfast. Somewhere nearby a woman talked and a child giggled.

"I've disturbed you," Perry said. "My apologies, but you need to see this." He handed over the paper, indicating the middle of the right-hand column.

"Odd," Cyn said, taking one of the chairs by the fireplace. "But important?"

Perry took the other. "Ryder lives in Jethro Street."

"So do many."

"And was engaged to wed."

"So are many, I'm sure. Why think this is about him?"

"We can find out, but it's stirred some thoughts. It appears the man in Jethro Street had everything to live for and no reason to kill himself, and yet he did."

"Being accused of treason might be cause. He was in deep distress over it."

"But why *now*?" Perry asked. "He's been in anguish over his sins for weeks."

"But now he's caught." Cyn put the paper down. "The country air's addled you."

"No, no, some idea is trying to form. There's a connection to another case." Perry hit his head with the palm of his hand, trying to shake the insight loose. "I have it! Did you hear about the case of Thomas and James Brown?"

"No."

"It occurred when you were in Canada. They were petty thieves, but they devised a novel way of going about it. They lurked at night in the shadowy parts of London, particularly those known for assignations of a certain sort, waiting for lone men to pass by. Then they dragged their victim aside, opened his breeches, and threatened to take him to court for sodomy if he didn't give up any valuables."

"'Struth. But their word against his."

"With the weight of proof on the accused, remember. How can a man prove he's not a sodomite when there's no obvious reason for a false accusation? Once caught on this hook, the victim could be milked again and again, and that was the Browns' way. None of their victims were brave enough to take them to court, and with reason. There have been men hanged for sodomy on very flimsy evidence. Enough to terrify anyone accused of the crime."

"Were all the Browns' victims innocent?" Cyn asked. "If so, why were they in such places at night?"

"Another point against them if it came to court. In the case brought to trial, the one that did it for the Browns, the victim was a servant simply taking the quickest way home after an errand. He was new to London and didn't know its ways. By singular good fortune, another man came by and saw what was happening, so he could testify to it. But as the case unfolded, it turned out that a previous victim had hanged himself in despair—over the constant payments but also over the shame of the accusation."

Cyn whistled. "Same pattern. Repeated demands on Ryder and Pierrepoint. Both would fear the accusation, and Ryder in particular wouldn't be able to face even the hint of suspicion. I see a flaw in your theory, however. Neither man would wander in such places at night."

"Their entrapment would have been more neatly devised. I suspect someone they trusted invited them to the Merry Maid."

"Pierrepoint would go out of stupidity, but Ryder?"

"The bait must have been right. There are groups devoted to ridding London of vice through prosecuting sinners. Any evidence he was part of one of those?"

"Yes. I didn't take much note of it, as he wouldn't be meeting a French spy there, but he did regularly attend meetings of the Society for the Moral Improvement of London."

"Why the devil do people skim over details? Never mind. He was tempted there to gain evidence, and foolishly went without another member of the society. Once through the door a number of seemingly worthy citizens would be ready to stand witness."

"Thereby incriminating themselves?"

"They could support each other's claims of innocence but agree on his guilt. He wouldn't have been willing to risk it."

Cyn shook his head. "I'd have sworn he'd go to the lions before giving in to blackmail."

"But that wasn't the torture he faced. It was trial in court, accused of a vile crime, with the terrifying possibility that he could be found guilty and shamed forever. One man—not a victim of the Browns, but merely unfortunate in where he was—was convicted even though many vouched for him, and he had a wife and three children."

"Gads."

"It's a fever at the moment, the desire to stamp out vice."

"But why shoot himself now?" Cyn inhaled and answered himself. "Because he was being pressured to explain how he was compelled, and he couldn't bear to even speak of it."

"In case some would believe the accusation true."

"Poor man," Cyn said. "He didn't deserve such torture."

"He did leak secrets. The fact they were minor doesn't excuse him. He'd have leaked bigger ones if squeezed hard enough."

"No," Cyn said. "He'd have shot himself sooner. Damn Guerchy and the French."

"I'm sure we do things as foul. It's the corruption of war. For now, we have hopes of ending this. Confronted with the truth, Pierrepoint will crack."

"Agreed, and the people at the Merry Maid will spill all they know under pressure. The weight of evidence will crush Guerchy and cripple French espionage, for now, at least. The French won't want such sordid means known."

"Can you report all this to Rothgar?" Perry asked. "I need to go home. A slight disagreement with my wife."

"Then make haste, my friend. Sooner is always better than later in that."

As they walked across the park, Claris asked, "Is London not suiting you, Ellie?"

"I must be getting old, for I enjoy country life now. Town has too much chatter, and I've never had the head for arguing about ideas. On liberty. On rights. On miracles, even. I remember Thenie talking about a time when men argued about how many angels could dance on the head of a pin. I ask you, why should they want to?"

Claris broke into laughter. "Oh, Ellie, you have such good sense."

"Well, I think so, dearie, and all this clever talk just causes troubles. Look at the Reformation."

"What about the Reformation?" Claris asked, fascinated.

"Nothing but trouble."

"The Roman Church was corrupt."

"And those that replaced it haven't been?"

"Ellie!"

"It's people that make saints or sinners, dearie. I've known saintly Papists and wicked ones, but as many of both among Protestants, and among Mohammedans too."

"You should speak your thoughts at one of the salons."

"Oh, no. I know my place."

Claris frowned at her. "You don't think your views would be respected? Perry pointed out that female rulers don't liberate their female subjects. Do female philosophers not liberate women of all classes?"

"Not that I've noticed. My odd notions would stir up a great deal of bother, and most of it would land on my back. I'm no martyr."

"It is hard to see why anyone would choose to be, but isn't it sometimes necessary? Change doesn't come easily."

"Now, that's the truth, dearie. Stuck in their ways,

most people are, and it's bloody war to change things. I can remember a time when I wanted to fight battles, but not anymore. Not anymore."

They fell into silence as they followed a path between lawns and trees, but Claris pondered the problem.

Why should Ellie "know her place"? Anyone was entitled to their thoughts, so why shouldn't they be entitled to speak them? And yet, in times like the Reformation people were burned at the stake for just that. If Ellie wouldn't be heard in a beau monde salon, were there salons for other sorts of people?

"Mistress Perriam! How delightful."

Claris blinked out of her thoughts to see the Fox, in company with two similar creatures in silken finery. And here she was, in her simplest clothing for this venture.

"Do please allow me to present my friends, Mistress Fayne and Miss Brokesby."

Claris curtsied and introduced Miss Gable, though she knew the three women would guess that Ellie wasn't their social equal. They couldn't, in courtesy, refuse to acknowledge her.

The Fox did so, but slightly, long nose pinched, then turned back to Claris. "I had no idea you meant to come to Town, Mistress Perriam. I would have offered to be your guide."

"How kind, ma'am, but I am well served in that way. Particularly by my husband."

"Oh, I'm sure he serves you well," the Fox said with a smirk, and at least one of the other women tittered. "But a man can't advise about mantua-makers and such as well as other women."

Claris heard the sly dig about her clothing. "How true," she said. "Lady Walgrave and Lady Ashart have been most generous with their advice."

It was almost as good as firing a pistol at them and left them dumbstruck.

Claris dipped a curtsy. "You must excuse me, ladies. I

have an appointment." Once out of earshot, she muttered, "Eat that and choke on it."

Ellie chuckled. "Silly widgeons. And that includes you for being jealous."

"I'm not!"

Ellie made no comment, so Claris pulled a face at her.

"You've no cause," Ellie said.

"You think not?"

"A woman like that beside you, dearie?"

"I'm no beauty."

"You're more than that, but in any case, he's not the sort."

"For what?"

"For adultery."

"I thought all men were. We're likely to spend a lot of time apart."

"It'll all work out," Ellie said comfortably, looking around. "We leave the park on this side, I believe."

As they entered a street, she asked a passing maidservant and was given directions. But the maid added, "It's not so nice a place, ma'am."

The maid went on her way, and Claris paused. "I wonder what that means."

"What it said, dearie."

"It can't be too bad. Aunt Clarrie approved of their lodgings, and this area seems respectable." A part of her wanted to give up this mission, but she wouldn't, for a great many reasons.

She led the way down the road as directed, and saw "Dun Street" painted on the wall of a corner house. It was the end house of a terrace that was not so different from Godwin Street except that the houses were two stories rather than three.

When they turned into the street, however, Claris saw what the maid might have meant, but surely the grim feel was simply a matter of light. Dun Street was narrow—only just wide enough for a carriage to pass along—and shaded by a large building on the right-hand side. A smell suggested that it was a brewery.

"That must be recently built," she said. "Aunt Clarrie mentioned being able to look out at fields."

"And pulled the street down," Ellie said. "Likely your Mistress Stallycombe has moved elsewhere."

Claris feared that was true. The quietness here should have felt safe, but she had to fight an urge to do as Ellie implied and abandon the mission. She only wanted some information. This wouldn't take long.

"What harm could there be in the middle of the morning?" she said, walking forward. "Someone here might know her new address. Look for doves painted over the doors."

"No point, dearie. They've converted to numbers."

Claris sighed. "So they have, but some of the signs are still visible. There's a yellow pig."

She walked along, trying to make out the designs. Three roses? A crown and spindle—

She was knocked against a wall by someone hurtling past.

The man grabbed for the box, but she held on by instinct, even as her shoes slipped and she fell. The assailant, a grubby young man with bad teeth, struck her arm with his fist. "Let go!"

In sheer fury, Claris yelled, "No!" and kicked him in the shin. Ellie was assailing him from the back, and he flailed out, knocking her down.

"Ellie!"

He wrenched at the box again but got only the lid.

Claris saw the forgotten pistol, grabbed it, cocked it, and fired.

The jolt threw her backward as the explosion rang in her ears. She stared in horror at the blood spreading down the man's dirty shirt. She'd killed a man!

Then she thought, *Ellie, Ellie?*

She shuffled sideways, still pointing the gun, even though it was now useless. "Ellie? Are you all right?"

"Not too bad," Ellie said, but faintly. At least she was sitting up, but hat askew, skin sallow with shock.

Claris knew she needed to stand, but she couldn't seem to find strength in her legs.

Thank God, help was coming.

No, not help.

Others like their attacker.

With knives.

"Help!" she tried to scream, but it came weakly from her throat.

She waved the empty pistol. "Keep off! Keep off!"

"You've bloody killed Bob!" snarled an older man. There were four, all ages. "You'll hang for that, you bitch, but we'll have your baubles anyway. And your clothes. And maybe more."

Claris cried out for help again, louder this time.

Why was no one responding?

The man leered. "None here'll help you, not against us...."

He was right. The street stayed silent.

"We'll start with this." The man grabbed the pistol.

Claris clung to it with idiotic desperation.

He raised a fist....

With a roar, a whirlwind arrived, slashing silver.

Claris covered her head, but it was Perry! A Perry she couldn't have imagined, furious, vengeful, stabbing one man after another with sword and dagger.

In moments, the ruffians were in flight, all bleeding, some supporting others, including Bob, who was alive enough to yell with pain as he was dragged away.

"What the devil did you think you were doing?" snarled this new Perry, bloody weapons in hand, blood splatters on his white linen....

Claris fainted.

Chapter 38

Perry fell to his knees and supported Claris up off the ground.

"She's not wounded," Ellie said, crawling to their side. "Just shocked. And the child as well, likely. Making her faint, I mean. Oh dear, oh dear."

Perry remembered the memorial of the wife shocked to death by a lightning bolt and held Claris closer. "You at least should have known better." No, he couldn't berate an old woman who was pasty white and had a lump swelling on her head. "I'm sorry."

Claris stirred. He turned all his attention back to her. "That's right, love. Look at me."

Her eyes fluttered open. "Love?"

"Are you all right?"

"I don't know. Did I faint? I've never fainted before...."

"You had cause."

She stared up at him, eyes huge. "I *shot* someone."

"Brave lady."

He heard a door open. A surly man was peering out of the nearest house. When his eyes met Perry's, he began to close the door again.

"A guinea," Perry said quickly. "For refuge for these ladies."

The man's eyes slid from side to side. Other doors were opening and some windows too as the residents cautiously assessed the situation. Perry could see the man's thoughts. If he didn't grab the guinea, someone else would.

"Come in, sir, come in. Izzy, come and 'elp these poor people!"

A young maid peered out around him and then ran forward to Ellie. "Oh, you poor lady. Come you in. Those bullies!"

Perry got Claris to her feet and made sure she was steady, leaning against the wall, while he collected his dropped sword and dagger and restored them to their sheaths.

"I'll carry you."

She held him off. "I can walk. I'm much better now." But then she clutched his arm. "Oh, Perry, thank God you came!"

He held her close as they entered the house. "Thank God indeed, but there's a reckoning to come, wife. I forbade this."

He saw her lips tighten and rejoiced. Her spirit was still strong.

They were ushered into a front parlor that showed signs of once having been decent if not elegant. Now it was dirty and shabby. He saw a mouse-gnawed hole in the skirting boards and a damp stain beneath the window.

The young maidservant had steered Ellie to an upholstered chair, showing more sense than he had. He settled Claris on the settee with her feet up.

"I'm all right," she protested. "See to Ellie."

"I'm all right, dearie, for all that my head hurts."

"Oh, Ellie. There's a lump!"

"Hit my head on the wall; that's all. No real harm done. I could do with a cup of tea, though."

Perry showed the man a guinea as proof. "Do you have tea?" he asked, without much hope.

The man shook his head.

"Brandy?"

"Only gin, sir."

"Then gin it is. And send your servant to fetch a hackney, if you please."

"Izzy."

The one word was apparently permission or command, for the girl ran off. Perry saw that she was barefooted and accustomed to it.

"This place was finer twenty years ago," Perry said.

"That it was, sir. It's the brewery wot changed everything. No one of the better sort wanted to rent rooms 'ere after that."

"Were you here in the better days?" Claris asked, suddenly alert and shifting to sit, feet on the floor.

Perry wanted to order her to lie quietly, but he supposed they might as well discover what they could now they were here, and she did seem restored. Except, that was, for dirty smears on her clothing and some splashes of blood from his violent foray.

The rage still seethed inside him, and he consciously calmed it before it erupted in undesirable ways. When he'd seen . . .

He'd called her "love," and he'd meant it.

Until that moment, he hadn't realized how crucial she was to him.

"Grew up 'ere," the man said. "Me mam kept this 'ouse and made a pretty living from it whilst raising me brother and me. Me brother works at the armories, but I went to sea. Ruined me back, came 'ome. When Mam died I stayed."

Claris asked, "Your mother wasn't Mistress Stallycombe, was she?"

"Nah, three doors down she was. Sign of the dove. Number seven, now. Numbers," he said and spat at the floor as if house numbers had caused all his woes.

"The gin?" Perry reminded him.

The man shuffled away.

"He can't be as old as he looks," Claris murmured.

"Life can wear people down," Ellie said, "and as he said, his back."

Perry saw Claris look at him and knew what she was going to say. "We must visit number seven before we leave."

He didn't want to fight with her. "We'll see what our benefactor has to say first."

The man returned with a pottery jug and three chipped cups. He poured the clear fluid into each and passed them round.

Perry tasted his quickly to see if it was drinkable, but it was good stuff as gin went. Claris sipped a little and wrinkled her nose. Ellie seemed to relish it.

"May I have your name, sir?" Perry asked. "We are Mr. and Mistress Perriam and Miss Gable."

"Williams, sir. 'Enry Williams."

"Can you tell us anything about Mistress Stally-combe? Does she still live here?"

"Her? Nah. Thought 'erself better even then. Left as soon as the brewery was planned."

"Do you know where she went?"

"Sorry, sir. You relations of 'ers, then?"

"No, but relations of my wife's rented rooms from her back in 1739. My wife is curious about their stay here."

"I was still 'ere back then. Delivery boy, I was, to an apothecary. Good job, but I took a notion to travel." His morose expression said that in hindsight that hadn't been a good idea. "Shot in the China Sea, I was, and sickened in Barbados; then me back went on me. Not 'ealthy in foreign parts, sir. Not 'ealthy at all."

"I'm sure you're right. The ladies we're interested in were the Misses Dunsworth."

The man shifted. It was subtle, but Perry saw it.

"You remember them?"

"I might," the man said, mouth working, probably on one or more loose teeth. "Dunsworth. Dun Street and worth," he said with a smirk. "Not thought of that afore. Worth a bit to you, is it, sir, to know what I know?"

"No." Perry sensed Claris's start of objection and quickly added, "It's merely curiosity, but you might think the guinea covers a bit of gossip."

He took Claris's hand and squeezed it, hoping she'd understand. He didn't want this man to think his knowledge important, particularly as there was clearly something to know.

Williams sucked his teeth a bit more, then gave in. "One of 'em died. That's why I remember 'em. Not many guests died 'ere back then. More now, though, if guests you can call 'em."

"How did she die? A fever?"

"Aye, that was it, sir. A fever."

Devil take it. He shouldn't have led him that way.

"Did she have a doctor?"

The man chuckled at that. "No, sir. No doctor, that's for sure."

Perry feared he knew what was to come. He let a silence run. Williams had come this far, so he wanted to tell the tale. Eventually the man said, "Mam was as close to a doctor as she 'ad."

"Your mother?"

"Aye, sir, she played that part on the street. Midwife, laying out, 'erbs and such."

As he feared. Perry hesitated, but Ellie said it. "Your mother helped one of the Miss Dunsworths to restore her courses."

That was the term, and Perry was grateful to her for finding it. Tonics to restore a lady's courses—in other words, to rid her of a child. He glanced at Claris and saw her beginning to understand.

"And that killed her?" she asked.

"No!" Williams protested. "All went as it should. Mam did nothing amiss. It was a week later the pretty sister sickened. The plain one wouldn't send for a doctor, even then, and it probably wouldn't 'ave done any good, so she was wise to save the silver. Took the body back to 'er village for burial and that was the last we saw of either."

The maidservant ran back in, looking as if she'd enjoyed her outing. "The 'ackney's 'ere, sir!"

Perry rose and turned to assist Claris, but she was already standing and looking steady. "The older sister must have been very distressed," she said.

"Distressed? Raving, is 'ow I'd put it. Vowing revenge on 'im. To those who didn't know, it seemed she was raging at God, but we knew. Raging against the man who'd done that. I pity 'im, for she was the sort to act on her fury."

"Indeed she was," Perry said.

"Mam said that Miss Clarrie swore she was married and that the child was legitimate. She didn't really want . . . . But her sister insisted."

"Poor Aunt Clarrie," Claris said.

Perry saw her hold back her thoughts, but he could imagine what they were. Giles had duped Clarrie Dunsworth into thinking she was married, probably with the help of his crony, Henry Mallow. Perhaps Mallow had stood as witness, then later denied it. Twenty years ago, marriage records were chaotic and witnesses were key.

Clarrie had clung to hope as long as she could, but in the end she would have felt like a harlot, even though she'd done no wrong.

"Perhaps the older sister raged against herself," Ellie said.

Williams looked at her and nodded. "Perhaps she did, ma'am; perhaps she did. I 'adn't thought of that afore, but there's no 'atred so deep as 'ating yerself."

"Thank you, Mr. Williams." Perry gave him the guinea. He found a sixpence and gave it to the maid. "And thank you too."

She blushed as she curtsied, bright eyed with her riches. He rather wanted to carry her away from Dun Street, but meddling always had consequences and should never be indulged on impulse.

He escorted Claris and Ellie out to the hackney, which was no worse than most of its sort. Once they were on their way, he said, "I hope you see that my warning not to come here was justified."

Claris met his eyes. "You didn't warn; you forbade. And in the end, we did learn something."

"Almost at cost of your life. And Ellie's."

"If you'd brought me here, we would have been safe!"

He broke the glare first. "Very well, we learned that your aunt Clarrie took a potion to rid herself of her child, and then died a week later of a fever, probably caused by that. Does any of that soothe your mind about the curse?"

To his surprise, she nodded. "It does, though I haven't quite sorted out why."

"Likely because your mother was mad with self-hatred," Ellie said. "As the man said, it's the sort to eat into the soul, for there's no one else to blame. She tried to blame Giles Perriam, but inside, she knew her sister's death was her fault."

Perry had never heard Ellie make such a long speech, and it was clear and cogent.

"If Giles was the villain, then Giles must pay," he said. "She might have thought of killing him, but that would be difficult and also too quick. She needed him to suffer as she must suffer, hoping his constant suffering might ease her own."

"That almost echoes the curse," Claris said. "Suffer as I must suffer."

"Indeed it does. She wrote mostly of herself."

"But how could she be sure he'd suffer as she dictated? Could she have killed his babies and wives? How horrible to even think that about my own mother!"

Perry shook his head. "Impossible. She wouldn't have access to Perriam Manor, and in a short while she was married to your father. She must have hoped that dread would be torment enough."

"Children do die," Ellie said.

"And she would remember the pestilence in Wellsted and the deaths of her own siblings. That must have made a deep impression upon her young mind. She might have thought that the probability of death for children was even higher than it is."

He sensed a reaction from Claris and wished his words unsaid.

He took her hand. "We'll do all we can to keep our children safe. That curse was the creation of your mother's deranged mind. Insofar as she was rational, she could only hope that he'd live in dread, especially of hell."

She clung to his hand. "Why did *she* not fear hell? She'd killed her sister, but all the days that I knew her, she seemed convinced of her own righteousness. Even on her deathbed she spoke of being with Clarrie again, and she must have believed Clarrie was in heaven."

"She probably changed the story in her mind," Ellie said. "I've known people who did that when the pain of the truth was too much to bear. After a while of telling their false story to themselves, they believe it as much as that the sun rises in the east."

Perry nodded. "Let's put the true story together. Your mother persuaded Clarrie to come to London and seek a fine husband. She pushed her into Giles's arms, for I can't believe Clarrie was truly in love with a man like that. Giles betrayed them, so Clarrie took Mistress Williams's potion."

"Reluctantly. Mother probably terrorized her into it."

"Because your mother still had her plan. Without the child, there was still hope of Clarrie making a good marriage. Harpy Mallow."

"Why do you call her that?"

"Giles described her that way. For once, he was right. All teeth and claws."

She shivered. "Yes."

He put an arm around her. "You are not at all like her."

"I pray not. Giles was vile, but she set out to torture him as surely as if she had him tied on a rack."

"And succeeded in the end, but by his ill luck, not a curse." He could see she still doubted. "Only think of the wording, Claris. It's all lies. The 'suffer as I must suffer' was about her, not Clarrie. The part about children dying as hers must die was perhaps most about Clarrie herself, whom she might have thought of as her child. She was already twisting it in her deranged mind. She was the victim, and Giles was entirely to blame. Giles alone had caused Clarrie's death, so he must pay. In composing that curse, she made herself the righteous vindicator." Perry thought for a moment. "And that's why she forced your father to marry her."

"What do you mean?"

"Once she'd established her version of the truth, she inherited the necessity of marrying well. It had to have been important, for it had led to Clarrie's death. So it must still be important. However, she didn't have the looks or charm, and she'd probably spent most of the money on the Town foray. There was one man she could get—a clergyman, but from a good family. She'd have sent a curse to your father for the part he'd played, and so she followed it up with a demand. Marry her and the curse against him will be nullified. He will escape hell."

"Oh, the *wickedness* of it. Father would have done anything, especially when he learned that Clarrie had died. Poor man."

"A kind heart, as always."

"He did his best to suffer for his sins on earth, and Mother helped him."

"Worrying again that you are like her? My dear, my dear, as Miss Pellew said, you're more like Clarrie, but with steel and spine. What's more, your father, though weak, was not a bad man. He probably only committed the one vile sin—to help Giles dupe Clarrie—and he truly felt his guilt. His pouring out money to the poor was unfair to his family but showed his contrition."

"He was truly compassionate," Claris said. "He felt the sufferings of others. Without Mother, he might have died a beloved rector rather than a mad one."

The carriage came to a stop and he thought quickly.

"Our explanation for our appearance is the truth. You ventured into a dubious part of Town and were assaulted. I rescued you."

"And all in search of a superior mender of stockings."

"What?"

She smiled at him, a wry smile but true. "I'll explain later."

The footman stared but accepted the explanation. Washing water was ordered for all of them and then Perry took Claris upstairs.

Chapter 39

Claris was glad of Perry's strong arm around her as she climbed the stairs. Her mind had slid back to that moment of terror, firing the shot, his arrival, his driving off four attackers.

Four.

Terror turned to thrill. He'd been magnificent!

When they arrived in their room, he gently removed her hat, smoothing her hair, looking at her with such tenderness. Perhaps more than tenderness? Hadn't he called her "love"?

The thrill swelled inside her, especially when he kissed her.

She clutched at him, wanted him—

Footsteps.

They broke apart.

Alice hurried in with the jug of hot water. "Oh, ma'am, thank the Lord you're safe. Let me get you out of those clothes."

"It's all right," Claris said as calmly as she could. "You may go for now."

Alice stared, but then bobbed a curtsy and left.

Perry was looking at her, amused, quizzical, but knowing.

"I want you," she breathed. "Now. This very moment. I know it's shocking. . . ."

He swept her up and laid her half on the bed so her legs dangled from the knees down. She went up on her elbows to shift further, but he already had his breeches undone.

He flipped up her skirts and slid right into her, hard, hot, and strong. Leaning forward, he caught his arm around her to hold her up for his searing kiss. It couldn't entirely stifle her sharp cries of pleasure as he thrust again and again. She brought up her legs around him, uncaringly bruised by his sword hanger.

They'd taken off nothing but her hat!

She thrust up to meet him again and again as the fever built and the ache exploded into a pleasure more intense than any she'd known.

He was braced on his arms over her, sucking in breaths, as she was heaving with them, but laughing down at her with such a light in his eyes. "My warrior bride."

"That was . . . That was . . ."

"What?"

"Naughty."

He hooted with laughter. "Then naughtiness is pure delight."

He pulled her up into his arms and rolled them both onto the bed, despite shoes, sword, and riotous clothing.

He cradled her face and kissed her again. "I love you, Claris. Say you love me too."

She searched him for humor, for a tease, but saw only honesty. "I love you, Perry. I didn't want to say. It wasn't in our agreement."

"I tear up any such agreement. We have love. We are blessed."

And a blessing was the opposite of a curse.

There and then, Claris ceased to believe that her mother's misbegotten curse could have any power over her. In the midst of such love, it simply wasn't possible. She tangled her fingers in his unruly hair. "If any powers come from beyond the grave, Aunt Clarrie will be working hard to make all right for me. For us."

He captured her hand and kissed her palm. "And she'll be particularly protective of our children."

"She will. She will."

They lay together as the clock ticked away the minutes, but when it chimed two, Claris pulled out of his arms and scrambled off the bed. "Dinner!" She stared at him. "Alice will guess."

That twinkle entered his eyes. "The whole house will guess. You were noisy."

"Oh, no!"

"We're married. It's blessed."

"Not that."

"Even that." He kissed her again. "I propose that we scandalize our households on a regular basis, even into our old age."

She pushed at him. "Don't say such things."

"I'm your lord and master and say as I please."

"Tyrant!" she exclaimed, pretending outrage.

"Have no doubt, love, you rule here. But we must change."

They acted as maid and valet for each other, stealing kisses as they stripped and as they dressed in fresh clothing. As he fixed a pin in his fresh neckcloth, Claris smoothed the bed as best she could. Smiling.

Idiotically, she was sure.

He loved her!

It was as if sun broke through on a gloomy day.

He loved her!

All was not perfect, for they must still be too much apart, but he loved her as she loved him, and that would be enough.

Claris went to make sure Ellie was all right, so Perry went down to the dining room alone. His amazing wife. Spirited, brave, and boldly wanton. He remembered at first sight thinking her ordinary. How wrong he had been.

She came down, sparkling with vitality and lovely

with it. "She's asleep. I think she's fine, but we'll summon a doctor if needed."

"Of course. As there's only the two of us, I'll move my place to your side."

She blushed at that. Did she too envision mad passion on the gleaming table, amid a scattering of sauces and fruits? He reminded himself that she must be bruised. In fact it was amazing that she wasn't as exhausted as Ellie, especially when she was with child.

When the meal was over, he suggested that she rest for the afternoon. "I plan a visit to the theater tonight, if you feel restored enough."

"Then perhaps I will lie down. Can the boys come with us?"

"Certainly. I've chosen a play they might enjoy."

She kissed him. "Of course you have. Do you not need to rest?"

Was that the invitation he thought it was? Regretfully, he declined. "I have some matters to attend to."

He escorted her upstairs but then made himself leave. He needed to deal with the men who'd attacked his wife.

He went to Bow Street to discover what he could about the Dun Street ruffians. They were known, as were some of their crimes, but none of their victims would prosecute. They were too poor and afraid.

Perry hired two Bow Street men to watch the street in order to catch them in a crime. Then he'd fund the prosecution. He hoped they'd hang, but transportation would do. That would remove only a ladleful from the swamp of crime in London, but Claris would in a small part be avenged.

He'd do something for the girl, Izzy, but he'd need to find out what she wanted. He could offer employment at the manor, but she looked like a London girl, so she'd probably not want that. She might not be comfortable in any fine establishment. He'd come up with the right plan.

He wished all his problems were so easily solved.

He took refuge in a coffeehouse again, hiding behind

a newspaper, trying to sort through the mess. He loved Claris, and he wanted to wake beside her every morning of his life, but she wanted to live at the manor and he was locked here.

She believed Perriam Manor was hers, hers for life and to pass on to her children and her children's children. It wasn't, and he should tell her that—now. Love demanded honesty, but honesty could destroy love.

Chapter 40

Claris spent the rest of the afternoon resting. She didn't sleep, but she daydreamed about Perry and all the ways in which their life could be perfect. She was sure he would be at Perriam Manor as much as possible, and she would visit him in Town when she could. She'd learned to celebrate the pleasures she had and not pine for more.

She'd moved to the drawing room by the time the twins came home full of stories about the river. Lovell had taken them on it to see the many important buildings along its banks. As they chattered, she smiled at their new confidence. They might even have grown, but perhaps that impression was because they carried themselves more erect. Lovell was having a good influence on their manner, but she suspected the main effect was from Perry.

When she'd been at the silk warehouse, he'd taken them to tour St. James's Palace, where court events took place, and also to a fencing academy. She'd been doubtful about that, but after this morning she saw that a man should be able to handle a sword.

"We dined at the Star and Garter," Peter said. "Such a grand place in Pall Mall. We saw a number of great men pass by. Lovell pointed out Lord Rockingham, Lord Greville, Lord Rothgar, and some others, gathering in a private room to discuss some weighty matter."

His eyes were bright with excitement, but Tom said, "The wild beasts in the Tower were better."

Claris shared a smile with Lovell, but the differences between the twins were becoming more pronounced and she worried what path they could find together.

The twins went off to their room, and Lovell said, "They'll each find their own way in time."

"Is my concern so obvious?"

"It's a reasonable concern. I knew a set of twins at school who were very close, but as they moved into manhood they looked in different directions and seemed to accept it. I knew another set who were at odds all the time. Now, that was unpleasant."

"Yes, they're blessed in that respect. Thank you for your care of them. They're coming along very well."

"They'll be fine men one day. They have good hearts."

She smiled. "Yes, they do."

When he'd left, Claris considered his words. She still worried at times about what she'd inherited from her parents, but she'd never worried that way about the twins. She realized now that was because they seemed so happy and sound.

Who could say why? She hoped it was in part because of her protection, but perhaps her father had been a good man once, or at least a normal one. Before he'd fallen into the company of Giles Perriam, and later into the claws of her mother.

Might Athena have been a good wife and mother if matched with the right man, a man she loved? Never sweet and docile, no, but not all men required that.

Perry didn't seem to mind her own thistly nature. . . .

She relaxed back into daydreams.

The theater, and then tender loving in the night.

She wore her wedding gown to the theater, for the memories it carried.

All her family were present, and Lovell as well, so she had to sit close to Perry. That was pure delight, but she wasn't so sure about the delights of the theater.

"It's so noisy. And pungent."

"I can't waft away the smells," he said, "but it will quiet when the music starts. As long as everyone approves of it, that is. Rebellion is always possible."

"Rebellion?"

"Theater audiences are easily roused, especially the servants up there."

Claris leaned forward to peer up at the highest level of seats. Someone up there threw orange peel down among the people sitting on benches in the center. A nimble young buck caught it and was applauded.

"I thought this would be a dignified occasion."

He chuckled. "Theater started in the marketplace and has never shed that ambience. Those bucks in the boxes on the stage could well cause trouble."

One row of boxes rose from the front edge of the stage, and one lower box was full of young men who were possibly drunk.

Perry took her hand and raised it for a kiss. "Don't look so worried. This will be magic."

Musicians filed into an area beneath the stage, sat, and began to play. The audience did quiet a little. Presumably they approved. Claris certainly did.

"An orchestra," she said with a happy sigh.

"A very small one. I forget all the things you haven't experienced." He was still holding her hand, and she was happy to have it so. "I hope to take you to hear a larger assembly, and your first large choir. Tomorrow we go to Ranelagh, so your first fireworks. What other wonders can I find for you?"

Claris leaned closer to whisper, "Only you."

He kissed her lips, but then a woman walked onto the front of the stage and sang an introduction to the play. Such a voice, and such a magical world revealed as the curtain slowly rose. Trees. A woodland glade. A castle in the distance.

Claris leaned forward as if drawn into that other world.

*   *   *

Perry watched her, amused to see her as absorbed as her brothers. The play was a light adventure involving a highwayman and an heiress fleeing a tyrannical father. Pure nonsense, but it was amusingly played, and the sword fighting was impressive. The dying villain spouted enough blood to satisfy the boys and to make one woman in the pit faint. All in all, a great success, but when they left the theater he was happy to be able to send the overexcited boys back with Lovell and escort the ladies in another carriage.

Predictably, Athena dismissed the play as folly. "For in reality he'd hang and she'd be whipped into marrying her gouty suitor."

"The theater is for fantasy, not reality," he said.

"And thus deludes the rabble. Perhaps I shall write a play that portrays truth."

"By all means."

And I hope it's a grand success, he thought, *providing funds for you to live here, where you wish to be.* Athena Mallow could well make life miserable for Claris back at Perriam Manor. How did he solve that problem?

He woke the next morning to find Claris smiling down at him.

"I've died and gone to heaven."

She chuckled and kissed him. "Then our bed is heaven."

"Which it is." He drew her in for a kiss, but no more. They'd made love last night, but gently, for she'd admitted to being sore from the attack.

He stroked her bruised hip. "Your grandmother should know a cream or liniment that would help."

"She's given up her witchy ways."

"Knowledge doesn't evaporate. Do you know how she learned herbal lore?"

"From some philosopher in Paris. Her memoirs would be interesting."

"And probably shocking, but I'd like to read them."

Claris chuckled. "Perhaps she could make a fortune from them, and be able to live in Town. I'm sure it's what she wants, but according to Ellie she's run through most of her money."

As he'd suspected.

"I could rent rooms here for her."

"Rooms she'd like?" she asked dubiously.

"Beggars can't be choosers? But yes."

She frowned. "I should pay it out of the manor's income, but . . ."

"But?"

"I have plans. For improvements, not just to the manor, but for the tenants and laborers. I want to pass on a thriving estate, but also one where everyone thrives, not just our family."

Pass on.

In the night he'd tried to come up with ways to live at the manor most of the year, but once she knew the truth she'd scarcely tolerate him for the thirty days. If he were to pay for rooms for Athena, he needed his father's allowance and his sinecures.

"My income can stretch to cover rooms, especially as I'll be giving up my establishment in the Lyceum."

"Why?"

"What use have I for a home which doesn't allow women? I hope you'll visit me in Town from time to time."

"From time to time," she agreed, smiling. "As you will visit me? Rather more often than thirty days a year?"

"From time to time to time," he said and kissed her again, restrained himself again. "You should linger in bed, for we go to Ranelagh tonight. And that's your lover speaking, not your master."

She laughed, glowing, her delightful freckles like gold on her skin. "Then I will obey, my lover. I will be indolent and thus ready for yet more pleasure. At Ranelagh and later."

He left her with a smile, but as he went downstairs the

smile died. Once he told the truth, she might never glow like that again.

Claris managed to be indolent for three hours but then rose to make full use of her last day in London. There were a number of items she wanted to buy for the manor, and Genova had agreed to accompany her.

When Genova arrived, Claris told her about Dun Street and the attack.

"You fired the pistol. You're a warrior at heart."

"I was simply terrified."

"But you took the pistol."

Dun Street had made Claris nervous. "Perhaps I should take it today."

"We're not going to any dubious parts of the city, so a pickpocket is the worst danger, and I have my footman as escort."

So Claris was able to enjoy the expedition, and she managed to acquire everything on her list, including an ingenious new form of bellows that she'd seen at Sappho's, and a supply of powder that she'd been told made ink that flowed smoothly and didn't fade.

At that shop she indulged in some writing paper of excellent quality and ordered a seal. There was a seal at Perriam Manor, but the bold P referred to the legal owner, Perry. The new one, with a CP design, would be her own.

In the early evening she helped Alice to pack, surprised by how much she'd managed to acquire in one week. As well as the silk, she'd purchased slippers, soap, and yards of ribbon and lace without any clear idea of what she'd trim with it. London could be dangerous to her income!

Even so, she'd return.

She and Perry went to Ranelagh alone, for Athena and Ellie were at another salon, and she hadn't thought her brothers should have another late evening. She'd bring them here someday, however, for they'd love it as much as she did.

She wandered in a daze through lamplit groves and around a pretty lake. She was amazed by the huge Rotunda. When they went inside, she looked up, up, up at the tiers of boxes lining the circular interior.

Perry said, "The tower in the middle can hold a fire in the winter to keep the place warm. Come, let's enjoy refreshments."

He'd reserved a box on the second row, and Claris saw that it was the best location. The lowest row was open to anyone strolling by. Clearly this suited some, but she wouldn't like it. Too high and it would be hard to watch the passersby.

Perry pointed out some famous people, but they were just names to her. She admired some of the ladies' gowns and saw details she might like to copy. For the most part she simply enjoyed the glittering ambience, the wine and ham, and her husband by her side.

And then came the fireworks.

Again, Perry found the perfect place from which to watch them explode fairy jewels into the sky. She gasped and cried out along with everyone else, and applauded vigorously at the end.

"That was astonishing! We could have fireworks at Perriam Manor."

He seemed taken aback. "At great expense."

"But perhaps once, for some grand occasion."

"What grand occasion do you anticipate? A visit from the king?"

"Of course not. But I want my people there to see fireworks, at least once. And I shall," she stated, remembering who was in charge at the manor.

"Then why not on the birth of our first child."

"Perfect!"

She traveled back to Godwin Street in a daze of happiness but woke the next day fighting tears. It was time to go home.

The house had been rented for only a week, so she

couldn't linger if she would, and she was as eager to return to the manor as she was sad to leave Perry. He was to escort them but would be able to stay only two days. She'd always known how it must be and would not put a sad face on it, though she wished he'd travel in the coach rather than riding.

There would be room, even in the one coach, for Athena had shocked her by declaring that she and Ellie would not return to bucolic misery. She'd suspected it would come to that, but not immediately.

"But where will you live?" she asked.

"Sappho has offered sanctuary for a while, and some other ladies are generous. I truly cannot bear the thought of country isolation, Claris, and you're well able to take care of yourself and your brothers. My duty there is done."

It was, and Claris was relieved. This might also mean that Perry wouldn't have to provide lodgings for her grandmother in Town. She couldn't help feeling a little hurt, however, that Athena could discard her and her brothers without a twinge.

That made her sharp when she said, "You could have mentioned this earlier. It disarranges the plans for the journey." She regretted that when she saw Ellie's unhappy face. She hugged her. "If you wish to visit Perriam Manor, you will always be welcome."

"That's kind of you, dearie, and perhaps I will now and then."

Claris didn't hug her grandmother.

She realized she never had.

When Perry handed her into the coach, he said, "Don't let her upset you, Claris. She is as she is."

"I only hope I'm not like her."

"Can a flame be ice?"

That comforted her, and as the miles passed, she accepted that she wouldn't miss her grandmother at all. She would miss Ellie, but not Athena, and without her dominating presence Perriam Manor would truly be her home. As they passed through the gryphons she smiled, because they guarded the treasure that was home.

It was a fine day, and the old brickwork glowed, already recovering from its ivy shrouds. The windows had been thoroughly cleaned, and they glinted like her diamond.

Perry handed her down and escorted her into the house.

"The dark paneling isn't oppressive anymore," she said. "It must be the light." But then she considered the portraits. "Giles must go. I doubt his ladies like his company."

"Perhaps they too should at least move to a less prominent spot."

She nodded. "No memories of that time. In fact, might their families like the pictures?"

He smiled. "Inspired."

"A new beginning."

"Then I must have your portrait done."

"Oh, no. . . ."

"Oh, yes."

"Together, then," she said. "The beginnings of a new Perriam line."

He seemed to disapprove, but then he said, "I'll consider which artist is most worthy of our patronage. I admire Mr. Gainsborough's work, but he's situated in Bath."

"We don't need a fashionable artist. A local one will do."

"Not unless he's skilled. I want you captured as in life, my love, in all your glory." The look in his eyes curled her toes. "Come, show me the improvements you've made."

He could stay only two days, and much of their time was taken by a stream of visitors come to welcome them back to the manor and to hear of the latest London styles and gossip. Claris told Jane Jordan about the child, and her friend shared her delight and gave some excellent advice. It was cheering to think that Jane had three healthy, thriving children.

When the time came for Perry to leave, Claris made

sure she presented a content face to her husband. However, he took her into the small waiting parlor and closed the door. "I have something I must tell you."

His expression frightened her. "What? What's amiss?"

He took her hands. "You know how important Perriam Manor is to my family. To my father in particular."

"Yes. That lies at the root of our happiness."

"If only that were true. My father was angry at the way things are, though he couldn't truly lay it at my door. He insisted that the manor be returned to the earldom on my death. I've willed it to my oldest brother, Pranksworth."

She frowned, trying to make sense of it. "Willed it . . . ?"

"Pranks promises you may live here all your life."

The truth hit and she snatched her hands free. "Oh, *does* he? And what of our children?"

"I'm sure he'll continue the indulgence. He has no true interest in this place."

"But wants it anyway!"

"He, like me, does as my father commands."

She was almost speechless. "So Perriam Manor isn't mine after all. You *promised*. It was part of our agreement!"

"I lacked foresight—"

"Lacked . . . Your father has no right! The manor is *yours* now, and you can will it as you wish."

He came toward her. "Claris, a father's word is law—"

She shoved him away, rocking him backward. "If I'd lived by that, we'd be in a sorry state! You're allowing a tyrant his way, and it's *wrong*."

"Have sense, you termagant! I'm dependent upon my father."

"By choice. We all have choice. You're just too weak to see that."

"Damn your vicious tongue! I must earn my living. I do it in service to my father. Through my positions in places of influence, through friends, through court, but at his will. Without his favor, I have nothing."

"You have Perriam Manor."

"Hah!"

"Your father is as obsessed as my mother," she spat, "and as destructively. All you Perriams are mad."

"Perhaps, but I'll not create a new schism in my family."

She stared at him, fists clenched. "*I'm* your family; *my child* is your family. You're destroying your family before it's begun."

He was as unmoved as a marble statue.

She turned away. "Get out. Go back to your beloved Town and your so important duties, and never come back."

From behind, he asked, "Can you forgive me?"

"How? You've broken your word to me."

"Then I can only ask your mercy." He walked past her and was gone.

She ran to the window to watch him mount and ride away, still angry enough to glare, but with tears streaming down her face.

All her bliss was dust. She'd let down her defenses and wrapped happiness around herself like a blanket, finally believing it hers for life. He'd snatched it away, leaving her nakedly cold.

She tried to tell herself Perry's betrayal didn't matter so very much. She'd be able to live her life here. Perhaps her children, or some of them, would do so when she was dead.

But they'd be tenants, depending on the fickle will of an Earl of Hernescroft.

They'd have no true right.

How could he do this to her?

Chapter 41

Perry rode away at speed. That had gone even worse than he'd expected.

There'd been tears in her eyes. Tears, fury, and wretched disappointment.

Yes, she had faced down a father, but not a father such as his.

The Earl of Hernescroft was God in his family. In many ways he was more powerful than God, because he was on earth to be faced now, rather than in the heavenly hereafter.

Othello stumbled on a rut and Perry slowed him, regaining control. The least he could do was to stay alive. If he broke his neck, the will would come into effect immediately.

He arrived back in London and left Othello at the livery stables close by the Lyceum. He entered his rooms, but they felt dead to him now. The expert ministrations of his servants didn't comfort. The peace and order grated on his nerves.

Claris wasn't here.

He missed Peter and Tom and their pestering attention.

He even missed Athena Mallow and Ellie Gable a little. In fact, he missed Ellie a lot. She had the kindest of hearts and a surprising wealth of wisdom once she felt free to speak.

As he'd had his post taken over to the house, only a

few letters and invitations offered distraction, and no event tempted him. He was strangely inclined to hide away from the world, but he sent a note round to Cyn to announce his return. The matter of the spies should be over now, but he should check.

He picked up the only letter of interest, one from Georgia. It was full of improvements she was making to her home.

> *And most frugally, I assure you. It astonishes me how cheap things are in the country, and how ingenious one can be if inspired. I've worked one wall in flowers using stencils. It truly has the appearance of fine wallpaper, and by stenciling I avoid the tax on purchased paper.*

Good God, she was running mad.

> *I do hope to see you soon, you and your wife. If you can't travel to the wilderness, I believe Dracy and I will be in Town whenever Parliament finally sits. He's resolved to do his duty, and I, of course, will delight in occasional sips at Town's heady brew.*

He refolded the letter. Was she truly happy, or masking her loss? Was love enough? If that were true, wouldn't he defy his father, lose his luxuries, and settle to rural life as cheerfully as Georgia?

He loved Claris, but he couldn't imagine a life watching turnips grow.

Claris wasted a day in feeling sorry for herself. Here she was in Perriam Manor, which had seemed her haven, her heaven even, but all was spoiled. What point in improving the house and the estate for the benefit of the Earls of Hernescroft, who didn't even want it except as a trophy in a meaningless feud?

When she sat to her first dinner, with only her brothers and Lovell as company at the big table, she had to force herself to eat. Soon the boys would leave, and Lovell too, and she would be alone. Her life had often been uncomfortable, but she'd never been alone.

After the meal she didn't bother with tea or coffee in the drawing room, but wandered the house, trying to recapture the excitement, the love. Empty corridors and empty rooms. Almost silence.

Yatta rubbed against her leg and she scooped him up, holding him close. "Athena abandoned you too, didn't she? Without a thought." She rubbed her cheek against his warm fur. "Why am I missing her? I don't even like her."

The cat only purred, but Claris's courage struggled out of the pit.

"I can do this," she said. "I have a lifetime here; my children will grow up here. What's more, I *will* find a way to keep it in my line."

My line.

Children?

Perhaps only the one now Perry had betrayed her. She'd come to trust him, she'd lowered her hard-built defenses, and he'd shattered her. She couldn't imagine sharing a bed with him again, no matter how he stirred her lust.

"You and me, then, Yatta," she said to the cat as she walked briskly down the corridor. "Back to work."

Cyn's arrival at Perry's rooms was a welcome distraction.

"All's well that ends well?" Perry said. "Except for Ryder and Pierrepoint, of course."

"I wonder if I could have done better by Ryder," Cyn said.

"That way leads madness."

"True."

"Of course, you've been an officer in wartime. You don't need that lesson from me. Do you return to your regiment?"

"I'm considering. Chastity will follow the drum if she must, but she's had her fill of distant lands, and motherhood seems to have turned her domestic."

"A natural urge, wouldn't you say, to want security and family?"

"I suppose so."

"But you want adventure?"

Cyn shrugged. "Above all I want her happiness, but also I've had my fill of war."

"Then why not leave the army? France will trigger a war sooner or later."

"And we might have to use military force against the American colonists. I certainly want no part of that. It will be like a civil war."

"The gods of war always seem more powerful than the gods of peace. Some government job, then?"

Cyn picked up a paperweight, then put it down again. "I'm more inclined toward commerce."

"A Malloren merchant?"

"We dabble in all things. Shipping, canals, silk, and cotton. I've learned something of Canada and its possibilities and have friends in the Hudson Bay Company. They trade mostly in furs, but it's a rich land that's only just being discovered."

"You could exploit that from here?"

"I believe so."

"No political work at all?" Perry asked, skeptical.

Cyn gave him a look. "With Rothgar as brother? He hopes to keep Canada out of the coming troubles. Trade, as always, will play a part."

Perry walked to the window and looked out at the busy street. "Why is life never simple for people like us?"

"Do you want simple?"

Perry heard the surprise and turned. "I too am considering, and I too want my wife's happiness."

"And she wants?"

"A tranquil life in the countryside."

"She has that, doesn't she?"

"But without me."

"Ah. What ties you here, then?"

"I'm beginning to wonder." With exasperation he added, "A month ago I'd have said that country living was intolerable, but now . . . Could I truly be content as a country squire?"

Perhaps he'd hoped for assurance, for he was shocked when Cyn said, "No. But you've no more need to be in London than I have to be in Canada, and you have the advantage of a short journey, whereas I'm unlikely to see Canada again."

"I can't do what I do now from Perriam Manor."

"Is that true? You have your friends and contacts, and letters travel speedily. You can travel up to London as often as need be, barring the worst weather."

"Perhaps thirty days a year here," Perry murmured.

"Will that suffice?"

Perry laughed. "A whimsy. Ignore me. You've given me much to think about."

"I hope to some purpose. Do you attend the Duchess of Ithorne's soiree tonight? A castrato is to perform."

"Always an alarming concept, despite the beauty of the voice. But yes, I'll be there."

It was time to pull free of maudlin dreams and resume his life.

Three days after Claris returned from London, Jane Jordan came over to talk about London and babies. She was a pretty, plump young woman with bouncing blond curls and a ready smile. She'd brought her three-year-old daughter, Ellen, with her, and they were remarkably alike.

"I've only been to London twice," she said. "I did enjoy it, but I was happy to return home."

"Yes, it's a spice to be used lightly. Yet some feast on it."

"Like your husband?" Jane asked cautiously.

Claris made sure to smile as she replied, "Exactly like

him. Town people are a different species, I think. Is it normal that I'm not sick?"

"Oh yes. I was with one, but not with the others."

When Jane left, Claris was in better spirits. She wasn't alone here, and there was plenty of work. She had a setback later when Alice nervously asked to return to Cheynings.

"You're settled back here, you see, ma'am, and have little need of me. And my brother's marrying next week and I'll like to be there."

Again, Claris made sure to smile. "Of course you would. It's been kind of you to stay so long."

"Oh, I've enjoyed it, ma'am. Especially London."

"Are you another who'd feast on London if you could?"

Clearly Alice didn't understand, but she said, "I'd like to serve a lady who spent time there, ma'am. But I'd not like to be far from my family all the time. I'd rather be a housemaid at Cheynings than away all the time."

Claris made the arrangements for Alice to travel back to Cheynings and consulted with Mistress Eavesham about a replacement. In the meantime, she accepted Deborah as maid. It might become permanent. A proper lady's maid wouldn't want to serve a rural lady who rarely attended any fashionable event or went to Town.

She might never go to Town again.

She would *not* mope, and so she flung herself into the projects she had planned. She wrote to Henry Cheere's workshop, asking for a sculptor to come to the manor. She told Parminter about some improved farming methods she'd read about in *The Gentleman's Magazine*. He was cautious but agreed they should investigate. He was less happy about the amount of money she wanted to spend on improving the cottages, but she was determined on that.

At one point he suggested she should consult with her husband.

"Mr. Perriam has given me complete authority here."
The brief rebellion subsided, and she had her way.

The sculptor arrived from London, but there were no letters. Not from Athena. Not from Perry. She didn't know why she'd expected a letter from him, but she had.

Did he think she wouldn't welcome letters?

She shouldn't, but she would. Foolish as it was, she wanted, needed, to know what he was doing day by day.

She could write to him, but that would let him off the hook, and he was in the wrong.

She plunged back into work.

On a day of torrential rain, she remembered the linen cupboards. Ripping frail sheets would suit her mood, but it was dull work without Ellie. She did miss Ellie and wondered how she was doing. Athena would be dragging her to the sorts of philosophical meetings that bored her. It didn't seem right, but despite everything, Ellie was a servant. She knew her place.

"Need some help with that, dearie?"

Claris stared.

It was as if she'd summoned Ellie here.

A ghost?

"What's the matter, dearie? You've gone white."

Claris ran over and hugged her. "It is you! I was just thinking how much I missed you. Is Athena here?"

Her dismay must have shown, for Ellie chuckled. "Not her. She's rooted in London now. I'm not. I thought perhaps you might find some work for me here?"

Claris hugged her again. "Can you imagine otherwise? But not work. This is your home. In fact, you can be my companion! I had that idea once but couldn't imagine anyone suiting."

Ellie beamed. "That's very kind of you, dearie. I'd like that. But I have to keep busy. Let's see about these sheets."

Claris almost agreed, but then she said, "Not yet.

You've been traveling, and in such weather. You'll want tea and food. Come along. You can tell me all the news."

Perhaps, said a weak voice, about Perry?

Over tea and cakes, Ellie related Athena's adventures. She was now the leader of a group of women working for the improved rights of women.

"Quite the lion, she is," Ellie said. "Or lioness, I suppose. What with her discarding her husband and traveling and having such adventures. Sometimes makes a bigger loaf of them than's true, but she's happy. A couple of grand ladies have given her annuities, so she's an income. Not as large as she'd like. Not yet, at least."

Claris shook her head. "I admire her, but she's so very wrapped up in herself."

"Always has been, dearie. But as you say, a remarkable woman."

"Will you miss her?" Claris asked.

"A little, but mostly out of habit. I'm not clever enough for all the things she's involved in now, and I don't like London. You sure you want me here, Claris? I don't want to be a burden."

"Sure and certain. I couldn't be happier. I've been feeling a bit lonely, you see." Ellie hadn't mentioned Perry, and Claris couldn't bear it. "Perriam?" she asked. "Did you see anything of him?"

Ellie's eyes were knowing. "No, dearie. But then, I heard he'd gone to Versailles. A restless sort of man, isn't he?"

Claris managed a calm smile. "Too restless for a country manor, that's for sure. Now, which room do you want? The one you shared with Athena is probably the nicest, but you must choose as you wish. And I'll arrange your salary."

"Oh, no . . ."

"Ellie! You're to be my companion and I intend to demand a great deal of companionship. I insist on paying you well."

When Ellie's eyes glistened and she pulled out a handkerchief to dab at them, Claris wondered if Athena had ever paid her, through all those years of devoted service.

She hugged her. Undutiful though it might be, she had no wish to see her grandmother ever again. "This is your home, Ellie, and we are your family. I'm so grateful that you're here."

Chapter 42

Perry suspected it was unwise to have come to Paris, but he had no idea how long his parents would remain, and matters could not wait. He couldn't bear it. A week severed from Claris had been too long, but he'd lasted two before traveling here.

His father kept a house in Paris, but when Perry arrived at the Hotel Hernescroft he learned that his parents were at Versailles. Hardly surprising, though he'd never liked the monstrous palace as much as they did. He left Auguste settling in and went out in search of amusement. Auguste was ecstatic to be back in France. He was going to be distraught when faced with life spent mostly in the countryside. Adieu, Auguste.

He went to a favorite coffeehouse and found some friends from a number of nationalities. They demanded the latest news from London and shared what they knew from Rome, Vienna, Madrid, and other cities. Familiar ground and he enjoyed it.

Could he do without it?

He was carried off to a card party and then to the theater and returned home late to find his parents already retired. Had he deliberately avoided an encounter?

He certainly wasn't looking forward to it.

If he sought to avoid it the next day, any chance was taken away when his father came into his room while he was still breakfasting. The earl was swathed in a robe of brown brocade with a red velvet turban on his bald head.

"What are you doing here?" he demanded, sitting on a chair. "Trouble?"

The piece of perfect brioche Perry had been enjoying turned dry in his mouth. He washed it down with coffee. "Not particularly, sir." He framed an excuse for his visit to Paris but made himself speak the truth. "I have a matter to discuss with you."

"Yes?"

"To do with Perriam Manor."

"Yes?"

If anything, his father was bored. The issue of Perriam Manor was settled and of no further interest.

"When I persuaded Claris to marry me, sir, I promised her Perriam Manor."

"Foolish of you. But I understand you've fixed it with Pranksworth that she'll be able to live out her life there if you die first. Weak of him, but then, he is."

"If I die whilst you're still alive, you'd throw her out?"

His father narrowed his eyes. "Watch your tone, sir. Watch your tone! I'd give the tenancy to Rupert."

The biggest bully of the lot.

This was the moment.

"I've come here, Father, to tell you that I intend to keep my promise to my wife. To change my will so that she inherits Perriam Manor, and our eldest son after her."

Purple rage rose in his father's face so quickly it brought back childhood fears. Perry couldn't stop himself from leaping to his feet and putting the table between them.

"You will not," his father stated.

Absolute.

Undeniable.

"I misspoke," Perry said, proud of his steady tone despite his hammering heart. His father had no physical power over him. He had to remember that. "I should have said, I have already changed my will. Murdering me now will not serve your purpose."

His father surged to his feet. "You dare to *joke* about this, to my face! Put this right, or you are no son of mine."

Worse than he'd expected, but suddenly, and blessedly, Perry didn't care. His father was ridiculous with his purple face and fat body. His parents had never shown any fondness for their offspring. They had simply regarded them as puppets, to do as they were bid.

"So be it," he said calmly. "I regret any division between us, Father, but I must do as the Bible says, and cleave to my wife."

"Bible! *Bible!* Do you dare claim moral superiority when you break the chief commandment? Honor thy father and thy mother, sir! Honor thy father and thy mother !"

He clearly expected instant repentance. When it didn't come, the purple drained away, leaving his father pale. It wasn't, however, a weak pallor.

"Leave this house immediately," the earl said in a flat tone. "I never want to see you again."

He turned and left the room.

Perry collapsed into his chair, not surprised to find he was shaking. He was very surprised by his reaction, however.

He felt free. Remarkably, astonishingly free.

Claris was in the frosted garden, surveying her work with satisfaction.

"What on earth's going on?"

She whirled, smiling. A second later she knew she should have frowned, but Perry was here! He was here. In riding clothes, as when they'd first met, and as back then, she was in her sole surviving black gown, made worse by an old knitted shawl against the sharp air. Old clothes had seemed necessary for this work.

She managed not to throw herself into his arms, but her heart was racing and she couldn't stop the smile.

"I've had all the yews cut down. The men and horses are pulling up the roots. Don't you dare disapprove."

"I don't. But why?"

"Look." She gestured to the memorials.

He came closer. "By God."

She couldn't read his reaction. "Do you think it a good idea?"

"Inspired. They look so peaceful."

He went closer and she walked with him.

The young sculptor sent by Cheere had instantly seen what she'd wanted and perhaps had felt as she did. Skillfully he'd chipped away the blankets and revealed, as if by magic, heads below. Sleeping babes, each a little different, but all looking peaceful and even happy in their sleep.

Instead of plinths, they lay on low stones carved to look like beds, their heads on soft pillows. One, the girl, Beatrice, had a sleeping kitten beneath a chubby hand.

Perry turned to her. "It's like a miracle."

"There'll be a flower bed around each. The sort of flowers to attract bees and butterflies so there'll always be life here. A fountain too once I work out how to make it play."

Even as she spoke, she was remembering. He'd betrayed her. He'd broken his word, and she shouldn't forgive him. He seemed to read her mind.

"I've come to throw myself on your mercy," he said. "I'm not asking for forgiveness, but for sustenance."

"What are you talking about?"

He indicated they should move away from the interested men, so she walked with him toward the front of the manor.

"I've corrected my misdeed. The manor will be yours upon my death, to do with as you wish."

She looked into his eyes. "Truly?"

"Truly. From now on, I promise you the complete truth."

"But your father?"

"Has disowned me. You'll have to feed and house me."

"Perry, I'm sorry. How could he?"

"Without a qualm. If I won't obey, I'm no use to him. I have some money, but the allowance he gave has stopped. My other income was from various positions in Town. I can't keep them if I'm here most of the time."

Claris was feeling breathless and seriously wondering if she'd fallen into a dreaming sleep. "Here? Most of the time?"

"If you'll have me. I won't break our agreement. Perriam Manor is yours, and you rule here."

She took both his hands. "Of course I'll have you! I've been miserable without you. But you don't have to spend most of your time here. Truly. We can manage."

His hands tightened on hers. "I want to be with you, day and night. I defy you to claim your misery has been greater than mine."

"Swords or pistols?" she demanded.

He matched her grin. "I'd win at either." He pulled her in for a hot kiss and then held her tight. "I never imagined a love like this, Claris. It's utterly deranged me, but I'd have it no other way."

"Nor I." She moved back to look at him. "But I hope you don't intend to avoid Town entirely. There's so much there I want to explore."

"I can't afford a home there."

She touched his cheek, moved by the sacrifice he'd made for her. "We'll find the money to rent one. I have a number of ideas to improve the manor's income."

He kissed her palm. "I'm sure you do, my amazing Claris. And I confess, I don't plan to be idle here. I believe I can still be useful, which might lead to remuneration, especially if the king continues to see me as a miracle worker."

"You've been performing miracles?" she said, smiling because she couldn't stop. She linked arms with him. "Come in and tell me all."

Despite it being not yet noon, she had a destination in mind, but Ellie came to meet them at the door. She seemed to understand the situation in a moment, for she beamed her special smile. "How lovely, dearies. You've finally sorted everything out."

How the twins knew, she couldn't imagine, but they came cantering up on their ponies and leapt off to rush over.

"Perry!"

"You're home!"

He let them crush him in a hug, though Claris could see he was for once unsure of what to do. A hand on each lad's head, he smiled over at her.

"Yes," he said. "I'm home."

Author's Note

I hope you've enjoyed Perry and Claris's dance of love in *Seduction in Silk*.

This book came to me with the opening scene, and then I had to figure out what it was all about. I loved the atmosphere of the curse, but, like Perry and Claris, I don't really believe in them, so what was I going on? I didn't find out until late in the book, because that's how I write—discovering as I go.

The political background of the book is accurate. The Seven Years' War is over, but France and Great Britain were still vying for control of the world—in Europe, North America, Asia, and on the high seas. It wouldn't truly end until Waterloo in 1815. Of course the American colonies are simmering, but as we know, Rothgar will succeed in keeping Canada for Britain. I'm sure Cyn will do well in his business dealings there.

There was plenty of espionage going on, but the events there are from my imagination. However, the way Thomas and James Brown stole from men in London is all true. Their trial is recorded at the Old Bailey. James was sentenced to death but Thomas was acquitted, for reasons that aren't clear to me.

There was also a case of a prosperous man, engaged to wed and with all to live for, who shot himself. As best I know no one had an explanation for that, but it gave me an idea for the novel. This is why I love browsing magazines, newspapers, and sites like the Old Bailey on-line. They're full of stories.

I can't explain the "smothered babes." They were just

there, and they certainly provided a challenge to Claris and to me. I was glad to discover that marble could be resculpted, and above all, patched. I hope you approve of Claris's solution.

The monument to Captain James Cornewall is real, and can be seen in Westminster Abbey. You can see it and other marble memorials on my Pinterest page: pinterest.com/jobeverley/seduction-in-silk/. There are a number of other pictures relevant to the novel.

Sir Henry Cheere was a real person (1703–January 15, 1781). He was a poor boy made good, rising from an apprentice to become knighted in 1760. Louis-François Roubiliac was also a real person.

Georgian London in the 1760s was a fascinating place, and the nobility didn't all fritter away their time and gamble away their inheritance. It was the Enlightenment, and many were fascinated by science and technology and helping Britain grow into the great industrial power it would become, either by being patrons of the enterprising or by being enterprising themselves.

James Ferguson was one person helped by the wealthy to develop his natural skills. He really did begin life as a poor country lad and rise to make wonderful models and machines and give lectures in London.

I like to use real people as background characters when I can—which means when they won't mess up my story!

Seduction in Silk is set in my Malloren World, so called because it began with five books about the Malloren family, ruled by the Marquess of Rothgar. Since then there have been eight other romances about people connected one way or another to the Mallorens, but I let them onstage only when they're relevant to the story at hand.

You can find a list of the Malloren World novels here: www.jobev.com/malloren.html.

Two of them—*My Lady Notorious* and *Devilish*—won RITA Awards, the top award in romance writing.

I also write in the Regency, and I have two series of books there. The first are traditional Regency romances (www.jobev.com/tradreg.html). Two of these won RITAs— *Emily and the Dark Angel* and *Deirdre and Don Juan*. The second series are Regency historicals woven around a group of men who met at Harrow School and stayed close. These are the Company of Rogues, but some of the books are about their friends, and even an enemy or two.

There's a RITA winner here too, *An Unwilling Bride* (http://www.jobev.com/reghist.html).

Please visit my Web site, hwww.jobev.com, for other interesting information about my books, and if you'd like to receive my occasional newsletter, you can sign up there.

I'm on Facebook at www.facebook.com/jo.beverley and occasionally I tweet.

Fiction serves many interesting purposes, but an important one is sheer pleasure. I hope that is what I have given you.

All best wishes,
Jo